THE SOCK MYSTERY

SHAWN LABAQUI

THE SOCK MYSTERY

Copyright © 2023 Shawn Labaqui
Cover Illustration Copyright © 2022 Kevin Keele
Internal Art Illustration Copyright © 2022 Shawn Labaqui

Publisher's Cataloging-in-Publication Data

Names: Labaqui, Shawn, author.
Title: The sock mystery / Shawn Labaqui.
Description: Los Angeles, CA : SML Story Design, 2023. | Audience: Ages 12 and up.
Identifiers: LCCN 2023907764 | ISBN 9781961184008 (softcover) | ISBN 9781961184015 (hardback) | ISBN 9781961184022 (ebook) | ISBN 9781961184039 (audiobook)
Subjects: LCSH: Interpersonal relationships –– Juvenile fiction. | Leadership –– Juvenile fiction. | Friendship –– Juvenile fiction. | CYAC: Interpersonal relationships –– Fiction. | Leadership –– Fiction. | Friendship –– Fiction. | LCGFT: Detective and mystery stories. | Science fiction. | BISAC: YOUNG ADULT FICTION / Mysteries & Detective Stories. | YOUNG ADULT FICTION / Science Fiction / General. | YOUNG ADULT FICTION / Humorous / General.
Classification: LCC PZ7.1 L33 2023 | [Fic]––dc22

Printed in the United States of America

Cover Illustration by Kevin Keele
Book Design by Shawn Michael.

For my family and friends

CHAPTER 1

When solving serious mysteries, there are three possible outcomes. One, you get killed. Two, you get embarrassed on a national level. Or, three, you live to see the world change.

Infamous for its secrets and billion-dollar vaults, the skyscraper towered over the city. Its sleek, silver frame reflected dark clouds and gloomy skies. Bolts of thunder and lightning flashed.

Armed guards defended every inch of the building. All the floors, the elevators, and crowding the entrance. Only insiders with high clearance could see the details of its nefarious secrets.

But today was different. Soon the world would know of the dirty connection between the guardians and power.

On the top floor, in the ceiling above the executive hallway, two silhouettes crept forward cautiously. Bill stopped, his nerves getting the best of him. "I don't know if I can do this." His breathing became erratic and his arms trembled.

"Why can't you trust me?" Brady whispered behind him. "Just do what I say."

Bill wanted to, but he couldn't move.

Try to be nice, thought Brady. No. He needs tough love. "Damn it, Bill. Yes. It's dangerous. But to get the truth, we have to tear down the lies. That's what we're doing. It would also include tearing down the lies we tell ourselves. Like whatever this scaredy-cat thing is you do. Show some courage for once. Get your head on straight, and let's steal that report."

There had always been distrust in the guardians. It came in the form of something mystical. You couldn't put your finger on it, but you knew they weren't trustworthy. And for the first time, actual evidence could be obtained. Tangible evidence. Something you could point to and say, See. It's right there.

"Ok. Ok," Bill finally said, trembling.

The job had been in planning for months. Last night, they had taken a helicopter ride high above the clouds, and skydived to the roof, barely avoiding a collision with a row of bulky A/C units. Then they used lasers to get in through the vent ducts and hid for the night. Now, when it was go time, Bill acted like this?

One might wonder why they skydived instead of using Lon Electric Flying Backpacks. A modern technology. However, Brady wanted to be untraceable, and electronics were easier to trace by enemies with Geo-Tracking. One might also think it better to do the job at night, with fewer security enforcements present. But if done at night, it required facial, voice, and fingerprint recognition—from different sources simultaneously. They had gotten the deepfake scan, a voice recording, and fingerprints three days before, then learned the combinations changed every other day. So, technically, they were a day late. Not to mention the nasty zap from the system after a second failed attempt.

This was the perfect time—a recent changing of the guards and the least expected time for an attack.

"C'mon. Pull yourself together," Brady whispered.

Down below, two guards stopped and looked around like they might be "hearing things." A short while after, they were back to patrolling mindlessly.

A woman in a tightly fitted uniform stepped out of the main office with a stack of forms. The door shut behind her, and the keypad lit up. She flipped through the papers.

"Must have been her," said the tall guard to the small one.

The woman pulled a titanium pen from her breast pocket and marked a page.

A shocked *gasp* sounded above—then a *crunch*—and the ceiling structure caved in! An overweight, orange-headed teen in a tuxedo crashed to the floor.

The woman shrieked, tossed her papers in the air, and ran away screaming.

In the ceiling, Brady ducked out of view as the papers see-sawed, and scattered unevenly around the hallway.

The smaller guard barked into his radio, "Code eight! Code eight! Top floor! We got a loony." They circled the unconscious kid, and pulled out their batons.

Bill awoke from his unplanned siesta, putting up an arm to block the blinding light. Unsure where he was or how he got there, he decided there was no point in figuring it out when there were guards in need of charming. He nonchalantly pushed away the ceiling debris. Wild Bill, as he affectionately nicknamed himself, got up and dusted off his tux. Then he pulled out a mini comb from his pocket and brushed his puffy mustache.

"This is a restricted area," barked the tall guard. "What are you doing here?"

"With all due respect, sirs," said Bill, "'restricted' is not in my vocabulary. Something can always be worked out. On that note, what do you think of these choices: Lincolns, Jacksons, or Benjamins?"

The guards looked perplexed. Not due to the attempted payoff. But because of his voice–so young coming from someone with a mustache. His Kent Clark mustache, that is.

"Or, do you want Grover Clevelands?" said Bill. "That's one thousand dollars. It would take me a tad longer. If you don't mind the wait."

The small guard squinted his eyes. "You want bribery added to the trespassing?"

"Wow. Just wow. Unable to read sarcasm." Bill took out a lint roller and began cleaning off his lapel. "We got off on the wrong foot. I was told the grand ballroom was on this floor. I'm the confetti guy." He pulled out a handful of confetti from his pocket and flung it at the guards. Some of it stuck in their mouths.

They spit it out. As Bill turned to run, the guards tackled him.

Squirming, Bill wriggled away from their grasp. His round figure was to blame. Turning on his back, he kicked the tall guard into the small one. Bill jumped to his feet and charged them. He stopped just before reaching them, and they drew back like a taut rubber band. He ripped a card from the tall guard's belt, threw it over their heads, turned around, and zoomed down the hallway.

The guards looked at each other, then sprang forward after him.

A briefcase plunked down next to the debris. Brady jumped from the ceiling and gracefully landed on his feet with a slight bend at the knees. His short brown hair bounced tidily back in place.

Also a teenager, eighteen years of age, he was three years older than Bill and wore the same tuxedo and puffy mustache. But unlike Bill's stretched clothes and protruding belly, Brady's tux fit perfectly. And his face was all business. He was mature beyond his age out of necessity. He had to be. For himself and Bill. He picked the briefcase and the security card off the floor, swiped the card on the keypad, and slipped inside the office.

The door closed. The keypad lit up.

A steady scream came from the hallway on the opposite side of the building, getting louder as Bill ran by.

Inside the office, Brady snuck past an unsuspecting dispatcher doing his rounds. He took a sharp right and slipped into the room with the digital filing cabinets. Several employees were rearranging files along the extended wall. He kept his head down and went straight for digital lock number 42. He pulled out an electronic key from his briefcase. Twisted the clicker and placed it on the lock.

Tic-tic-tic-tic.

As it did its thing, he pretended to enter the assigned code.

From outside the office, an unclear jumble of warnings came from Bill. "Uh, another...guard...Four." The sound was muffled, coming through the ceiling. Finance Office employees looked up from their desks.

Tic-tic-tic-tic.

"C'mon," Brady whispered. He peeked around to make sure no one was the wiser and turned his back to the room. One employee looked at him, squinted his eyes, then headed to the back office.

A low beep came from the gadget, and the drawer slid open. Brady rapidly leafed through the folders. *Confidential, Secret, Top Secret, Super Secret*, and he stopped at a file named *Super Duper Top Secret—Don't Even Start Thinking About It*.

Another muffled warning came from outside. "Three more... Seven now...."

Brady pulled out the bribe report. He tried quelling his excitement, but it felt like holding the Declaration of Independence. A smile crept on his face. Mystery Solvers could only dream of getting their hands on something like this. Evidence that could crumble coldhearted conglomerates. It had the list of corporations and the multi-millions they paid guardians, with every detail, from connections to the offshore accounts, illicit payments, and the fake names they used.

He pulled out his camera, switched off the flash, and snapped a picture with his Memo App. He attached the photo and pressed "send." It twisted and disappeared in a vortex. Rolling up the national treasure, he delicately twisted it into a cardboard tube, and placed it in his briefcase. Quickly and quietly, he made his way out.

Heading to the exit, he pulled out his magnetic rope. He wasn't abashed if anyone saw him now.

Confidence brimmed out of every cell in his body.

CHAPTER 2

Right outside the office, Bill was amazed with himself as he held off the guards with his maneuvers and blocks, able to get out of any hold with ease. But really, it was because of his physical shape. Others called it *rotund*, *protruding*. He called it *fun size*. And with the added sweat from the friction, it was hard for them to get a hold of him. Philosophically, there's good and bad to everything. See? It justified his diet failures. A good diet would have messed this moment up!

The guards were tired, sporting splotchy sweat stains and flushed cheeks. They had stopped grabbing Bill and waited for the guards with stun guns. Bill continued twisting around and karate-blocking the air.

Brady kicked the door open and sprang into the hall. He whipped the magnetic rope around the crowd of men, and it latched onto itself, making a sort of lasso. He yanked back as Bill jumped, the rope tightened, and the cluster of guards sprawled on the floor.

With Bill's butt above the rope, Brady pulled him from the pile.

"Somebody deserves a new title." Bill winked.

Brady ignored him. It wasn't the time to celebrate yet. "Are you okay from the fall?"

"Fall?" said Bill. "I jumped, no?"

Brady pressed a button on the magnetic handle, disconnecting it from the rope. He placed the handle in the briefcase. "You went unconscious again."

It wasn't the first time Bill had blacked out during a mission. It happened more times than was respectable. Kind of embarrassing for a mystery solver, really. Brady didn't understand how he would name himself "Wild Bill" with that kind of track record. But if he was being honest with himself, he loved Bill too much—he'd let him get away with anything.

Deep in thought, Brady hadn't noticed Bill pulled out his phone and took a few quick selfies with the guards. He had gotten a selfie with a guard who was holding his side in pain where the rope had tightened. Another while tickling a guard. And another where a guard was doing his darndest to avoid Bill's wet, puckered lips. The last selfie wasn't technically a selfie but a blur–Brady yanked him from the scene as the flash went off.

Brady pulled Bill down the hall. "Now's not the time."

"You realize Natty's going to demand to join even more when this is over. You'll have the power to do it," said Bill with a smirk. He knew that would ruffle feathers and divert the attention from him.

"Don't bring up my sister right now. Please."

Bill smiled inwardly.

They tried opening the last three doors at the back corner of the building with no luck. Brady checked the corner door one last time, twisting with all his might.

Failing that, he pulled out a Key Bullet from his briefcase and delicately inserted it into the lock. A tiny melting spring sat between metal contacts at the end, keeping the circuit disconnected.

He pushed it in–Pop. The door released.

They hurried inside. Brady locked the door. He attached a Deadbolt Infuser for extra strength. He opened the window and attached a Descender 500 to the sill. Five hundred feet of Kevlar rope uncoiled with a long whir and a snap. He tugged on it, confirming its stability.

Bill breathed heavy, and wiped his clammy hands on his pants. "The stairs feel a lot safer. Can't we just talk to them and sort it out?"

Annoyed, Brady clipped the briefcase to his cummerbund. "Why does everything turn into a frick'n joke with you? This is important. You know why I'm doing this."

Bill wasn't joking this time, but got the message. "Alright. Okay."

"You need to remember who we represent, Bill. People count on us. And try considering my review. You reflect on me. You understand, we can't be caught."

"Firstly, it's not Bill. It's *Wild* Bill. And *dos*: You're making a big deal of nothing. I would never let you let your father down. And besides, we won't be caught–"

A loud *CRASH* jolted the door. Bill flinched. His hand slapped his chest. "Gosh darn it."

"You have nowhere to go!" A deep voice bellowed.

Brady adjusted his bowtie and tightened his suspenders with a jerk. Bill was too himself to reason with. "Okay, *Wild Bill*. It might become a big deal if you can't get yourself out the window." Brady put his cufflinks in his pocket and folded up his sleeves. "How the heck do you go from terrified to goofing around at the drop of a hat? Then you go right back to being terrified."

"I'm not perfect like you. I'm sorry." Bill's throat tightened.

Another heavy thud hit the door.

Out the window, the tops of the palm trees swayed in the wind, the fronds and the leaflets were fighting among each other. All the way at the bottom were tiny dots moving on the ground. The dots were people! Bill clenched his hands and rubbed his fingers. Then he tried calming himself with a slow-breathing technique.

It didn't work. He leaped onto Brady's back.

Brady shook his head. Just last night, they had skydived out of a helicopter onto the high-rise, and he wasn't this scared. Truth is, Bill was strapped to his back and blindfolded. And his mouth was taped to subdue any potential screams. The things he had to do for Bill.

Bang. The door rattled. The deadbolt was starting to give way. Brady nudged Bill off his back and jumped out the window. "You're going to have to learn sometime. Fate doesn't cuddle."

Another crash in the door and the lock clanked.

Bill stared off into nothingness.

"C'mon," said Brady. "Man up."

Bill stood still, not responding.

Brady didn't believe nor disbelieve in past lives, but something like this made him wonder if maybe they were true. There was a lot of new-age thinking about spirituality and simulations. Who knows? All he knew was Bill shouldn't be this scared. "Snap out of it!" he said.

Bill looked at him.

"How long are you going to be a child?" As Brady said it, he felt bad. He knew Bill wasn't doing it for effect. He was genuinely terrified. Brady gathered his thoughts and tried again, this time softer. "Nothing will happen. I'm right here."

Bang–Clank. Bill's eyes snapped toward the door, then back at Brady. "Promise?" said Bill.

"Promise," Brady replied in a hurry.

"Cross your heart, hope to die, stick a needle inside your eyeballs?" Bill forced a smile.

"Yes, you can stick a needle inside my eyeballs." Though Brady didn't like it, he knew a joke could relax Bill. It was his coping mechanism.

Bill inched his way to the window.

"A little faster, buddy."

Bill got his legs over the edge and grabbed the rope. Deliberately, slowly, he turned onto his stomach. The trembling got more intense.

Bang–Crack. The deadbolt snapped. Bill jerked back and fell off the ledge. He barely got a hold of the rope, hitting into Brady.

The rope stretched...

Brady felt a pain in his tongue and the taste of blood. No time to worry about a little cut. He put a hand on Bill. "Don't let go. Get on my back." He angled his head out of the way, and Bill swiftly adjusted his position.

Down the rope they went.

"Wait!" said Bill, gripping with all his might.

"No time!" Switching from hand to hand, Brady descended as smoothly as possible while carrying his unwieldy friend. The whites around Bill's knuckles and nails contrasted with the pink from the rest of his fingers. He'd have sore hands for days. Brady, a sore body.

A loud crack-thud sounded above, and three guards peered over the ledge. Bill looked up. A guard took out a portable electric saw and placed the blade against the rope. Zzzzzzzzzz.

"Faster!" yelled Bill.

Brady extended the distance between each grab of the rope as the vibrating jagged metal pressed against the Kevlar.

Zzzzzzzzzzz–snap–snap–snap–snap–snap–snap–snap–snap.

The last fiber stretched to full tension, holding on for dear life.

The guard lifted the saw above his head, scowled, then chopped down. The rope burst—the two ends frayed.

Brady's and Bill's eyes widened, and the pits of their stomachs flew up into their ribcages.

They went into free fall. The friction of air rippled their faces, flapped their ears and tuxedos, rustled their mustache hairs. It kept up for what felt like one of those long elevator rides. Bill screaming the entire way down.

"Aaaaaaaaaaaaaaaagggggghhh." They bounced off a first-floor awning, flew up a couple of stories, and came hurtling back down. They bounced off the awning again.

Brady landed on the ground with a *thud*. As he looked up, Bill crashed down on him. The end of the frayed rope missed Bill and smacked him on the head.

Bill rolled off of him and frantically patted his body. He relaxed. "Phew. I thought it'd be much worse."

Touching his tongue, Brady painted his finger with a speck of red. He quickly wiped it off. No one would see it. He unhooked the briefcase, double-checked that his tools, and more importantly, the bribe report, were still there. Once assured, he ripped off the mustache from his upper lip. He did the same with Bill, who wasn't ready for it.

"Ow, dude." Bill gasped and rubbed his upper lip.

Brady smiled. The sun was breaking through the clouds. The day had turned from dismal and gray to sunny within the hour, and he could feel the excitement building. "You realize how many people have tried to do what we just did? People have died for less. I'll be the talk of the town."

As he said it, a gang of burly security guards flew around the corner and tackled them—Brady's and Bill's heads whip-lashed, their bodies flying to the ground. The briefcase broke from Brady's cummerbund, popped open, and slid under a bush.

Bill's hands went out in surrender.

Brady squirmed vigorously, getting his upper body free. He elbowed the guard off of him. As he struggled to his feet, two more guards tackled him to the ground like hungry line-backers.

With leverage, the guard on Brady kept an angry, hairy forearm to his neck, Brady's head squished against the pavement. He couldn't budge. Could barely breathe. The other guard tied his hands behind his back with a prickly rope. Brady grunted loudly.

"Be quiet." The guard pushed harder on Brady's neck.

They picked Bill up and, gently, with his cooperation, tied his hands, too. "I'm so sorry. I'll go home," Bill pleaded.

The guard tightened the rope and dragged Brady to his feet.

"You think I didn't catch your little trick?" A guard with a walrus mustache went into Brady's pocket and pulled out his phone. "What do we have here?" He opened the photo icon and found the bribe report on top. Swiping through, the only other photos were of Brady and a blond girl. He deleted the bribe report picture, including the one in the "sent" folder. He went to slip the phone back in Brady's pocket, but dropped it on the ground. "Oops."

The phone crunched under the guard's heel. He pointed to the bush where the briefcase slid. "Grab it."

A guard with an Afro pulled the briefcase from under the shrub and picked out the bark and broken twigs. He grabbed the cardboard tube with the Bribe Report.

"Take them to the woods," said Mustache guard.

The men dragged the teenagers in their scuffed-up tuxedos to the sidewalk.

A black Plymouth Fury with a crimson-red interior screeched to a halt. Two large agents in trench coats and bowler hats got out.

They forced burlap bags over Brady's and Bill's heads, shoved them in the trunk, and slammed it shut.

CHAPTER 3

No one on the outside knew it was the Mystery Solvers Inc. main office. Neighbors looked at it like some abandoned house from the 1950s with its torn laced curtains covering the windows and splintered wood and faded teal paint overlaying the facade. It was an old classic by today's standards. The surrounding houses were a mix of modern, New Age custom, and metallic veneer.

On the other side of the house, stone steps guided a winding staircase to the back door. The structure was oddly perched six feet above ground level on a bank.

A lanky man with peppered hair and a rugged face leaped up the steps, tightly clutching a sealed envelope. His suit and bowtie looked slightly off at a close distance, but to a casual observer appeared proper.

The door creaked open. As he walked through, the floorboards whimpered. The sofa and furniture in the living room were dusty and faded. The floors and walls dilapidated. Cat footprints were the only sign of traffic.

The gentleman stopped at a bronze bust of a bearded man. On its face was a shocked expression. He pressed his finger in the open mouth—*Clink*. Hydraulic sounds accompanied a transformation of the floorboards into stairs. He headed down into the secret underground headquarters.

At the bottom of the steps, he pressed a red, flashing button. The mechanical stairs retracted into the ceiling.

The walls and floors shined a metallic glow, far different from the outside facade. The man grabbed near the seams on either side of his suit and ripped them off. He threw the suit and bowtie into a hole on the wall. Sensors detected the clothes and sucked them into a laundry chute.

Underneath the rip-away outfit was his Mystery Solvers Suit. A blue and silver, full-body spandex with an "M" encircled on the chest. The uniform of everyone in this establishment. Made of Elastatuff, it was an interwoven combination of Kevlar fiber and spandex, giving it the strength to make a blow less ouchie while simultaneously stretching to any angle. And it dispersed the impact point throughout the suit, making it easier to take a hit. But don't get cocky, as the instructions noted. It still hurts.

The "Mystery Solvers Inc." sign was displayed in the hall. Just below it, a framed quote read, "Be suspicious when you hear 'Everybody knows....'" and, below that, another framed quote, "Look Deeper."

Through the hall and down a couple of steps was the Mystery Solvers office bay. There was a noticeable energy about the place. An excitement mixed with nerves.

As the gray-haired Mystery Solver strode through the bay toward his office, everyone's attention was on him. Much more than usual today.

Near the back wall, a petite Mystery Solver named Curls scanned the day's news into her Organizing Application. Or O-APP for short. She spoke with a soft voice in contrast with her crazy, curly hair. When she scanned in the news article, the data organizer created multiple folders with dates, names, and subjects, then cross-organized names, dates, and other information from previous scans. The O-APP helped Mystery Solvers make connections fast, solving mysteries with just a few clicks.

"Looks pretty good," she said loudly. Then, with her stylus pen, she transferred the view from the mini-pad to the screen on the back wall.

Ignoring her, the stately man continued through.

Two tables over, a Mystery Solver wearing inch-thick glasses took fast food meat from under his microscope. He placed it on the Toxic Shelf next to a cup of sewage. The items on the shelf were separated from most toxic to least harmful, and color coded by black, red, purple, yellow, then white. If Glasses weren't in his uniform, he'd be wearing his red suspenders and green pickle cap. He was a nerd as a badge of honor.

"They really do poithon people," Glasses said with a lisp. "You thee...." He said it loud enough for the older man to hear, but the boss wasn't listening.

Harry, who ironically had no hair on his head, angled the large monitor so the stately man could see the replay of him catching Bigfoot in a net. "Now, that's catching a mystery."

"I cannot lie," said a strong-built Latino, looking up from his book, *Lemming Humanity*. "That is a great catchphrase." The swirl of hair on his forehead bounced around as he took another bite of his beef stick. "At least somebody will give young Brady a run for his money." His nickname was Army, of course, because of his flat face, ten abs, and the fact that he always had beef jerky on hand.

The others shook their heads at Army in disagreement. It was a corny catchphrase.

Curls said, "Army, are you only saying that to get on Harry's good side in case he wins?"

"Just speaking *verdad*, also known as the truth." Army went back to reading *Lemming Humanity*.

The gray-haired boss walked by an open gym filled with equipment—dumbbell racks, squat stands, an elliptical treadmill, and more. Gunner, a buff black man, was kicking dents into the punching bag–worn down from only a few weeks of use. He swiped the sides of his flattop fade and made his pecs dance. "If a bad guy asks for trouble, I deliver the goods." He went back to pounding away at the bag.

The gentleman stopped outside the door that read "President." An enormous cluster of balloons huddled at the ceiling and held a note chest-high.

"Congratulations, Dan!"

He let out a long, disgruntled sigh. He'd been dealing with this since the announcement. But it was getting out of hand.

Dan went back to the bay and waited until all eyes were on him.

"Thanks, guys. I appreciate everything. I love the enthusiasm. But this has to stop. And, no, I haven't decided...."

Now, eyes of wholesome shame were staring. He'd gotten his point across. To most of them. He took a gander at the empty desks that belonged to Brady Watts and Wild Bill. Whom the note and balloons were from, based on the handwriting. The desks were next to a cabinet titled "Emergency Arsenal Armament," fortified with black steel, and had a fingerprint access mechanism.

Dan headed back to his office and pulled the note and balloons inside. He let them float to the ceiling. Tired, he plopped down at his desk. He had a lot to think about and wasn't looking forward to the task.

The photo on the wall of Palm Islands looked so beautiful and inviting. There would be an abundance of coconuts, sunshine, and all-you-can-drink drinks. He couldn't wait for his future.

When the daydreaming faded, he got to work. He opened the envelope and spread its contents on the table. The Mystery Solver's data sheets sat on top, each with a form—"Transferring Title and Responsibilities." It was time for someone younger, more enthusiastic to take over. After much deliberation, he moved aside Army's and Slick's photos, and put those of Brady and Harry on top.

Outside the office, at the far end of the hall, Slick fiddled with a Magneeto pen in front of the soundproof door. Never without slicked back hair, he had applied a thicker-than-usual goop this morning. He held coins in one hand and the Magneeto pen above it. Pressing the button, coins flew up and stuck to the point. Letting go, the coins dropped back into his hand.

He leaned near the soundproof door and whispered, "Slick is the best candidate by far. You, on the other hand, have no chance...."

The vibrations of Slick's words traveled through the door, then through a cone with an attached headset—the Elephant Ears—to an Asian lady with a bowl cut. You can guess what they called her. She had actually insisted on the nickname above other nicknames—including *"chili soup"* for how often she ate soup and *"cayenne pepper"* for thinking it solved every sickness. She took off the headset and popped her head out the door. "I can't tell if the Elephant Ears work. I heard you speak well of yourself."

"Shut up, Bowl cut. I'm just testing them."

"Riiiight," she said.

"I haven't seen Brady or his weirdo sidekick today," Slick said.

Bowl Cut smiled. "I heard Brady and Bill were on a block-buster mystery. Something you've never done." She fake-coughed, then looked at her watch. "They should have completed the mission by now. Word on the street is, if Brady solved it, it'll put him at the top of the list, regardless of his age."

"He's not as special as you think. He's a whiner who isn't owed anything." Slick pushed her back in the room and closed the door.

He sat back down, muttering to himself.

Later, the Latino knocked on the president's door.

Dan poked his head out and lifted his eyelids, fighting to stay awake. "I'm busy, Army. Can you come tomorrow?"

Before the door closed, Army held out a padded square envelope with scrapes on it. "I found this as I was leaving. Thought you'd want to see it."

A sticker on top of the envelope read: Important. Watch before making any decisions.

Dan took it and yawned. "I'll check it out."

♪ ♪ ♪

Rough twine from the bag scratched and prickled Brady's face and ears as he squirmed around in the trunk. They had been driving for a while, and the car suddenly went up a steep incline. Bill rolled into Brady, smushing him against the frame.

Added to the grunt, a chill shivered ominously through Brady's body. From his best understanding of the direction and time, they were headed to the infamous Park Forest Hills. The one where the dead bodies were found. The bodies belonging to research maven, Miss Pinky, and the Hardy Men—Jimbo and Topher. All said to be accidents. All of them truth seekers.

Brady would have to talk Bill off the ledge again. Bill had stayed silent since the trunk slammed shut, except for nervous breathing. What Brady would say, he didn't know. But they would have to be alive for him to say it.

He reached with his hands tied behind his back and felt around for a release latch. He checked near the lock where it should be as well as the bottom edges. Nothing.

The car turned onto a bumpy road and they started bouncing around. Brady hit his head against a metal corner. He held a yelp in, gritted his teeth.

When the searing pain dipped from the height of its power, he let out a couple long, slow breaths. It forced him into a Zen state. Right then he realized it was an old-timer's car. It wouldn't have the usual setup. Ignoring the bump that started to grow on his forehead, he exerted himself, lifting his back up to the top of the trunk. The upper edges were empty. Tired, he fell back down. He lifted his back again, searching the left corner this time.

A flat handle. That was it! The ridges and size were the same as those retrofitted trunk releases.

Don't do it yet, thought Brady. Be strategic. "Hey, Bill. I need you to listen very carefully. I found the release latch. It's above my shoulder. When we pull it, we need to get out without wasting time. But we can't shake the car. We have to do it as smoothly as possible. Alright?"

"Okay," Bill said, quietly.

"You're going to roll on top of me, facing the opening. I'll hold you there as long as I can. Find the latch with your teeth, and pull. It'll be right by your face. When the trunk pops, roll out immediately."

"How the heck do I get the latch with this over my head?"

"Feel it through the burlap."

Bill said nothing. He just nodded through shaky breaths.

"Let's do it." Brady squirmed around to face the opening with his hands behind his back.

The first attempt failed miserably. As Bill rolled up onto Brady, the car hit a dip and they crumbled. On the second heave, Bill got up and Brady held him in place for only a few seconds. Just when Bill felt the latch, Brady's strength gave out and Bill fell back down.

Outside, the sun was fading into the horizon and the sky was turning dark. The car headlights blinked on. In the front seat, the agents watched the road as the Plymouth Fury illuminated the beaten path, going over sticks and rocks up the hill, winding left and right. Classical music poured out of the speakers with its rhythms and whines. As the car hit another bump in the road, the trunk popped open in the background and ricocheted shut.

The car continued up the hill, the agent's faces quietly enjoying the symphony. The trunk popped open again, and Bill's round body fell out and rolled, bouncing down the hill littered with pine needles and cones. Following him, Brady dropped out and rolled after him.

A tree stopped Bill's momentum. He groaned. Brady crunched into a tree twenty feet down the hill.

Head swirling, Brady called out. "Bill!? Are you okay?" Wisps of frigid air escaped through the burlap.

"I can't see anything." Bill's voice trembled.

"I'm coming. Keep talking." Brady rolled and wiggled closer and closer to Bill's voice. The ground was pokey with needles and small rocks. He sat up and scooted backwards until he was touching Bill.

The crisp air swirled through the trees as twilight disappeared into darkness. Brady grabbed Bill's shivering hands and warmed them. "Turn your hands to the left."

"You should get someone else," Bill said. He began sniffling. "All I do is mess everything up."

"What are you talking about?" Brady said as he picked at the rope. "I only get mad because I know you can do better." He bent far to the right, almost pulling his shoulder socket out, and reached in his pocket. He grabbed the cufflinks.

"They could've killed us." Bill sniffled. His teeth chattered.

Brady had to tread lightly. One wrong word and he might lose him. "We're too young," he said. "They don't kill people like us. It would inspire more people to join our ranks. They're just trying to scare us into stopping." He said it with relief in his voice because he convinced himself he believed it, too.

Flipping the toggle clasp on the cufflink so it was straight, Brady shoved it between the knot. Then he moved it in a circle until it broke up the tightness. "I won't let anything happen to you. Plus, who would I work with? It wouldn't be the same." He pulled out the cufflink, got ahold of the two fibers, twisting until he worked Bill's rope loose. "I wouldn't be caught dead with Slick."

Bill untangled the rope and pulled his hands apart. "If that's what you want." He took off the burlap bag, and blew hot air into his hands. Then he untied Brady.

"Let's get home before people start worrying," said Brady.

CHAPTER 4

Across town, in the center of the city, streetlights glowed through the fog, tinting the alley walls a dingy yellow.

Two hooligans pulled out blasters from a duffle bag and scoped the scene with eager eyes. Calculating. Cunning.

Azin, the slightly thinner one, picked his nose diligently, trying to get at a stubborn green. Okay, maybe this one wasn't so cunning.

Lievy, the one who clearly made the decisions of the two, smacked Azin's finger away and handed him a large white sock with holes cut out for the eyes. They slid the socks over their heads.

"To Mr. Sock." Lievy lifted his blaster with reverence. Azin lifted his blaster, and they clinked them together like a toast of champagne.

Inside the laundromat, customers loaded washers and dryers, folded clothes, and watched videos on their phones.

The double doors burst open, and the hooligans rushed in with their blasters up. "This is not a game!" Lievy yelled. "Give us all your socks!"

The customers went in shock, going stiff as if time stopped.

"Socks! Now!" yelled Azin.

As if time restarted, customers frantically removed their shoes and socks while others raked through their baskets.

Azin flung several washers and dryers open. He rifled through the clothes, and stuffed socks in his duffle bag—adding the occasional unintended underwear. Then picking those out and throwing them away in disgust.

Lievy walked around with a threatening blaster barrel and an open duffle bag.

Trembling customers tossed their socks in.

Darting eyes and uneven breathing drew Azin's attention to a woman on a squeaky wood bench. One of the few unresponsive to their demands.

"What are you waiting for?" said Azin. The woman pulled out her wallet and offered it. He slapped it to the ground. "Your socks, dummy."

A jittery, courageous man, with his shoes still intact, stepped to the middle of the laundromat. His eyes blinking uncontrollably. "I'm...not giving...you...anything. P-p-please...leave these good people...alone."

A dude in a do-rag smoothly took a hit of his e-cig, and coughed. "Give them your socks, bro. You crazy?"

Taking it as a challenge, Lievy stepped up to the brave man. "Is that so? You won't do anything?" He pointed the blaster between the brave man's eyes, the barrel taunting him. "Dance!"

The man went straight into his own rendition of the Scottish Highlands Dance: Hop. Kick. Switch. Kick. Hop. Kick. Switch. Kick. Twirl. Bounce. Bounce. Heel. Heel. Toe. Toe. Heel. Toe. Heel. Twirl. Kick.

"Now give me your socks," said Lievy. "And don't stop dancing." Mid-dance, the brave man kicked off his shoes and, with his toes, slipped off his socks and flicked them at the duffle bag. He finished another round of: Hop. Kick. Switch. Kick. Hop. Kick. Switch. Kick. Twirl. Bounce. Bounce. Heel. Heel. Toe. Toe.

Then he bowed. "Anything else, sire?"

"Have a seat and don't utter another word."

The brave man settled on a bench, crossed his legs, and put his hands in his lap like a good little boy.

At the end of the aisle, Azin sat down next to a sniffling young girl and mimicked her exaggerated sob. "Wa-wa-wa. We have a wittle kwy-baby, do we?" She went silent. He snatched her socks and put them near his buttocks. An unexpected loudness *rattled* out. "Oh!"

The unfriendly smell transformed the girl's fear into disgust. She turned away and plugged her nose. He giggled.

The hooligans grabbed a few more socks from a bin and fled the laundromat.

An hour later, four police cars had sealed off the front entrance with an accumulation of spectators peering from the yellow tape.

Officer Tager and Officer Martin interviewed a disheveled woman with smeared mascara.

"You know you sound crazy, right?" said Martin.

Tager elbowed Martin. "Maybe it sounds a bit far-fetched. So you're saying two men wearing socks as masks stood everyone up with blasters? And they forced you to give them your socks, but not money?"

Sniffling, the girl tucked her chin in her jacket and nodded.

"Did you hear a name? See a face?" Tager pulled out a notepad to jot down the answer.

"No," she said, "But one of the robbers took a poor girl's sock and did something incredibly rude to it...."

In the background, a flash of mixed colors lit up the spectators behind the yellow tape. Unaware of what had happened, the crowd of faces stared, expressionless.

♩ ♩ ♩

Brady's and Tammy's home was located on a residential street at the end of a cul-de-sac. Shiny gray plaster covered the exterior walls with large glass windows and canary-yellow curtains lining the left-hand side.

Brady's *Mysterymobile*—his sleek silver sports car with triangular headlights—wasn't parked in the driveway. It was on the street two houses over. Most people might think that was going too far "to be safe." But not in his business. Not during a mission to expose the guardians.

Tammy got up from the living room couch and powered off the projector. She had wavy, blond hair, and was wearing short shorts and an oversized white button-up. When the projector screen disappeared into the ceiling, it revealed the bookshelf along the wall. The setup was intentional. With no TV mounted, it was more inviting to read. Better than constantly being programmed by a rectangular box with colored lights shooting out at you.

She grabbed a novel from the bookshelf, passed by the bedroom, and headed upstairs.

In the study, on the second floor, Brady placed his book, *If Aliens Attack,* on the shelf next to *The Pyramid Mystery, The Not So Obvious Establishment*, and *News: A Facade.* Above the bookshelf was a TV mounted to the wall. Attached to it, a note: "For research only!" That was intentional, too. Don't get suckered into brainless TV watching.

Brady's Mystery Board was set on an easel and included all the mysteries he was investigating. He placed a "solved" stamp on the Financial Establishment section, which had a photo of the recently scaled skyscraper. The rest of the board was filled with photos, notes, and, when necessary, red strings. Including the Tooth Fairy section, Treasure Island, and more.

The boys at the office made fun of him for not using the digital O-APP. He didn't care. He loved the tangible earthy corkboard with the rich and delightful red strings. How others would only use an O-APP was mad to him. A healthy paranoia about technology and mysteries kept him with both new and old technologies. In a pinch, he could swap them out. His preference was old school. His dad had enlightened him that nostalgia lives better in tangible things. A letter more nostalgic than an email. A paperback more than an eBook. The mystery board over the O-APP.

On the opposite side of the study was another desk. Above it hung Tammy's vision board, plastered with inspirational quotes including, "Don't wait for the perfect moment, take the moment and make it perfect," and a bundle of pictures, including one of the Eiffel Tower and another of her and Brady. It helped remind her to go after her goals. She had it made before she started seeing him a year ago and "manifested" him into her life. Only a few pictures were on the board that she hadn't "thought into existence" yet—specifically, the section *Vacation in Paris*.

Tammy put the novel on the desk, and went to the aquarium by the railing. She grabbed a jar and shook the green pellets in the mini pond. "My sweet Little Toby." She patted the baby turtle on the head.

Her wavy blonde hair was bright and bouncy and her hazel eyes nestled in her delightful, round face. She had no shoes on and was wearing only one sock. Her favorite one with the spy turtle design.

It didn't make sense to Brady how he was with her. He was hardheaded, and she was super adorable. Even he could admit she was in a different league.

His smart wristwatch beeped, taking him out of his musings. *Protest* flashing on the screen. It was time to prep for City Hall.

He opened the *Memo App* on his wristwatch and clicked the "poof" symbol. He scrolled to the top. The bribe report photo had made it through. He smiled. Don't underestimate a Mystery Solver.

Connecting to the printer through Wi-Fi, he made two copies of the report. One he left on the printer and the other he placed inside a hidden drawer at the base of the cabinet. It felt good to be a step ahead of the bastards.

In the reflection of the Gadget Rack, he smoothed out his hair. Then "wiped off" the shoulders of his mystery solver suit.

From the time he was a little kid he was always searching for answers. No matter the question. It was an itch he had to scratch. For his first ever investigation, he remembered the ant trail in the kitchen. Instinctively, he followed it to a hole in the tile. Any normal person would plug the hole and call it a day. But he couldn't. He had to know where it came from, and why. He put on thick overalls and boots and crawled under the dusty house. You had to get down and dirty to get the truth sometimes. He found an ant hill. Next to it was a leak in a water pipe. Not only did the ants have their designated food hole, they also had their water source. He had told his poppa, and they fixed the leak and handled both problems at the source.

He had never correlated those earlier moments to who he would become. Until now. And soon he would be promoted to the leader of a group best known for that activity. Life was making sense.

As Tammy adjusted rocks in the turtle aquarium, Brady snuck up behind her. Little Toby craned his head to get a glimpse of Brady and smiled with his baby tongue sticking out.

"You could be looking at the new president of Mystery Solvers Inc.," Brady said to her, and winked at Little Toby. Toby's mouth opened wider in excitement.

Tammy's mouth curved into a smile. "That calls for a celebration." She spun around, grabbed Brady's mystery suit, and pulled him in close. "We have enough saved up for a trip."

He glanced down and away, then turned back quickly, knowing better than to shoot her suggestion down completely. "Soon, babe."

Her posture slumped and she scrunched her lips. "What's the big deal about taking a week off?"

"What do you want me to say? If I become president, I'll only get busier." He rubbed his neck. "We'll still have date night."

Tammy did that thing when she wanted to change the subject. She pretended the conversation didn't happen. She lowered her head, glanced up at him, and touched him with her naked foot. "Can you help me find my other sock? Maybe that's a mystery. Socks disappear all the time."

Brady looked at her, unsure if she was being serious. Then he chuckled. "Very cute, honey. Let us deal with the mysteries." It reminded him of the infamous bum who begged for socks. He'd never seen the bum in person, but it was mentioned at headquarters many times. He glanced at his watch. "Check the dryer. I got to go." He grabbed the bribe report copy from the printer.

Next to the Gadget Rack was an open container of liquid toxin tester. No use for that today. He opened the gadget door full of his special devices: Microscopes, Magneeto pens, key molders, Key Bullets, and other gizmos.

He reached past the front row and grabbed a red smoke bomb from the back. He liked its patented squishy, round texture. It was made to explode on impact and required speeds of forty miles an hour to break the seal. He probably wouldn't need it but took it just in case. You could never be too sure at a protest. He kissed Tammy on the forehead and trotted down the steps.

She crossed her arms. "If you're not going to give me what I want, at least give one girl in your life a win. Let your sister join."

Brady almost stopped to respond. His sister had been bugging him ad nauseam and telling everyone else to remind him, and it was getting annoying. He realized it was better to ignore any mention of his sister and Mystery Solvers, and it would go away. Bickering only egged it on. He continued, at the same speed, down the steps and out the front door as if he didn't hear her. She had mumbled it, so, in his defense, that would work.

Sunbeams shone through the fluffy clouds, catching Brady's face at a cinematic angle. He put on his Top Gun aviator shades. Today was going to be a good day. No—a great day. When he exposed the truth, it would mark a new standard for Mystery Solvers.

His next-door neighbor, Ardy, was directing a fat technician and a hairy technician who fumbled a washer and dryer set on a dolly. Ardy spotted Brady and waved, yelling louder than necessary. "Have a fantabulous day, Brady!"

Brady nodded. "You too, Ardy. What you got there?"

"These fine, strapping men are helping me load in my new Super Laundry set. No need for laundromats no more."

The back of the truck was open. Bags were strewn about. On the side of the truck was a flashy promotion. "Super Laundry: A Lifetime of FREE Service," and at the bottom was a sponsored LFS circled logo.

"Not a bad idea," said Brady. He put a hand in the air to Ardy. "Later."

Bill came up the driveway in his green, ball-shaped buggy car. The window was down, and upbeat music was blaring. His face went awestruck when he saw the bribe report in Brady's hand. "How? They destroyed the evidence." Then he smiled ear-to-ear. "Why didn't you tell me?"

"Had to make sure, first." Brady winked. "I have a duty to this world."

"Yeah, you do." Bill leaned over and drummed on the side of the car door. "Time to seal the deal, baby."

CHAPTER 5

A sea of protesters surrounded City Hall. Helicopters circled the scene. Police waited in riot gear. Protesters raised their picket signs in unison.

"We are the majority! We are the majority!! We are the majority of the majority!!!" The chant grew to a crescendo.

Some protest signs were holographic, edited by color and design in the software. One sign had "BIG BANKS" engulfed in the classic red circle with the slash-line crossing it out. Another read, "DON'T POISON US," with pills rotating on the frame. Other signs were old-school white boards with a stick handle attached. One old-time sign read, "The people behind me can't see." Another read, "This is a protest sign," and next to it, "His protest sign is smaller than mine."

A crowd stood in a half-circle around the news correspondent and Brady in his Mystery Solver suit. Bill was next to him.

The correspondent raised the microphone to her lips. "It's been remarked that with so much pressure on Mystery Solvers Inc., you could end up going backward if you make one wrong move. What do you say to the haters?" She flipped the mic to Brady.

He put his hand to his chin, thoughtful about the answer.... "As long as we persevere with the truth, we'll be okay."

Off to the side of the crowd, two tall hooligans scoped out the scene. They were the same two men in black hoodies at the laundromat stick up. Lievy and Azin. Spotting Brady and Bill, they looked back at each other, nodded, and moved in closer.

Out of nowhere, a group of juvenile delinquents pushed the hooligans aside and intruded on the crowd.

"Mystery Solvers and your wannabe superhero spandex," said the leader of the delinquents. "You guys believe the craziest things!"

The other delinquents laughed.

Brady scanned the crowd, moving his eyes only, and got a glimpse of the troublemakers. He tightened his stance and quietly put his hand in his pocket to make sure the smoke bomb was there.

"Yeah," said one of them. "You believe in aliens, don't you?"

"Only crazy people believe in aliens," another chimed in.

Wild Bill turned with a disgusted face. "Huh? How do you not believe in aliens? UFOs. UAPs. Heard of them?"

"Yeah, they're made up," said the leader. "They said Area 51 is a lie. It doesn't have alien technology."

Brady relaxed and took his hand off the smoke bomb. "If you looked, you'd know Area 51 is a cover. S4 is the real location."

"Yeah," said Bill. "Try checking past page one of the internet."

"You believe anything," said the delinquent leader. "Always have something handy to replace earlier lies. How do you know S4 isn't fake? Don't you think we'd see more UFOs? The news would've shown the evidence. Not CGI. It's bullcrap!"

Bill looked at the empty air beside him. "Hear that? He said 'the news'. Have you noticed that Big News spins the narrative of only one side of a story? They do it to create a highly charged emotional response." He unfurled his hand toward the delinquents as an example. "And do you know why that is? So they can sell more advertisements." He nodded proudly. "You can listen to the TV and continue to be mad at your family, friends, and society all you want. That's a 'No, thank you' from me."

In the background, a man and a woman turned to each other and apologetically embraced.

The second delinquent called out, "Of course you believe in aliens. You're crazy mystery theorists!"

Still disappointed, Bill said, "You've seen pictures of the galaxy. And you think we're the only intelligent life in the universe? Cool story, bruh."

Brady added, "Do yourself a favor. Read *If Aliens Attack*."

"You mean the fantasy/sci-fi book?" said the third delinquent.

The leader said, "It was written by that crazy guy who said he was abducted. He had zero proof." The delinquents laughed.

Brady knew that even if there was proof, they wouldn't believe it. Sometimes disbelief can be stronger than belief. It wasn't lost on him in that moment that he hadn't seen proof for himself, either. They were on different sides of the same coin. But his belief would be stronger than theirs. "Take it or leave it," he said, "here's my favorite line from the book: 'Some alien brains are in the pelvis or stomach; it's not always the head.' A biological protective mechanism." Brady raised his brows. "You're welcome."

The crowd applauded.

The delinquents flipped them off and walked away.

Bill waved at them. "Bye-bye."

As the delinquents disappeared, the hooligans moved a little closer. Then a little closer.

The correspondent took back control of the interview, pulling Brady's arm and turning him to face the camera.

"What would you say is the purpose of these protests and do you think you're making headway?"

Brady stood tall with conviction. "The wool has been pulled over our eyes for too long. More and more people are waking up. The powers that be can't control us anymore. We have people willing to fight for the truth and the evidence to stand up." He unrolled the bribe report.

Gasps and cheers bubbled in the crowd. Faces in disbelief.

"And that's all from City Hall. Todd, back to you in the studio." The camera feed cut out. The correspondent dropped her jaw to the cameraman, who showed her two thumbs and a payday smile.

The crowd clapped and cheered! Brady and Bill did an elaborate handshake. Bill did the dab, then a robot dance, then pointed to the crowd—who erupted with applause. Brady nodded proudly.

Now flustered, Lievy and Azin pushed their way through the cheering mob toward Brady and Bill.

Three girls swooned and batted their eyes. Brady and Wild Bill puffed out their chests and took it all in, letting the cascade of admiration wash over them. As the joyful noise simmered, Brady whispered something into Bill's ear. The hooligans moved in closer.

Brady flung the red smoke bomb into the ground. Up it went in a puff of smoke!

Faces looked on in suspense. When the smoke settled, the Mystery Solvers were gone. The hooligans frowned. The crowd went wild!

CHAPTER 6

It was the day of the big announcement. Brady, Bill, and the rest of the mystery solvers were leaning in around the table. They held their breath as Dan prepared his thoughts.

Photographs of each installment of Mystery Solvers ran along the meeting room wall, from the ORIGINAL group, including a younger Dan, to the current outfit. With the chosen successor, a new picture would go up. And picture day was an exciting tradition.

They looked around at each other, sizing up the competition. Who was going to take over in the changing of the guard? Every one of them thought they would make a great leader, which added up. Being in the group by itself was a sign of strength and perseverance. All necessary qualities. But who was kidding whom? It was between Harry and Brady.

Harry had taken Brady under his wing when he first joined as a young buck with Bill. He showed them the ropes and was even there for Brady's first-ever mystery—The Chicken or the Egg Mystery.

They both liked each other, and each had the other as their second choice. Yet there was an unspoken desire to hold the title.

Harry had solved many big-time mysteries, including the Big Foot and Pyramid mysteries. He'd been with Mystery Solvers the longest of the current group, not including Dan.

Brady was the second youngest. One of his few "drawbacks." Most of them started in their twenties or early thirties—not in their early to mid-teens like Brady and Bill.

Even without his latest triumph, Brady was the current favorite. He gave himself a 55-60% chance. The bribe report was but a megaton cherry on top. He'd prepared for this moment his whole life. Being chosen would help him achieve his life's goal and make his father proud. He had to fight off emotions just thinking about it.

Dan cleared his throat. "What do we know is behind every bad condition in the world?"

Without skipping a beat, the group chanted, "Someone is actively making it that way! So, turn every rock, pull every string, follow every crumb until you find out who it is!"

"Still on your toes," said Dan. He let the moment breathe. "You all know the importance of this meeting. It's time I passed the torch. Let's cut to the chase."

The anticipation had Brady tickled pink. Through excited nerves, he winked at Bill with bad timing.

On the other side of the table, Slick whispered something to Harry, who rejected him, clearly not interested in his negativity.

Dan continued, "I've looked through everything. And as hard as it was, I have come to my decision....

"It's down to Brady and Slick."

A collective disbelief spread on everyone's face. Some heads tilted. They looked at Harry, worried about his reaction. He sat there in shock. Slick ran his fingers through his greasy hair with a smirk in his eyes.

"Brady and Slick?" Army questioned out loud.

"Are you sure?" said Bowl cut.

Brady felt a twinge of irritation. When Dan had introduced him and Bill as Mystery Solvers, the first thing that came out of Slick's dirty mouth was, "Why would we let children in? They're stupid and weak."

Ignore him, Harry had said. If they're here for the cause, that's all that matters to me and anyone worth their salt.

On character alone, how could Dan put Slick ahead of Harry? It wasn't only Brady who disliked Slick. Harry saw what he saw, and others did as well, even if it wasn't spoken. It would be wrong to root for Slick, even with the better odds.

"Drumroll, please," said Dan. The table rumbled. Hands bounced off the wood in a barrage of blurry strikes.

Suddenly, Brady felt a touch of calm, followed by a wave of guilty relief. It should've been between him and Harry. This made it easy for Dan to pick him as the new president! A faint smile started to show. The relief turned to a quiet excitement, and he thought of his dad.

The Mystery Solvers continued feverishly rattling the table.

Nerves came on strong for Brady and Slick, who both tried to control their breathing, in anticipation.

Gunner stared intently at Dan's mouth for the first clue.

Bowl Cut smiled in amusement.

Bill slowly scrunched his neck, leaned back, and closed one eye.

Army rattled the edge of the table faster with the last of his strength. Tatatatatatatatatatatatatatatatatat....

In a sweep of his arms, Dan directed the rattling to stop.

"Brady. You're the most impressive Mystery Solver we've ever had. We shouldn't be surprised."

Brady hadn't realized he was holding his breath. He exhaled in a release of joy. Standing up, the buzz of euphoria lit up his face, and he headed toward the front.

"However," said Dan, "I had to go with longevity. I chose Slick."

Brady didn't hear what he said. He shook Dan's unoffered hand and turned around, smiling. Beaming.

Hesitant, Dan put a confused hand on Brady's shoulder.

Suddenly, Brady noticed the energy in the room felt off. A line of blank faces were staring at him. Did they not think he'd be chosen? He was the front runner. That other asshole was barely 3rd or 4th in line. Why was this a surprise?

Slick walked up with a crazy look in his eyes. "What the hell are you doing?"

A jolt of revelation made its way in his mind as time rewound. He was now hearing the words he had missed.

♪ ♪ ♪

It took a moment for the embarrassment to hit, having blacked out for a nanosecond at the twist of outcome. Like your crush telling you they liked you only to reveal moments later, it was a joke, a dare. The anguish so fresh you forgot where you were.

When Brady came back to his surroundings, a wave of nerves tightened his throat and his heart pounded out of his chest.

The rest of the Mystery Solvers stayed silent.

Keeping his expression detached, Brady did his best not to let his appearance match his emotions. But it would be impossible. He had let his father down. Everything he taught him went to waste. What would the rest of his family think? Would Tammy still want to be with him? Did everyone here think he was a sham?

He couldn't hold it anymore. Anxiety broke through the surface. He became visibly distraught, taking in heavy breaths through his nose, and slid his trembling hand in his pocket.

"I made the choice," said Dan. "It was a tough call."

Slick scanned the room, smiling at the shocked expressions.

Brady sat back in his chair, despondent. Of all people, how could Dan let Slick run Mystery Solvers Inc.? He shook his head. "You can't tell me one person who would follow his lead." As much as he wanted to believe that, he knew it wasn't true, or fair.

People might not have liked Slick as much, but they followed and worked with him, solving mysteries at a much faster clip than on their own.

"What do you think this is doing for you?" Dan asked. "I can tell you it isn't helping."

"I solved the biggest mystery on corruption. How could you pick him over me? Has anyone done anything close to that? Honestly." Brady bit his inner cheek, averting some of his mental pain to physical.

"Calm down, child. The grown-ups have deliberated." Slick smiled his annoying smile.

Brady stood up, stuck his fist out, and his middle finger sprang up.

A "Whoa!" jumped out of Gunner's mouth.

Army jostled around in his chair, holding his mouth shut to keep from bursting out laughing.

"Some professionalism, please," said Dan. He rubbed his forehead, chewing over something on his mind. Then he grabbed the remote from the board. "I didn't want to do this, Brady." He clicked the remote.

The projection screen crept down. The gentle purr of the screen coming down, to him, felt like a horn blaring to get him off the train tracks while being held in place by titanium straps. He wasn't going to avoid the impact.

The screen stopped.

Brady's chest tightened. He looked up, then at the others, and cleared the lump in his throat. Did they know what this was?

Lit up on the screen was the file room where he extracted the bribe report. An officer in uniform appeared to be looking directly at him through the camera.

"Are we ready?" The man adjusted the lens. Off to the side, a hand removed a note marked "Fake" from the bribe report. "He won't know what hit him. I wish I could see the dumb look on his face when he sees this. Hi there, Brady," said the officer with a wide grin. He looked off-camera again. "Make sure everyone knows not to take the bribe report unless he captured a picture with the Memo App. If he did, you can destroy his evidence. He needs to think he outwitted us." The officer faced forward. "I hope you see this soon."

The video paused. An eerie silence swept over the room.

If Brady could have a superpower, it would be to disappear. The day of the mission rushed through his mind. Almost ten guards couldn't take Bill. How easy it was to retrieve the bribe report. The dangling carrot of the file name—*Super Duper Top Secret*. It was all too perfect. With the adrenaline pumping, he hadn't noticed.

Army palmed his face. "You always confirm twice."

In the era of narrative news and AI, it was Investigation 101 to verify every source twice, at a minimum. Some did three, and some went as far as four or five. You could never be too certain.

Dan rewound the video and stopped it with the "Fake" note in the center of the frame.

"It was better in the long run if you found out sooner," said Dan, almost apologetic. "We can't put out false claims. It looks bad on the Mystery Solver name. I wanted it to be you. I really did."

"This isn't fair. It could've happened to anyone."

"But it didn't happen to anyone, did it?" Slick forced a chuckle, twisting the screws. "It was you. This is embarrassing. You weren't chosen, Brady, it's okay."

Brady grinded his teeth and tightened his fists. "You're a pretender. I should be president and you know it."

Dan placed the remote back on the board. "A leader doesn't have to urge people to follow him. There's a natural gravitation. And by more than one person. No offense."

"Why should it matter?" said Brady. "Outside the sting operation, my production speaks for itself. I worked my ass off."

Slick made a cynical face. "Accept your mistake and move on."

Gunner piled on, "I'm not sure if I agree with them or if I'm just mad at you, Brady, for not taking me on that mission. Which definitely should've included blasters."

Brady crossed his arms and stared pleadingly at the room. "I deserve this...."

Dan sighed. "Brady. You've told me how much you look up to your father. Do you think he'd be proud of you right now?"

It hit Brady like a ten-ton weight. His heart sagged, and he slid down in his seat.

"Sorry," said Dan. "Let's pretend none of this happened. And show some respect for my decision."

The room got quiet.

"Alright. Come on up, Slick. Everyone, this is your new president."

Slick took center stage and the group clapped lightly while Dan eyed Brady to make sure another outburst wouldn't come.

Slick acknowledged the soft congratulations with a couple of nods. Then a small bow to Dan. "You're an impossible follow, sir. I'll try my best. From all of us, have a great retirement."

Breaking up the tension, Glasses and Bowl Cut whistled. Gunner and Army cheered. Curls and Bill clapped lightly. The striking hands got louder as the group let the embarrassing moment fade into the past. This was for Dan.

He had been a great president the last couple of years and deserved a good farewell. He was in the group itself for two decades. They made a lot of progress, exposing mysteries on a larger scale during his time. From the Museum of Fake Artifacts to the revelation of Narrative News and many others. Dan reflected on his time and shared a few stories. The group got a kick out of hearing about his younger days and how it made him who he was today.

When he finished, he changed his tone to a serious one. "Thank you all. I'm going to miss you. But it's time to turn over a new leaf. You each have a responsibility to keep our message strong. And to fight for the will of the people. Always remember that." They nodded. "Slick, this is you now. It's time to wrap up the meeting."

"Of course," said Slick. "Announcements." He addressed the group, making sure not to make eye contact with Brady. "Due to our reputation being under rebuild, Brady, sadly, I must let you go. You put unnecessary hardship on the group at this time. When things are back to normal, I'll check in with you. Until then, work on yourself."

Dead silence.

Once the title transfer was finalized, Dan had no say. He apologized with a shrug.

Brady rose to his feet with what little energy he had left. "This is my life. This is who I am. You can't do this."

Slick glared down at him from his new perch. "I just did.... Sorry, but your daddy ain't getting you out of this one."

CHAPTER 7

Sock Street spanned several blocks and overflowed with production facilities. A prominent street in the district, it boasted the largest export of socks in the western world.

Outside Quality Sock Maker Factory, lackeys, in gray uniforms, and enforcers, in navy blue uniforms, shoved the factory workers in the back of the vans. Along the face of the building, the convoy of black vehicles started up. The fleet drove down Sock Street and stopped at the next factory—Mill's Sock Plant.

Hundreds of automated machines buzzed and whirled on the knitting room floor, churning out a surplus of product. James Lin pulled out a cloth, wiped the speckled sweat from his forehead, and adjusted his large-framed glasses. He stepped up on a stool, leveling himself with the machine console. It appeared massive next to him. After punching in the details of the next order, the machine came to life with hums and clicks and flashing lights.

The manager came over, fidgeting with his stylus pen. He double-checked the notes on his electronic pad. "I have to do it again, Mr. Lin. The owner ordered me to cut more hours. We can't afford your rate."

James hopped down from the stool and took the family photo off his desk. The picture showed him, his wife, and his son laughing on the teacup ride, with chocolate smeared all over their faces. "I teach my son always to protect famiry. What I tell him if I can not support us like real mans?"

"It's not my decision. If it were up to me, nothing would change. The schedule starts next week. Notes will be in your basket by the weekend." He rubbed his neck. With nothing else to say, he left.

In the lobby, the receptionist dropped a form in the basket system. A gang of lackeys and enforcers crowded in through the entrance, openly parading their blasters.

Ivan, the man in charge, had a buzzed head and wore a brown leather jacket. He stepped forward, rested the blaster on his cheek scar, and eyed her until she became flustered.

"Uh, hi—you have an appointment?" She straightened the papers and placed her pen in a coffee mug.

"Tell your manager he has visitors. Nothing else," said Ivan. "'You. Have. Visitors.' Got that?"

She fumbled with the phone and dialed line "1" for the manager. The receiver vibrated nervously against her head. It rang twice before connecting.

"What do you need?" The manager spoke with an irritable tone.

"You have visitors.... Got that?" she looked at Ivan for approval of her delivery.

Ivan nodded, and a twinkle passed across his eyes.

"I don't know. They're here. You have visitors. Got that?" She hung up and began shuffling papers. She opened and closed the drawers pointlessly, trying to look busy, and added a few smiles, hoping the intruders wouldn't include her any further.

Ivan tilted his head in her direction. A lackey grabbed her and pulled her up.

The manager came in, irritated, ready for a fight. "What is going on here?"

"Your duties are finished." Ivan grinned, with his blaster resting on his shoulder.

"On what grounds? Who are you?"

"Your new boss." Ivan pointed the blaster at the manager. "This socks, doesn't it? Get it? Socks. Sucks. Similar but different. Pun-y."

The manager said, "Your joke sucks. Get it?"

Ivan yanked the manager by the collar. "I make the jokes!" He shoved him toward an enforcer and called out to the lackeys, "Round everyone up."

In the yarn room, lackeys torpedoed the employees with a deluge of threaded yarn balls until they surrendered with their hands up.

In the wrapping room, an enforcer held an employee to his rolling chair as another fastened shrink wrap to it. They twirled him into a ball on wheels.

In the knitting room, two lackeys forced the smaller James Lin forward while another trained a blaster on him. James struggled against their constraint. "You need weapon to hold down a old man like me? You is cowad."

♪ ♪ ♪

Unable to move, Brady lay face up in bed. His life energy draining into the mattress. With his dream unceremoniously ripped away, it had become a struggle to do the small things. Like getting out of bed. Changing. Doing laundry. He peered through the apathetic blur as the ceiling fan rotated in a slow, hypnotic hum....

The day he decided to be a Mystery Solver created a vivid impression in his mind. When he was much younger, his dad was about to go on a mission in his old-timers' Mystery Solver suit—faded gray—a prominent color at the time.

"What do you do, Daddy?" he had asked.

The look on his dad's face brightened. Like seeing your baby's first steps, an elation only parents could understand. It was the first time Brady had asked him about his life. He got choked up, and swallowed his excitement. "I protect innocent people from the big bullies of the world. By exposing their dark secrets."

"But—but you can get hurt," said young Brady.

"Most of the bullies I deal with are hiding. So I have to find them and expose them."

Young Brady's eyes worried. "But a kid at school tried to stop a bully, and the bully made him go to a hospital."

"A handful of people can make the world seem scary. But if you stand up to them, they eventually shrink, and the world doesn't seem so scary anymore."

"Is it hard to stop bullies?" young Brady asked.

Dad got down on a knee and patted his head. "That's why there aren't many of us doing it. The really brave ones are willing to give themselves up so everyone else can be safe. They have big hearts."

And that's when it was. Brady beamed up at his dad with a child's wonder. "I want to help people. I want to be like you, Daddy."

"One day you can." Dad hugged him tight. "You can be the best Mystery Solver there ever was." He kissed Brady and headed out the front door.

Brady would go back to that memory whenever he felt he was losing his way.

His father, Clark Watts, was one of the original Mystery Solvers. A photo of him hung in the meeting room at Mystery Solvers Inc. He was in the original members' photo and several pictures after it. A true Mystery Solver. Clark Watts had a reputation for taking on the dangerous assignments. He solved one mystery after another without a hitch until that last mission.

When Momma Jan broke the news of his father's death, it sent Brady spiraling. Nightmares woke him from his sleep. Anxiety guided his waking hours. It took months to get over the initial shock, but under the surface, the pain stayed with him for years.

Eventually, Mom said something that stuck with him and helped him through it. "Your father will always be with you." She would cover her heart whenever she said it. For a kid who lost his hero, it was hopeful. And to him, it felt true. His dad was looking over him.

When he was older, a notorious bully at the school playground was picking on him. With the thought of his father, he faced the bully and didn't back down. He took several knockdowns, but got back up each time. Other children pleaded with him to stop getting up. He paid them no mind. After the fourth time, the bully ran away, scared that the tenacious kid might retaliate.

Brady learned a valuable lesson. By facing bullies without flinching, they eventually gave up. Bullies, deep down, were cowards.

He would help other kids when bullies tormented them, and he became known as the "Bully Destroyer." When a prominent bully, Dovinic, got wind of this, he came to destroy Brady and take back control of his imagined superiority.

With foresight and sharp-witted tactics, Brady set a trap to squelch the attempt. Dovinic happen to be bullying Bill at the time. Brady convinced Bill, despite his shortcomings, to stand up for himself.

They were eating at Bill's lunch table when Dovinic burst into the lunchroom, and stood over them with a mischievous grin and a pair of brass knuckles. "Two-for-one. Just my lucky day."

The other kids kept their eyes on their food, wanting no part of any retaliation.

Brady signaled to Bill, whose hands were trembling, gripping a handle under the table. Bill wasn't ready to deal with the potential backlash. That's why Brady was there. He grabbed Bill's hands and yanked them. The attached string veered, by carefully placed pulley wheels, to the left, under the table, then across to another table and shot up into the ceiling behind a pillar. With a couple of precisely placed bars, the string shot around the pillar and directly above Dovinic. The tile above him had been removed, and down came a tub of scalding hot soup.

After a moment of shock, before anger could take over, Dovinic felt the hot sizzle against his scalp. He grabbed his head in agony. The pain was so intense he ran off crying.

Word got around, and bullies disappeared from the school, setting off a chain reaction in neighboring schools where bullies were confronted and destroyed. His actions had a rippling effect. In the same way, bad actions can have a rippling effect, too. It matters who wins.

Maybe that was why he worked so hard to become a Mystery Solver. To carry on his father's legacy and expose bullies on a larger scale. Perhaps that was why his sister, Natasha, was begging to join, too. The DNA ran in the family.

♪   ♪   ♪

Over the next couple of days, Brady tossed and turned, agonizing over Slick's words ... *I just did ... your daddy ain't getting you out of this one.*

Anger and sadness took their turns, twisting him up, only giving him a break here and there, then back to the torment.

Tammy's attempts to uncover what was going on were met with a cold shoulder. No matter how much she asked, he couldn't let her find out. It would stamp him as a true failure.

When he first tried to eat, the food came back up minutes later. He could only keep down small portions of water or tea. Eventually, when he was able to have solids, he ate applesauce and chicken soup. Tammy was sneaking Echinacea into his liquid nourishment. She had assumed it was simply an illness.

On the third day of his personal hell, Brady put his Mystery Solver suit on the dresser. He was determined to return to headquarters and plead his case. He would show them he still belonged. He had written out a detailed monologue with an apology. But in the end, he couldn't muster the courage. It would destroy him if he got shot down again in his frail state. So the suit lay on the dresser, collecting dust.

After the fourth day, he decided to go outside and take a long walk. Being holed up too long, added stir-crazy to his already long list of problems. He needed to make a change.

When his neighbor greeted him, he didn't look up. He lugged his disheveled body along the streets.

People gave him weird looks, but he hadn't noticed. He was stuck in a tumbling current of thoughts.

An hour into the walk, looking out at the houses, the cars, the people, the trees, the birds, the buildings, it was starting to help. He could sense his mind untangling and the emotions starting to dissipate. Though it was slight, it was a welcome change. Maybe it could get better.

He passed by a newsstand that carried Electronic Newspads, magazines, and old-school newspapers. Photos of a young man in a Mystery Solvers suit were plastered over all the headlines.

He did a double take. The images came into focus.

They were pictures of *HIM*.

In bold headlines:

"PUSHING FINANCIAL LIES: BEHIND THE SCENES"
"FAKE MYSTERIES SOLD TO YOU"
"MYSTERY SOLVERS INC. IS THE REAL MYSTERY"
"BRIBED"

A shock wave of embarrassment overwhelmed him. His upper body got weak and his knees buckled. He reached out, breaking his fall with the shelf, inadvertently knocking down a row of news tablets. Quickly, he stood them back upright.

The sunlight felt like a spotlight on him, with the world staring. Judging. A quick forehead massage obscured his face from passersby as he darted away.

Taking a shortcut, he rushed across the street and walked fast through a small city park. An old man on a bench looked up from his electronic news pad. Brady veered off. The man made the connection that it was the same face on his screen, and he scowled. Brady hurried through an alley and across a road. A mother grabbed her kids in horror and ushered them back into their house. A kid riding by on a bike saw him and threw his Sloshy drink. Brady ducked. The blue ice splattered on the building behind him.

It was said as a Mystery Solver, if you haven't been attacked by the news, you haven't done enough. He found it hard to imagine that proved any value. This was much harder to deal with in real life than he imagined.

Before long he made it home, slumped face down in his bed, wishing the excruciating nightmare would end.

Circles of dampness bled onto the comforter. He had been putting on a brave face when Tammy was around. He couldn't show weakness in her presence. When she was gone, the emotions rushed out.

What could there be to live for if he couldn't solve mysteries? He chastised Slick in his head, vividly picturing an onslaught of words, and a horror on Slick's face. If only it were to his actual face, man to man.

After twenty minutes, Brady snapped himself out of it. He couldn't let that disgusting excuse of a man get the best of him. He made his way to the closet with his Mystery Solver suit and rolled the sliding door open. He dropped the suit behind the hamper.

I can do better on my own. Just watch.

CHAPTER 8

Moonlight glared on the compound. Glints of light reflected off two circular windows—like wicked eyes looking down on an inferior world.

Surrounded by ten-foot-high walls and a jungle of palms, the compound bristled with sentries. Soft swishing fronds and the occasional buzz of a green fig beetle were the only sounds in the monotony of a 24-hour surveillance.

Inside the boardroom, an enormous map of the city covered an entire wall. It was filled with two kinds of magnets. Ones with a picture of a Super Laundry building, which represented the locations of the laundromats, and ones with a picture of a Super Laundry washer/dryer set, representing household owners.

Lackeys cowered in their seats, waiting anxiously for the boss to lay down the law. They could see it in his eyes. One of their own had messed up, and they weren't looking forward to the tongue-lashing that would undoubtedly be aimed at all of them.

Vance held up a silver pocket watch by the chain, letting each second tick. Each strike louder than the last, blending with the dim flickers of light. Vance wore a purple fedora and Italian suit. His face was skinny with hollow, sunken eyes, and he sported a pencil mustache.

Next to him, Ivan twisted his neck, popping his vertebrae in place. In the light, his cheek scar was thick and dark like a branding. "A couple of you decided to stray from the guidelines."

The door opened, and a large brute of a man dragged in the two laundromat hooligans by their collars. With his thick neck, broad shoulders, and bowling ball arms, Mooch planted them in front of the meeting.

The room went still.

"It's natural to lose socks...." Vance said. "That narrative took a long time to instill in this society." He pocketed the ticking watch. "When you jeopardize that, you put us in a predicament. Don't you?"

Heads in the room nodded, terrified.

The hooligans in the tight grip of Mooch swallowed the lumps in their throats.

A biker girl with black hair and leather pants placed a white case on the table. With her nose pierced, dark lipstick and eyeliner, it always appeared as if she had a scowl. Even when she smiled. She unlatched the snaps and opened the case, revealing a trigger-controlled light gun. It had a clear body and mixed colors in the chamber.

Wary eyes followed the blaster as she handed it to Vance, who spun and faced the hooligans. He pulled a lever, initiating a whirling sound. Then, slowly and with precision, he adjusted the red translucent power nob.

The hooded robbers struggled, unable to escape Mooch's clutch. They grabbed at his leotard, and his bowl cut hair, to which he twisted his grip on their collars, tightening against their necks. They let go.

"It–it was intended to be a surprise," pleaded Lievy.

Azin cowered to the glowing blaster. "They caught it. It won't get out."

"We didn't let it get out!" Vance boomed.

The front door slammed against the wall! The lackeys turned their heads in unison as a massive body entered. A shadow cast on the wall, engulfing the entire room.

Teeth chattered. Faces froze.

"Mr. Sock," said Biker Girl. She added a devilish smirk and a lick of her lips.

Dead eyes pierced the hooligans' souls, and their neck hairs shot up. They clenched their teeth.

Vance pulled the trigger and colors burst into the hooligan's eyes. Their faces set in rigid horror.

Slowly, they drifted, like molasses, into another dimension. Their eyes dimmed, and their bodies went limp. They dangled in Mooch's grip.

"Send them home," said Vance.

Mooch dragged the slumped bodies away. The lackeys watched as the hooligans' feet disappeared across the threshold.

"If a good cop or one of those pesky Mystery Solvers got wind of what we were up to, I might not be so nice," Vance added an *X* to *10th street* on the city map. "If you see anyone catching onto our scheme, you better do something about it."

The group nodded anxiously.

Vance turned around. "Now, get to the next phase of business."

♪   ♪   ♪

The extra activity in the newsroom was to be expected with the agenda of the day and the live broadcast around the corner. The anchor desk was lit perfectly for Todd Strout in his sharp designer suit. The makeup artist combed Todd's thick brown hair for him and added powder to his cheeks. She gave him a flirtatious smile. He reciprocated with a furrowed brow.

The news director, eating a slice of greasy pizza, deleted the news copy from the computer and added an edited report to the teleprompter. He waddled to the anchor desk and leaned over to Todd. "Give them your vintage."

"Of course, sir," said Todd. He quickly inhaled and exhaled three times. "A–E–I–O–U, and sometimes Whyy-whhy-whhy-yyyyyyyah!" He stretched and opened his mouth wide. He contorted his jaw, working his face muscles. Straightened his note cards.

An announcement came over the loudspeaker: "Everyone clear the desk. We start in ten seconds." The makeup lady came back and did one last dab on Todd, staring at him with playful eyes. She and her assistant scurried off the set.

Todd looked up as the fat news director, eating another slice of pizza, counted down with his greasy fingers: Five. Four. Three. Two. One, and pointed to Todd.

"Hi, I'm Todd Strout," he winked, then gave his irresistible slanted smile, "and here's the news. A laundromat downtown was robbed. One victim insisted to the police that only their money was taken." Todd squinted at the teleprompter. "Their laundry was left alone completely...."

...Open City Grill had customers packed in like sardines, with the big screens broadcasting the news at each corner of the restaurant.

A waitress pulled out a mini e-pad. "Is there anything else we can get you?"

"I said, we're good. Thank you." Brady pulled his baseball cap down, covering his face.

The waitress scooted back. "Sorry."

As hard as Brady had been trying, he hadn't done well getting back on the mystery train. And he hadn't told Tammy he was kicked out of the group. He dragged food around his half-empty plate, occasionally scanning the restaurant to make sure no one noticed him.

Tammy adjusted her hair and realigned the cutlery the way she did when she was upset. She took another sip of sparkling wine. It had already flattened, frustrating her more. "Can you try to make the date fun? Remember when we first met?"

He stared at his food.

"Turtles ring a bell?" she said.

He mumbled, "Can right now be later?"

She tucked her hands under her legs. "You messed up one time. Nobody's perfect. The Mystery Solvers know who you are."

Brady closed his eyes.

"You're not telling me what's going on. I'm trying here."

"I'd like it if we didn't talk about it."

She wiped her mouth. "If it's hurting you this much, why don't you take some time away?"

"Please stop," he blurted out. Her face flushed, and he angled his eyes up at the news broadcast.

She let out a disgruntled breath, her frustration turning to silence.

Good. Give it a rest, Brady thought. A good intention doesn't always equal a good outcome.

She angled her body away and pushed the sparkling wine to the edge of the table.

A minute later, Brady glanced over. Tammy's arms were crossed, and her brows were arching high. Expecting an apology. Brady turned away. She was the one who brought it up. She should be the first to apologize.

Tammy cast a sideways glance. "Why is he doing this? What did I do?" she said loud enough, hoping for him to respond.

Brady looked up at the TV. Todd Strout put his hands together and looked at the camera. "Here's the latest...."

A small box on the top-right zoomed into the entire screen: The mayor was speaking to a sea of reporters. Bulbs flashed and popped as he spoke. "We are going to clean up the streets. And I won't sleep until it's a safe place for everyone. So let's hurry. I want some sleep!" The reporters laughed. "And allow the police to do their jobs, okay? To the Mystery Solvers out there, please leave it to the pros."

The screen shrank and disappeared, with Todd back in full view.

"You heard it from the mayor," said Todd. "The Mystery Solvers have been Unincorporated...." Then he looked off camera. "Don't they have jobs? Or are they volunteers?" He chuckled softly. "Either way, if I had a rich family, I'd just go be rich and enjoy life. Just a suggestion." Todd smiled a big grin.

Brady dropped his head, and clenched his teeth. "Why did we come here?" He lowered his cap even more.

Tammy put her hand on his shoulder. "You deserve time off if anyone does. It could be good to have a break."

Pain set in his jaw.

"It is the police's job, anyways," Tammy added. "Let them take the slack for a little while."

He darted a glance at her. "You make a good point. The police should help find your spy turtle sock. It's their job. Right, honey?"

She looked at him with a pain in her eyes. One of emotional betrayal.

He wouldn't admit it, but he enjoyed seeing her bothered by the comment. She could join in some of his torment. "Socks, huh? Most ridiculous mystery I've ever heard. No one in their right mind would look into it."

"Why are you doing this?" she said.

Brady knew he would probably be kicked out of the house at this point, so what the hell, might as well go for broke. "I'm sure the infamous bum knows what's happening with your socks." Brady waved his hand as if announcing the newest magazine issue, "Investigation: The Sock Mystery."

"That's it!" Tammy threw her napkin on the table and stormed out. The electro-chime at the entrance rang as the door opened and closed.

"What is wrong with me?" Brady leaned forward, catching his face with his hands.

The waitress was standing off to the side, awkwardly silent.

"Check, please," said Brady.

That night, the lights were out and Brady lay on the living room couch. The blanket was up to his neck, and his feet were exposed to the cold. He looked at the bedroom door, then up to the high ceiling—eyes filled with guilt.

He cuddled into a ball under the blanket.

CHAPTER 9

By the next day, the Tooth Fairy section of Brady's mystery board was stamped, *Solved*, wrapping up all of his current investigations. Yet he didn't feel accomplished.

Stubble had grown in patches on his face and his hair was greasy, shooting out in spikes on the right side. Not from a product, but from lack of attention and care. Uninvited thoughts of Slick sent him into a fit, and he knocked the easel over. The board slapped on the floor. Pins and cards broke free, scattering in the study.

Begrudgingly, he collected the cards and put the board back together, pin by pin.

He sighed. He needed to fix his self-authored mess if he was going to get his life back on track. And he knew where to start. Happy wife, happy life. Happy girlfriend, happy world, friend. Right?

But since he got nowhere talking to Tammy—she had him in silent treatment—he did the next best thing. He shaved off the stubble, washed his hair, and headed out.

Driving in the afternoon traffic, the Mysterymobile drifted in the lane, almost hitting a curb. After several honks from a worried driver, Brady straightened up.

He adjusted his sitting position and gripped tight on the wheel, thinking about his time at Mystery Solvers Inc. With all the days they spent together, it pained him how easily they let him go. Not one of them stood up to bat for him. Strangely, it hurt more to think of the good times. The pushup contests with Gunner and Army, where he came in last place every time. But he didn't care because he was one of the macho boys for a brief moment. Or when Glasses or Curls helped him understand a new device, including how and why it worked. Or Dan as a father figure, and Harry as a mentor. Thinking about it got him feeling insecure.

"Have they mentioned me?" Brady asked.

Bill was in the passenger seat, riding his hand on a wave of the rushing wind. "We ain't going into that. First, you need to focus on sweet Tammy. You done messed up with her. You handle that, then we deal with the others." Bill attached his phone to the auxiliary frequency through Digital Hotspot. A Wi-Fi on steroids with no buffering. He synced it up and pressed his Beats app.

Rap beats pumped through the speakers. He bobbed his head to the rhythm. "MC Wild Billy ... You know what it is ... Yeah. Yeah. Yeah... Yeah, she's upset, and rightfully so—but don't fret. There's always a way to catch karma in a net. Get it back on your team. We know exactly how 'cause we create the means. Dun-dun-dun–"

Brady disconnected the hotspot.

"Hey, man. I was on a roll."

"You need help."

"Would you rather me sing the investigation song?"

Brady looked at him, very serious. "You really need help."

Something caught their attention. Outside the passenger window was the infamous bum, dejected in ragged clothes. Several pairs of socks hung over the edge of a bucket. A note taped to the side of the bucket read, "Help. Need Loss Free Socks."

It was odd seeing the bum after everything he'd just gone through.

"Brady!" Bill yelled, pointing forward. They were in the middle of the street with oncoming traffic and horns blaring. The car screeched, Brady swerved back into his lane. Bill braced his hand on the dashboard and clutched the grab handle.

Brady kept his eyes ahead, sitting upright. As the street rushed by, the oddity of the moment struck him again. He had gotten in a fight with Tammy, and it was a joke specifically about missing socks and this bum that got him in trouble. Maybe it was a sign from the universe....

No. He didn't believe in that sort of thing, universe signs or symbols. You do things, or you don't do things. That was the sign.

They got onto the freeway east, continued several miles, exited Flower Lane, and drove through Industry City.

Street signs "Honduras," then "Costa Rica," passed by the window.

"That would be funny," said Bill. "What if the people on Honduras Street only use Honduras money and speak only Honduras?"

"Honduras is not a language," said Brady.

"Or what if you could get some good coffee on Costa Rica street? Cuz they're known for coffee. Honduras, too."

"Can you be quiet for one minute of your life?" Brady asked rhetorically.

"Nope. Where are we going again?"

"You never listen, do you? I had the gift sent to my parent's house. Where else would we be going?"

Bill's clenched, shaking fist went up to Brady's face. "This is where else we'd be going."

Brady smiled, but quickly smothered it and got serious. "When we get there, I don't want to see you doing anything crazy. She's off limits."

♪   ♪   ♪

Momma Jan's house had a front garden adorned with flowers, herbs, roses, and a lemon tree. Keeping up a garden brought her peace. By watering the plants, she felt she was also nurturing the planet. That was the story she told Brady when she started filling the garage with gardening tools.

Wearing her usual—the floral headband, the tapered trousers, and denim shirt—Momma Jan pulled Brady in and hugged him tight, swaying him back and forth like a metronome. The hug was a family tradition passed down from his musical grandparents. "It's so nice to see you." She finished swaying him and put her hands on his shoulders. "Natty and I were heading out. Before we go, I want to make sure you're okay. We can always talk about it."

He took her hands off his shoulders. "I can handle myself, Mom. I'm a grown up."

She squeezed his cheek. "Never. Not while I have a say." She pulled out a lip balm from her fanny pack and applied it. "I know I can't stop you from being a Mystery Solver, but it doesn't mean I want to see you hurt."

He looked away. "I'm fine."

The front door opened, and his sister came skipping toward them. She had shoulder-length brown hair and a bubbly personality to match. A female spitting image of her brother.

Bill, attempting to act nonchalant, leaned on the hood with his legs open—slightly too wide for "cool." He was entranced at the sight of her. Unmistakably "chalant." Her hair swayed to and fro as she skipped. Bill put a hand up. "Hey, Natasha. How is–you?"

"Hey, Bill." She couldn't have turned from him any faster, addressing Brady. "Give it up already. I'm joining."

"Are you really going to do this right now?"

"You're not Dad," she said. "You don't get to say what I do."

Brady gave her dagger eyes. "Don't go there."

"You know how I mean it." She had wanted to join Mystery Solvers ever since he joined. "He would let me."

"You have no idea what it's like. It's not happening," said Brady, "so stop bringing it up."

"It is happening–"

"Nope. How loud do I need to say it?"

Natasha rolled her eyes.

Momma Jan stayed quiet. She was used to them bickering over anything. In the past, she would interject and try to get them in agreement. Later she learned it was best to set ground rules and let them sort it out on their own. Like the sibling food splitting solution. Where the first child cuts the portions, but the second child picks first. You never saw more laser focused cutting in your life.

After a few back-and-forths, they stopped arguing. "You're done. Good," said Momma Jan. "Brady, I put the delivery on your bed. Natty and I are going shopping."

"Why doesn't she get a license? Isn't she old enough?"

"Shut up, turd-noodle," said Natasha.

"You want poor momma with an empty nest? We're going. Love ya. Call me if you need anything." She rummaged through her fanny pack, and found the keys. They got in the electric minivan.

As they drove away, Natasha rolled the window down and yelled, "I'm a future Mystery Solver!"

Siblings truly knew how to get under each other's skin. And getting in the last word was an effective technique.

"He's just being a protective brother," said Momma Jan. "That's all it is, honey." She didn't want Natty to be a Mystery Solver either, but wasn't going to tell her that. Otherwise, it would have the same effect as it did when she warned Brady. If you tell a kid not to do something, it only gives them a strong desire, almost a superpower, to do it. It was best not to mention it and hope it became a passing phase.

Natasha aimed the A/C at her face. "If the past doesn't have to define him, why does it have to define me? Why does he get to decide?"

"You're right. And you will." Then Momma Jan used another motherly trick. "What do you think about Bill? He likes you. He's a nice kid."

She took the bait. "Mommmm... I like him as a friend. But he calls himself 'Wild Bill.' I don't know."

"Think about it. In the meantime, let's go shopping."

Hook. Line. And sinker. She wasn't thinking about her brother or Mystery Solvers.

Back at the house, Brady groaned as the minivan disappeared down the street. "Why are sisters so annoying? She'd run for the hills if she knew what I had to deal with this week."

"You haven't told them?"

Brady looked at him. Which sounded very similar to *they don't need to know and don't think about saying anything.* "It'll only make them want to check in on me more. Can't have that."

"It might be hard to share at first," said Bill. "Truth is always the best policy."

Brady walked away from him to the house.

"You're right. They don't need to know." Bill rushed to catch up.

On the second floor, at the end of the hallway, Brady grabbed the doorknob to his old room. He looked across to his sister's door. "Want to see her room?"

"Yeah, for sure," Bill said, excited, then quickly changed his demeanor to dismissive. "I mean, maybe? Not a big deal. Either way. Whatevs. Your call. Nah. Yeah?"

Clothes were everywhere. On Natasha's bed, the dresser, the floor. Her pink comforter was balled up in the far corner of the bed. Her dresser drawers sat askew on broken drawer slides. Photos of teen heartthrobs filled the edges of the Girl Power poster frame. Through the crack of the open bathroom door, her excessive collection of makeup could be seen huddled on the sink. "Not surprising," said Brady. He pushed aside a mound of dirty laundry with his foot.

"She can be as messy as she wants," said Bill. "Just clean it up by the end of each week. I'd do it for her."

Pretending not to hear him, Brady opened the bottom drawer. He found what he was looking for, pulling out a case of adrenal boost shots. "Don't mention I showed you this. When her Acute Fatigue Syndrome kicks in, she has to drink one within ten minutes, or she takes two hours to recover. And she's the one who doesn't want to listen to me?"

"I'd totally take care of her," said Bill.

"Uh, yeah–No, Bill. That's my sister." He waited until Bill acknowledged the seriousness of the matter. Then put the adrenal boosts back in the drawer.

Brady's room was as he left it. The board games were stacked neatly in the corner, with "Lazer Shooter" on top. His bed, the dresser, the art, and everything was tidy, ready for a sailor's inspection. And his Spy Turtles poster frame hung above the headboard.

In the middle of the sharply tucked bed was a silver box with a bow on top. "Here it is." He picked it up. "If she doesn't like it, I might have to move to the center of Earth."

"To fix an upset, get her a gift," said Bill. "A reminder you still love her."

"I know the quote," said Brady.

Bill continued, "The gift: That universal solvent for female upsets. A subconscious reminder they're still loved."

Brady kept it going. "Since the dawn of humanity, when a woman felt unheard or unloved, however slight it might be, she became upset."

"Hell hath no fury like a woman scorned," said Bill.

They laughed.

Brady said, "I deserved it."

He slipped off the top of the silver box with the attached ribbon. Flickers of color lit up his face.

Bill peered over his shoulder, and his jaw dropped. "O... M... G..." He hugged Brady from behind and gave him a peck on the cheek. "Say bye-bye to bad karma. You done good."

"You have personal space issues."

"Hey, man," said Bill. "Space determines love, baby. That's why I'm close to you. And you'll be even closer to Tammy tonight, eh?" He pushed Brady with his elbow. "Eh?"

CHAPTER 10

When Brady got home, he walked in with the box behind his back, wholeheartedly uncertain how she would receive it.

She was at the kitchen island putting away the dishes, doing her best to ignore him. Since the fight, he was still sleeping on the couch, and she had only shared a few sentences with him. Mostly assertive assaults under her breath like, "Where did you hide the charging plate this time?" and "Don't you have important mysteries to solve?" She walked around the kitchen, passing Brady. She was wearing her turtle pajamas and her loose white V-neck with her hair in a ponytail.

"Honey," he said.

She glanced up with an attitude and blew a strand of hair away from her face. "What?"

He held out the silver box and a red rose. "I know I screwed up. I have to make it right somehow."

She took them, but kept them at a distance like they might give her the cooties. "If you wanted to make it right, you would've handled it that night, so I don't want to hear it."

"I thought you needed space. You wouldn't have spoken to me, anyway."

"Bullcrap." She tossed the box and rose on Brady's makeshift bed. "Don't put it on me. That's such an easy out."

He put his head down. He was hoping she'd accept the gift and forgive him so he wouldn't have to tell her the whole truth. Sure, being scared to admit such a "simple" thing as being kicked out of a group was ridiculous. Simple to others. To him, it was much more. It was his identity. His life.

"I need to tell you something," he said. Fear and worry seeped in his mind. She might not understand. She might change her mind about him. "Never mind."

She frowned. "Don't do that. What is it?"

Pressure came up from his chest to his neck. The back of his ears felt hot, then his head. He couldn't deal with the angst much longer. It would go away if he just spoke the truth.

He mustered the courage and said, "I haven't told you this because I was hurting...." He looked at her.

She waited quietly, rubbing her fingers together behind her back.

No. It would be the end of him. He couldn't.... Just say it, he thought. Get it over with.... He finally let it out, "I'm not a Mystery Solver anymore."

Tammy stared blankly.

Brady rubbed the back of his neck.

"What are you talking about?" she asked.

"I was kicked out." He rubbed his forehead. "If that makes you want to rethink us, I understand." His mind went numb. This was a bad idea.

"That's what this was all about?" Her face relaxed, and the misunderstanding dissipated. "Why wouldn't you tell me? And why would you ever think that I'd rethink us?" She seemed more upset at that.

A weight lifted off his shoulders. He looked at her.

"When did that happen?"

Before he could answer, her mind returned to the date night. Then it hit her. "That whole time, I was telling you to take a break," she said. "That's terrible."

"I couldn't bring myself to say it." Brady rubbed his neck again. "If it helps, you were right. Taking time off would be good for me. We can go on that vacation."

They stared at each other in awkward silence. They were both out of character, and now he was agreeing to a vacation he wasn't ready for.

Tammy laughed in a moment of levity. "I assumed you were lying around because you planned to apologize. I thought I was doing the best silent treatment. You simply had nowhere to go...."

"I'll be completely honest. You not wanting to talk helped me," he said, half-smiling. "I needed it." Then he backtracked, "No, I mean–I was lost. I didn't know what to do."

"I guess I deserve some of the blame, too. I'm sorry, babe." She kissed him on the cheek. "And I would never leave you. Get rid of that thought."

"We can set up the trip if you want," he said.

She looked at him. "What? And ruin my vacation? No, thanks."

Brady plucked the rose and silver box off the couch and held them out. "At least let me make up for the date."

She grabbed them and put them on the kitchen island. "Not until you're Brady Watts again. No lying around anymore. Find a mystery to lift your spirit. When you're back on your feet, and you're yourself again, we can talk about trips and dates."

"I completed my board."

"What about the Tooth Fairy mystery?" she asked.

"It wasn't the Tooth Fairy stealing the money. It was a clone from an east coast robotics company. They paid the news to run the fake story."

She tilted her head toward Brady's makeshift bed. "Well, you're not sleeping out here anymore. Do whatever you have to do to get your spark back. And please move your stuff inside. I miss you."

The worry washed away, and his eyes perked up. He gathered the blanket and pillow from the couch and swung them over his shoulder.

Tammy took the box and rose from the kitchen island and placed them on the coffee table. "When the real you is back, I'll accept these. And you can take me on a date."

Brady smiled.

CHAPTER 11

With a real chance to redeem himself, Brady looked for a new mystery to solve. He scrolled the internet. He checked every news source, and the Private Detective Pages for personal hire. Nothing sparked his interest.

Usually, he'd dive into the first thing he came across and go from there. But the enthusiasm he once had was gone. By the end of three long hours, he had melted in his chair. Eyes blurred, limbs like weights, staring at nothing.

He closed his eyes tight. If he didn't get out of this head-space, it would destroy him. He couldn't live like this. It wasn't how he was raised.

He looked at the old photo on the wall. "Dad," he said. "What do I do?"

In the photo, Poppa Clark was standing tall with his chest out. The "M" on his suit sparkled in the sunlight.

Be like dad, he told himself. Take charge.

The thought rattled in his head: Socks.

C'mon. That's ridiculous. Trying to rekindle your life purpose, and this is what you come up with?

You can dig into it a little. If you find something, take it to its conclusion. If you don't, you don't. And you can move on. But get out of the house. If there's a real mystery there, Tammy can be proven right and you can both have a laugh.

Okay…. I'll look into it…. But it's going to be nothing.

As he peeled himself off the chair, a sixth sense of danger stirred in his mind.

That was weird. It felt like someone was watching him. He looked around the room. The blinds were covering the windows. Little Toby was talking in his sleep on the aquarium rocks. The A/C was humming downstairs. Everything else was eerily quiet.

He sighed and shook his head. Stop getting in your own way.

Yet something about it gnawed at him. As a mystery solver, you knew if something felt off there was a reason for it. And you better be willing to find out what it is. Anything you wanted to understand in life, you had to confront. You had to go towards the unknown. Towards the danger. Everyone else ran from it. That's what made Mystery Solvers different.

And there it was. That itch he had to scratch. The need to know why. He grabbed his keys from the mini bowl and headed out.

The silver Mysterymobile came to life and he drove off. Where was the guy? Brady remembered being on the way to his mom's with Bill when he had seen him. That could jog his memory. He went through the route in his head: Go past downtown. Onto the freeway. Get off Flower Lane in Factory City…. It had been after the near-accident when they got onto the freeway. It was on the outskirts of downtown. Yep. He sped ahead. He knew exactly where it was.

He stopped the Mysterymobile and got out. It was here that he had seen the man begging. Brady was standing in an empty spot on the sidewalk, several feet from the corner store. He looked around the empty street. What a letdown. The bum was the main reason to give socks a chance.

As he turned to leave, the annoying ditty started in his head.

Oh, no. Not this. Please no. He hated the song. And the melody was super annoying. It rattled through his head again.

Ugh. It wasn't only bad. It was corny, too!

He couldn't lie and pretend the song didn't work. That's why Mystery Solvers used it at the beginning of many cases. It reminded them to do the small things that got investigations going. In many of the cases Brady solved, it started with the tune incessantly pinging around in his head. It wasn't even properly catchy. It rumbled again:

Make the notes, ask the questions, see if anything starts connecting.

Make the notes, ask the questions, see if anything starts connecting.

Make the notes, ask the questions, see if anything starts connecting.

My goodness. Please stop. Having a song you liked stuck in your head was already annoying. The investigation song was another thing entirely. Like getting "It's a Small Planet" stuck in your head. Unbearable. Where's a cartoon mallet to smash your own brains in?

To add to the torture, Bill used to prank him at the office. He'd sneak behind him and quietly hum the melody in his ear while he was on an important internet search. He'd do it again on lunch break. Then in the meeting room. Any chance he got until Brady would find himself wistfully humming along. It would get to the point where he would sing the lyrics, "Make the notes, ask the questions, see if anything starts connect—Bill!"

The whole point of the song was to remind you to ask enough questions, make enough notes and see if the little crumbs led to bigger crumbs and more strings to pull. The more strings you pulled, the more the mystery unraveled.

Brady took out his e-notepad. "Okay. Fine."

♪   ♪   ♪

He walked into the corner store, passing by a customer with an overflowing bag of snacks. Probably for a one-man movie night, Brady guessed. He'd been there many times in his single life.

The store owner was looking through his phone, mumbling swear words under his breath. He was in his sixties. Bald head. Five o'clock shadow. And wearing a wife beater and jean shorts. Brady could sympathize with whatever he might be dealing with.

"Can I ask you something?" Brady said with his stylus pen ready.

The owner looked up with zero emotion. "Are you going to buy something?"

Brady pulled a five-dollar note from his pocket and slid it to him. "An interview?"

"Just buy something." The owner pushed the money back.

Cash notes were tax-free. Brady knew that. Mom-and-pop shops would usually take it when they could get it. He added another five-dollar note and slid the pile back furtively. The owner shook his head. Brady went into his pocket, added a ten-dollar note, and slid the money to the owner.

The old man gathered the money, wadded it up, and shoved it into his pocket. "Make it fast."

Brady got right to it. "Several days ago, there was a bum outside begging for socks. Do you know him?"

A layer of disgust passed over the owner's face. He couldn't do anything about the bum. Stupid laws. "You just missed him. He loitered all day yesterday."

"Do you know where I can find him?"

"Why would I know? Or want to? Unless you're offering to get rid of him."

"I'm investigating something he's involved in," said Brady. He flipped his screen to a new note. "Has he been coming here for a while?"

"Off and on for a couple of years. Anything else, Mr. Hardy Boy?"

"Sure. Do you ever wonder why he begs for socks?"

The owner let out a disgruntled breath. "No. I don't. You get one more question."

"That's fair," said Brady. "Do you ever lose socks?"

The owner looked more annoyed than ever. "You used your last question on that? They fall behind the dresser. They get sucked into the lint catcher. Everybody knows that. Just buy a new pair." He angled out his leg to show Brady his fresh knee-high socks with the LFS logo at the top. Then he pointed to the imaginary source of annoyance outside. "That dirty vagrant creating a ruckus about socks is making a fool of himself."

Brady attempted to sneak in another question, but the owner saw it and cut him off before he could start.

"That was it." The owner removed the wadded-up bills and slid back a five-dollar note. "Go bother someone else."

It was strange how upset the guy was. That could be something. When beginning investigations, anything could be something. You wrote it all down. Though, most likely, it would be nothing.

Brady took a cherry lollipop from the candy jar and slid the money back. "Thanks for your time." He crunched the lollipop in his mouth.

Moving methodically through the cement metropolis, in and out of stores, parks, and alleyways, Brady asked random people about their experiences with missing socks. He got a couple of weird looks, including some people recognizing him from the news. But the looks weren't as personal this time. He could deal with that.

After several hours, he got a lot of the same answers. Yes, they lost socks. So what, everybody does. Some hadn't lost any recently, but they did in the past. Only one or two people admitted they weren't sure how, but it didn't matter. It was probably the monsters that got them, haha. They're small. They fall into the cracks. The dryer demon sucks them in through the lint catcher. They just get lost.

Dejected, Brady plodded back to his car. It went the way he expected. Everybody loses socks. And nobody cares. It's the way it's always been. "It's probably the dryer," he said to himself. "Everybody knows that." He'd heard it too many times for that not to be true–

A lightbulb went off.

"My goodness. Everybody knows."

He was going along with the sin of Investigation 101. When everybody "knows" something that they don't really know: red flag.

Everybody thought the earth was flat.... Until Pythagoras and others questioned it. The Earth was considered the center of the galaxy.... Until telescopes were invented and other discoveries revealed that nobody really knew. Everyone "knew" BIGFOOT was fake. Until he was caught!

Socks just get lost, right? Everybody knows that. But do they really?

Brady's face brightened, and a surge of enthusiasm jolted through his body. For the first time, he had a genuine interest in socks as a mystery. Maybe they did get sucked into the lint catcher. Maybe there were sock monsters. Or maybe they were simply hiding behind dressers. He knew he didn't know. That was the important thing. Now he was determined to find out.

With his newfound outlook, he headed back out. It wasn't much later that he spotted a man in grubby attire sitting alone on a bench. The only clothes on him that didn't match the grime level were brand-new socks. Why only the socks?

Brady quietly took a seat next to him. He waited a polite amount of time until the man eyed him, and he introduced himself. After the usual questions, he got a new thought. He asked, "Where did you get your socks from?"

"The Ginormous Discount on 3rd Street," said the man, a little wary of the question. "Who's asking?"

Brady looked around like it should be obvious. "I am."

That's a new wrinkle. Start asking that.

He continued, this time only searching for people with brand-new socks. He didn't know why that was important but sometimes you went with your gut. The next person he interviewed said she recently lost several socks but replenished them, so it didn't matter. He asked her where she had bought them. She responded, "At the Tarjay."

Interviewing another ten people, he got another eye roll and a few headshakes. He looked at his e-notepad. There were a couple of new crumbs. Everyone single one of them had lost socks recently, and seven of the twelve had gotten their new socks from Ginormous Discount.

And something else interesting. More than half of the people with new socks seemed lethargic or sad. Maybe *sad* wasn't the right word. Bothered. Irritated. When he asked if anything upset them in their life, they all responded no.

The last person he interviewed was a man, much older than him, with a colorfully patched bucket hat, and wide, baggy, denim overalls. The man thought he looked cool, as evidenced by the way he bit his lip and slid his fingers back and forth on the brim of his hat. "I got these beautiful socks from Ginormous Discount. Which is funny because, technically, the socks aren't discounted. Haha. I'm all good, though," he said with a starry-eyed gaze. "I got those Loss Free Socks. They have that good YOU KNOW, if you know what I mean. Ya heard?"

Over the last several months, there had been billboards and commercials on TV, and internet pop-up ads, promoting new socks with the tagline: "Get fresh–with Loss Free Socks. No deductible sock insurance." The LFS logo flashed in his mind. He'd seen it several times recently. On the bum's sign. The first store owner he interviewed was wearing LFS socks. There had been many commercials with celebrities promoting them. Special Air Force pilots endorsed them. Even guardians. It was being promoted everywhere. Brady noted it. People will really do anything for a buck.

"Loss Free Socks?" Brady tapped the stylus pen to his mouth.

"You betcha, holla," said the man. He pointed at the LFS logo on his socks, then turned around and cool-walked away as limp-y as possible. Arms swinging for balance.

CHAPTER 12

On the way to Ginormous Discount, Brady passed a digital billboard of a Super Laundry store, and under it: *See our newest Super Laundry on Broadway: Revolutionize Laundry.*

The air smelled of fresh lilies and jasmine from the plant shop and incense from the neighboring smoke shop, the smells battling it out for the domain of the street.

Ginormous Discount was located at the corner of a busy intersection. The display had shirts, pants, and underwear on sale. Socks were overpriced. A sign and stack of cards by the display read "Loss Free Socks. Ask for details." Two kids were rummaging through the piles.

Brady grabbed an LFS card and a pair of plain white socks. He headed to the register and put the merchandise on the counter. Right as the manager began his rote greeting, there was a loud commotion outside. The manager excused himself.

Intrigued, Brady followed the manager halfway, and poked his head outside.

The two kids were scrutinizing a pair of Superdude socks. The blond boy showed his freckle-faced buddy the faded initials. "See? They are my Superdude socks."

"Take them," said the freckled boy.

"Not so fast," said the manager, coming around the other side of the sock display. "Put them back." The blond boy looked at the socks in his hand, then at the display. "Put them down," the manager reiterated.

Freckle boy grabbed the blond boy's shirt. "Run!" They dashed away with the socks.

The manager leaped for them, barely missing, and tumbled to the ground. "Get back here, you little runts."

The kids hopped a stone wall and raced down the street, trying to get as much distance from the crazy-eyed manager.

Two blocks down, when they turned the next corner, a hand grabbed them, and their smaller bodies whiplashed to a halt.

"They're mine. They're mine," cried the blond boy.

Brady let go of their shirts. His chest was puffing. "How do you know?"

"You can ask my mom. Look. She initials all my stuff." The blond boy showed Brady the BB initials. "They stole them."

"When?" Brady put his hands on his knees, wheezing.

"I promise they're mine. I never even wore them."

"How did the store get them?"

"I don't know. My mom puts them in the laundry to do that pre-shrinking thing. Then they were gone."

"My gosh," said Freckle boy. "That was up north."

The blond boy scrunched his forehead. "You're right. We moved a half year ago. How the heck did they get here?"

"What do you mean?" Brady asked.

"I lost them before I moved."

"Can you do me a favor?" Brady asked. He sensed some distrust, so added, "Don't worry. It'll be worth your while."

The manager at Ginormous Discount was muttering to himself as he handed a customer their receipt. His face turned to relief when Brady returned with the boys. "Thank you for catching them." He looked at the youngsters. "You're in big trouble. Where are your parents?"

Brady pushed the Superdude socks in the manager's face. "The more pressing question is: Where did you get these?"

"We order them," said the manager. He pushed Brady's extended arm away. "What are you hinting at? You saw them steal it."

The freckled boy retaliated, "You stole them from my friend."

Brady placed a hand on the kid's shoulder, indicating he would handle it. "What is this from?" He showed the manager the BB initials.

"I don't report to you," said the manager. "And besides, they just wrote that."

Blond boy said in a snide tone, "We don't have faded ink pens. My mom wrote that a long time ago."

Something changed in the manager's eyes. The way he positioned his eyebrows in a condescending slant. The manager recognized who Brady was.

Just then, a happy southern couple got in line behind Brady and the boys, holding a pair of socks. The manager glared at Brady with a betrayed disdain. "I have customers."

Brady stepped aside, letting the couple by, and eyed the goods as they put them on the counter. "You're okay with the high prices?"

The southern lady showed Brady her Loss Free Sock card. "We got that good old insurance. We get 'em for free."

"Not none deductible either," said her husband. "And that's on top of a low monthly rate. Done wonders for us." He put his index finger to his mouth with a shhhh, and winked. "I suggest Sock Loss Consultations. Best deal out there."

The manager fake smiled at Brady and the boys. "Leave my store."

An old employee walking by with a mound of socks said, "Be nice to the customers." She was past the age when people weren't shy to speak their minds, even if it ruffled feathers.

"Quiet, Gilda. They're not customers," the manager replied.

Gilda stopped and turned around. "If you're nice, they might buy something, making them customers. In turn, that will help us survive."

Brady grabbed several socks from her pile. "I'll gladly support you, Gilda." He looked at the manager. "I'll pay full price, too."

"Thank you, young man," she said, then lowered her voice to a whisper. "We appreciate it."

The manager grumbled.

After the southern couple left, Brady paid full price for the socks, including the Superdude pair.

Outside, he handed the blond boy a twenty-dollar note. "Go get yourself a video game. Or whatever you want."

Seeing the money, the friend with the freckles jumped out of his shoes, slipped off his socks, and offered them to Brady with puppy eyes.

Later inside the store office, the desk was covered in paper notes, returned purchases, and torn order forms. The manager leaned back in his chair, aggressively twirling his finger in the old-time curly phone cord. The door crept ajar. He angled out to get a view. Nothing was there. It must have been a draft of wind, he figured.

He snarled and rubbed his right temple as he spoke into the phone. "The Mystery Solver came by... The kid on the news. Also, someone forgot to use the special bleach. Initials were visible.... and Gilda thinks she can talk back."

In the shadows, Brady reached behind the manager and snatched a form from the New Order basket.

From every store in the area, Brady bought a pair of socks and snatched an order form if they promoted sock insurance. When he got home, he went up to the study and put all the forms and socks on his desk.

The old notes from the mystery board were unpinned and discarded. Then he added his new investigation, taking up the entire board.

The Sock Mystery.

Brady couldn't help the smile that smash-stamped his face. His spark was back. He was invigorated for the first time in what felt like forever. And what were the odds? It was socks that brought him back! A mystery she told him about. When he solved it, he'd definitely be invited back to the group.

"Honey!" he shouted. "I found it."

Tammy came out of the bedroom, intrigued. "What?" she said, smiling. She could sense the change in him.

"Come up," he said.

She glided up the steps. "You have me on pins and needles. What is it?"

"I found my mystery."

She shared a glance with him. "I knew you would." She stopped at the top of the steps and looked at the board. Her face turned sour. "Are you making fun of me? If you're trying to make me feel stupid, it will piss me off."

"Babe. It's for real. You know I, of all people, wouldn't expect this. Something is happening with socks. You were right."

Her demeanor softened, and she walked toward him. "Are you saying you should listen to me more often?"

"The only time I'm wrong is when I don't."

She let on a flirtatious smile and tucked her hair behind her ear.

He pulled her in and kissed her forehead. "Socks are being stolen. I don't know how yet, but they are. And I'm going to solve it. Because of you."

She blushed and looked up. He kissed her again.

Tammy grabbed his shoulders and guided him to the edge of the balcony. She faced him toward the living room.

What was she trying to show him? The kitchen island was tidy. Couldn't be that. The windows and front door were locked and secure as they should be. He looked to the couch. The silver box and rose waited patiently on the coffee table.

His eyes brightened. "I get to take you on a date."

"I'm going to get ready."

♩ ♩ ♩

Twinkling lights and vines climbed the lattice wall. Fine dining and conversation mixed beautifully with the push and pull of sultry jazz melodies. Romance was in the air.

Tammy's luscious, wavy hair bounced and shined. Her flowy top, buttoned skirt, and hoop earrings said *I'm a snack* as she gazed at Brady with smitten eyes.

He was in his white button-up shirt and black tie filled with tiny polka dots. His good posture was back. Even how he cut his food and wiped his mouth had purpose. He was *him.*

She took a sip of sparkling juice, reminiscing on their first encounter. "It was the best costume party."

Brady slurped up the last bite of his juicy sirloin steak. "I recall saving a beautiful Spy Turtle from the Turtle Destroyer. He didn't stand a chance."

"No, he didn't." She giggled.

"Her eyes were begging for a hero." Brady pulled a fresh new rose from behind his back. "And if I recall correctly, the hero saved her at the last second." He handed it to her.

She closed her eyes and smelled the petals, the scent whisking her along. "He swept me off my feet."

"Yes, he did." Brady reached into a white paper bag by the chair.

When Tammy opened her eyes, the silver box was in front of her. "Oh, my." He nodded, and she pulled the ends of the bow, unraveling the knot. She removed the lid. Her eyes lit up. "It's us." She scrunched her lips, emotional. "You did good, Baby."

The music turned to slow jazz. Brady went around to her chair and kneeled beside her.

In the background, six men in ski masks and gloves scuttled behind the hedges. They double-checked that their masks were covering their faces. One peeked out to get another look at the unsuspecting couple.

When Brady was done with what he was doing, he hopped to his feet and reached his hand out, inviting Tammy to join him.

She put her hand on his, and he pulled her up, leading her into a slow dance.

Swaying side to side.

Back and forth.

He took her hand, spun her out, then spun her back in and to a dip. Tammy smiled.

They clasped their hands together and spun in a circle, gazing into each other's eyes. As they twirled, their feet glowed with a faint trailing light. When they came to a stop, they weren't in their shoes. On their feet were blue cashmere socks, each with an embroidery of dancing turtles—tastefully done with sparkling jewels.

Patrons and staffers gave Tammy and Brady weird looks for dancing in the middle of the restaurant. The lovebirds wouldn't have cared even if they noticed. Oblivious, they sat back down.

"When I wrap up the sock mystery, I'm taking you somewhere special."

Tammy twirled her hair. "With bright lights?"

"I guess you'll have to wait and see."

She frowned playfully.

"Close your eyes."

Her eyelids settled above her freckles and rosy cheeks. "What now?"

He waved a hand in front of her face, making sure she wasn't peeking. He reached into the white paper bag.

Her smile stretched wider in anticipation.

The sound of the bag crinkling.

A glove covered Tammy's mouth! Two men in ski masks restrained her and another four grabbed Brady.

The waiter dropped a large tray. Glass shattered, and patrons scattered in a frenzy.

The leader of the gang threw a bag over Brady's head, creating *blackness*.

A yelp came from Tammy.

"You feisty little girl!" barked a voice.

"Oooh. He's super feisty, too."

"Shut up with that!"

"Now you're getting feisty."

"Hold him!"

"Feisty!"

Swinging his head around, Brady flung the bag off. A couple was hiding under a table. Tammy's eyes screamed in terror, her mouth still sealed by the glove. Her arms and legs were strapped to the chair with electromagnetic wrap ties.

He twisted and yanked to no avail. They cuffed his wrists to the chair while two of them held his legs. He glared at the the ring leader. "Think hard about what you're doing."

The bag went back over his head.

In the next several moments, a series of blunt force trauma rendered Brady senseless. At some point, the bag came off again, but he couldn't see a thing. No hint of details. Only pain and blur.

He strained his eyes. "I'll find you, whoever you are."

Something came out of the leader's jacket he couldn't recognize. A low whirring motor rumbled in his head. Then a muffled bang.

A flurry of dim colors struck him in the face, followed by a bout of vertigo.

The lights went out.

CHAPTER 13

Brady lay in last night's outfit, dirty and disheveled. His head throbbed, and his hands ached from heavy clenching. Where was Tammy? How much time had passed? Through the pain, he scanned his surroundings. His blanket was balled up on the floor. The bedroom door was wide open.

Frantically, he scooted back to the headboard. How did he get home? The last thing he remembered was a crowd of pedestrians hovering over him.

Then, suddenly, he could feel—a faint memory—the magnetic-ties. They had held him to the chair on his side. He could feel the cold, hard ground. He could hear the worried screams. In the confusion, he had struggled awake, looking helplessly for her.

As he sat in bed, searching anxiously for details, his mind overflowed with guilt. A painful memory resurfaced, and an ominous shudder snaked down his spine.

His grandparents had died in a car crash on their way to the opera. A man in a trance drove through a red light, T-boning them. Before that, the family was a complete unit, full of love. The crash was the first break in the armor.

Brady's heart was crushed when he later discovered it wasn't an accident. His grandparents were killed to intimidate his father. But Dad never stopped exposing mysteries. And a year later, he died.

Deep down, he knew they took Tammy to get at him, too.

He reached his hand to Tammy's side of the bed, wishing it wasn't a dream.

Against the headboard, he sat there ruminating. Tormented. All the heartache he endured revolved around mystery-solving. From his grandparents to his father. And now his Tammy. All because he wanted to help people. To expose truth. Was it worth it?

Brady pressed his palms into his eyes. Don't think like that. You can't let them win. There was only one thing he could do to stay sane. Just make it simple: Solve the next mystery. Find her. That's how you're wired when you're born into a Mystery Solver family.

Dad wouldn't sit around. He wouldn't mope. He'd use the loss to inspire action.

Brady shook himself out of it, and raced upstairs.

Pacing back and forth, he tried to recall more about the assailants. A clue to who they were and what they would do next. But all he could see was a blur. The more he tried to focus on a single visual, the quicker the memory faded, frustrating him.

That's when he heard the crinkle in his pant leg. A piece of paper. Dread seeped into his bones and he suddenly felt ten pounds of mental mass weighing on him. That wasn't there before. Uneasy, he reached in his pocket and pulled out a note:

STAY AWAY OR THE
REST OF THEM PAY

His cheeks flushed red. A whine rang in his ear. The floor, the table, the mystery board, and the entire room was warping in and out. He grabbed the sides of the table, steadying himself.

How he hated he was right. And he was the reason.

Slowly, he looked at his phone. There was no avoiding it. He had to make sure they were okay.

His eyes closed as he put the receiver to his ear.

Maybe it was better not to know. He put the phone down....

Guilt forced him to pick the phone back up.

Anxiously, he dialed.

The phone rang for an excruciating fifteen seconds before he pulled the phone away again.

"Hi honey. Are you calling to give me good news?"

The phone rested back against his ear.

"Hey, mom."

"So, did she like the gift?"

Brady's voice was soft, a pretended innocence. "Yeah."

"And..."

"She forgave me." He winced.

"That's so great. I told you. I knew she would."

The note stared at him.

In the background, Natty called out, "Congrats, bro. Good work."

"Listen," said Brady. "I got to go. Something came up."

"You called me. I would love to hear more details."

"I know. I just wanted to thank you for helping. I got to handle something."

"Of course, honey. I love you."

"Love you, too, mom." Brady hung up.

They can't know. Just act fast, and handle it. They don't need to worry.

Brady crushed the note in his hand. Heavy breathing mixed with anger and revenge; like a piston, he was ready to explode.

He got right to work, transferring all his notes onto rectangular cards. "THE BUM" card. The "EVERYBODY KNOWS" card. "GINORMOUS DISCOUNT," "SUPERDUDE SOCKS—SLOLEN FROM UP NORTH," "FADED INITIALS," "SPECIAL BLEACH," "ORDER FORMS," "LOSS FREE SOCKS—LFS," "SOCK INSURANCE," "SOCK LOSS CONSULTATIONS."

A map of the city took center stage on the board, and pins held the blue cards around the outer edges. Red strings were added from the cards to the locations on the map where he discovered the clue. And also from one card to another when there was a connection.

First, he scrutinized the BB initials on the Superdude socks. The ink appeared normal. He rolled to the gadget shelf and pulled out his microscope. Under magnification, the faded ink kept its consistency. On the *Ink Time Stamp* webpage, he entered the month and the ink used per the kid. It pulled up samples of the time period—a perfect match. The ink on the socks weren't new.

His leg bounced up and down as he went over a theory: They steal socks from the dryer/lint catcher. They wash them and use a special bleach to erase any ink. They repackage them in a new city and sell them again, doubling their money. Outside that mistake, it's been a perfect plan.

Something didn't make sense. Sock insurance signs people up, then they steal the socks over and over? Customers get replacement socks for free. But that loses money.... "What am I missing?" Brady rubbed his forehead.

He logged online and typed in "Why insurance for socks?"

The first article spoke about grief re-activated in people who lost their most-beloved socks. Brady shook his head. More mumbo jumbo society would eat up because it was emotional and "sounded" smart.

He thought about Tammy. Depression from losing a loved one, sure. But socks?

"Think," he said, half-zoned out, staring at the socks on his desk.

His mind wandered back to the last mission. Something else about it bothered him. The awning into which he and Bill fell was right where it needed to be to break their fall. They would've been in a hospital if it was one foot over. A single foot. What if that was intentional? Part of the set up.

Sometimes he went too far in theorizing. "Look deeper" was the motto. But not too deep. Everyone knows you never go full mystery theorist.

However, being hospitalized would've created sympathy for Brady, making the media attack on his reputation much harder. The awning could've been a coincidence. But it was on the back corner of a building where no door or window existed.

Was he also being set up with the sock mystery? Did they know he would go to Ginormous Discount? The kids happened to be arguing about initials at the first store he checked. The manager definitely knew who he was. He could see it in his eyes. And the manager's office was conveniently open, and the order forms easily accessible.

Brady felt sick to his stomach. He was being played like a marionette. A toy. He let out a deep breath, dropping his head. "Why didn't you just take me, cowards."

A picture of a shark flickered in his mind.

Then another flash.

It was a shark tattoo on the leader's forearm.

A grip of hopelessness and anguish twisted him in a knot.

More flash memories of the night with Tammy flooded in.

The concealed men.

A pressure holding his arms and legs.

The blur of his turtle socks swaying back and forth.

The ring leader.

And Tammy's eyes full of terror.

Brady's ears turned red-hot. Slowly, he gritted his teeth. His fists balled up, fingers digging into his palms. What he would do to them if they were in his grasp. The pain they would feel.

In a burst of rage, he grabbed the pile of socks and flung them across the room. The exiting of emotion had him slumped over the table, drained of energy.

Thoughts of that night wandered back.

The shark tattoo.

The turtle socks being yanked off.

The blur of precious stones swaying in his face.

Mid thought, his attention drifted to the socks around the room. They were on the ground, on the bookshelf, Tammy's desk, the windowsill. One sock had landed on the printer above the Gadget Rack. Another had landed halfway in the clear liquid toxin tester. The toe was submerged, and a mist of purple bled into the liquid.

He squinted his eyes, not sure if he was imagining it.

He rolled over in the chair, keeping his eyes on the container. The clear liquid had turned purple.

Holy s%#. He opened a drawer at the bottom of the shelf and pulled out the Toxicity Chart. He ran his finger near the bottom. "Category 5, purple," he read it out loud. "Toxin five-dash-zero to five-dash-nine. Effect: dangerous with prolonged contact." This was a darker purple—closer to five-dash-nine. It was the type of toxin that stayed in the system, seeped through the skin, traveled past the blood-brain barrier, and gradually destroyed the gray matter in your brain.

He grabbed a sock off the printer and turned it inside out.

Lining the toe was a faint shiny film, too slight to notice if you weren't searching. He felt it. Sniffed it.

He filled another container with the toxin tester, and dunked the sock three-quarters the way in, leaving out the toe. The chemical solution didn't change. He dropped the whole sock in, and within seconds, the bleeding of purple began. He grabbed a sock that landed on the bookshelf and another by his foot. Turning them inside out, he found the same shiny film.

That familiar saying from his father crystallized in his mind and exited his mouth in a whisper...

"Hidden Bullies."

CHAPTER 14

After a concealed man had threatened him, the infamous bum re-wrote his sign without a mention of Loss Free Socks. With his arms around his knees, the bum was curled up on the sidewalk, rocking back and forth.

A five-dollar note dropped in the bucket.

"Thank you," said the bum, looking up.

Brady got down on a knee. "I have a few questions."

The bum leaned back, putting his hands out for protection. "I fixed it already."

Brady wasn't trying for that response. He softened his face, making himself more friendly. "I know something's going on with socks. I think you can help me."

"Really?" The bum peered around. "But they'll hurt me."

Brady followed the bum's eyes, but nobody was around. He turned back. "For me to do something, I need any information I can get."

"What do you want to know?" the bum whispered.

"Why don't we go somewhere more comfortable?" Brady offered a hand. The bum mumbled something to himself. After thinking about it, he warily put out his dirt-stained hand. Suddenly, he retreated.

Brady kept his hand out with gentle urging until the bum reached out again. Brady wrapped the dirty hand with a sock and pulled him up.

Pedestrians walking by gave Brady disappointed looks.

"You'd do the same thing," said Brady. "That was within reason."

In the park, birds chirped. A squirrel raced up a sycamore tree with acorns in its cheeks. Jogger's feet kicked up dirt.

Brady and the bum sat at opposite ends of a bench, pretending not to know each other. A jogger in slick running tights went to sit between them, but Brady's quick hand denied her. "We're meeting," he said. He had to do that with another jogger before he inched a little closer.

The bum leaned over and whispered, "I was leading the protest at Super Laundry, but the news blurred our picket signs. They said we were 'traumatized' about losing socks. They're big fat liars."

"Do you have names I can look into?" Brady kept his head forward while noting the bum's response.

"Vance runs Super Laundry. He's off the grid. He has no legal connection with the company. His boss is a monster who goes by the title...." He made sure no one else was within earshot, then said, "Mr. Sock. No one has seen his face." The bum's eyes dropped to his soiled hands. "I shouldn't have fought them."

Brady moved closer. "Hey. The only wrong thing you can do is nothing."

The bum scratched his head. "My life is destroyed."

"What life do you have if you don't have your truth?" said Brady. "Many people sell their souls. That's a worse life, I promise." He moved a little closer. "My name is Brady. What's your name?"

The bum moved closer to Brady. "I'm Oliver."

Brady moved even closer. "Listen. I will get to the bottom of this. You have my word."

"You can't." Oliver covered his eyes. "Not against them. They will destroy you without a care in the world."

"I won't let them," said Brady.

The bum continued as if he didn't say anything. "Even when you think you're making headway, they're already two steps ahead. You can't win."

Brady looked away, then back, frustrated. "Yes, I can."

"Not by yourself."

A pack of schoolchildren stopped near them. Brady and Oliver sat up straight and scooted away a few wriggles. The teacher counted heads. One boy was missing. Down the way, the straggler dragged a stick as he meandered on the trail. "We have to wait for everyone!" the teacher hollered. Brady and Oliver waited as the slowest kid looked up and shuffled toward them. When he caught up, the teacher softly scolded him and took his stick as punishment. The group went on their way.

"I can," said Brady, moving next to Oliver. "And I will." He pulled down his shirt, revealing his Mystery Solver suit.

It would've produced a bigger effect if Brady had shown him a toy blaster. "I'm telling you," said Oliver, "don't take them on alone. You're not enough. They have big plans and they won't let anyone get in their way."

Brady leaned in. "I've already been investigating it. They're putting poison in the socks. Don't wear them." That ought to impress him, thought Brady.

Oliver gave him a timid shush sign with his dirty finger to his mouth. "That's why I beg for them. To get rid of them."

Brady leaned in. "Good. See? I'm quite capable."

Oliver shook his head in disagreement. "They will shamelessly post story after story, taking anything and everything out of context until even your friends turn on you. Get a group."

Doubt finally materialized in Brady's mind. "I don't need one."

"Do you see me?" Oliver looked down. "I used to be enthusiastic about life. The best I can do is get socks out of circulation. When people like you ask, I share the information I have. It's rare for people to think there's a problem, let alone do anything about it. And besides, I already helped the other Mystery Solver."

The words stopped Brady in his tracks. "Someone from Mystery Solvers Inc.?"

"He had the same 'M' on his suit."

"Who? What did he look like?"

"He was about your size, I think.... I don't know. It was dark. He had a hat on."

Brady's gut twisted. Someone at Mystery Solvers Inc. was involved in the sock mystery.

CHAPTER 15

It took Brady a while to get over. The group the world trusted to expose the dangerous mysteries and there was a bad apple among them.

What made it worse was every Mystery Solver had made jokes about the sock beggar. An effective ploy to keep Brady off the scent. And why wouldn't they? "Poisoning the name" has been used by evil people since social orders began. You take a person or a subject and attach a negative word to them and, through twisted stories and outright lies, you can get a mob to attack even a smiling humanitarian grandma.

Brady couldn't remember who started the derision at the office. Bowl Cut was the first to bring it up to him at the water cooler, but surely, she heard it from one of the boys. There was an obvious suspect number one. However, he wouldn't rule anybody out. More than one of them could be involved.

He loaded socks into the Ginormous Discount bag and grabbed his e-notepad from the charging station. He decided that when he got to the meeting he would just come out and say it. Tell them someone in the group was involved and watch the cornered snake hiss. It could turn ugly. Get ready to be a punching bag, he told himself.

On the way, he changed his mind. It was better to play ignorant, and find out who met the bum without letting on what he knew. Whoever was involved would shut down the subject. Cloak-and-dagger. And they'd try to knock Brady down in the process. He could sniff them out that way.

Time to play chess.

The weekly meeting was underway. Slick pressed a few buttons and shot a message on the screen with the flick of his wrist and the Smart Remote in his hand. He coughed, and swallowed ever so gently.

Brady entered, a little on edge. The group barely looked at him as he put the bag of socks on the meeting table. Only Bill acknowledged his presence with a wave. It struck a nerve. They were a little too comfortable with him being gone. What bothered him more was seeing the new team photo on the wall with Slick in the center. The smiles. The fun they must've been having. He had only glanced at the picture for a split-second and a bubbling resentment started to build.

"What are you doing here?" Slick asked.

Brady cleared his throat. "I need to show you something."

Slick smacked the remote on the table. The rest of the Mystery Solvers sat up straight. "I didn't give you permission to come back, did I?"

"It can't wait," said Brady.

"Find someone else who's interested. Maybe call a different group... in your...Rolodex."

Army spit out his jalapeño jerky and grabbed his mouth, almost bursting out laughing. Slick smiled.

Brady kept his composure. "This mystery isn't a joke."

"I really don't care for your bull$%#. Or, maybe I do," Slick said. "What is it?" He stared warily at him. "This better be good."

It took a moment for Brady to realize he could proceed. "Uh, here's the evidence I have so far." He fumbled with the bag while paying close attention to the group. "At first glance, it seems–"

"Get to the point, Brady," Slick said, cutting him off.

Brady pulled out several socks, looking directly at Slick, then searched the rest of the team for knowing eyes. He received only blank stares.

The temperature in the room changed as they made the connection. Army raised his brows. Gunner rubbed his forehead. Glasses covered his face.

"Oh, no," said Harry under his breath, embarrassed.

The group looked at each other with side glances, unsure whether to take him seriously or laugh. Bowl Cut tensed her teeth to go along with a worried expression.

A pin randomly dropped from the ledge of a small corkboard and bounced around and around, slowing to a stop.

Then silence.

"Socks aren't lost," Brady blurted out. "They're stolen. And poison is being added to new socks to make people sick."

More silence...

Then the meeting erupted in laughter. Army slapped his knee. Gunner hooted and hollered. Bowl Cut wiped away a tear, smiling. Bill covered his face. Slick shook his head.

Cracks were showing in the armor. Brady held it together. He wouldn't let the bastard take him down another peg. He had something for him, alright. He tossed several pairs of socks to Slick. "Then what are these? Check the inside. A poison film on the inner toe correlates with toxic level five-dash-nine. Dark purple."

"Fine," Slick said in a condescending tone. "Let's look them over, shall we." He dropped them mockingly on Harry's lap. "You believe in him, don't you. You pass them around."

Harry looked at Brady apologetically and handed them out.

Brady glared at Slick. He couldn't wait to turn the tables on him. The group inspected the socks, one by one, turning them inside out.

"What film? It's pure cotton," said Bowl Cut. She threw a sock back to Brady, who caught it. He inspected the inner toe, and to his surprise, there was no poison. He felt it, sniffed it. It was untarnished.

He raced out of the office and came back with a container of liquid toxin tester. He dropped the sock in. After ten seconds, he shook the container. Nothing changed. "There was poison, I swear." Another sock smacked him in the face, followed by laughter.

Army showed reluctance to say it in fear of hurting Brady, but pointed it out anyway. "Didn't we used to make fun of that bum and say how crazy it would be if someone came in here saying they were investigating socks?"

"Oh, yeah!" Gunner started cackling and fell off his chair.

Curls giggled. Bill watched, mortified. The rest of the team joined in the laughter as Gunner held his stomach.

The blur of muted laughter. The blushing faces. Brady felt alone in a crowd of old friends. Each stomp of a foot, each bark of a laugh, like a slap across his face.

Keeping his gaze down, Brady simmered. If he saw a smirk on Slick's face one more time, he might black out with swinging fists.

Lowering his hands like a conductor, Slick quieted the room. "The media fiasco is finally behind us, and you come with socks?"

"You acting crazy, dude," Gunner said as he got back in his chair. He wiped his eyes. "Come back when you have a mystery where I get to use blasters. Socks definitely wouldn't do it. Hahaha." He kept a hand on his stomach.

"*Te has vuelto loco*," said Army. "Translation: You gone loco."

Brady got defensive. "There was a poison."

"But not these?" said Slick. "For your own sake. And I say this with all due respect to your family name, don't click the share button on this story." He smirked and quickly frowned to hide his enjoyment. "Do you, by chance, take crazy pills?"

That's enough. Brady turned to Slick, ready to catch him off guard. "I spoke with Oliver."

A vacant stare from Slick. "Who?"

"You know who. The sock bum." Brady glanced at the others. Nothing changed in their demeanor. Except perhaps some more embarrassment for Brady.

"And?" said Slick.

Brady's mind scrambled for a response, but nothing came. Had he imagined the poison? What happened to him that night with Tammy? Had his memory been betraying him.

"You're dismissed. But before that, let me help you with a little suggestion. Find a real mystery." Slick pushed Brady's notepad into the trash and coughed. "Please make it easier on all of us and let yourself out."

CHAPTER 16

Back home, Brady locked the deadbolt and rested against the door. His chest rising and falling in tiny breaths. A lot of weird things had happened since they took Tammy. Had he imagined the poison?

Unmoving, he peered at the steps.

If he had double-checked every sock and brought the purple poison to the meeting, they would've at least given him a chance.

Recent experience smothered the thought. Slick would've made him look bad no matter what, saying he fabricated the liquid or some other lie.

A sudden bout of panic.

Maybe there wasn't poison. He hadn't checked every sock. After the liquid went dark purple, he checked a few more and rushed to a conclusion. Some tests could give false readings. He never gave the liquid time to correct itself and fade back to clear.

What if he had gone crazy? The turtle socks were expensive. It could've been a random attack. And his mystery-leaning mind made up something to prove itself right.

Against his will, he headed upstairs. It was time to face the music.

The bag of socks dropped onto the desk. Brady bit his thumbnail and waited a little to give the universe enough time to put things where they rightfully belonged. Then he took a deep breath. And looked.

The liquid was dark purple. Brady dropped his head. *What is wrong with me?*

Brady checked every sock this time. None of the ones he brought to the meeting had the shiny film. He looked inside the Superdude socks—both had the poison. He checked the rest of the socks and, one by one, confirmed that all but two pairs had the shiny film.

A new container came out of the cabinet and he filled it with the toxin tester. He dropped in one of the socks from the meeting. After a few seconds, the chemical solution barely changed. Not noticeable unless one watched closely. And certainly not enough to be deemed "toxic."

Not poisoning every sock would make it difficult to pin the crime on anyone. Like that infamous confidential project where the guardian administration force-tested a "new vitamin" on the public. They secretly added a category six poison to every fiftieth vitamin and placed those mostly in poor neighborhoods. When one of the unsuspecting subjects died, and you spoke up about it, the guardians and Big Pharma would show that the forty-nine other vitamins were okay and thereby prove it wasn't the vitamin that caused the "side effect," giving them plausible deniability. Then they'd slander your name, telling everyone that you were <u>one of those Mystery Solvers</u>.

Brady added more cards to the board. "PURPLE POISON––FIVE-DASH-NINE," "VANCE," "MR. SOCK," "SUPER LAUNDRY," and "SHARK TATTOO." He wrote *Oliver* on "THE BUM" note, and, with a red string, connected it to the new note, "A MYSTERY SOLVER IS INVOLVED."

Next, he logged onto the internet and pulled up the magnifying glass icon. He typed in each new note, then scoured and searched far down from the first page results. As expected, he found nothing acknowledging the existence of poison. Also, nothing on Mr. Sock.

On Vance, there was a story from ten years ago, lauding the mystery man as "The Diamond Smuggler—gone into hiding," with the sub-caption, "He lurks in the shadows, taking whatever he pleases." No photos or videos existed of the elusive Vance.

Also, there was a story about the sock bum. "Oliver, of *Family Laundry* fame, gone batty. Name tarnished." His family had owned an enormous chain of laundromats. The family lost their fortune along with their majority ownership in the company due to outstanding debts.

In the photos of his protest, all the signs were blurred out.

By the time Brady found an article on banned sock fasteners, and the many couples who went missing after their complaints against a local laundromat, he came to the conclusion that the bum was right. It wasn't to be undertaken alone.

And there was only one person he would ask. Brady rolled a pen between his thumb and index finger, working out how to get Bill on board without mentioning Tammy. It would be mentally draining to tip-toe around.

As he thought about it, the sound of moaning turned Brady's head. Near the railing, the aquarium tank had fogged up and the water was algae-green. Little Toby lay at the back with half-crusted eyes.

"Toby." He rushed to the aquarium. He took his little buddy out and placed him on the table. "My goodness. I'm so sorry."

After cleaning the tank and refilling it with water, he put Toby back, and shook green pellets in the small pond. Toby didn't budge. Brady shook more in. Toby half-submerged himself in the water and turned away, resting his head on a rock.

"I'm going to find her. I promise," said Brady.

Sad and weak, Toby raised his head and swam to the glass. Brady picked him up. "I'm working on it. I'll get her back.... Please eat." Brady kissed him. Toby snuggled up against his cheek. Brady placed Toby back in the tank, and to his relief, he began eating.

♪　♪　♪

When Bill arrived, the door was unlocked. He slipped inside with two coffees, doing his best to keep spurts from coming out of the holes. As he locked the door, a droplet catapulted out of the cup. He caught it with a fast-acting foot. "I got us organic mushroom coffee, sir!"

Through the open bedroom door, Brady called from the bathroom. "I'll be out in a minute."

Bill entered the bedroom and excitedly placed Brady's coffee on the dresser. The smile on his face was subtle but growing. This is what it felt like to be in a superior position? He was looking forward to helping Brady for once. To help him relax a little. Learn to let things go. Not take every moment too seriously. Yeah. That's what he was here for. His smile got a little bigger.

He took a sip from his cup. In pain, he immediately began sucking in air and smacking the roof of his mouth with his tongue. Ooh. Ooh. He blew at the treacherous hot steam rising from the sippy hole. After adjusting to the burnt tongue, Bill said "Hey. Harry and the guys apologized after you left. They wanted you to know."

"You can't tell them about this meeting."

"I'm calling them this instant. J-k. J-k."

The bathroom door was open and, even though Brady could barely grow stubble, he was shaving. He buzzed the left side of his face.

Bill poked his head in. "Where's Tammy?"

"With a friend," said Brady, hiding his eyes. He shaved his chin and neck.

"So, are we really doing this?" Bill asked.

"It might seem crazy, but you'll see." Brady shaved his right side. All that was left was the dreaded shaving cream square under his nose.

Bill looked suspiciously at Brady's unfinished shaving job. "It's the sock mystery...so yeah...naturally...it sounds a bit much."

Noticing the white square, Brady quickly shaved it off. "Are you going to be annoying, or are you going to help?"

"Does the doughnut's center, with the hole in it, have zero calories? Then, yes, I'm gonna help." Bill pulled up his pant legs, revealing he had no socks on. "If you don't wear socks, they can't be stolen. Equals, no worries. For the rest of your days. It's my problem free philosophy." He put the coffee cup to his mouth and delicately sipped. "Don't wear socks. That's my help."

Brady washed his face and turned to Bill, serious. "Did you ever notice Superdude is professional? He takes his job seriously when he's saving people. He's not goofing around, making childish jokes."

Wild Bill smiled. "Humor saves people."

Brady closed his eyes.

"Is everything okay?" said Bill, showing concern for the first time. It dawned on him. "It's not just about socks, is it?"

Ignoring him, Brady exited the bathroom, and opened the drawer. He put on a shirt and baseball cap, then went upstairs.

He showed Bill the sock mystery board and handed him a printout of the news articles.

Bill read, "Sock Fasteners Banned," and started chuckling.

"This hasn't been easy for me." Brady took the articles back.

"I'm sorry. It's a story about banned sock fasteners. That's pretty funny. I'm not even trying to be mean."

"Lives are at stake." Brady's voice was stern.

"Because of socks?"

Brady released an angry breath and spread a few socks on the table.

Bill gave him a sideways glance. "I get it. I know what's going on…. Imma drop some life knowledge on you right quick. People can only affect you if you agree that they will. Now, Tammy affecting you, that's one thing. Good or bad, you want to be affected by someone you love. That's part of the deal. But Slick? You're letting him affect you? Stop agreeing to *that*. It's not okay."

"I'm annoyed with you right now," said Brady. "Not him. So how do I get you to stop being so annoying and take something serious for once in your damn life?"

"Okay, then, don't let me get to you. And definitely not Slick. Because that's what you're agreeing to. If you're around someone who gets under your skin, do this. First, close your eyes. With no light, there is no visual to trigger you. Now, empty your mind so the negative energy of the past can't be used against you. Like so." Bill breathed in deeply and exhaled, running his fingers down his face and ignoring the pain in Brady's. "It will get you in the moment of now. Try it, Brady. Let it flow."

A gloss of sorrow filled Brady's eyes. He hadn't heard Bill's words, but they were so inviting and so soft that he found himself following along. He inhaled, exhaled, and glided his hand down his face.

Bill's eyes went wide. He was shocked and excited that he was getting through to Brady. He could even see misty eyes—

"This is stupid." Brady snapped out of it. "I brought you here to talk about important things. Not some mumbo jumbo. Are you in or out?"

"You might not see it right now," said Bill, "but lightness and humor will save you one day. If you let it in."

Brady stared at the ground, disappointed with himself. Why did he think Bill would change.

"Scrap that," said Bill. "It's a power I'm forcibly bestowing on you. For your future is in danger if I don't." Bill jiggled his own body before grabbing Brady's shoulders, and shaking him. "Transferring humor now!" They were both vibrating.

Mental frustration hit its boiling point. "Stop it!" Brady hit Bill's hands away. "Your humor wouldn't save anyone in the face of evil."

Bill stopped smiling.

"You don't have to help me. I'll do it myself. Get out."

Bill froze, confused.

"You never take me seriously. Just go."

"Dude, I'm playing."

"Please, leave."

They stood there uncomfortably quiet, unable to make eye contact.

🧦 🧦 🧦

Slumped in the chair with his head on the table, Brady sat there, not saying a word.

Not sure what else to do, Bill put a gentle hand on his shoulder.

Ater a minute of silence, Brady's bloodshot eyes met Bill. "They took Tammy."

"What?!" Bill's hands shot to his mouth. "Oh my gosh. Who? When? Oh my gosh."

Brady dropped his head.

"I'm here for you," said Bill.

Brady picked himself up, and wiped his eyes with a sleeve. "Solving the sock mystery is my best chance to find her."

When the emotions subsided, and Brady had Bill's full attention, he handed him a Superdude sock. "This sock disappeared from a kid's laundry up north and wound up at a store here. They forgot to use a special bleach that erases ink, so the kid found the initials. Based on my preliminary data, all stores selling LFS socks are involved." He turned a white sock inside out and showed Bill the poison film. He pointed to the purple toxic liquid. "That's the poison in the new socks."

Bill dropped the Superdude sock on the table. "Maybe give me a warning?"

Brady looked at him.

"Sorry."

"It's on the inside. You're fine." Brady grabbed another container from the gadget shelf and filled it with the toxin tester. He handed Bill the turned-out sock. "Drop it in."

Bill did, and instantly a purple mist bled into the liquid. "Geez. The poison is real. Damn. That means they don't poison every sock so they can keep plausible deniability alive. Cherokeet Project, anyone? See, I know stuff."

Brady placed his new cell phone on the table and spread out the order forms. He put it on speakerphone and dialed the first number.

It rang a couple of times and gave a dial tone.... "We're sorry. You have reached a number that is no longer in service. If–"

Click. Brady handed Bill the next order form. "Go ahead."

Bill put a retro wall-phone receiver to his ear, connected the adapter to his cell phone, and dialed the next number.

"We're sorry. You have reached a number that is no longer–"

Click. Bill slammed the retro receiver hard on the table, and the sound reverberated. He unplugged the adapter from his cell phone. "Back in the day, they used to get to hang up like that if they were mad."

Unevenly piled on the desk, the same address appeared at the bottom of each order form. Brady lined them up.

"Oh snap," said Bill. He looked back at the sock mystery board. "How did you find all this?"

"I followed the crumbs. And I'd like it if my best friend helped me find more."

Bill nodded, excited.

Wind moved violently, thrusting a whirling echo low to the ground. The gust propelled random trash across an empty parking lot. Moments later, an old-time newspaper swirled through the lot. Then an electronic tablet tumbled by with the news displayed on the screen.

Brady and Bill pulled up in the Mysterymobile, the front wheel crunching an aluminum soda can by the curb. They verified the address on the order forms and looked at the empty lot in front of them.

"Oh, double-snap," said Bill. "Fake address."

"Make up a good sob story," said Brady. "We're getting sock insurance."

"You know I can cry on command, right?" Bill said it with a quiet excitement.

Unexpectedly, Brady leaned over and hugged Bill, resting his head on his shoulder. "This means a lot to me."

Bill hugged him back. "I'm your right-hand man."

CHAPTER 17

The Sock Loss Consultation parking lot was almost full, with one spot left. Two 1960s Cadillacs, one red and one black, at opposite ends of the lane got eyes on the last open space. They revved their engines. Screeching wheels left skid marks behind as they raced forward. Just then, a blue sedan pulled out next to the empty spot, leaving two open spots right next to each other. The racing cars let go of their pedals, slowing down, and glided into the two spaces.

Eyes from the cars locked onto each other. Engines stopped abruptly, and the car doors swung open.

Walkers planted on the ground.

Two old ladies got out, shut the car doors, and pressed their remote keys—Beep-beep.

They put on identical shiny green visors, readied their walkers on the ground, and gave one more glance at the competition. Go.

They raced forward, jostling each other for position all the way to the entrance. Atop the pole at the front of the building a flag flapped in the wind. The flag's design was a sock clutched in an owl's talons.

The reception area had a doctor's office feel. There was an electronic sign-in tablet situated next to a couple of small cactus plants. The waiting room was full of faces with no hopes or dreams.

Brochures were neatly piled on the coffee tables, including one for a Super Laundry set. One brochure read, "Sock Insurance. The only insurance where we give you what you paid for immediately, no questions asked, because we truly care." A customer picked it up and flipped through it.

The two old ladies pushed their way into the waiting room, and both yelled, "I got here first!"

Then, "No, you didn't. I did. Jinx! You owe me a soda!"

Patients turned their heads for a gander, then went back to reading their magazines.

A lady in scrubs called out, "Josh. We're ready for you. Josh?" A man in a business suit put down his magazine, grabbed his briefcase, and followed the lady into the hall.

They passed by Consultant Office #1.

The lamp inside the #1 consultant's office gave off a warm, relaxing light, making the antique furniture and the earthy colors charming. Sitting behind the consultant's desk was a large and unwieldy man who had never seen a gym, let alone a piece of equipment. He was facing away in his swivel chair.

Brady waited impatiently. It had been a minute since he sat down, and the consultant hadn't responded to him. If this was some new negotiation tactic where you made the client as uncomfortable as possible before starting, it was working.

Quietly, he looked around, searching for clues. There was a bookshelf to the left. On the wall behind the big man was a framed diploma of Ethan Stilter from Pawn State, and, next to it, a framed Certificate "Sock Consultant" to the right. On top of a file cabinet was a rip-away countdown: *Days left: 8*.

An abrupt movement from the big guy had Brady facing forward. The consultant swiveled around in his chair, set his elbows on the table, and touched his fingertips together. "Hi, Brady. I'm your consultant." Without looking, he pointed to the diploma behind him. "Ethan Stilter." His fingertips landed back together. "First, I'd like to hear your story. Because everyone has one." He smiled, revealing stained, crooked teeth. His jacket was stretched taut, the buttons held on with barely any hope.

Brady put on an act of subtle angst. "I'm–I'm losing socks. But I-I don't know how."

"Fantastic," said Ethan.

Across the hall in room #2, consultant Cliff Jackson adjusted his reading glasses, and pulled out a tissue from a thin cardboard box covered in yellow flowers. "Here you are."

Bill accepted the tissue and dabbed his stuffy, red nose. Unbeknownst to the consultant, the red nose was caused by a stiff pinching before Bill entered the office. And soon after his sob story began, the reaction blossomed perfectly. To add to the charade, under the table, Bill squirted stinging liquid in his eyes from a thick onion slice.

"Tell me more," said Cliff, "it helps to get it all out."

Bill sniffed and wrinkled his nose. "And–and–and–he ripped holes in my socks... on purpose!"

Compared to Brady's subtle actions, Bill's were melodramatic. Nevertheless, Bill was proud of his acting, slowly but surely pulling Cliff into the story, ready to turn on him at the last second and reveal his cards.

To the right of Cliff, on the cabinet, was the same countdown: *Days left: 8.*

In office #1, Ethan nodded profusely. He clapped lightly in Brady's direction as if he were a hoity-toity instructor celebrating a student after they finally got one answer right. "It first takes admitting to the problem on the road to solving it," said Ethan. "I applaud that in you. And I know it's not easy." He handed Brady a pamphlet on sock insurance. "The good thing is, with insurance, anytime you lose a sock, you get an LFS reimbursement card, no questions asked. Except we do make sure you're wearing the socks. Having worn them and then losing them proves no funny business."

So you can poison people, Brady thought.

In office #2, Bill had Cliff reeled in and was ready to pounce. He finished the last of his sob story with tears in his eyes, genuinely burning from squeezing a little too much of the onion juice.

Like a light switch, he flipped to gotcha journalism and stared down Cliff. "You're stealing socks, aren't you? You sock theeeeeefff!" Pronouncing it wrong intentionally.

Cliff scratched his head.

"Explain exactly how you're stealing socks, and I won't tell on you." Bill held up the onion slice above his head, waiting till Cliff saw it. Then dropped it like a mic.

In Office #1, Brady considered bringing up the poison but decided not to tip his hand. "I know you're stealing socks. I don't know why."

Ethan kept his cool. "It's simple. We're not. We're on your side." He grabbed Brady's hand and patted it like he was a toddler.

Brady pulled away. "If that's so, answer the first thing that comes to your mind: What's the countdown for?"

"Uh...," Ethan was trying to understand.

"Hmm," said Brady in a hinting tone.

Ethan turned and saw the rip-away countdown. "Oh. That. That's a–something big," said Ethan. "It's–our anniversary. Of helping people."

It was the only moment of hesitation from Ethan. Brady took note.

"Listen, Mr. Brady Watts. Our favorite part of this job is getting you the socks you so desperately need. And these deals will save you from any future loss. That's a promise. And it costs almost nothing."

"All right," Brady said reluctantly. "Sign me up."

Ethan grinned from ear to ear, showing his horrendous teeth. In a blur of hands—which may have been three, possibly four, Brady wasn't fully paying attention—Ethan passed him several forms from the cabinet. Brady rubbed his eyes, and gave them a once-over. On the back was a tiny, point-two font size with legal nomenclature protecting them from all legal liability into the future and possibly giving up rights.

"Am I signing my life away and all my bank accounts if I put my signature down?" Brady asked.

"You betcha." Ethan fake-smiled, indulging in the joke he'd heard a million times.

It was seamless for Cliff. He handled the accusations with ease. And Bill was none too pleased about it. Bill signed up because, admittedly, it was a great deal.

"One more thing," Cliff added with a gentle smile.

Bill raised a clenched fist. "If you show me another brochure, I'll show you this."

Ignoring the hinted threat, Cliff swiveled around, opened the closet and pulled out a gift bag. Bill's eyes became soft, and his fist went down.

The street was glossed in a moody orange from the fading sunlight. They entered Brady's home, and Brady tossed his gift in the kitchen trash. His mind was on his consultant. Did the guy really have three arms? Nah. Couldn't be. He chalked it up to being tired.

Bill had a tight hold on his gift bag. "I couldn't shake my guy. It's actually a good deal." He looked at Brady's bag in the trash. "That was your choice."

Brady said, "I saw a countdown on my consultant's cabinet. When I asked him about it, he hesitated. There's something to it."

"My guy had a countdown, too," said Bill.

"We're scoping out Super Laundry tomorrow." Brady squinted and turned to Bill. "We have eight days to solve this."

"That's one week per the Beetles," said Bill.

"Huh?"

In his best English accent, Bill repeated it, "Ats wun woik pa tha Bee-els."

CHAPTER 18

Large, neon-blue lights spelled "Super Laundry" on the marquee. The laundromat stretched the size of two buildings and was made of coated steel and transparent aluminum glass. The grand size perfectly represented their slogan. *This is where laundry is done.*

Wearing colorful sweats, a headband, and, of course, their Kent Clark mustaches, Brady and Bill stealthily snuck through the sliding glass doors as customers passed right by them.

Hundreds of digital washers and dryers pulsated in the sprawling laundromat. Through the glass ceiling, all the straps, hangers, and ducts were visible, giving the already expansive space a more open feel. The only part not see-through was a four-foot walkway down the middle.

Brady and Bill swiftly darted around customers, scouring every square foot of the laundromat. Inside the dryers. Behind them. Underneath. Anytime the patrolling security officer glanced their way, they ducked or waited stiffly by a basket that wasn't theirs. The guard was packing a blaster on his hip. For a laundromat, overdoing it much?

Discouraged, Brady closed another dryer door. On the wall ahead he saw a sign. He read it. *"Management responsibility. New Code 345: The management assumes no responsibility for articles lost, stolen, or damaged."* He pulled out his phone and zoomed the camera to a readable distance. *Flash*. "I guess customers are wrong now?"

Nearby, a woman with long acrylic nails held a single sock out to her boyfriend. She rechecked the dryer. "Every single time!" she said, and threw the sock at him. He shuffled through the hamper.

Bill snuck over with his ears angled toward them.

The boyfriend, noticing him, grabbed the hamper, put his arm around his girl, and distanced them from the redheaded eavesdropper.

"Didn't mean nothing by it," said Bill. He peered in the dryer, pulling and yanking and spinning the insides. Firm and structurally sound.

"It's got to be the lint catcher, right?" He removed a ball of lint and flashed his light in the small opening of the lint trap. Nothing out of the ordinary.

It was never best to focus on one trail of evidence, or assume a single outcome, so Brady inspected a washing machine. The rubber edges around the opening was solid. No crack for a sock to slip through. The drum was a metal frame with water holes, like a silver honeycomb. He moved it around, listening for loose parts. None detected. At the back was a Super Laundry logo. He picked at it and tried twisting it off with no luck. He closed the washer door, and called out to Bill, "Have you found anything?"

Bill shook his head. "What if the dryer is a teleportation device for socks?"

Brady sighed. "Look deeper. Not too deep."

"I heard scientists are already teleporting photons and atoms. They're closer than you think."

"Come on, Bill."

"Yes, sir. Sorry, sir."

On the wall straight ahead, and to the right, two cameras systematically panned back and forth, covering the entire laundromat. The cameras stopped at a door titled *mechanical room* in the corner, then panned away. There was an old-time lock on the door. It would be easy to pick. Brady timed how long each rotation took before the cameras faced the door. Twenty seconds in total. Based on the calculation, it gave him less than half that time before the cameras would catch a clear view. "I think we have our next move."

When the guard wasn't looking and the cameras panned away, he slipped over and inserted a key molder with the spring-loaded edges. The activator in the gadget clicked and pattered, molding to the proper cuts.

The cameras panned back toward the door. Bill grabbed an unattended laundry bin and stationed himself in front of Brady. The cameras stopped, played the waiting game for a moment, then panned away. The gadget let out a low beep. Brady turned it in the keyhole, and the lock released. He stepped inside.

It was a five-by-twelve-foot room. There was a desk littered with receipts for machine parts and metal springs. Next to it, on the wall, was an electrical panel. And at the left end of the room was a circular chute leading to the ceiling walk space.

The Super Laundry guard noticed Bill standing in front of the door, put his hand on the blaster and headed toward him.

"Cough," Bill blurted out. When that didn't work, he called out, "Security's coming, Brady. Cough!" Saliva found itself down the wrong pipe in Bill's throat, and he started coughing for real.

Brady stepped out and patted Bill's back. "Are you okay?"

"What's going on here?" the guard asked. He nervously squeezed the blaster handle.

"Sorry," Bill said, clearing his throat. "We're not allowed here?"

"It was unlocked. I only looked," said Brady.

Bill stared at the guard's mouth. "There's something in your teeth. You should probably get that. Ew."

Seeing the guard's attention go inward on himself, Brady and Bill walked away.

The guard peered around sheepishly. He felt his front teeth with the tip of his tongue before going in with a searching finger, then shouted, "Stay away from that door!" Then he mumbled to himself, "One hundred people probably saw it. Oh no."

Bill tossed the bin on the counter. Brady nudged him and eyed the mechanical room door.

♪　♪　♪

That night, near closing time, the guard escorted the last customers outside. "Please leave. Thank you."

"We still have ten minutes," said the last customer. He pointed at his sock on the ground. "That's my favorite sock."

A lackey stomped on it. "Too bad."

The guard closed the sliding doors and locked it.

In the dusty ceiling, Brady and Bill peered down through the transparent aluminum glass, lying on the four-foot strip. They were in their Mystery Solver suits now, with only their heads visible from below.

The manager's door opened. Cliff Johnson exited with an enforcer. Bill's jaw dropped to the floor. He blindly searched for Brady's shoulder, tapping him, and whispered, "Sniggity snap times ten. That's my consultant, Cliff, from sock insurance."

Brady's index finger flew to his mouth with urgent shush motions.

Cliff searched around for the noise above, eventually blaming the machines for their awkward cranks and whines. He gathered the lackeys and guards in a semi-huddle. "Pay attention. Especially what not to do."

Up in the ceiling, a swirl of dust entered Bill's nose. He squinted. "Uh–Uh–Uh–" Brady pinched Bill's nostrils.

The sneeze died down. Brady shook his head.

Cliff waved the lackeys in closer. "I don't want to yell." They huddled tighter around him. "At the end of the week, we retrieve the socks when the customers leave for the day. Listen close...."

Brady got super focused on his hearing.

"This is how we do it," Cliff continued. He waited until they were all quiet.... We take–"

Sneeze!

Bill covered his mouth. His face turned ghost white.

Cliff and the lackeys looked up as Brady and Bill ducked out of sight. Cliff yelled, "Get them! Don't let them escape!"

Several lackeys unloaded their blasters at the ceiling. The transparent aluminum glass crunched and cracked under the onslaught, but held firm.

Two unarmed lackeys headed for the mechanical room.

Cliff turned to an enforcer. "Double security at every location. And tell the boss we should send someone to Brady's house. He needs to know who he's messing with."

With no time to chastise, Brady grabbed Bill, and they scrambled to their feet. Bill flipped the bird down to Cliff as they darted along the edge and ran to the mini set of stairs leading to the roof exit.

The push handle had a long red sticker, *Warning Alarm.*

The door flung open. Brady and Bill rushed out with their fingers in their ears.

Through the wailing of the alarm, Brady squinted, surveying the scene. Telephone wires hung four feet from the building along the right side. They ran to the corner. Brady pulled Bill back several steps. "You ready?"

Bill nodded as the two lackeys rushed onto the roof.

"Let's do this," said Brady. They ran and jumped... They held onto the phone wire as their momentum swung them back and forth. When their bodies settled, Brady pointed with his head. "Go that way." They scooted along the wire.

Frustration started building in Brady. "What the heck happened back there? He was about to reveal the secret."

"I'm sorry," Bill said, remorsefully. "That dust thought it was white and that I was Scarface. There's nothing I could've done."

One of the lackeys on the roof readied himself with a silent prayer, then dashed forward, and jumped off the building.

"Hold on!" Brady pulled out cutters and snipped the wire. They dropped. "Let go on the upswing!"

Bill screamed.

The lackey grabbed onto thin air, missing the boys and the wire, and fell straight down, crunching into a large bush.

Brady and Bill swung out and up. "Now!" They flew off the wire...

...and onto the back side of a slanted roof. They rolled off and, smack-smack, hit the ground.

They lay there grimacing in pain, looking up at the night sky.

When they caught their breath, Brady said, "You need to do better. This can't keep happening. Seriously. If you didn't sneeze."

"I will." But Bill didn't sound like he believed his answer.

Brady went back to thinking. What could the secret have been? It had to be the Super Laundry dryers. They had a way of siphoning socks. Then it hit him. "Super Laundry dryers," said Brady. "My neighbor has a Super Laundry set."

Momma Jan and Natasha wandered through the Organic Farmer's Market. They passed smoothie stands, meat stands, and vegetable stands, coming to the fresh fruit section, which stretched half a block by itself. Each fruit had its own booth and a touchscreen vending machine. The customer could swipe left and right on the screen to check each fruit in separate pods, and when they selected one, they could turn the fruit around to check the back or sides. Each pod gave statistics on the fruit's age, ripeness, origins, and other pertinent information. After the farming crisis, the public wanted to know exactly where their food came from and how it was grown.

Natasha selected an orange and a cantaloupe. She felt orange was good for her energy and gave her good luck. Momma Jan chose a honeydew melon because of the taste. Mom paid with her digital Moolah app, touching her phone screen to the payment terminal.

"Thank you for choosing us." The clerk bagged the fruit and handed them to Momma Jan.

They pushed through the crowd of shoppers to the end of the street. On a light pole, the missing person notice of an old Chinese man with big square glasses grabbed Natasha's attention. It mentioned the raided sock factory and had the man's personal details. Height, weight, and more. She read it out loud, "Missing person notice. James Lin of Mill's Sock Plant vanished last week during the sock factory strike. There were no signs of anything wrong with him or his work. If you have any information, including his whereabouts, contact me or my son at.... With best regards, Adeline Lin."

Out of nowhere, Natasha felt woozy and plopped on her butt.

"Oh dear." Momma Jan let go of the fruit bag and sat next to her. "Do you need your medicine?" Natasha braced herself with her palms on the pavement, keeping her head down. Mom shuffled through her fanny pack, pulling out an adrenal boost. "Here, honey."

Natasha grabbed it, and sighed. Down the gullet it flowed. Her energy lifted instantly. She picked herself up and stared at the notice of James Lin. Doctors had determined her father's death set off her condition when she was younger, and reminders could reactivate it. The mention of a missing father did the trick.

"I don't need permission to do my own investigations." Natasha ripped the notice off the pole.

Momma Jan spoke softly. "Honey. I don't know if it's a good idea to have a constant reminder."

"I can't let it control me forever."

♪ ♪ ♪

Not accustomed to guests, Brady's neighbor, Ardy, relished any opportunity he could get. He had invited Brady and Tammy over several times, but their schedules never matched up.

When Brady and Bill showed up at his door, Ardy invited them in before they could change their minds. Having company was a routine activity where he came from, and he had clearly been missing it.

Ardy inquired what the unscheduled visit was about. As Brady explained their suspicions of the Super Laundry sets and the sock siphoning, Ardy smiled and nodded like he didn't believe it, but it was worth going along with because he had them as company!

Brady probed inside the dryer. Similar to Super Laundry, he found zero evidence.

"Is this for actual real?" Ardy asked.

"No, bits bor bactual beal," said Bill sarcastically. "Of course, it's for actual real."

Brady asked, "Can you call your technician?"

"I would. But there isn't a problem, silly."

"Winky winky. Hinty hinty," said Bill.

"I don't know what your problem is with me," Ardy said to Bill and smiled. "But I like it." Then he realized. "Oh. Winky-wink." He chuckled. "I'll call them at once."

It had been a busy day for the mobile Super Laundry techs. But what was one more call? Hairy technician and fat technician bobbed up and down, back and forth, as the truck rolled jaggedly along the bumpy roads. The hairy technician spoke into his headset. "See you soon, Ardy." He disconnected the call and put the earbuds in the cupholder.

"It's our civic duty to steal from morons, right?" said the fat technician. They chuckled. But under the veil of laughter were frenetic nerves.

The truck entered the driveway and stopped behind Ardy's tan-colored station wagon. The hairy man got down from the driver's seat with his loaded tool pouch. The fat man squeezed out of the passenger seat with his clipboard.

"Thanks for coming on such short notice," Ardy said, waving them in. "You're simply a top-notch outfit, aren't ya?" He walked them past the living room where Brady and Bill were hiding behind the couch and took them to the laundry room.

"We take pride in our job," said the hairy technician.

"It'll only take a couple minutes," said the fat one. "We don't want him being distracted. If that's okay, I'll hang with you in the living room. We can chat."

Ardy smiled. "Of course, good sir." They both knew, small talk was his favorite pastime. He excitedly took him to the living room.

"Good weather, am I right?" "How's the fam?" "If it ain't broke, don't fix it," "...but if it is, do fix it," and "That's what my grandma swears by," were a few of the expressions Ardy shoehorned into the conversation before saying, "It's amazing you come out to service for free. You must be busy all the time, my friend."

"Yeah, but we enjoy our duty," said the fat man, silently chuckling to himself through heavy, muffled breaths.

Behind the couch, Brady signaled to Bill that it was time.

The fat man sensed movement. As he went to peek, Ardy interjected, "The more socks I clean, the more the machine breaks down. But it's only when I clean my socks. Is that weird?"

The fat technician hemmed and hawed.

Brady hit the bend on the fat man's knee and pulled him down on his back. A thud and a reverberation echoed. Bill placed duct tape over the fat man's mouth and whispered, "Shhhh. Shhhhhhhh."

Fat man's nostrils flared in and out, his eyes filled with panic. Brady heaved and rolled him onto his stomach with all his strength. After a breather, he zip-tied his arms and legs.

Bill peeked in the laundry room. A box with baseball gloves and a Louisville Slugger sat in the right corner. To the left, butted up against the wall were the washer and dryer.

The hairy technician was bent over on his knees with his head inside the washer, looking at the back of the silver honeycomb drum. He placed a magnetic key fob on the top edge of the Super Laundry logo. It released a clamp. He slid the logo to the side, exposing a keyhole and thin retractable claws.

Sidestepping Bill, Brady got behind the technician with the Louisville Slugger.

The hairy man leaned out of the washer to talk to his partner. The unexpected face holding a bat had him fumbling the keys. "Hey, I—hi?"

Brady tapped the bat against his hand. "Tell me exactly how you steal socks, or you'll end up like your fat friend."

"I'm j-just a worker," said the hairy man.

The bat made contact with the laundry basket and it flew off the counter against the wall with a slap. Dirty clothes spilled out. "My bat thinks there's more."

"Okay-okay. I'll show you. Please don't hurt me."

"I don't know. I might," said Brady, in a non-serious tone.

Bill hopped on the counter for a better view and Ardy poked his head in. The technician cowered at the unexpected group forming.

"Thorough details," said Brady, the bat rotating in his hand. "Let's go."

"Ok. Ok." The technician swallowed. "When you press the start button, the door locks, and the smart glass fogs up.

"Water fills the drum. But soap isn't released yet. As the clothes separate in the water, invisible green lasers scan the clothes, detecting any socks.

"Once it chooses a sock, the software digitally marks it through a wave sensor. Then, the Super Laundry logo slides open and the hidden metal claw snatches the chosen sock and pulls it through the back."

The hairy man put his hands up in defense from an attack that wasn't there, then slowly pointed, showing him the logo to the side with the claws exposed. "Once it pulls the sock in, it gets placed on a conveyor belt. Rolling sponges squeeze the water out. Then they're flash heated and fanned. The belt loops back around and drops the socks into the cylindrical container. Only then does soap get dispensed into the load. That all happens in twenty-five seconds."

Although they tried not to show it, Brady and Bill were astonished. Their eyes were subtly bulging. And their shocked expressions were erroneously taken for threats.

"Alright! Okay!" said the hairy technician. His hands went back up. "When the container is full, the machine alerts the customer for a free service checkup. It stops working if they ignore it for a week.

"They call us, and we come out and fix the problem. It's that simple. We use this key fob to unhinge the cover. That accesses the container." He entered the key and turned it. The container ejected from the back. He twisted it, disconnected it from the machine, and emptied the socks into his bag. "That's all they tell us, I swear."

"Wait," said Bill, pausing. "Holy moly. It's not the dryer!?"

"I just showed you. It's the washer." The technician put his hands together, begging for mercy with praying hands.

"The washer. Before the dryer. Socks already gone," said Bill. "That's uh-mazing!"

The hairy man jerked back and raised his arms to block the imagined threat. "Okay! Okay!" he continued hastily. "We put them in these bags marked by zip codes and owner." He offered the bag to Brady. The serial number and zip code were stitched at the top of the bag.

Noticing the ease with which they were getting information, Brady simply stared at the technician.

"Noooooo! I'm sorry, please! We don't deal with laundromats. Only the higher-ups deal with them. We send the bags to Super Laundry headquarters as 'lost and found.' That's as far as we go. They send it on some train."

"Where?" Brady asked very nicely. He wasn't even holding the bat anymore. He had put it down a bit ago.

"Oh gosh. You're really going to give it to me, aren't you?" His eyes were big and glossy, fearing whips and lashes. "It's high clearance. I don't know where they go. It's not my department. Give me mercy, please!"

"Hey, man. Calm down." Brady lightly slapped him a few times. "What about the countdown? There's less than a week left. What's it for?"

"A countdown?" The hairy man wiped his forehead. "We're at the bottom of the totem pole. He doesn't tell us anything."

"Who?" Brady asked.

"We get encrypted texts."

"Don't lie to these friendly faces," Brady said, pointing to Ardy and Bill, who put on smiles. "Who's your boss?"

"Oh no," cried the hairy technician. "Not again." He looked at the bat leaning on the wall, then back to Brady and the scary, calm, smiling faces. "Uh, our boss, Ivan. He's nuts. Please.... Please...."

"Your bosses treat you badly, don't they?" said Bill. "Am I right to think that?"

The hairy technician nodded, terrified.

Outside, while Bill held the back door of the truck open, Brady pushed the fat man, still zip-tied, face-first into the seat. It took many shoves and lost sweat to get him there. Tired, he went to the driver's side and gave the hairy man a threatening stare. "Go before I change my mind."

He slammed the door.

The hairy technician started the truck. Brady knocked on the window. "I know who your boss is. If you tell one person about this, he'll know you shared everything."

The truck backed out with a loud screech, and drove off, swerving down the street.

At Brady's house, they tossed the loot on the living room coffee table. The key fob. The cylindrical container. The bag marked with the serial number and zip code. Brady rubbed his chin. "Legally, headquarters have to have all affiliate's locations in their records per code 879. Can you get the Super Laundry Headquarters blueprint?"

"Best believe it," said Bill. "Do criminals love getting caught, or do criminals love getting caught? They're like," he paused, changing his voice to a high pitch, "Hey, we're doing crimes over here. Look at all the evidence." He changed his voice to a low bass. "Thanks, criminal. Come with me. You're going to the world's stupidest criminal jail." He laughed in his normal voice.

"We'll go as plumbers," Brady said. "And we'll need a distraction for the guards."

"Natasha." Bill showed hopeful teeth.

"I was thinking an explosion," said Brady.

"She'd be more effective."

"No. It's dangerous."

"She doesn't have to do anything," Bill pleaded. "She can be the distraction."

"I'd barely be okay if it was a onetime thing," said Brady. "Which is impossible. She'll just be annoying. And she'll never agree to my terms."

"There's always something you can do." Bill whispered something in Brady's ear.

"What? That's a horrible idea."

"It's a good idea if it works. Nothing drastic."

♪ ♪ ♪

"Eat up," said the sentry. A tray of sloppy oatmeal clashed on the cold ground.

Tammy coiled into a ball and covered her head. She waited silently as she did every day. When the cage door shut, and the guard left the room, she pulled the chains and brace that was around her waist to the tray. Working the spoon, she scattered the oatmeal apart and found the bleed of a substance. She pushed it down the drain and shoveled clean scoops in her mouth. Then a couple more.

The cage filled half the room, its only visibility from a flickering candlelight. There was a maroon couch, and above it a machine contraption with an attached screen. Whatever it was, it was only used when she was asleep.

Thinking about Brady, she let herself cry. It had been almost a week. And she was losing hope. The worst part of it was she probably had it easier than him. The guilt he must be feeling. Please don't blame yourself. Just keep looking. She wiped her eyes.

The door creaked open. She kicked the tray at the cage walls and scooted back, putting her head between her legs.

A looming shadow glided over the wall, stopping at the cage door. Green eyes glowed, observing her.

"You'll starve if you don't eat." The voice was deep, guttural.

Her heart pounded in her chest. She kept her head down, not making a sound. Stay strong, she told herself. Don't let the monster win.

The cage door opened, and the shadow loomed over her body.

"I get the sense you're hoping he finds you."

She said nothing.

In shadow, the monster grabbed her neck and lifted her against the cage wall. "You should hope he doesn't."

The monster let go. She dropped to the floor, gasping for air.

CHAPTER 20

Although the bigger laundromats like Super Laundry had high-tech equipment, Natasha liked Family Laundry. Half of the machines were inoperable, so traffic was slow. She could take her time.

She sat on top of the dryer and laughed at funny internet videos while her rump radiated in warmth.

The dryer buzzed.

Natasha hopped down and opened the door. The cozy heat snuggled her hands as she transferred her clothes to the laundry basket.

Slinking into the aisle, two men in ski masks snuck behind her. The taller one forced her arms behind her back.

"Help!" she said. "Help—" A hand covered her mouth.

The chubby, slightly shorter one raked through the basket, taking out socks.

The only other customer swiftly sidestepped out the front door.

After the chubby one stole her socks, the taller one pushed her onto the laundry bin, and they ran off, the chubby one quickly lagging behind.

In a flash of inspiration and anger, she grabbed her detergent bottle and hurled it at the chubby criminal. It hit his leg, tripping him. He got up, frantically gathered the socks he had dropped, and scuttled toward the exit. Without thinking, she ran after them. At the end of the aisle, near the entrance, she jumped on the chubby man's back.

"Mmmhhh," mumbled the chubby criminal.

She lost her grip and slid down, latching onto his back pocket. The taller criminal grabbed the chubby one's arms and pulled him along.

The tension of the weight tore the pocket off, and Natasha hit the deck. The criminals fled out the door.

She rested against the far dryer, grimacing. Her stupidity in the moment struck her. They could've hurt her. Chastising herself, she threw the pocket away and started hyperventilating.

Suddenly, her blood pressure shot down, and she became weak. She closed her eyes, breathed in, and exhaled. Breathed in, and exhaled. Don't do it. You don't need it...

She couldn't help it. She pulled out an adrenal boost from her pocket and downed it.

♩ ♩ ♩

The sock mystery board and easel were newly set up downstairs in the living room, along with several gadgets. Brady was pacing back and forth, his mind on Tammy. *We're figuring it out. Stay strong, honey.* He placed the sock bag and cylindrical container with the other gadgets on the coffee table. Then he added new cards to the board. "IT'S THE WASHER." "LOST AND FOUND TRAIN." "SUPER LAUNDRY HQ." "IVAN."

While looking over the clues, Brady felt an itch on his nose. He scratched it.

"Pick 'em, lick 'em. Roll 'em, flick 'em," Bill said as he came down from the second floor with a couple of electronic keys.

"It was the outside. Look." Brady scratched his nose again. "Just hand me the blueprint."

"Okay. I trust you." Bill put the electronic keys on the table, then passed him the cardboard tube with the blueprint. "Some good news. I will fit in the ducts. They don't have the Smart Air Systems. Thank goodness for historical building laws, am I right?"

"You should really try to get healthy," said Brady.

"I know, and I will. But, let me have the win."

"Congratulations." Brady pulled out the blueprint. "We also need *elephant ears*. They're in the top drawer."

"On it like gronnit," said Bill, and he was right back upstairs.

Brady took out the spool of red string and a pair of scissors. "While you're at it, can you feed Toby?"

"Yes, sir, boss man." Bill raised a thumb. "Honorary spy turtle Toby shall be fed like a king. Isn't that right, little buddy?"

"The food is to the left of the tank," Brady called out. "Just a few sprinkles." Brady added a red string from the card IT'S THE WASHER to the card SUPER LAUNDRY HQ and LOST AND FOUND TRAIN.

Noises of struggle came from upstairs.

"Do you need help up there?"

"Nah, I'm good. It's the cap. It's not coming off." The struggles continued.

Brady called out, "You don't take it off."

Clank. The cap and pellets poured into the water. "Oh no," said Bill. "I'm sorry, little duder." He retrieved the cap. "I hope you're hungry."

Little Toby smiled up at him half-heartedly.

Bill leaned over the railing, biting his lip. "I spilled half the container in…. I'll clean it up."

"Just bring the *elephant ears*," Brady said. "Maybe it was a happy accident. He hasn't eaten much since Tammy's been gone."

Bill brought the elephant ears down.

"We need to hurry." Brady began adding notes on the new cards. "And I thought about it. We'll go with a smoke bomb."

Bill's face scrunched together in disappointment.

A barrage of knocks suddenly struck the front door, startling Bill. His hand went to his chest. "My goodness."

They got quiet.

Brady crept over on his tiptoes. There was another rattle of knocks. He slowly raised his head and peered through the spyhole. The tension in his body relaxed, and he opened the door. "What are you doing here?"

Natasha pushed past him with her backpack. "I'm helping you with the sock mystery."

Brady looked at Bill. Bill raised his shoulders.

"How do you know about it?" Brady headed back to the board.

She unzipped the backpack. "The missing person notice." After he didn't respond, she thought about it and zipped up the backpack. "I was robbed at Family Laundry."

"Oh no!" Bill was a little overdramatic. "What happened?"

"That still doesn't answer how you would know about the sock mystery," said Brady.

"So, you don't even care that I was robbed? If it makes you feel better, they only took my socks. Happy?"

"Why do you love putting words in my mouth? It just doesn't make sense that you know what I'm doing. You're okay. That's good, isn't it?"

"Ugh, I hate you," she said. "Tammy texted me the night you found the sock mystery. I knew you were dealing with a lot. I was checking in on you. At least I care."

Brady felt a twinge of guilt. No-no—it was irritation.

"Go ahead, ask her," said Natasha. "She's the one who told me. Are you going to be mad at her now? Tammy! Can you tell this nincompoop that you told me about the sock mystery so he can get off my case already?" She looked in the bedroom. "Tammy?" She looked at Brady. "Where's Tammy?"

"She's out. Lower your voice. You don't need to yell."

"I wasn't yelling. You need to clean your ears."

Bill got awfully quiet. He looked at Brady, and Brady subtly shook his head, no.

"I should be able to help," said Natasha. "And because they robbed me, you can't just deny me. That would be so wrong."

"I feel bad about that, Natty, but it doesn't mean I should involve you in something dangerous. Why do you think I won't let you join? To be mean? I couldn't live with myself if something happened."

"You always do that," she said, getting angrier. "You don't get to tell me how I can and can't live. If you won't let me help, I'll do my own investigations. I'll give you that choice. You can't stop me from both."

"Does Mom know where you are right now?" Brady asked.

"I told her I was going out. As long as I'm back by twilight. Mom's not a tyrant like you."

He pulled out his phone. "I can call her."

"Go ahead, a-hole. You can't keep me from living."

"I'm right here, guys," said Bill.

"I can't believe you're making me do this, Natty. Don't get ahead of yourself. You can help this one time. But it isn't a trial for Mystery Solvers. Those are my only terms."

"Deal!" she said. "See, that's all I ever asked. I just want to help." She hugged him. He awkwardly patted her on the back, shocked at how easily she agreed to the terms.

Bill's attitude shifted to excitement, his eyebrows bouncing up and down.

"Okay then, let's get to work," said Brady. "Grab the blueprint."

Bill and Natasha reached for it, touching hands. Bill gulped, and rosy cheeks blossomed.

"You're too funny," she said.

"I shouldn't have," Bill said with a nervous tic.

"Can we focus?" Brady took the blueprint from them and rolled it out onto the table. It took only a brief explanation of the sock mystery before Natasha was primed, fired up, and ready to go. Brady showed her the information necessary for her task, which wasn't a lot. "Natasha, it's that simple. Give it a minute, then get out of there and go home. Don't get it wrong. That's important."

"Easiest job you'll ever do," said Bill.

She rolled her eyes.

"Once we get to the file room and break the vent cover seal, officials are alerted. Bill, we'll have three minutes to retrieve the records and get out of there. We have no time to waste."

"Yes, boss," he replied.

"I can do more if you need," said Natasha. Her face brightened. "Just saying."

Brady didn't look at her. "We had a deal."

"Fine."

CHAPTER 21

Like a band of badass young superheroes, Brady, Bill, and Natasha walked toward Super Laundry headquarters as if they were moving in slow-motion. Natasha sparkled in a bright red dress and matching lipstick. Brady and Bill flanked her a few feet behind in plumber uniforms and their go-to puffy mustaches, each holding a briefcase. Bill secretly stole a glance at Natasha.

The grand lobby had a high ceiling. The walls and floors were lined with white marble and quartz. At the front desk, two massive receptionists directed calls, routed packages, and took notes.

Natasha headed toward the receptionists with an extreme catwalk stride. The excessive switch of weight from leg to leg and hip bouncing out at each landing was comical. But effective. The receptionists looked up as she whipped her hair back. Her lips sparkled.

Brady and Bill, taking it as their cue, headed toward the hallway.

Natasha leaned over the desk, cupping her hands on her chin. "How are you, Mr. Guards?"

The first receptionist crossed his arms. The other squinted, untrusting of her motive. "Where are your parents?"

She peeked behind her. Brady and Bill were already gone. She turned to the guards and smiled.

In the bathroom, a bald man in an executive's suit walked to the sink. He washed his hands and checked his hairline in the mirror. On his belt, reflecting in the light, was a security access card attached to a retractable chain.

Through the crack in the middle stall, Brady signaled to Bill.

"Sir, can I shine your shoes?" Bill said as he got up from under the far sink in his plumbers suit. "Also, can I measure you for a fitting?"

The exec rubbed his forehead, confused. "No, thank you?"

"I know how this seems. Actually, I'm doing tailoring as an extra revenue source." Bill took out a mini measuring tape and did a lightning-quick, full body assessment—arm, true bust, true waist, high hip, outer leg. "I'm an entrepreneur. You should support that," he said, twisting the man around. He measured across the shoulder, across the back, and true hip. "Look at yourself. You could use a shine and much more. I'm all about discounts, too."

Quietly, Brady leaned out from the middle stall, aiming a Magneeto pen at the access card.

The exec put his hand to his chin, giving it honest consideration. The retractable card moved and the corner caught on the man's belt loop. Brady let go of the button. The card retracted back, settling in place. He pressed the button again. The card came toward him, and this time it got about halfway when the man felt a slight tug. Brady let go of the button. The man looked down. The card snapped back to his belt–

Bill grabbed the man's face. "Look into my eyes. You should support small business!" The man stared back. An executive in headlights.

Brady pressed the button again, and the card started toward him.

"Okay, I'll do it," said the man. "I'll get a shoe shine."

"Yes! You're my first customer!" Bill gave the man an overaggressive hug and a circular back rub. He threw a thumbs up to Brady.

The chain and card stretched out, coming within Brady's reach. He unhooked it, showed Bill, then mouthed, "One, two, three." He let go of the chain—it snapped back to the belt. Bill slapped the man's butt! "Haha," said Bill, "totally joking, of course."

"What are you waiting for?" said the man. "I want my shoes shined."

"Can we do it tomorrow? Same time, same place. See you then? Love ya." Bill ushered him out. The man stared back, perplexed, as the door shut in his face. Bill kicked in the door-stop.

They ripped off the plumber's uniforms and shoved them in the briefcases. Underneath, they were dressed in their Mystery Solver suits.

"Ugh," said Bill, pretending frustration. "I made a deal with him, and now he's gonna expect me back."

In the middle stall was a large vent cover high on the wall with a hinge at the top and screws on the sides and bottom. Brady snatched the electric drill from his briefcase and stepped up on the toilet seat.

The bathroom door screeched ajar, halted by the door-stop. A hand from outside came through the crack, feeling around. The door pushed more. "I got to go so bad!"

Like a NASCAR tire changer, Brady unzipped the screws––Zip-zip-zip-zip-zip-zip.

Bill held his briefcase open, letting the screws drop in, then closed it. Brady put the drill in his briefcase and took Bill's. He lifted the vent cover and tossed in the briefcases as far as he could. They hit the back wall at the cross-section.

"You go first," said Brady.

Bill struggled into the duct, getting caught a few times by the ever-dropping vent cover. Brady helped with a little shove at the end. Bill squirmed forward, turned around, then helped pull Brady up and in. Head to feet.

Brady scooted in as far as the enclosed space allowed.

The man squeezed through the bathroom doors and glanced at the urinals. They were too far. The first stall appeared locked, so he busted into the middle stall and unzipped. "Ahhhhhhhhhhhh...." The sound of relief.

Keeping his eyes away from the action below, Bill held the vent closed.

The man finished with a couple shakes, then zipped up his pants, and walked to the sink. He turned the nozzle on and off without washing, then exited the bathroom. Bill relaxed, letting his head down. "Phew.... And gross. And gross. Ew. I would never.... Well, I shouldn't lie. I did it once." That was a lie. He had done it three times.

Brady handed Bill magnets from the case. Bill snapped them onto the bottom corners of the vent, holding it in place.

Crawling through the duct, Brady maneuvered stealthily, like a spy turtle, while Bill clanged along.

"Can you at least try?" said Brady.

Bill's stomach rumbled. "Uh oh."

"You better not," Brady whispered. "In this space?"

Fart. The sound echoed through the duct. Brady's eyes widened in terror, and he scrambled ahead quickly—and quietly. The menacing cloud billowed after him. When it caught up, he took a deep breath, flattened to the duct, and closed his face holes.

Bill chuckled. "It's not that bad."

Waving the fart away, Brady held his breath then blew at it. "If I can't breathe, it is that bad, Bill."

Above the file room, Brady placed magnets in the corners of the vent, and pulled out a curved-bit screwdriver. He inserted it through the vent fins, angled it in alignment with the screws and, one by one, unscrewed them. Meanwhile, Bill attached a digitally controlled winch to the metal framing. He put on his touch-screen gloves, then handed Brady a waist harness and a rope.

The office ceiling reached twenty feet, a consistent design throughout the building. The floor shined with slick white tiles, and digital cabinets were double-stacked along the walls, except for the corners to leave an access for maintenance.

The vent cover swung down, breaking the seal. Beep-Beep. Brady started his stopwatch. "Three minutes." His head poked down. He looked around and went back up. A moment later, Brady roped down slowly into view, his arms and legs stretched out.

The door rattled.

"Stop—stop—stop," Brady whispered.

Bill pressed the stop button on the winch. The screen scrambled colors then went black—clunk—the mechanism broke, sending Brady falling. Bill grabbed the rope and squeezed tight. Brady slowed to a stop fifteen feet up.

Regaining his balance, Brady steadied his arms and legs. The door swung open. The tension of the rope rubbed against the frame. Bill held on, arms trembling.

A chubby woman in a green dress walked in backwards, guided by a tall, gangly man. He looked like part of the geek squad with his freckles and glasses.

"We'll be in a lot of trouble if we're caught," she said.

"I like it that way," said the geek, as they playfully maneuvered in a flirtatious dance.

Breathing silently, Brady was holding as still as possible when a smooch sounded below. For goodness' sake.

Then his right arm began trembling. He focused on it, and it stopped.

His left leg started shaking. He looked at his leg, it stopped.

The other leg started trembling, then both. He stared at both. His arms joined in, and now all his limbs were trembling. His eyes darted around at his limbs to no avail.

He changed his tactics and concentrated on holding his position to a quiet hum.

The strain intensified. His core temperature rose. His pores opened up and a sheen of sweat trickled across his face.

The geeky man pushed his glasses in and showered Chubby with peck kisses all over her face. She giggled. He walked her further back, stopping directly under Brady.

The sweat on Brady's forehead gathered, swelling to a bulge.

"Hehe," said the geeky man. "You're super cute."

The sweat hit its apex. Brady watched as it glided down his nose, and dropped. The four-eyed man moved the woman to the cabinets, and the sweat hit the floor behind them with a mini splash.

Drip....

Drip....

Drip....

Brady watched helplessly at the falling sweat.

In the duct, Bill held on for dear life. Hands numb, fore-arms sore, and arms shaking. His grip slipped an inch!

Squeak–Shoes rubbed against the wood flooring as Chubby and Geek attacked each other with more peck kisses.

"You're so handsome," she said.

"You're so pretty," he replied coyly.

Something caught Chubby's attention, and she angled her head out. The geek turned back to see what she was looking at. A small puddle of water reflected ever so slightly on the floor. They walked over to it and stopped. Their heads craned up. The vent was in place.

"Hmm. Condensation," he said.

Brady dropped silently to the floor by the far cabinet.

The time hit three minutes and counting.

"Where were we?" said the woman. "Oh yeah. The part where you're so handsome." She kissed him again.

The duct rumbled above, and their heads shot up to the vent. "What was that?" asked the geek.

A magnet in Brady's pocket snapped against the far cabinet! Their heads jerked at the new sound.

"What was that?" said Chubby.

Geek stepped in front of her. He gulped, then crept cautiously toward the corner cabinet.

From the duct, Bill watched the man close in on Brady. Bill searched for something to use. With no other solution, he took a deep breath, speaking in a deep, sonorous voice, and said, "You two are in a lot of trouble."

Chubby and Geek went stiff. They looked at each other. Then neatened their clothes and scurried out the door.

"What are you doing?" said Brady.

Bill swung the vent cover open. "I think you meant 'Thank you for saving me again,'" said Bill. "And not a chance. They were spooked like a Stevie King story."

"It did work," Brady conceded.

"That's right, it worked," said Bill, proud of his improvisation.

Brady looked at his watch. The time hit three minutes and forty-five seconds. He rapidly scoured the wall for the cabinet number. Finding it, he swiped the access card over the digital drawer marked S800-S899. It slid open. He flipped through and pulled out a file.

"Authorized eyes only – S879
From: Mr. Sock
To: Vance.
Subject: Factories and Super Laundry.
"File with the Administration per the Building Code (BLC) 2085-1915311-1325192051825-0-31513."

Brady glanced at the door, then opened the article.

"APPROVED: WE'RE CREATING A GLOBAL NETWORK. MOVE THE COMPOUND OF THE SECRET SOCK CORPORATION (SSC) TO CENTRAL AMERICA. THE LOCATIONS TO BE ENCRYPTED"

"Central America...," Brady said, thinking out loud. "Compound.... The Secret Sock Corporation...." He snapped a photo and flipped the page.

"SUPER LAUNDRY HEADQUARTERS, THE SPEED TRAIN, AND THE COMPOUND TO BE COMPLETELY SEPARATE—LEGALLY AND BY LOCATION"

Flash. He snapped another photo and flipped to a diagram.

"SPEED TRAIN–ROUTE"
"*BOXCAR–265C*"
"CODE: 3069"

The diagram showed a docking station, tracks going over mountains, through tunnels, and to open land with sporadic posts along the path, then fading to a blank area with no destination.... A secret. He snapped another photo.

There was a commotion of footsteps crowding outside the door.

CHAPTER 22

"Drop the rope," Brady yell-whispered. He slid the file back in the cabinet and shut it as quickly and quietly as possible. The rope unfurled. He clicked it to his waist harness and tugged on the line.

The doorhandle made a squeaky sound. It slowly turned. Bill strained, muscles fatigued, as he pulled Brady up. Slink... Slink... Slink. Toot—out came a little fart. "Oh–my goodness, so sorry."

Slink... Slink. Brady's worried face zoomed in closer with each pull of the rope.

"I couldn't help it," Bill whispered. Slink... Slink.

Brady grabbed the edge of the frame and pulled himself in. The door flung open. Brady quietly pulled the vent cover in place.

Three militia-looking officials raced in with blasters drawn. They wore dark gray wool suits, slick shin-high boots, and a hard-brimmed boat captain's hat. The patch on the gray vest was an owl.

The head official had thick bushy eyebrows almost hiding his eyes. He pointed with his sharp nose toward the access corners. They each checked one. One official noticed the indent mark left by the magnet from Brady's pocket. "Hmm."

The shimmer from the tiny puddle caught the head official's eye. He put his index finger in the air. Looked up at the vent, then back down to the puddle.

"What's that smell?" said the third. "Burnt broccoli?"

The head man raised his blaster to the ceiling. The others nodded.

Along the line of the duct, he swung his arm, pulling the trigger several times—*BANG-BANG-BANG*. Small chunks of tile fell to the floor, exposing punctured holes. The officials listened closely.

Dead silence.

In the duct, the temperature escalated. Sweat formed on Brady's and Bill's foreheads, their skin clammy and hot against their suits. They exhaled slowly, and with each breath, sun motes swirled in the light beams between their legs.

"Search the building and don't let any suspicious people leave," the head official said. They marched out.

After another minute of silence, Bill wiped his arm across his forehead and flung off the sweat.

They crawled their way back to the bathroom. The coast was clear. They got down, changed back into their plumber uniforms.

The lobby was too quiet for comfort. Brady peeked his head out. One of the receptionists looked stressed as the phone spewed orders in his ear. "Yes, sir," the receptionist replied. "We will keep an eye out."

Bill bumped forward as Brady turned back to tell him something and they knocked heads. A door had hit Bill with a line of employees passing through. Brady rubbed his forehead.

Now was a good time as any. He tugged Bill's shirt. "Let's go. Stay calm and collected." They followed the group of employees into the lobby, then broke off toward the front doors.

"Hey, you. Stop!" said the receptionist.

They stopped. Brady shut his eyes and let out a sigh. They turned around to meet their doom. Both massive receptionists hurried dutifully around the desk toward them.

Down the hall, the three militant officials headed toward the lobby. "Go-Go!" barked the head official with the eyebrows. "Suspicious men think they're making it out of here?"

Brady prepared to grab Bill and run. When the three officials got to the lobby, they took a sharp left, with an accompanying squeak of their boots, and went down the other hallway.

"Oh," said the first receptionist, getting closer. "Sorry. I thought you were Johnny."

Face cool as a cucumber, Brady's mind let out an irresistible "phew." He nodded.

The way Bill was holding the briefcase to his body caught the second receptionist's eye. "What's in your case?"

"Nothing. Some plumbing tools," said Bill. He nonchalantly—chalantly—relaxed his grip and let the briefcase hang to his side.

"Show me," said the second receptionist.

Bill cleared the lump in his throat. He put the case on the ground, unsnapped the latches, and opened it slowly. Inside was a plumber's snake and the corner magnets.

"Very well." He looked them up and down. "Have a good day."

They thanked the receptionists and headed for the exit. As they put their hands on the front door, the first big man yelled, "Wait a sec!"

They turned around again. Busted.

"Charles," he said, "I thought you were Charles, not Johnny. My bad. They look similar. Have a good one." Brady forced a smile. They pushed the front doors open and fled.

The three officials came running to the front desk. The head official scrunched his thick eyebrows. "Who were they?"

Outside, Brady and Bill moved quickly but calmly away from the building, not wanting to grab too much attention.

Brady's mind went to the files. "The train must go to the secret location."

"Sounds about right." Bill nodded. "They're officially in the Hall of Fame for covering their tracks. I don't like them because they're bad and all, but you must give respect where respect is due. On that aspect only, though—covering their tracks. Let's not take this out of context and say how I respect bad people. Okay?"

"Focus."

"Yes, sir."

The first massive receptionist came rolling out of the building on a Segway. Brady and Bill heard the roll of motors and looked back.

"Uh oh," said Bill.

"Go!" said Brady. They went into a full sprint. Brady's feet lightly pattered along, while Bill's thudded pavement.

The big man leaned on the Segway at full speed. He caught up pretty fast, getting close on their trail. "I wanted to apologize," he said. "I was only joking! Seriously, have a good day." He slowed down, swerved around, and headed back to the building.

♩ ♩ ♩

At home, Brady inserted a flash drive into the projector, and a picture diagram appeared on screen. He adjusted the image. A note at the bottom read: *Box Car 265C. Code: 3069*.

"They might lose their Hall of Fame status," Bill said as he enlarged the view on his laptop. "Earth View blocks a close-up of that blank area. It doesn't let you zoom in. When you deny people access, it only makes them want to find out more. They could've put in a fake view. I hate to say it, but if they want to keep that Hall of Fame status they better fix it. Or they can consider it revoked."

"Help me load the backpacks. We're short on time," said Brady.

Bill helped fill the bags with body straps, wires, a hammer, strength magnets, an "electronic key," and other gadgets.

"Here, this too." Brady tossed him a sticker with an image of a digital keypad with an "error code." It looked surprisingly authentic.

"They won't know what hit 'em," said Bill.

Brady directed his laser pointer at Natasha, who was lying on the couch. The possibility of her asking about Tammy ate at him. "You're not supposed to be here. This is what I meant. Go home."

"Be nice," said Bill.

Brady said, "Doesn't it cost money to get all these ride-shares and lie to Mom?"

"It's worth the price if I get to annoy you," she said. "Relax, big bro. I'm only watching."

"That's right," said Brady. "Only watching."

He didn't know how long he could hold her off from her passion, knowing she was just as smart as him. But he'd protect her from herself as long as he could. This was a dangerous business.

Flushing the thoughts out of his mind, he turned to Bill and pointed the red laser on the screen. The red dot hit the docking station. "There's a lot of security here. To avoid it, we'll enter here at Rock Tunnel." He pointed to the tracks going into a natural tunnel on a rocky hillside.

"Oh. How high is it?" Bill asked.

"It's pretty high, and these tunnels and posts are only a foot out from the train, specifically to keep people like us from getting in. I'd barely make it. You definitely wouldn't. So be ready. We need to get inside the boxcar fast, or we're goners."

"Easy, peezy. Lemon squeezy," said Bill, creating his confidence until he makes his confidence.

"I'm also going to point out that boxcar 265C is near the front of the train." Brady made sure Bill was listening. "I don't plan to travel many boxcars to get to it. We'll need to jump as soon as the train shoots out of the tunnel, or it'll be more work."

"I'll be ready," said Bill. "I'm pretty sure I've conquered my fear."

"Good." Brady turned to Natasha. "Go home."

She made a face.

CHAPTER 23

The speed train was sleek, gray, and aerodynamic, and each boxcar had its own access panel. Inspectors exited onto the platform. They nodded to the guards and put their hands together in an "O" shape. The indication of approval.

The station director entered the code into the control console.

A horn sounded. Green lights flashed along the platform in succession out toward the open land. The train started on its course, chugging along slowly, then gradually speeding up until it was soaring along the tracks.

An aerial view above the train station showed the path snaking far into open land toward rocky terrain.

Many miles out, above Rock Tunnel, the whir of the train echoed in the distance. Air swirled in currents, and dust from the rocky hillside joined a gust of wind. Brady squinted to protect his eyes as he braced against the rock. His fingers were dusty to the touch. The utility backpack hung over his shoulder.

A pale, petrified Bill inched beside Brady with his own utility bag. "I'm not sure we should do this!" Bill shouted over the wind.

Brady adjusted his bag. He should've known this would happen. It would've been a bigger shock if it hadn't. "You're Wild Bill!" he said. "Not Wimp Bill!"

"Oh gosh!" Bill gulped. The train whizzed out of the tunnel, and dust shot up in Bill's face. His fingers met his eyes, and he wobbled, losing his footing on the rock. Brady grabbed him and yanked him back to safety. Bill nervously twisted around and clung to the side of the dusty boulder as the train continued at neck-breaking speed.

They peered over the edge. The train was ten feet below them.

"Maybe there's another way!" said Bill.

The end of the train was almost out of the tunnel. "We have to jump!" shouted Brady. "It's time to earn your name!" He grabbed Bill's wrist and jumped. Bill tried screaming, but nothing came out.

As they fell, Bill frantically moved Brady's body under his and landed on top of him. They hit the train and bounced backwards. Bill's backpack ripped off on impact and flew away. The momentum tumbled Bill and Brady toward the end of the last boxcar.

They put their hands out, sliding ten feet, and coming to a halt with their legs off the edge. They dropped their heads to the train.

"What a day," said Bill.

Brady looked back at the tracks.

He got up in a crouched position and helped Bill to his feet. They braced against the flapping wind.

From a distance, they were two tiny figures on the last boxcar—a good twenty boxcars from their destination. Brady threw his hands up in dismay. "C'mon, Bill."

They jumped boxcars all the way to 265C.

Against the roar of the wind, Brady kneeled down. From the utility bag, he pulled out a strength magnet. It had a flat bottom for contact with the train and an iron ring on top. He placed it a foot from the edge and pressed the magnet app on his phone. It strengthened tenfold to the train—clunk—solid as a rock.

Secured to the iron ring with the waist strap and wire apparatus, Brady lowered down the side, getting level with the boxcar door.

Bill lay flat on his stomach, holding onto the ring, then slowly inched backward until his legs stuck out over the sharp edge. He felt around for the wire with the other hand. He got hold of it and went down. As he inched lower, the wire stretched.

Brady looked up. "What are you doing?"

"I can't be up there by myself," said Bill.

"Maybe you shouldn't have lost your bag." Suddenly, the train track curved out, extending over a lake, and the force pulled them away from the train.

"Whoooaaa." The track curved back onto land, quickly straightened up, and they smacked into the side. It jerked Bill's grip, and he slid down the wire, stopping two feet from Brady.

Brady entered 3-0-6-9 into the keypad. A small red light flashed. He tried the code again. Denied. Tried it backward. 9-6-0-3. Denied. Thinking for a moment, he got an idea. He pressed. 2-6-5-3. Denied. He pulled out his "electronic key" gadget and put it on the keypad. Beep. Beep. Red flash. He tried again. Beep. Rad flash. Denied.

Thank goodness he thought of old-school solutions as well. He went into his utility bag and pulled out the can of compressed air. Turning it upside down, he sprayed the keypad copiously. It frosted over. Out came the hammer.

Suddenly, the train track turned invisible, and the train swerved in a new direction, veering right, toward open land. Bill lost his grip and slid down, hitting the hammer out of Brady's hand.

It fell to the ground and bounced away.

"Do you see that?" Bill said excitedly. "We're definitely going to their secret place!"

"The hammer!" said Brady.

Bill inched back up. The wire continued rubbing against the edge.

Brady closed his eyes. It was these moments that Bill didn't seem to grasp. Be a pro at everything. The little things matter. He had told him often. And every time he did, it seemed to go over his head.

Frustrated, Brady shuffled through the bag, causing more tension on the line. A fiber snapped.

Their eyes shot up to the partially frayed metal.

Ahead in the distance, another natural tunnel was coming fast.

"We got problems!" Bill cried out.

Brady grabbed the keypad and his hand rejected the freezing cold. A quick hot breath into his fingers, then he stretched his suit over the keypad and pulled. It didn't budge.

The train continued barreling toward the tunnel.

The wire rubbed against the edge—more fibers snapped! Brady turned the can upside down and sprayed the last of it. With the edge of the can, he feverishly banged at the keypad.

Dssht-dsshht-dssht-dsshht-dssht-dsshht-dssht-dsshht.

The screen cracked internally and went black.

The door disconnected from the lock.

Dangling, Brady pulled the sliding door apart with all his strength. It started moving, then slowly rolled open, and clicked in place. Brady reached for the handle.

The wire snapped.

Missing the handle, they fell. Brady stuck his fingers in the grooves on the train floor. He stretched out for Bill with his other hand. They grabbed each other's forearms. Their grip slid, and their hands interlocked at the wrists.

Fear of losing each other flashed through their eyes.

Ahead, the tunnel was 500 yards away and coming in hot. No time to think. Brady tried lifting him. That wasn't going to happen. "Push along the side!" he said. "I'll sway you!"

The tunnel was 400 yards away.

Bill pushed off the hull with his feet. Brady held on. The howl of the speed train hit a high pitch.

The tunnel was 300 yards out.

Bill pushed along the edge, gaining momentum.

Brady swayed him side to side—200 yards—side to side—150 yards. Losing grip, their hands slipped—fingers locked in place—100 yards.

The tunnel came screaming in—50 yards.

One more time, swinging back—30 yards—forward and up into the boxcar—20 yards.

Brady grabbed the ledge and Bill's hand—10 yards— and pulled himself onto the train. The rock tunnel *WHOOSHED* by.

The boxcar went pitch black.

In the darkness, a roaring flurry of wind streaked through the cab. Brady and Bill lay on their backs, exhausted. Intermittent flashes came alive with tunnel lights racing by. The train went dark again with the roar of wind and the whine of electromagnetic friction on the tracks.

The cab burst with light as the train flew out the other side of the tunnel. Open desert rushed by. They rested on their backs, relieved. Their arms and legs stretched out like snow angels.

"Somehow, we need to stop ending up like this," said Brady.

He unhooked the utility backpack and threw it off to the side. He tossed the strap and frayed wire out of the cab. Then he opened the magnet app and lowered the strength to 0. Above them, the magnet tumbled off the train.

A motion detector above the door activated a hidden camera.

When they started searching the cab, they both went slack-jawed. Mounds of sock bags littered the boxcar. To the right, a row of five-by-five-by-five rolling bins sat in the corner.

In the security boxcar, near the front of the train, a red light was blinking on a panel: *Boxcar 265C*. The panel displayed each boxcar's temperature, pressure level, and other details. The head security guard, who had a square jaw, turned to his junior. "We got motion. Check it out."

Back in Boxcar 256C, Brady took out his camera phone. *Flash*. Bags were labeled by customer number and zip code, and by laundromat number and zip code. Some laundromat bags were four times the size. One large bag was full of socks with holes and worn-out markings. *Flash*.

Two of the rolling bins were full of worn socks with no initials, and the other two were empty. *Flash*.

"We can hide in the bins," said Bill. He jumped in one filled with socks and wiggled under several layers. A moment later, he came up pantomiming, "guns blazing" with hand pistols.

A digital clock on the wall was counting down: *4 days, 4 hours, 56 minutes*. Brady calculated the timeline in his head. That's about what it should be from when they got the consultations. The rip-away countdown. He aligned his digital smartwatch with the clock on the wall. The screen outlined the countdown, registered the time code, and transferred to his watch. He double-tapped the screen and said "Countdown" into the microphone.

Footsteps on the roof thudded toward the opening. Brady put his phone in his pocket. Bill ducked into the bin.

The junior guard swung in the boxcar, rolled to his feet and drew his blaster.

Brady shot forward—foot out—and kicked the blaster out of his hands. It skidded near the open door.

Crouching and gaining a foothold, they both jumped for the blaster, knocking it off the train.

The guard palmed Brady's face, pushing his head into the howling wind. Bill sheepishly peered out from the bin. Not sure what to do, he lowered back down. The guard pushed harder on Brady's head. A line of posts along the track were rushing at him. Brady hit the guard's arm away and angled his head in the boxcar. The posts rushed by, barely missing. He kicked the man back, and got up.

The guard pulled a knife out of its sheath. He pointed it at Brady, and charged.

In one motion, Brady grabbed the man's wrist, spun into him, connecting the back of his head to the man's nose. He jarred the knife loose.

"Do something, Bill!"

Bill peeked out from the bin.

The guard pushed off Brady and jumped for the knife. Brady got on his back. His arm went under the man's chin. The guard swung around in circles, trying to get him off. Brady held on, tightening his grip in a chokehold. The man stopped to gain equilibrium, then stabbed Brady's leg with the knife—crunch.

Brady ignored the impact. He squeezed tighter until the guard went pale and dropped to the floor.

Sheepishly, Bill came up from the bin.

Brady pointed at the knife in his leg. "Yo, man?" He pulled it out, then took his phone from his pocket. His leg was saved by the phone.

"I'm a lover, not a fighter," said Bill as he hopped out of the bin. His stomach gurgled, and he rubbed his belly. "Plus, I knew you had it. I would've just got in the way." He crouched by the unconscious guard and made him look like a baby sucking his thumb. Bill took a selfie with him. *Flash.* "That'll be a great Insta pic."

Brady pocketed the cracked phone and tossed the knife off the train. Expecting something different from Bill wasn't good for his mindset. Get his assistance when possible. That was the best he could hope for. "Help me move him."

They rolled the guard to the opening and, with a last heave, shoved him off the train. His body tumbled out of view in a trail of dust.

Above them, more footsteps thudded toward the opening.

Brady grabbed a sock bag from a pile and got in a batting position.

The head security guard swung in—smack—Brady hit him right off—Clang! A post whizzing by flattened him.

Brady looked out to see if there were any more signs of guards. He went to the utility backpack, pulled out the "Error Signal" sticker and placed it over the broken keypad. He forced the door shut.

"Quick. Get in a bin," said Brady.

"Let it be noted here." Bill raised his eyebrows. "My idea. Credit goes a-this way."

"Just get in a bin and cover yourself."

"My idea," said Bill.

They hopped in separate bins and dug under layers of socks.

The train sped over rolling hills, through green landscapes, and through a green hill tunnel, then made its way back to the open desert. A few miles later, the train stopped at a loading dock.

A slick concrete base soared above the desert, blotting out the sky. It was an enormous enclosure with no windows. Clearly intending to keep the outside world out.

A line of armed sentries stood guard at the entrance.

Four men in scrub-looking uniforms and latex gloves stepped up to boxcar 256C. The front man slid his card on the keypad without looking. No access indicator beeped. He noticed the error signal and slid the door open.

"Malfunctioning," he said into the tablet microphone. He entered ERROR and REPORTS. "Reporting a keypad and door malfunction to the authorities." He said it aloud as he pressed enter on the tablet.

Once the boxcar was unloaded, the four men rolled out with the bins, including the two that were empty, now filled with individual sock bags. They headed toward the base. Sentries waved them in.

Sixteen wheels and eight steps marched in sync as the bins rolled through large corridors. At the end of the hall, the men rolled the bins through a magnetic, thermal curtain that separated on contact and reattached after they passed. They pushed forward into an enormous loading dock of an airport hangar. Single terminal.

Socks moved around in the front bin. Brady's eyes explored. Holy moly. The scope of this was much bigger than he ever could've imagined. Super Laundries. Poisoned socks. Insurance. Discount stores. Speed trains. And a hidden international airport? It takes a lot of complicit people to keep a secret of this magnitude.

There was Big Pharma, Big Tech, Big Media, and Big Food. Who knew there was Big Sock?

Undercover security agents were scattered throughout the hangar with their bowler hats, trench coats, and sunglasses.

At a window, a line of men and women in colorful clothes waited. The clerk stamped passports and signed them. On it was the stamp of an owl, and, circling it, in small capital letters, *"HIGH SECURITY CLEARANCE."*

A lady in a purple dress took her passport from the clerk. She was the nice older lady from Ginormous Discount who gave Brady the socks. An undercover agent escorted her, and she rolled her suitcase to a platform.

Airport security took her papers. "Suitcase right here," said the officer. "Please stand in the circle on the platform."

She placed the suitcase in the designated area and stood where she was told. He frisked her. Then he nodded to the undercover agent and pressed a code on the panel. A flash from a camera took a photo of the lady and the agent.

From above the enclosure, a slanted escalating belt extended from the top of the hangar, 500 feet long, and touched down to the platform.

The men with the four large bins rolled past the photo station platform onto the rolling belt. Brady's eyes looked out from the first bin. Socks from the second bin moved, revealing Bill's eyes.

From above and outside the enclosure, the rolling bins were escalating up to...

...a spaceship. A geodesic structure of connected triangles in the shape of an enormous flying saucer.

In the first bin, Brady's eyes stared in disbelief.

In the second bin, Bill's eyes darted around and locked onto the spaceship. His eyes widened.

He fainted.

CHAPTER 24

Outside light shone through tinted windows in the cargo hold. It was mostly dark with tiny dim lights along the floors. The men in scrubs pushed the bins to designated spots against the wall under color-coded curtains—silver, green, blue, and red. Sensors triggered clamps on the wheels and mechanical straps shot out from the wall and tightened around the bins. Electromagnetic cloth—also silver, green, blue, and red—settled over the tops and clamped to the sides, holding the socks in.

The men tugged on the straps, then left the cargo hold.

Above the first bin, the silver cloth moved. Forcing his arm through, then a shoulder, Brady pushed his upper body out and plopped on the floor. He staggered to his feet. "Bill," he whispered. He reached his arm in the next bin, feeling the rough texture of a sock bag.

"Over here." Bill fell onto the floor from the furthest bin and got up groggily. "Where are we?"

"This might be S4. We got to get out of here."

Bill looked around, unsettled. "Wait, what?"

"I think this is S4. The real Area 51 place. We're in a space-ship."

By the windows, a gold-mustard light shone down on three round helmets with mechanical corrugated rubber at the base. The seating area had belt straps, chains, and clasps for the feet.

"What is that...?" Bill's face turned white like he already knew the answer. He fainted.

"Yep," Brady said to himself. "That's my best friend."

A siren blared. "Lift off in progress," a speaker announced. The floor hummed.

Brady rushed to the cargo exit and yanked on the handle. It didn't budge. He whirled around. The utility bag. He raced to the bin and reached through the socks as far as he could when he realized he left the bag on the train!

Vibration hummed the bins. Lights flickered.

With no other choice, he rushed to the seating area, unhooked a space helmet from the shelf, and shoved it over his head. The sensors detected body heat, and the mechanical rubber extended down, closing the gap to his neck. Oxygen released into the helmet. He took another helmet and slipped it over Bill's sleeping head.

With a thrust of energy, the spaceship took off, and Brady flattened to the floor next to Bill.

The saucer raced up to the sky, through the clouds, through the stratosphere, into OUTER SPACE...

QUIET.

ZERO GRAVITY.

Brady flailed around, floating directionless in the cargo hold, trying to grab anything. He bounced off the floor and headed toward the rolling bins. As it came within reach, he got hold of the edge of the red-covered bin and his feet swung up, flipping him upside down. His back into the tall curtain. He contorted his body and turned around.

Bill's body bounced off the ceiling, and his eyes opened. As he came to, he noticed the windows getting closer. Then Bill saw the floor. He wasn't on the floor! He hit the window and bounced off, staring at the magnificent view of the black backdrop with speckled lights.

"No-no-no-no-no," said Brady. It was happening again. He sprang like a rocket to Bill. It was too late. Bill fainted.

Not accounting for Bill's movement, Brady found himself off course. As he flew by, he reached out, grabbing Bill's arm, and they went spinning. They bounced off the wall. Brady frantically swiped at it, hitting it on the wrong side of the momentum. The spinning escalated.

Dizziness supplanted his equilibrium, and they spun toward the door. The view began blending together. Ceiling. Wall. Floor. Windows. Ceiling. Wall. Floor.... He held onto Bill, fighting the reeling, but his eyes pulled him back to disorientation. Through the rotation, he noticed the cargo door getting closer. Swiping made it worse last time. Don't make the same mistake. When they got close, he stuck his foot straight out, and it hit the door, stopping the revolutions with a thud.

He blinked and joggled his head to fend off some of the dizziness. Looking through the blur, he could see a hint of his target. The seats were warping in and out. With his knee bent, and holding Bill, he pushed off the door handle. He floated straight at them—so he thought, gradually drifting left. They ended up at the wall between the bins and the window. Brady stopped the trajectory with a steady hand. He swiped the wall, turned around, and recalculated the distance to the seats. He sprang forward. Off course, again, but close enough this time. He flailed his free arm, correcting course ever so slightly, and got hold of the seat cushion.

Head still wobbly, Brady found the belt strap and pushed Bill down. The moment he grabbed for the other strap, Bill started floating away. He pulled him back down. Closing his eyes helped with the dizziness. He held Bill in place with his shoulder, felt around, got ahold of the belts, and buckled him in.

Once Bill was secure, he got into the middle seat. He looked down at the belt—made for prisoners—and strapped himself in.

Bill partially came to, his eyes flickering. He moved his nose around, attempting to satisfy an itch. It didn't go away. His hand hit the helmet. Then scratched at it. Kept scratching at it. His eyes shot open.

"Buddy," said Brady, "we're in space. We have to find out what's happening. But to do that, you're going to have to stop fainting. Okay? You'll be fine."

"I'm not fine," said Bill. "I can't scratch my nose! Why is this over my head?"

"To breathe. We can't breathe in space."

Bill turned his head and looked out the window, eyes filled with trepidation. Space, and all its terrifying wonder, stared back. Growing up, they had seen all the movies of men in space. Which never ended well for them. He faced forward. "Where are we going, Brady?"

"That's included in the things to figure out," Brady said calmly. "Which we will do." Under the surface, his mind was racing in a million directions. When did earth have alien saucers like this? Why are there shackles? And what does it have to do with socks? He felt around the sides of his helmet and the corrugated rubber. It had strong suction to his clothes and was oddly stable, putting him at ease for a moment. At least they could breathe.

Overhead, the speakers crackled. "Super warp speed will start after the countdown. Keep fastened and safe travels. We'll touch down outside home planet's orbit in no time.... 10... 9... 8... 7... 6..."

They both grabbed the armrests, their hearts pounding.

"OMG-OMG-OMG!" said Bill.

"5... 4... 3... 2... 1..."

A vortex materialized around the saucer. The spaceship shot forward, disappearing into the haze.

Brady and Bill jolted back. The bins rattled. Lights flickered. They strained against the pulsating straps. Snot slowly leaked out their noses. Simultaneously, they rage-sniffed the snot back in.

The rattling, the lights, and the shaking intensified. Brady instinctively put his arm across Bill's chest like a grown-up driver protecting a child in the passenger's seat.

Far out in the solar system, the vastness of SATURN and its RINGS glowed.

A nebulous circle appeared, and the spaceship shot through the haze, gliding toward the planet. The vortex disappeared behind it.

QUIET.

ZERO GRAVITY.

Their weight loosened in their seats, and they floated. Breathing heavy, Brady scanned the cab and spotted double doors at the far end of the cargo hold.

Bill squished his hands together. "We're gonna die."

"You have to stop that. I need you."

Out the window, Bill caught a glimpse of Saturn. His jaw dropped. Holy mother of planets. He could see its outer rings in the distance. But it didn't look the way he had imagined. "What the fudgesicle," he said, shaking Brady's arm.

The "rings" of Saturn were trillions of clusters of moon rocks and dust. It was much different seeing it up close than a photo from a billion miles away. In school, Saturn's rings were the flat bands going around the planet. The photos still looked cool, but to tell you it was a lousy comparison was an understatement. Real life was more magnificent. And scary.

As the spaceship glided toward the planet, Brady and Bill were in a trance at the extraordinary view. They forgot about S4, the saucer, and where they were going. They just stared.

When they passed the inner ring, something was distinctly different about it. They did a whiplashing double take. Full-blown shock.

The inner ring was socks.

A small, one-man spaceship hovered close to the inner "ring." An apparatus extended out from the side and sucked in a load.

Brady snapped himself out of it. The view might be fun to watch, but they were getting closer to the surface of a foreign world. He looked back to the other side of the cargo hold.

"Follow me," Brady said urgently. He unstrapped the buckles, pushed off the seat, and floated toward the double doors.

Reluctantly, Bill followed. "Can't we wait 'til it goes back to Earth?"

After the brief journey, Brady and Bill smacked into the double doors. They grabbed the handles affixed to the walls on either side. It appeared to be an elevator.

On the right side was a panel with a button. It had a strange, foreign symbol with circles and twirls. Brady pressed it. Digital lines appeared in the helmet's glass. As it outlined the panel, trying to "focus" on the button, the doors opened. Brady and Bill floated in.

"What are we doing?" said Bill.

Brady pretended not to hear him and looked around.

Three buttons in the elevator were marked with similar symbols. Unmistakably foreign. As he focused on the buttons, the screen in his helmet outlined the panel.

The characters digitally converted to COCKPIT, PASSENGER, and CARGO.

"The helmets translate," said Brady. Unsure if this was a good idea, he pressed the PASSENGER button.

The doors closed.

They had always talked about saucers and aliens when they were younger. But not like this. Not where man was working with them.

"I don't know what we're thinking." Bill rubbed his arms. "We're gonna die, man. We're gonna die."

"Hey," said Brady. "We'll figure this out." Though he wasn't so sure he believed it.

The double doors opened to the seating area. Brady stealthily leaned out. A large, curving partition walled off the passenger section. The wall was high, yet you could float over it. To the far right was a stewardess compartment, and about ten feet to the left of the elevator was a walkway to the two sections of the seating area.

Clamoring voices drifted over the walls, the words muffled. Brady and Bill quietly pushed toward the partition and grabbed the top edge. They popped their heads above the wall. Their faces set in shock.

The passenger cab was filled with aliens.

CHAPTER 25

Brady grabbed Bill's suit and yanked him below the top of the partition. They held themselves there as the color drained from their faces. Luckily, they were in shock or they'd be screaming. At least Bill would be.

They had dealt with crazy mysteries in the past. But this was different. This was real aliens. In the flesh. Should they run? Escape? Hide? Those didn't feel good in the pit of Brady's stomach. It was best to face problems. Not avoid them. But what could they do? Should they fight? If he had his book, *If Aliens Attack*, maybe something would work there. That didn't feel right, either. Just thinking about it eased the stress a little, and the color in his face returned.

Then a weird thought occurred to him. It wasn't some elaborate plan. He didn't know enough to hatch one of those. It was the simplest plan he could think of. And, as crazy as it sounded in this situation, it felt right.

Act normal.

Whatever was going on has apparently been a regular occurrence. It had the sounds of a typical passenger cab. The murmurs, clicks, and snores. It was just another day for them. As new and scary as it was for him and Bill, it didn't seem frightening to anyone else. He decided that's what he'd go with—acting normal.

He took a breath, ignoring his beating heart, and rose above the partition to get another peek. Instantly, he got the chills. These weren't the aliens we've all seen in documentaries, or on TV. They were not gray. They were green. And they weren't the small ones you hear about with the enormous heads and big eyes. These ones had a variety of body structures. A lot of them were human-like, with two arms and two legs. Some were animal-like, with four legs. Some were husky, some small, and some jelly-like. But they all had a similar scaly, light-to-dark greenish skin tone.

Each passenger compartment had six seats, which were high end, heavily padded theater chairs with lean-back capabilities, and a tray for food.

A slender alien with punk hair was listening to music. A giant alien with a potbelly, and mini horns for eyebrows was reading a book. An octopus-looking alien with glasses worked up a frenzy on her laptop, her many two-pronged fingers blurring the keys.

Above each seat was a contraption with attached handles and a curved screen. Probably some state-of-the-art, new-age, immersive entertainment.

He was in awe, but kept his face matter-of-fact for Bill. If not, Bill might scream, and he could sense Bill was looking at him for comfort. It didn't work.

Mouth quivering, Bill abruptly said, "I gotta go." He turned around and headed for the elevator.

Brady grabbed his foot and pulled him back. "Wait," he whispered. "I need you to keep an eye out."

"Why don't you announce you're here and have a party with them while I go hide?"

"You don't have to come as far as me, but I need eyes. Come to the walkway." Brady pointed with his head.

Sweat speckled on Bill's forehead. He forced some fast-twitch nods. "Okay. But, remember, you're forcing me. I don't want to do this." Bill followed closely behind, focusing on his breathing and quiet hand placements.

They stopped at the walkway to the passenger area. Brady peered out. Along the walkway at each ten-foot interval was a seating cubby.

Further down on the left side, he heard a strained conversation. An argument with the tone of a subordinate against authority. He noticed he could make out words. The helmet had vocal translation, too!

He cautiously floated toward the quarrel, and stopped near the opening. He peeked over the partition.

Sitting rigidly was a female alien in a purple dress. She was small, thin, and older, with buggy eyes and bright silver-white hair. She wore a loose scarf around her neck. Large for an older lady, but she was small compared to the other aliens. She crossed her arms as the authority figure spoke.

The monster in uniform pulled out a recording device. His face was stone-green, he had sharp teeth, and a solid overpowering stature. Medals, ribbons, and ten breast pockets covered his officer's jacket, and his name tag read, Norbo. He was a high-level executive for the security administration of Saturn. "I take my duty very seriously. I'm sure you understand." He finished spelling out a few things off the record, then flipped his recording device on. It had two small microphones and speakers on either side.

Bill's eyes shot back and forth from Brady to the elevator. Brady gave him an encouraging thumbs up and went back to the conversation.

"Working with humans against our species is a planetary crime," said Norbo.

"I'm being wrongfully charged," she responded stubbornly, "and you know it."

Norbo gave her a cynical squint, then he turned off the recording device. "It doesn't matter who's right or wrong. It only matters what can be proven with evidence. As of now, it's one word against another." He turned the recorder on again. "You'll be going straight to the grand jury. You better hope your story hits hard. It's all you'll get." He powered the device off. "There are alternatives we can work out. You don't want to be tagged for treason."

She crossed her arms and went silent.

Further down the walkway from Brady, at the opening of another passenger cubby, a stewardess alien with a tail was backing out with a snack tray and a trash bin. She wore Traxtanium Magnetic Slippers that held her to the floor.

Brady zipped around and pushed off toward Bill.

An announcement came over the speakers. "Approaching Saturn. We'll be touching down shortly. Be seated and strapped in until we reach the atmosphere."

"Go," Brady whispered. He turned the corner outside the partition and grabbed Bill. They pushed off for the cargo elevator.

When they floated near it, Brady got hold of the inlet and stopped their momentum. He rattled the down button. It lit up, but the elevator didn't open. He continued quietly pushing it. "C'mon."

As he hit the button, it dawned on him that another alien could be in the elevator. But what other choice did they have? They pressed their bodies against the double doors, keeping out of view.

The stewardess turned the corner into the outside partition circle. They could only hope she would go the opposite way, but she rolled the snack cart straight toward them. They pressed harder against the doors.

Brady slipped his hand out and pressed the elevator button again.

Bill mumbled a prayer to himself.

As the stewardess passed by the elevator, the doors were open.

Brady and Bill were floating in place against the ceiling. After a few seconds had passed and the alien hadn't come in, Brady reached down and pressed the cargo button.

"Can you get the elevator for me?" said another waitress. Footsteps hurried to the doors. Brady rattled the cargo button in a frenzy while Bill focused on the doors, doing his best to use "the intention."

The door closed.

"Never mind," said a muffled voice, "I'll do it later."

When the doors opened in the cargo hold, Bill pressed the *passenger* and *pilot* buttons before they floated out.

"Purple Dress is our crumb," said Brady.

"What do you mean?" Bill was appalled.

"There's an alien in a purple dress. That's who we're following."

"Why?"

"I have a gut feeling," said Brady.

"You can't just go with that every time."

"What the heck is that supposed to mean?" Brady asked.

"Remember the guy you thought was a scheming criminal, and it turned out he only wore the dark glasses because he was blind? Your gut feeling isn't always right. Why don't we hide until it goes back to Earth?"

Brady stared at him. "Bill, it's what we're doing."

The saucer descended through the clouds and an enormous transparent dome appeared.

Made of the extraterrestrial element—translucent traxtanium—the outside base of the dome was pliable to any surface condition. It could float on Saturn's gas surface and stay in position because traxtanium had a binding and looping magnetic pole to anything it touched, holding it in place while never fully touching. Like a magnet with both the pull and push force simultaneously. The outside surface of the dome didn't affect the weight inside because it was disconnected from the rest of the atoms, almost buffering them like they didn't exist. Yet it didn't change the natural pull of the planet's gravity inside the dome.

A crackle sounded through the speakers. "Touching Saturn's atmosphere in 3…2…1…"

"Uh oh." Gravity took hold. Brady and Bill crashed to the floor.

A giant mechanical door on top of the dome opened. The saucer glided in.

CHAPTER 26

On Earth, in the security office at the Secret Sock Corporation, stacks of surveillance monitors blanketed a curved wall. The large desk with the primary controls anchored the middle of the room, flanked by two smaller desks.

Vance adjusted his red tie and nodded to Ivan, who handed a disc to the guard.

"Play it," said Ivan.

The guard inserted the disc into the video slot and entered a few commands.

A visual appeared on the large middle screen, then spread throughout all the monitors as one screen. Other than a faint red dot, the screen was dark.

Vance glanced at his pocket watch. "Bring him in."

A guard opened the door. Biker girl strode in with a white case and a scowl on her face. Behind her, Mooch dragged the train conductor by the collar.

She opened the case and handed Vance the light blaster.

Mooch easily held the conductor in the air with one arm.

"How would I know?" the conductor pleaded as he flailed. "I'm not security."

Vance pulled the lever on the blaster, initiating a whirling sound. "Cue it to the alarm."

The guard fast-forwarded the video. It sped through the train door opening, the lights going on, Brady taking photos, Bill jumping in the bin, and–He paused it.

On screen was Bill coming out of the sock bin, pantomiming "guns blazing" with finger pistols, and Brady looking at the countdown on the wall.

"Did you see an alert in your cab?" Vance asked.

The conductor quit moving and held on to the brute's arm. "The video goes straight to the security boxcar. Not mine."

"Why isn't it set up in yours?"

"I can do it. In fact, I'll do it right now."

Vance pointed to the monitor wall. "Get a close-up on the skinnier one." The wall of screens zoomed in on Brady's face. Vance grumbled. "Brady Watts. Mystery Solver. Just what we &$%# needed." With a death-stare, he aimed the light blaster and pulled the trigger.

Mooch turned his eyes away as lights spun in the chamber and shot into the conductor's eyes. The man stared into a colored abyss, an unknown dimension. When the light faded, he mumbled incoherent gibberish, and slunk over.

"Get rid of him," said Vance. "Does anyone else want to join him?" He handed Ivan the light blaster.

Silent stares from the guards as Mooch hauled the conductor away.

Ivan strolled around the room, holding up the light blaster. All the guard's eyes locked onto it, and they squirmed in their seats. He pointed the blaster at them. They flinched. He pointed it away from them, then back at them. They flinched again. He slowly pointed it at them. They flinched slowly. He pointed it at them quickly. They flinched quickly. He pretended like he was going to point it, but didn't. They flinched. He smiled.

"Warn the authorities back home," Ivan said.

♪ ♪ ♪

Back on the spaceship, Brady and Bill frantically paced up and down the cargo hold. Though Brady generally stayed positive, he couldn't see how they'd get out of this one.

"They're going to torture us," said Bill.

"I don't think so," said Brady. "They kind of seem like humans."

"Then they're definitely going to torture us!"

"We'll figure something out. Get your head in the game." They peered out the window. Alien airport mechanics were guiding the saucer forward with blue, glowing traffic wands.

A crowd of aliens waited impatiently for their family members coming home. Most aliens were in suits and posh clothes. Some wore very little. A few "hipster types" were dressed head to toe in artsy clothes, including one with a face covering. Next to the hipsters was an invalid with a helmet, presumably for gas medicine intake or to protect him from an allergy. "That's it," Brady said. "We'll be ill hipsters."

The ship's base opened, and the escalating belt extended down to the platform.

Flashy smoke and lights were met with cheers from the crowd. Impatient loved ones waved excitedly as the alien passengers descended the ramp. Two small, out-of-place hipsters, concealed in curtain cloth from helmet to toe, moved with the arrivals. Brady was covered by the blue curtain, and Bill by the red curtain, held together by safety pins from the cargo hold. Separate pieces covered their helmets and were tied at the neck.

Bill waved vigorously in his red disguise, trying to mesh with the exuberant home comers.

"Overdoing it, buddy." Brady pulled his arm down.

A two-headed female alien cried double the happy tears as she rushed by them. She jumped into her husband's four arms, and he spun her around. Kiss marks stamped both of his cheeks simultaneously.

Norbo and Purple Dress passed through the crowd, flanked by two undercover officers. Norbo held a tight grip on her arm.

Brady followed, pulling Bill along. "We can't lose them."

The bright light made it harder to see clearly through the cloth, but it was enough to identify faces and the purple dress. They clumsily scooted through the crowd, garnering a few strange looks.

Behind them, as they followed Purple Dress through the crowd, the escalating belt retracted into the saucer, and a gigantic shaft of light shone down on it. The light beamed it up, and moved it 200 yards away into a half-circled structure.

Suddenly, red lights were flashing, and horns were going off. Teams of armed officials descended on the geodesic saucer. Bill looked back as the teams rushed in.

Brady pulled him away. "Not such a bad idea now." His gut was right. They kept their heads low, and followed the crumb of the purple dress.

Down the block, orange taxis and hover buses waited for passengers. A dark blue, six-seater police craft stopped at the corner. Norbo, Purple Dress, and the undercover officers got in.

A taxi hovercraft stopped nearby, and a passenger got out. Brady hailed it down with his blue flapping curtain arms. The hovercraft glided over and abruptly stopped. They got in.

The helmets translated alien to English, but would they translate English to alien? Brady wasn't sure and didn't want to risk it. He pointed to the police hovercraft and shook his curtain forward aggressively.

The taxi driver was in a charcoal-colored suit, had an octopus-looking head, a large mustache, and wore wraparound sunglasses. "What's your destination?" he asked.

The blue cloth vigorously pointed toward the police craft speeding away.

"I'm not sure what that means," said the taxi driver.

Brady kept pointing with the cloth.

"Hello?" said the driver. "Where am I taking you? In that general direction?"

Brady spoke slowly, "Follow... that... police car–aft?"

The driver shook his head and glided after the hovercraft, which had almost disappeared down the street. "Jallywoks," said he driver in a condescending tone under his breath.

The taxi stayed a reasonable distance behind the police craft. They went under a tunnel, turned several corners, and over a bridge. Brady tried to trace the turns but lost it by the fourth corner.

They continued a few blocks, turned one last street, and slowed to a crawl outside the massive structure of the Saturn council dome.

Norbo and the security escorted Purple Dress inside, passing a throng of aliens dressed in formal attire eagerly waiting to enter.

"Right here," said Brady.

The taxi stopped. "Twenty crups," said the driver.

"Give me a second." Brady pretended to reach in his nonexistent curtain pockets. "I can't get at my wallet." He scooted Bill out of the taxi. Brady faced the driver and pretended to recheck. They bolted away from the cab and hurried toward the dome entrance.

Bill yelled to the taxi, "We'll pay you back!"

The taxi driver honked his horn and raised his tentacles. "I was expecting a tip. Assholes." He glided off.

They got in the back of the line. A few aliens stared at them a little too long for comfort, making them antsy.

The longer they stood there, the more aliens stared, and Bill became fidgety, turning his body left and right. Brady grabbed his jittery arms and settled him. Under the cloth, Bill took in a deep breath, but his nerves only got worse. He pulled Brady from the line and went around the curved corner under the sky-walk so no one could hear them. "What are we doing?"

Brady put his hands on Bill's shoulders. "You have to trust me."

"Yeah. I usually do," said Bill. "This is crazy."

"It's better than being in the saucer. Whatever's happening is big. The Purple Dress girl knows something. We'll be careful."

They got back in line, which was moving.

A hexagon skyscraper loomed high in the dome city. Its control and eyes were everywhere like tentacles. At the top floor in the executive office, a red light blinked above a desk. The executive commander of planetary defense turned from the window. "What is it now?" He glided over in his hover-chair.

In slick uniforms, two female assistants with droopy ears and tails stood at attention by the door, not saying a word.

A glass tube extended down from the ceiling. A memo stuck halfway out. The commander took the digital message and read it. He glided over to the MEMO RELAY STATION and placed the memo inside. HIGH ALERT then COPY were pressed in the relay receiver—the memo shot up to the ceiling. A red light scanned it, capturing the "data," turned around, and transferred the digital copy to several other tubes. The memos shot up the wall, across the ceiling, down the other side, then into the floor. They branched out to different locations.

Following the original memo, it whisked straight down, twisted, turned inside the building walls, curving left, then right, and went into a mini underground tunnel. It shot down the street several blocks all the way to the Saturn dome building.

In the Saturn Dome's main office, the red interplanetary alarm blinked rapidly. The tube with the original memo popped up on the minister's desk.

Over in the assembly hall, the place was buzzing with excitement. Lights from the chandeliers bounced off the expansive walls. Purple drapes with a gold design of swirling socks overhung the balconies. The proceedings of the grand jury were about to commence. Anyone in the public could witness the testimonies, as evidenced by the large turnout. It promoted public trust in the law and the authorities if anyone could stand in and watch high-level cases. Live video coverage was also available so that anyone could tune in. Based on the dome map grid, the stand-in witnesses were grouped by sector.

Purple Dress wasn't fooled. The media manipulated the truth and, having the public able to "see" what was going on, could still pull the wool over their eyes with propaganda. History showed the same tactics employed on every planet and every city in the interplanetary alliance, including the dome cities on the other side of Saturn. However, it still gave her a better chance than nothing.

The hall was filled to capacity and conversations were spreading around. The council sat on a raised platform with various planetary flags behind them. A line of media members took photos and recorded the proceedings from the ground.

In the middle of the stage, the council minister, with his pale green head and droopy eyes, stood. He was in his black judge robe with a frilly white bowtie. "Settle down. Settle down," he said. "The case of the Gilda Report will be heard. Have her face the front, please."

The guards faced Purple Dress before the council.

"Traitor!" yelled an old, hunched-over alien, jamming her cane into the floor. The crash echoed as if the sound reflected off the golden socks in the drapes. The crowd rumbled with whispers.

"Quiet!" The minister raised his three-pronged hand, and the room settled. "The case you bring against the SSC, Secret Sock Corporation, is serious. Do you understand the ramifications, and do you wish to proceed?"

Purple Dress stepped forward, unwavering. "I do."

Near the back of the crowd, Brady whispered to Bill, "Let's break up. We'll attract less attention. Be cool, okay?" Without giving him a chance to reject, he went right. Bill tried to grab him, but he had already slipped past a large-bodied alien with tusks.

Bill nervously pushed his way to the left, bouncing off a few strange creatures. It included a small alien with spiked hair and no nose, who watched him curiously.

The council minister continued, "Start with your name and occupation."

Bill spotted up behind a group of teenagers thinly scattered about. The less of a crowded area, the better for him. Or his claustrophobia would set in. He pulled out his phone, fumbling with unsteady hands, and started the video recorder.

Purple Dress pulled out a note. "Thank you, Minister. My name is Gilda Rici. For the last seventy-five years, I worked for the Secret Sock Corporation on Planet Human. I worked at the stores and different laundromats. I helped manufacture the original Super Laundry sets and their yearly upgrades. In the last couple of years, unfortunately, I started noticing crimes against the human treaty agreement... by Mr. Sock."

"Ooohs" from the crowd.

The no-nose alien with spiked hair slipped through the crowd and got up close to the small, chubby hipster. He reached for Bill's phone.

Bill moved it away and went stiff, keeping his arm up. The alien reached for the phone again, and Bill brought it down to his side. "Shoo." Bill waved the nosy alien away.

Sensing more eyeballs on him, Bill stopped the recording and put the phone under the sheets and in his pocket. He kept as still as possible. "Go...away," he whispered, terrified.

Gilda continued, "When I looked, I found poison hidden in—"

A siren wailed in the assembly hall, echoing off the walls.

Aliens covered their ears. Some covered their stomach because of the tummy ache it caused or the back of their necks, a lower headache.

Bill could only turn away. It was the best he could do, unable to reach his ears.

A voice came over the loudspeakers. "There's been a planet breach. The meeting will commence tomorrow."

Security staff and Norbo busted through the side door to the stage, and grabbed Gilda.

"Gilda," said the security staffer. "You are hereby detained for conspiracy with humans."

A gasp in the crowd.

"I did no such thing," she retorted.

"Take her away!" ordered Norbo.

Clamoring spread in the crowd as they escorted Gilda out. Bill pulled his phone from his pocket. He pressed the record button—*Flash*.

Uh-oh. He had accidentally set it to photo when putting it away. The surrounding aliens faced him. He shoved the camera back in his pocket and put his hands up.

Green faces inched toward him, bodies gathering around.

An innocent fuzzy-haired face looked at Bill. "Why would you do that?" She pointed to the *NO PICTURES* sign on the wall.

Brady swung by, grabbed Bill, and pulled him past the crowd. He veered around a pillar and face-planted into the belly of a giant alien.

A face with strong cheekbones and a thick unibrow peered down at them.

Brady and Bill angled their heads up, then slowly backed away.

The no-nose alien slid up behind Brady and Bill. "Who are you two? Show your faces."

Bill stared through the drapes as large, green bodies inched closer and closer, gradually surrounding them.

More heads popped up in the crowd to get a better look.

"We have face deformities!" Bill blurted out.

A few aliens backed off.

Brady elbowed Bill. "We have rights," said Brady. "We don't have to show you anything."

The aliens looked at each other, then closed a circle around them.

CHAPTER 27

A thick, scaly creature with three fangs and three eyes stepped forward. "Show your face."

Behind Brady and Bill, the no-nose alien ripped off the red and blue cloth from their helmets.

Aliens backed away, horrified. Murmurs echoed in the crowd.

"Humans!"

"Security!"

"The humans!"

A discreet figure slipped out from the shadows on the balcony. He was in his purple camouflage and dark glasses. An officer from the Saturn Watch Against Treason—S.W.A.T. He hopped up on the railing and jumped off, flinging out a precisely aimed net over Brady and Bill. Magnets at the ends of the circular net converged under Brady and Bill, gathering them into a ball.

The crowd dispersed. A female with ram horns from Sector 17 put the back of her hand to her forehead and fainted. Her male counterpart broke her fall. A few shocked aliens ignored the rules and started recording the scene with their phones.

Windows lined the skyline walkway from the Saturn council dome across the street to the jail, so citizens could watch felons go to lockup after a trial. It was additional transparency to keep the public happy.

The S.W.A.T. officers escorted Brady and Bill across the skyway with their helmets exposed. Bill was so out of it that his body was being moved for him. At least he hadn't fainted. Somehow, that was an improvement.

At the jail entrance, a S.W.A.T. officer placed his seven-finger hand on the scanner.

In the circular jail room—the Circle of Doom—Gilda leaned against the electromagnetic chains, her silver-white head hanging low in defeat. Next to her were two eight-foot-tall aliens in all-black outfits. One sported a mohawk hairstyle, and the other had a French crop hairstyle with a ring in his nose.

Cables came down from the ceiling and held a curved screen that went around in a complete circle. You could watch the screen from any vantage point in the padded cell. As needed, propaganda against the accused got played on a loop so they stayed in line.

A small room connected to the circle jail room was visible through a glass wall. An alien with an elongated egg-shaped head was strapped to a slanting metal table connected to electrodes. And a loin cloth covered his family jewels. He had marks all over his bare chest, arms, and legs, with green blood smeared on the cuts. You could smell the stench of sweat and burnt skin.

Norbo crouched to Gilda's height, devilish eyes slanting across his face. "Would you like to be next?" He pressed a button on the back of his remote. The alien on the torture table writhed in agony, flapping against the metal table. Norbo lifted Gilda's chin. "You're going to tell us where you're hiding the humans."

She tried to look away, but he held her chin.

He let go. "We'll find them."

Just then, the jail doors opened. S.W.A.T. officers forced Brady and Bill inside.

Norbo looked over, then back to Gilda. "What do we have here?"

"What do they have to do with me?" Her eyes changed when she recognized Brady.

"You do know them."

"I've seen one of them. That doesn't mean anything."

"Do you forget what the penalty is for treason?" Norbo put a hand on his blaster.

The officers released Brady's and Bill's cuffs and placed them against the wall. Norbo clicked the remote, and electro-magnetic chains shot out from the padded walls, strapping their arms and legs.

The S.W.A.T. officers left.

"Death is the punishment for treason." Norbo let it simmer. "There's nothing you can do, Gilda. Nobody will believe you, and nobody will care." As he sauntered over to the humans, the remote swayed on his hip.

Bill trembled, staring at his feet, while Brady kept a stone-cool expression, staring straight ahead.

Norbo whacked the side of Brady's helmet.

The impact shot through his skull, and a piercing whine rang in his ear. He tried staying calm, but his eyes couldn't lie.

Bill's breathing became erratic. Shock setting in. He closed his eyes.

"Why would you investigate socks?" Norbo said, grinning, exposing his sharp, jagged teeth. He pointed to the alien on the torture table and pressed the button. "This is what happens to humans like you."

The alien flapped against the clasps. The thrashing of body to metal got louder and louder until the alien jerked uncontrollably and went stiff. His body slumped back and his mouth drooped open. A splintered tongue fell out.

"You two are next." Norbo flipped a switch on the remote. "I want to show you something first. It'll give me time to prepare for your rank skin." He powered on the curved monitor.

Four screen segments separated in Brady's direct view. It was security footage from The Red Café, a high-end café in downtown—Planet Human. The top left view was from the camera outside the café. The top right was from the camera inside, facing the bar. The bottom left was from the customer seating area, and the bottom right was aimed at a door near the back of the café.

"What's on your mind, Mystery Solver?"

Brady was unsure what he was looking at, and suddenly, he felt anxious. Not this again. The screen was taunting him.

From outside the café, Ivan opened the front door for Vance and the Biker girl. A stretch hummer pulled up to the entrance. Mooch, the large brute, opened the back door. Sock loss consultants Cliff and Ethan, who he recognized, exited with the fat news director, who ate mini pizza bites from a small snack box. Then the mayor scooted out, followed by the three army-looking officials from the Super Laundry Headquarters. Lastly, a blur on the screen emerged from the back seat. A large specimen of a man—or monster. Completely concealed in all black, and a vague green shot from the eyes. A reflection off the camera.

He knew it right away. Mr. Sock.

The seating area outside *The Red Café* was bustling with customers. A woman got a view of Mr. Sock and turned the other way. A man pretended not to see him, dropping his phone on the ground. Three birds flew away, and a puppy whimpered behind its owner.

The café door opened, and the parade of characters headed to the back—where the bottom right camera was aimed. A blurred Mr. Sock and the three officials entered last.

In the customer seating area, the bottom left view zoomed in close to a table by the far wall.

When Brady saw her on the screen, his heart sank.

His sister was seated near the back wall of the café. She masqueraded in black clothes and mascara, and was bobbing to music on her headphones.

She had done her research and pulled her own strings, following the trail of crumbs. After she had found the Missing Person Notice at the farmers market, she decided she would give the information to Brady. He didn't respond when she brought it up. So she kept it stashed away. She helped them on the Super Laundry mission. Then, after they left for Rock Tunnel, she called the number on the notice. It led her to Adeline—the wife of James Lin—who gave her the address to Mill's Sock Plant.

She got a ride-share to Sock Street and snooped around the factories. They were mostly brick buildings, and a few stainless steel ones. Although she'd never been there, she could tell it was recently abandoned. The streets were freshly paved, but barely a soul to be found. It looked like a renovated ghost town. She saw a strange overweight character with a grease stain on his tie coming out of Mill's Sock Plant. The big guy met a shady man in an Italian suit with a thin, long mustache. Thin Mustache Man handed him a card from his back pocket, and another card fell out. After they left, she grabbed it. The card was to *The Red Café*, which had a note of a meeting the next day.

When the time came, Natasha got a ride to *The Red Café* with Momma Jan, who was now bringing water and snacks from the bar.

It wasn't Brady's imagination. There they were on screen. Norbo stood over him, smirking. Brady lashed out, struggling valiantly against the clasps. It lasted only a short while before he lost strength and sank back to the wall. Chained to an outcome he couldn't control. He tried his hardest not to look at the screen, but couldn't help himself.

Momma Jan handed Natty a snack and put a receipt in her fanny pack. "Why are we here?"

"Brady said it was a new café I should check out." She waited for Mom to look away, then quietly took out the elephant ears she had stolen from Brady's place, and plugged in her headset. She pressed the record button and connected the vibration sensor to the wall.

The sound crackled, then cleared up. She could hear a deep guttural voice....

"The Mystery Solvers know too much. Put them in the morgue!" a voice thundered.

Another voice chimed in, "They're only kids."

"Do you want to join them?" A fist to a table—Boom.

Natasha jolted from the wall.

Worry appeared on Momma Jan's face. "What's wrong?"

Natasha looked behind Mom and flinched again in a panic. Two intimidating men were standing over her shoulder.

"Why are we really here?" Momma Jan asked.

A guard yanked Momma Jan out of the chair.

Ivan ripped Natasha's bag away, and grabbed her wrist. "To the compound."

In menacing ink, on his forearm was a tattoo of a shark.

The screen went black.

Against the magnetic clasps, blank-faced, Brady stared at nothing. He wanted to be mad at Natasha for going against him, but he only had himself to blame. She would've listened if she knew more details. If she saw the dangers of the business. Had he not constantly pushed her away, she would've stayed out of it on her own decision.

The light in Brady's eyes dimmed.

Norbo chuckled. "I was told you were a formidable opponent. This is disappointing."

Brady looked at Norbo, hoping to find some humanity. There was none.

"You want to know what I love about people like you?" Norbo swung the remote around his finger. "You look into a mystery like socks and find yourself here.... And I get to kill you." He clipped the remote back to his belt, and poked Brady's helmet. "No more fight in you?"

The best Brady could do was lift his head for Bill. It was all he had to give. Bill wasn't fairing much better. He was leaning on the straps, mumbling to himself.

A joke about the alien popped in Brady's head. Something Bill might say about the alien's breath being horrendous to distract him. He thought of when Bill jiggled, then grabbed his shoulders, and shook him vigorously, saying he transferred his humor. What if humor would work? Bill seemed to think it could.

He looked at Bill—pale and cowered in fear.

Who was he kidding? Jokes don't work against evil. And you can't simply wish its effects away. It's evil. You have to be strong.

Norbo tilted Bill's helmet up. "Your friend here is more pitiful than you."

Brady mustered what energy he had left. He gritted his teeth and glared at Norbo. "If I got out of these straps, I would destroy you."

The monster was taken aback. He leaned in close. "I'm so scared. What will the little human do to me?" Norbo belted out, laughing.

The sound knocked Bill out of his funk. He glanced at the aliens on the wall—resigned to their fate. He looked at the dead green alien on the torture table. Then at Norbo, who was uncomfortably close to Brady.

Brady gained a little more energy. "You'd have a different attitude if I wasn't chained to the wall."

Norbo laughed the way one would laugh at a baby boy swatting a doll to show his power. "Is that so?" He smashed his fists into the wall on either side of Brady's head. Brady kept his gaze. Unfazed.

The monster gripped Brady's helmet with his colossal hands and twisted, loosening the suction against his body. Brady squirmed as the helmet rose above his head. He shut his mouth tight.

"How long can you hold it?" Norbo taunted.

Bill's eyes went big. He had a mini panic attack, and started hyperventilating. Straining against the clasps, he unhooked a safety pin from his outfit and passed it off to his other hand.

Brady's face was turning pink.

Trembling, Bill extended his arm. With his thumb and index finger, he thrust forward, stabbing Norbo in the back of the elbow.

"Ow." Norbo dropped the helmet back on Brady's head. He looked at the source of pain in his arm. Then pulled out the pin. "Very impressive coming from you." He put the pin up in the light. Green blood trickled down.

Norbo turned and shoved the pin into Bill's side. "I guess it'll be you first." He twisted Bill's helmet off and threw it across the room.

Shock hit Bill. He tried blocking out the pain, holding his breath. Norbo smacked him in the chest, and he began convulsing, gasping for air that wasn't there.

He lost consciousness and slumped in place.

"I don't mess around," said Norbo.

Brady pulled the blaster from Norbo's belt. Norbo looked down, dumbfounded. Brady showed him the remote, then the blaster.

Bang! Norbo's eyes glazed over, then he fell flat on his face.

Brady stunned him again.

The aliens on the wall kept to themselves, avoiding eye contact.

Snatching Bill's helmet off the floor, Brady rushed over, and put it over his head.

The room was quiet.

The gadget extended to his neck and released oxygen. Brady waited restlessly as Bill's body hung limp over the electro-chains.

He tilted Bill's helmet up. His eyes were still closed.

"C'mon," said Brady. "Please."

No response.

"Wake up, buddy." He shook Bill's body. "The oxygen should be working by now. C'mon."

The silence was deafening.

He shook him again. "Bill?"

There was nothing. He shook him again.

Loneliness fell over the space.

Brady unchained Bill with the remote and slumped with him to the ground.

"You can't go. I can't lose you, too," he said, holding back tears. "You're my right-hand man." He forced a smile, and a tear rolled down his cheek.

Bill lay motionless.

Brady leaned against the wall, tears rolling down. He sat quietly in misery, holding Bill's limp body.

CHAPTER 28

After Brady and Bill had taken care of the school bully Dovinic Tarke in the lunchroom, an unlikely friendship formed. Bill followed Brady everywhere, and insisted on helping him take care of more bullies. Against Brady's rejections, Bill persisted, and Brady finally gave in, allowing Bill to join his one-man squad.

Though Brady had pretended he didn't care, he was happy Bill was around. They had no other real friends in school, which helped Brady at the time he lost his father. They could always count on each other to be there. Outside of school, they began spending time together. Sleepovers turned into hanging with the family. That's where Bill met Natasha. And he had been smitten with her ever since, even if it was a one-sided affair.

Once they got rid of the bullies at school, they joined Mystery Solvers. The president, at first, was reluctant to let Bill in the group for obvious reasons, but Brady insisted on it, or he wouldn't join. With the Watts family name, it was a no-brainer.

As bothered as he was that Bill liked his sister, or that Bill wasn't courageous enough in life and in mystery solving, he hated now that he ever wanted him to be brave. He wished he'd never uttered, "Be a man," or "Show more courage." It was courage that killed him.

He wished he could be annoyed with Bill again for not being properly prepared. For slowing Brady's progress on an investigation. For goofing on the job. For getting the investigation song stuck in his head. Anything as long as it meant he was still here.

If he had a do-over, he'd say to be who you are, go at your pace. As long as you work to improve, you'll get there. He wished he focused on that instead of his superdude perfectionism.

He went back to memories of laughing with Bill at the fair when they made the impossible basketball shot in that tiny rim. And taking home the giant teddy bear. More like Bill laughing, and him being intense and determined, then giving in and slightly smiling. He recalled the short videos they made for the latest social media craze, and having dance-offs in their pajamas, Natasha even joining a few times. At the brightest moment, he could see Bill's face when he finally let him join his one-man crew. The smile. His eyes. A look of pure elation.

A small puddle formed in Brady's helmet.

"What's going on?" Bill asked, looking around in confusion. He felt his side and winced.

Brady opened his eyes. "Bill? Bill!" He hugged him tight. The puddle of tears rolled around in the helmet. "You didn't go." Brady noticed Bill gasping and released his grip. "You did good, buddy. You did good."

Grimacing, Bill pulled the pin out of his side. The red curtain concealed the blood well enough.

Brady held his head back, letting the tears fall out of the helmet and soak into his outfit.

"Were those tears for me?" Bill tossed the safety pin.

Brady wanted to laugh, but all he could get out was, "You saved us."

"I did?" A tired smile from Bill.

Brady pointed with his head at Norbo's body.

"I did that? You got to be kidding me."

"Well, technically, you pricked him with the pin, which helped me get the remote and blaster. But it couldn't have been done without you."

"I like that. Let's keep it," said Bill. "The narrative should be that we wouldn't have done it without you—me. You know what I mean. We wouldn't have done it without Bill."

Brady laughed through welled-up eyes. "We have to get out of here." He helped Bill to his feet. "Are you okay?"

Bill moved his arm and torso around to test the pain. "I'll probably need a lifetime of workman's compensation."

"Ok, we'll get you that," Brady said. "Let's chain him to the wall. Grab his arms." He crouched next to Norbo's feet.

Bill bent down at the monster's shoulders. That's when he noticed the alien's chest rising and falling. He looked up at Brady, petrified.

Norbo snatched Bill's legs, and kicked Brady back to the mat.

A shrill scream blasted from Bill's throat. His uvula bounced around. Norbo shoved Bill backward at the front of the knees, flipping him head over feet in a failed somersault. Bill landed on his rear, crashing to the floor.

Norbo went for Brady, who jumped for the blaster.

Brady landed a foot short. Norbo got hold of his leg and pulled back. With a thrust, Brady kicked back, breaking Norbo's finger. A muffled grunt, Norbo released his grip. Brady leaped again.

Norbo lunged forward and latched onto his ankle.

Brady extended his arm, barely getting a handle on the blaster. As Norbo pulled him, Brady contorted his body and unloaded into the monster's chest. Norbo blacked out, and flopped on top of him.

The large body was an overly-weighted blanket with a husky smell. Brady exhaled, and closed his eyes, taking a moment for himself.

He called out to Bill as he squirmed out from under Norbo. "How are we doing over there?"

Bill dragged himself to his feet, holding his back and sides. "Never been better."

They strained, pulled, and lifted Norbo into a sitting position against the padded wall. Before Brady could press the remote, the monster's body fell over.

They heaved his body upright, this time with his legs spread at a 45-degree angle for balance. Brady pressed the remote and the electromagnetic chains wrapped around his torso.

Bill tore a piece of the red curtain fabric and shoved it into Norbo's bladed mouth. "Eat that."

Brady looked over to Gilda and the criminals, having forgotten they were there. They had stayed silent.

"We're not your enemy," Gilda said calmly.

Brady tucked the blaster under the blue sheets, clicking it onto his Mystery Solver belt. "All we care about is getting home."

The criminal alien with the mohawk hairstyle spoke up, "The most we can do is break you out of here. They'll kill us if we try to help you off Saturn."

Brady reminded them. "He already mentioned treason."

A silence among the aliens.

"Our only chance is to expose them," Gilda looked at the aliens. Without speaking, an understanding was shared. There's no telling what would happen if they were still here after the humans escaped. "We'll help get you back to Earth."

"I don't want to die," said the alien with the French crop hairstyle.

Mohawk thought about it, coming to the same conclusion.

"We love you so much." Bill went in for an awkward hug with his outstretched hands touching the hairdo aliens on the wall. They leaned away from him.

Brady released Gilda, Mohawk, then Frenchie.

In the jail office, staff kept an eye on the monitors. Cameras covered the entire Saturn council dome. Inside the assembly hall, the skywalk to the jail, the jail entrance, and the adjacent offices outside the Circle of Doom. That was where it stopped. Many hits were carried out in jail, and they couldn't have evidence of the dirty deeds getting out. Naturally, they prohibited cameras inside, or the facade of "transparency" would disintegrate.

On one monitor, Mohawk and Frenchie were knocking out two guards by the jail entrance. On the next monitor, the fugitives snuck into the skywalk. Mohawk placed a beeping gadget next to the glass wall. They disappeared out of the camera's view.

"Send the planet distress signal!" The monitor watch flipped a switch on the panel, inserted a key, and turned it counterclockwise.

The first guard pushed the alarm. "Red alert—Saturn jail!"

A hole exploded in the skywalk. The rubble under the window crumbled, and the glass shattered. Nearby pedestrians scattered from the falling debris.

Mohawk quickly got down and hung onto a rebar jutting out from the crumbled ledge.

Frenchie slid down his backside and stopped at his ankles, creating an alien body ladder.

Gilda made her way down.

Brady asked Bill, "Want to get on my back?"

Bill peeked over the ledge at the rubble. "I want to do it on my own."

"Are you sure...? OK. I'll be ready to catch you." Brady slid down the aliens and landed on his feet.

Bill inched his way down.

"We have to hurry," said Gilda. "Police will be here any minute."

"Do it. Don't get in your head about it," said Brady.

Bill scooted down, his big belly bumping by Mohawk's, then Frenchie's head, and he got to Frenchie's ankles. He hung there for a moment. Then, at Brady's urging, he let go. Brady broke his fall for an easy landing.

Brady patted his back. "Good to see improvement, dude."

"I feel like I'm on your level now," Bill said as he dusted himself off. "We should point at each other like that Spider-dude meme."

Frenchie dropped, then Mohawk.

"Follow us," said Mohawk. They took off.

Police hovercraft roared to a stop outside the rubble. The vehicles were dark blue with a picture design on the side—a green mole's pointy face, a shiny hat, and jazz hands. The officers hopped off and spread out with searching blasters.

Several pedestrians pointed to where the fugitives fled.

Above the dome city, red lights were blinking at each mile. The signal for planetary danger—high alert.

The fugitives ran down the street, keeping low behind parked hover vehicles. Up ahead, a group of teenage aliens played catch, and further down, two officers on hovercraft were gliding around, searching between cars and houses with their big bug eyes. Brady and the fugitives changed direction and bolted for an alley under a bridge.

The kid aliens stopped passing the ball around, transfixed by the human faces in the helmets and bodies draped in curtains. The kid with a backward baseball cap turned back to see what the fugitives had reacted to. He spotted the police and yelled, "The humans are in the alley!" He pointed frantically. "The humans went to the alley!"

With no openings between the bridge walls, the alley was longer than expected. A wrong choice. But they couldn't turn back now. Brady and Bill ran as fast as their little legs could carry them. Gilda, being older, was behind Mohawk and Frenchie, but still quicker than the humans.

Pushing his legs faster, Bill stepped on a stretched portion of his red curtain and spilled to the ground.

Sirens pulsated behind them, getting louder.

Bill groaned. He was in too much pain to move.

Brady rushed over, and yanked Bill to his feet. "Let's go."

"I'm too tired." Bill rubbed his elbows and hands tenderly. "Maybe I can talk to them."

Brady wasn't about to argue. "That's the funniest thing you've ever said." He bunched the curtain cloth in Bill's hands, hooked his arm, and scampered forward.

The sound of the cop's sirens turning into the alley had them running harder. Engines revved behind them. The cops shot forward like mad dogs, and the distance quickly evaporated.

"As soon as they're in range, throw the sheets at them." Brady let go of Bill, who was running on his own now. They pulled the curtains off their bodies.

When the police were ten feet out, Bill blindly flung the red cloth behind him. It missed and fluttered to the side. Brady's throw went to the right, hitting the closer police officer in the face—who lost control, jerked his hands, and swerved into the other hovercraft. They ricocheted, and the first craft slammed into a light pole. The second one crashed into the side of the alley, the rearview mirror popped off on impact.

The loud collision stopped Mohawk and Frenchie in their tracks. They looked back.

Mohawk said, "Get the hovercrafts." They raced over. One of the alien cops got up groggily, pointing at the fugitives.

Brady pulled the blaster off his belt.

The bug-eyed cop backed away. "I wouldn't do that."

Mohawk and Frenchie lifted the hovercraft upright. The power lights were still on. Not quite to full capability, but were serviceable. Brady jumped on with Mohawk.

Gilda hopped on with Frenchie and grabbed his waist. As Bill got on behind Gilda, the hovercraft scraped the ground, then corrected itself, staying an inch off the pavement.

"Let me switch. No offense," said Gilda. Frenchie stopped, and she got off.

Mohawk and Brady swung by and picked her up. She held onto Brady's waist. They sped away.

The police alien pressed the talk button on his radio—no indicator light. "Stop them!" he yelled to no one.

The fugitives glided through the streets, turning at random corners, avoiding any traceable pattern, and veering in a new direction at any sign of witnesses.

As they rode through the streets, Gilda spoke in Brady's ear. "I have a place in the Underground where we can stay for a couple of days until things calm down."

"We don't have a couple days. We have to go now," said Brady.

"The airport will be shut down with search parties at every exit. There will be no luck with that for several days. When it reopens, I have a friend with clearance for baggage emergencies. We can sneak you on the next shuttle out." Brady's nonrebuttal was his understanding. "For now," she said, "we go to the Underground. It's the best place to hide. But we need to make a pit stop."

Videos of the fugitives escaping the skywalk were broadcast on digital billboards and tall buildings around the dome city. The incident quickly made its way onto every news channel.

Red lights flashed throughout the dome.

As the fugitives glided ahead in the police-hovercraft, Gilda gave Mohawk the directions and went over the plan with Brady.

"Here's your backstory," she said. "You stole money from a kid who turned out to be the son of a rich energy owner from Sector 5C. It's important to say Sector 5C because it's new, and they won't know much about it. Criminals in the Underground are hiding. And a lot of rich folks live in Sector 5C and have tight security. Criminals won't mess with that."

"We're going to a criminal's house?" Brady asked.

Mohawk let out a disagreeable grunt. As they turned the next corner, he said, "Many people would like to get reinstated, and turning in a human would do wonders. I don't know if this is a good idea."

"We're short on solutions," said Gilda. "Nita is my friend. She wouldn't do that. And she won't know you're human. We're going to conceal you properly. In fact, it's important she doesn't know who you are. If she does, and they catch you, she'll be charged with harboring a human. I have to look out for her, too."

"She could see the news, couldn't she?" said Brady.

"She doesn't own a TV," Gilda said. They stopped at a circular house. The garage door opened, and they glided in.

The hovercraft stopped. Gilda got off. "Brady, go over the backstory with Bill. When we get to my friend's place, you shouldn't have a reason to say anything to her. But if she, or anyone, probes deeper, say you aren't allowed to talk about it."

"Where are we now?" Brady asked.

"My home," said Gilda.

"Why don't we stay here?" said Bill.

"There's a good reason," Gilda said rhetorically. "And while you think about why, give me a minute." She rushed inside.

Bill got off the hovercraft and stretched his back.

Going over the backstory, Brady had to repeat some details because Bill, nodding as he listened, was more interested in the garage. In the corner was a broken-down robot maid, and a rotating mini-dry-cleaning system built into the wall. Saturnites cared a lot about their fashion sense. It added up as they had yet to see one appearing indecent.

Bill glanced inside a trash bin. There was an oblong teapot and a few wet cloth pieces shredded to bits.

"You shouldn't look in other people's trash," said Mohawk.

"Sorry." Bill dropped the lid.

Gilda returned in a loose frock with daisy petals that she wore over her purple dress. She brought a couple of one-piece gray suits for Mohawk and Frenchie. A bundle of pastel green and brown sheets for Brady and Bill. Scissors. Clips. A mini-electric hand sewing kit. And a black spray paint canister attached to a brush. She also had a small container of ointment for Bill. "Here. Put this directly on the cut. But before that...." She put down the rest of the stuff and took out a sopping wet cloth. She rubbed it over the blood spot on Bill's suit, and the stain dissolved on contact. "Now, apply the ointment."

Unable to detect a stain, Bill said, "Nifty." He applied the ointment and immediately felt relief. "Ohhh. Wow. That's wild. Can I buy the rights for earth? For both."

"Sorry. It can only be determined by the Saturn council." She handed the spray brush to Mohawk. "Paint over the police symbols." The electric hand-sewing kit went to Frenchie. "Let's get these humans looking more Saturn."

After a short time, Brady was covered space-helmet-to-toe in green cloth, and Bill was covered in brown. They looked the part, passing off as artsy musical teenagers.

CHAPTER 29

Pink hues lit up the dome, reflecting off the planet's fog. The skyline was a rich water-color painting.

Headed for the Underground, the fugitives glided out of the garage in their altered looks. Mohawk and Frenchie drove while Brady, Bill, and Gilda held on. When they passed the second block, sirens wailed behind them. They looked back as police amassed in front of Gilda's house.

"Perfect timing," she said.

After fifteen minutes of zigzagging the map, they came upon a worn-out bench under an awning. It was an old Sector 35 bus stop, the route long since discontinued. And a block from Nita's house.

Half of the buildings and houses in the Underground were new and sparkly, and the other half were old, dull, and worn out. Sometimes on the same block. Half of the inhabitants didn't even know this was the Underground.

"We're not under the ground," said Bill.

Mohawk said, "And so the police won't be looking."

To which Bill nodded. He liked that.

Nita's house had white stucco with Spanish roof tiles. A fence surrounded the property, and sat between two neon pink and purple apartment complexes.

The sun, already half the intensity of a normal Earth day, was dipping below the dome. The streetlights sparked on.

Gilda knocked on the curved door. After an anxious minute, a shadow rolled through the hazy glass at the top, and the door opened. A cute female appeared, noticeably smaller than Gilda. Her hair was curly tentacles, she wore pointy glasses, and had on a bright yellow dress that matched the old 1950s human-style fashion.

"You've got to be kidding me! OMG!" Nita hugged Gilda, then kissed her cheek. "You look as fierce as ever. What's what? We've got to catch up, my lady." She looked at the others.

"Thank you so much," said Gilda, apologetic in tone. "I know it's last second. I'll explain everything."

"Don't you utter another word. Come on in. You are always welcome in my abode." She ushered them in.

The living room had a circular design with yellow, rounded seats lining the back wall. An aroma of eucalyptus and peppermint wafted out from the air-ionization and air-conditioning smart system unit.

In the center of the room was a tune player. She set it to the classical signal. "This is my favorite." Nita swayed her head to the music, her hair tentacles in step. "If you need to be soothed, make sure your body moves."

Frenchie joined in the swaying. "I dig it."

Mohawk smacked Frenchie, stopping him real quick.

Gilda and Nita romanticized about the past. They spoke of their younger days, chasing guys at school and later in the clubs. Especially the men in uniform: Raid Boys and S.W.A.T. Officers. They giggled. Nita talked about dating one of the young Raid Boy trainees. His name was Tanex. What a hunk he was. Nita secretly stayed in touch with him, and they saw each other, even to this day. But she had to keep it a secret due to her legal troubles. Military men were the hunkiest saturnites. They agreed by the way they bashfully covered their mouths and raised their shoulders. Nita spoke of becoming a singer and how it changed her life. When she became famous, that's when Gilda went to Earth on her latest mission. Gilda told her about her Earth experience, saying she was glad to be home for good. Pretty dull on Earth, Gilda added.

"So, what's the story on these two?" Nita pointed to Brady, concealed in green, and Bill, concealed in brown. "And why are they so artsy?" She laughed warmheartedly.

"They're helping me with a couple of things. I can't tell you about it," said Gilda. "Without going into too many details, they got into a mess in Sector 5C. If you see their faces, it'll put you in a scenario you don't deserve.... Think of them as artsy artists, if that's okay. You know how ridiculous sentencing is."

"Don't remind me," said Nita. "Of course, booboo. Not another word."

"I appreciate it," Gilda said. "Listen, I have to get a Live View Code as well as a few things from Defense Depot with these two," she pointed to Mohawk and Frenchie. "Can you watch my artist friends for a little bit, make them comfortable? We'll be back in an hour."

"Sure thing, hun."

Gilda and the hairdo aliens got up and headed to the front door. She took three hats from the coat rack and Nita's Mini-Bubble Hover keys. She passed hats to Mohawk and Frenchie, and called to Brady and Bill. "Whatever you need, she's good for it. Okay?"

Brady acknowledged her with a thumbs up. Bill made a bow.

"See you soon," Gilda said, and they left.

The large round seats engulfed Nita and the boys as they sat in awkward silence.

Brady twiddled his fingers. Bill adjusted his outfit.

Nita looked them over carefully. "Can I get you guys a drink? I make a good Sequila."

That was a grown-up drink, for sure. So Brady said, "Thank you. But we're underage."

"Yeah, we're good," said Bill. "We just had a few sodas. At that place—back. You know."

"I don't know," said Nita, touching her chin.

Brady cut Bill off before he could add to the story. "It's not important."

"How old are you?" Nita asked.

"I'm fifteen–almost sixteen," said Bill. "He's eighteen."

Brady nudged Bill again.

"The legal limit here is sixteen." Nita squinted. "But, it's not a big deal to drink when you're in the Underground, even if you are underage." She added a smile. "My drinks are exceptional."

C'mon, thought Brady. Think.... Right. "Unfortunately, we're from Sector 5C. The legal limit is high there. Pretty uptight with all the pretentious lords. We don't want to mess up the legal situation more than we already have."

Disappointed, Nita sighed and grabbed the remote. She brought the music low and switched on the TV. A screen lowered down from the ceiling. "Wonder what's on the news lately."

Brady turned his head to the front door in vain. Gilda said she didn't have a TV. He turned back to her. "We'd rather not watch anything," he said. "It's been a long day. Music is better."

"Yeah, TV's boring," said Bill. "Can you turn it off? We'd rather talk about how you're such an elusive criminal."

Nita was taken aback. She clicked the remote, and put it in the cupholder. The screen stopped halfway down. Luckily, the TV was still at low volume—not loud enough unless you were paying close attention. A video of Gilda and the fugitives escaping the skyway played at the top.

Catching Brady's eyes up at the screen, Nita angled to look.

Brady pulled her attention away. "Nita, so sorry about that. What he's trying to say is—what we want to know is—what's your life story? How did you get away? Must have been a harrowing experience."

A slight blush painted her green cheeks. She hadn't gotten this kind of attention in a while.

"The more details, the better," Bill added.

"Well," she said, excited to relive her past, "I was a rambunctious kid. I was always looking for attention. When I found music, I started singing right away. A gig here, a show there. Right after school, things took off. I had four number one songs within the year." She tipped her glasses down, showing off her famous glance. "Right...?" It went clear over Bill's and Brady's concealed heads. "I was making loads of crups. Living lavishly, going on retreats regularly, always 5-star meals. Until one day, I learned my books were off. My tax guy ran away, and it turns out he was cutting off the top. He'd been forging my signature, and I was held responsible. The banks wouldn't cover me, and I found myself in debt.

"I didn't know what to do, so I evaded taxes completely. I did that for two years. Unfortunately, I got caught, and they sentenced me to fifteen years in prison. Fifteen! When Bleeko did the same crime, he got one year. I have given more crups to the SRS in a year than most have given their entire lives! On top of that, I was a famous singer. Give me a frigging break.

"During my one-week pre-jail period, I couldn't come up with the crups, so I ran to the Underground and have been here since. The SRS is so grimy. They take way too much. Make you always feel like you're treading water."

"SRS?" said Bill.

Brady quickly turned to him.

"Duh, joking," Bill added. "Stupid SRS."

"Saturn Revenue Service is the worst," said Nita. "You wait until you start working for a living. They take-take. Take-

take-take. And we vote for that. Everyone wants to be in a rat race, never able to relax. Screw that. I don't regret leaving the spotlight one bit." She looked at the ground, preoccupied. "I lost my way during that time. Since I've been here, I've regained my level-headedness. I don't have to sing for anyone else anymore. I can siiing for meee-eeeeeeeeee!" She whipped her head toward Brady and Bill, glimpses of her old life sparkling in her eyes.

Under their helmets, Brady and Bill watched in awe. "Your voice is amazing," Brady said.

"You sing like Mariah," said Bill.

"Who?"

As Bill was about to reply, Brady jumped in with the save, "Sector 5C."

She trailed off in thought. She was feeling good. "Those were the days." She looked back at them. "Has anyone ever told you that you look like those electro dance music guys? They keep their identity hidden."

"Yeah. But we only like the style. We don't play music. It's never been our thing," said Brady.

"Yeah, I'm over it, too." She turned around and looked up at the TV. It was onto another news story. She clicked the remote, and the screen disappeared into the ceiling. "Whatever happened to the governor in 5C?" she asked. "I heard he was kicked out of the election."

"Oh, he's a—" said Bill, stopping his response. "Honestly, I'm not familiar with what happened to him. I don't follow the guardians here."

Brady nodded.

"Well, I thought he was a good governor. It's a shame." She went to the kitchen. She grabbed a couple packs of chocolate rolls from the snack bowl. Then she took two cups from the cupboard. Got a pitcher from the fridge, and poured two glasses of lemon soda. With her back to them, she sprinkled in a packet of white powder and mixed it. She came back to the living room. "Here you go. It's one of my favorites. My specialty. Non-alcoholic."

"Thank you. Truly," said Brady. "But we had a big meal with drinks just before we got here."

"Can I save them for later?" Bill said, indicating the chocolate rolls.

"You can always eat later if you wake up hungry. I get it if you're shy about eating in front of strangers," said Nita. "You should have a drink, at least."

They sat there silently.

Bill put the chocolate snacks in his makeshift pockets.

"Mind if we see our room? We've had a long day. We're pretty tired," said Brady.

"Yeah. All because of that Sector 5C," said Bill.

"Of course. I'd be glad to. Follow me." She led them to a dimly lit hall near the back. The door at the far end was the guest room. "You'll like the beds. I'm sure I'll catch you so comfortable that I'll have to shake you to wake you up." She laughed.

Brady felt a sudden pang of doubt. Why did Gilda leave them alone? Had she been playing them for fools? She lied about the TV. But she seemed genuine. Now he wasn't sure anymore. It struck him that they might be alone on Saturn with no help.

She opened the door. There was art and photos on the walls. In the right corner were two beds connected in an L-shape.

"You can fight over who gets what bed, but it won't matter. They're both velvety smooth, and they have the new memory foam. Let me know if you need anything. Oh, and Gilda just texted me. She'll be by to get you in the morning." She opened the door to leave.

"Perfect," said Brady. "A good night of sleep will help a lot."

Bill added, "That Sector 5C got us tired."

"Thanks so much, Nita," said Brady. "We appreciate it."

The door closed behind her.

Nita danced and spun and hummed her way past the living room to the counter where the phone was. She unclipped the ear-pods, put them in, and dialed a number.

"Hi................ I have the humans."

CHAPTER 30

"I'm only giving them up if I can get my life back. Total forgiveness," said Nita. "Deal...? I'll send the coordinates." She smiled, twirling her tentacles.

At Defense Depot, Gilda pushed the cart along the aisles, taking a camera pen off a shelf. Mohawk added net shooters to the cart, similar to the one used on Brady and Bill at the Saturn council dome. Frenchie added a 10x10 field vision blocker. One could put the four pieces at any angle within a ten-foot radius, and it blended the view in front, or projected any visual that was programmed. Gilda dropped a pack of mouth-shooting darts and a smoke bomb in the cart. Mohawk added an armor chest plate.

Gilda made sure she was out of the camera's view, and slipped a Live View Code into her pocket. There couldn't be any evidence of where she got it from or the guardians would cancel all Live View Codes from the store's records just to stop hers.

"We should get back," said Gilda. She rolled the cart in line behind a group of shady-looking characters.

Her attention wandered to the front of the line and she froze—unable to believe her eyes. Above the crups register was a digital-wanted sign that flashed a photo of Gilda in her new white daisy dress, Mohawk and Frenchie in their gray suits, and the humans in their freshly disguised outfits of pastel green and brown. The screen outlined their bodies and blacked out the background, leaving out clues as to their location.

The three of them lowered their caps simultaneously.

"The kids," she whispered. She peered around the store. Thankfully, no one had noticed them. They left the cart and rushed to the exit.

In the parking lot, Frenchie stared suspiciously at Nita's Mini-Bubble hovercraft. "She gave us up?"

"It appears so." Mohawk looked around for any signs of officers.

Gilda said, "The police would've been here by now if it was tracked."

Mohawk got in the driver's seat, Gilda in shotgun, and Frenchie in the back. They sped off.

Rushing through red lights. Weaving dangerously in and out of lanes. Honked at by offended vehicles. Going against traffic on a one-way street. They ignored all signs, especially ones commanding a full stop.

At Nita's house, a throng of police officers and hovercraft crowded the entrance with their headlights dimmed. Spectators in the neon apartments watched from their balconies.

Back in the Mini-Bubble, Mohawk zoomed through another red light. Gilda put in her ear-pods and pressed the voice sensor. "Call Nita." The phone rang several times before Nita picked up.

"I'm sorry, Gilda," Nita said with remorse, but her tone hinted it was a justified trade-off.

"How could you do this?"

"You're going to be acknowledged for helping me turn them in. Plus, they're just humans. You'll get over it."

"They're not just humans. They're helping expose the corruption. The same kind that has you hiding in the first place."

"I can't keep living like this, booboo. I had the decency to wait 'til you were gone. Can you at least give me that?"

Gilda hung up and flung the earpieces out the window. There was most likely a tracer on the line.

Nita took out her ear-pods and nodded to Officer Lungeer. He had an elongated head, big nostrils, tall ears, and small eyes—a horse-shaped head. On his breast pocket design—the one with the mole—the hat was shiny gold instead of shiny blue, indicating he was a superior.

"She understands." Nita beckoned them to the hall and took them to the guest room. The three cops crept closer, surrounding the door.

Officer Lungeer tested the handle. It was locked. "On the count of four," he whispered.

They got into a barging stance. The police positioned themselves, locked and loaded.

"One... Two... Three... Four!" The cops kicked the door in. Police swarmed inside.

The youngest officer snuck over to the L-shaped double bed with a bulging mass under the blankets. He reached for a corner.

"What are you doing?" Lungeer yanked him back. "Do you not remember anything from detective school? What does that look like?"

It was clearly pillows arranged in the shape of a body. The young officer knew he messed up. "Pillows."

"We don't even want to give them the satisfaction of pulling the blankets off, now do we?" said Lungeer.

The young officer shook his head remorsefully.

"Rookie." On his way to the window, Lungeer pulled out a mini flashlight from his leg pocket, and, like an overly pensive detective at a crime scene, scoped for anything out of place. He checked under the beds. In the closet. Behind the framed photo of Saturn. Opening the curtains, he angled the flashlight on the window diagonally from upper left to lower right.

A faint circle reflected back. He reversed his motion with the same result. He pushed in close to get a better look. There was a large circle etched in the glass.

With the back of his flashlight, he hit the glass. It fell, rolled around in a loop, then tipped over to one side. It wobbled, rotating in its circle, lowering gradually to the ground, to a vibrating hum, and stopped.

"Dang it," said Nita.

Lungeer looked at her. "You get one week."

She shook her head, dismayed.

Back in the Mini-Bubble, Mohawk turned onto Nita's street. Police were everywhere. He hovered down a couple of houses out of view from law enforcement, and pulled into a parking spot.

Gilda rubbed her forehead, stressing over Nita. "It's not like her. Why?" The pain of betrayal stung worse by a friend.

Across the street, pastel green Brady and pastel brown Bill poked their heads out from the dilapidated bus stop. They could vaguely make out Gilda and the criminals in the Mini-Bubble. Gilda was shaking her head.

"Maybe they didn't know Nita would turn on us," said Brady. Half hoping. Half relieved. But part of him wasn't sure. He strained his eyes through the green cloth, studying her body language. He'd seen that type of headshake before. From his own experience. He did it many times when Bill had done something he shouldn't have. It was an expression of annoyance. She was annoyed with Nita.

Into the light, Brady angled out from the bus stop and waved his arms. Bill joined in. Mohawk and Frenchie noticed the movement and got Gilda's attention. Her face brightened.

Shielding from view, they got out of the vehicle and snuck down the street. They crossed at the old bus stop and huddled by the hovercraft.

"I'm sorry about Nita," Gilda said. "How did you get away?"

Brady showed her the safety pin he saved from the cargo hold. "I was worried you might've set us up."

"Nita has been a lifelong friend. I never would've guessed that." Gilda shook her head. "Let's get to a safe area so we can make a new plan."

Irritated, Mohawk powered up his hovercraft. Frenchie powered up the other one. Brady, Gilda, and Bill got on, and they drove several blocks, stopping in the shadows of an old, rundown building with broken windows and flickering lights.

"Why are you willing to help us?" Brady asked.

Gilda thought about it. "When we were in jail, I was resigned to the fact I was going to die. I've been fighting the corruption for years with nothing to show for. It felt like there was no way to beat them. Then, you took down Norbo. That rekindled my hope that maybe something could be done."

Brady was relieved to be right about her. And that he was right about something on the positive side. He smiled.

"We're far from out of the woods," she said, turning the mood back to sour. "We have to come up with something. Any ideas?"

Mohawk hinted his disappointment at Brady and Bill. "We had the perfect plan. What happened? How did she find out?"

"Probably the news," Brady said. "She has a TV. And she kept asking questions."

"None of this is going to change anything. Let's focus on what we can do now," Gilda said.

Bill raised his hand. "If anything, it was my bad. Don't take anything out on Brady. I spoke the most. She tried to ask about the governor in 5C who was kicked out of the election. I said we didn't know much about what happened to him because we don't follow that stuff. Good save, eh?"

Mohawk gave him a deadpan stare. "There's no governor in 5C. It's an energy sector."

"No more talking to anyone about anything, okay?" said Gilda.

Bill nodded, scratching the cloth over his helmet. "I took some of her snacks." He showed them the chocolate rolls. "Am I allowed to keep these?"

"I don't think you'll like it. It's Saturn food," said Gilda.

Bill slid the chocolate rolls back in his pocket with a look and shrugged.

Brady ripped off his green disguise from his helmet. Then he took the cloth off the rest of his body. "It's not making a difference. I'd rather have my sight."

Bill happily copied him, and they threw the disguises into some spongy-looking bushes. Gilda joined in, unzipping the white daisy outfit, and added it to the pile. The aliens all tossed their hats.

Mohawk peered up at the dome structure. It was halfway open. "This might be out there. It's been a long time, but I trained in the old saucers at school. I'm willing if you are." Gilda looked at him like he was crazy. "I know," said Mohawk. "What other choice do we have?"

"Are you chipped? Are you a master flyer?" Gilda asked.

It was a fitting question. With the chip, a pilot controls the saucer with their thoughts. In the beginning, they don't have the best hold on mental control, so they start with manual. They gradually move up to chipped control. If something goes wrong with the chip, they can always resort back to manual. But manual doesn't work without the chip. Unless you're a master. Real masters don't need a chip at all.

Similarly, it's the same way a human can move his hand by deciding he wants to move it. At the beginning stages, one can't do it without the help of a parent moving their baby arms for them. Eventually, they grow muscles and move for themselves as they gain control. After a while, it becomes automatic.

Mohawk said, "I'm neither a master nor chipped. But all the older spaceships have basic manual."

Frenchie raised his hand. "Behind Fluffy's restaurant, past the edge of Sector 50, is the old repair yard. There may be a functional spaceship we can steal."

"It's worth a shot," said Mohawk. "If we're lucky, we'll find one that works. But there's no guarantee we'll get out."

They all looked at each other.

"Why not," said Brady. "Let's go for it."

CHAPTER 31

In the parking lot of Fluffy's restaurant, a reptile-looking family with webbed hands and feet pointed to a small spacecraft flying up behind the building. "That's so cool, daddy," said a young saturnite.

The fugitives glided to the left. "Keep going. It's beyond there." Mohawk pointed.

As they got closer, flashlight beams sliced around the side and back of the restaurant. Two police hovercraft turned the corner, heading in their direction. The fugitives swerved, and zoomed toward the entrance. "We can go through the kitchen," said Frenchie.

They parked in the restricted zone, and rushed inside.

"Stand behind us," Gilda said. Brady and Bill crouched behind the half-circle wall of Gilda, Mohawk, and Frenchie. The host's desk was empty. Brady and Bill kept low as they moved forward, avoiding the diner seating area to the right.

Just as they passed the host's desk, a voice shouted, "Hold on!" The host quickly handed menus to the customers she was tending to and hurried over. "Wait on that side, please."

Gilda, Mohawk, and Frenchie closed tighter around Brady and Bill. They awkwardly scooted back to the other side of the desk. Unfortunately, the body wall didn't completely seal them from all sides and Brady and Bill found themselves exposed to the only customer on the waiting bench. A short, plump, light green creature with eyeballs at the end of antlers. Both her eyes were bending over, directly leveled at her e-phone.

Bill released the knot in his throat.

Brady faced him the other way, and whispered, "Play invisible."

"Thank you for waiting," the host said to the group. "Name on the reservation? And how many?"

"Four, please," Gilda said, then intentionally gave a false name. "Should be under Milda." As the host looked down at her list, the fugitives inched forward another step.

"Ah-ah-ah." She pointed at them. "Stay right there." The fugitives stopped. "I don't see you on the list."

Gilda smiled. "That's impossible."

Peaking over the alien body-wall, Brady looked distressed. The TVs around the joint were broadcasting the fugitives. He tapped Frenchie, whispering, "We're on the TV."

Gilda and Mohawk rubbed their foreheads to conceal their faces.

"Is everything okay?" asked the host.

"No," she said, keeping her voice down. "Everything isn't okay. You're telling me we're not on the list when we made reservations a week ago? This is not like Fluffy's. And, I will say, quite concerning. Might write a review. Might not. It's up to you."

The host looked over the list again, flipping pages. "Milda, you said? We can make an exception. Give me one sec." She forced a smile and took out her pen.

Brady and Bill snuck another peek around the body-wall, and their faces slowly morphed into shock.

Blinking eyes.

Mouths gaped open.

Customers were eating away at their tasteful entrées—socks!

♪   ♪   ♪

Brady and Bill hid behind the body wall. Slowly, they peered out again.

A table of rich aliens scrutinized the menus. Socks from specific regions of Earth cost more. The 100% cotton socks cost even more than that. And cashmere costs the most.

A large businessman in a suit and top hat dabbed his mouth with a handkerchief. "Apparently, all of our great singers are on a diet of human crooner socks. If you don't believe it, my friend ate a Sinatra sock once and his singing got better instantly.

"I call BS," said his assistant.

The boss took a sip of his drink. "He has a cellar collection of socks owned by legends. I believe him."

"Gym socks are tasty," said an alien with a headband and eight small muscular arms. "Could you imagine an NBA sock? A Jordan sock would be unbelievable. Even an old, retired Jordan. I'd take that over any other sock."

"Of course you would," said his girlfriend. They laughed.

A six-handed waiter brought a few large trays to the table. He pulled off the five silver dome covers to reveal tender cashmere and 100% cotton socks. "Enjoy your delicacy."

At the next table, a youngin spit out his sock. "Half-polyester is awful! That's it. We're making money. I want to have the cashmere-mix any time. At least 100% cotton."

"One day," said his friend. They looked over at the rich table.

For a moment, Brady and Bill forgot they were human fugitives and stepped out to get a better look. They watched dumbfounded.

Mohawk pulled them back in.

Bill took out the chocolate snacks from his pocket, able to distinguish sock lines in the rolled-up treat. "Darn. Why didn't you tell us?"

Mohawk gave him the shush sign.

The only customer on the waiting bench casually looked up from her phone, eyes raising with her antlers. She caught sight of the humans and blinked. Brady made eye contact. He shook his head and put out his hands to calm the situation.

Outside, police spotted the damaged hovercraft and glided over. The paint hiding the police symbol was chipped, revealing the top of the shiny blue police hat on the green mole. A shrieking cry squealed from inside the restaurant. The officer barked into his radio. "All units converge on Fluffy's in Sector 50!"

The police burst through the front doors. "Everybody, get down! The place went frantic. Customers ducked under the tables. Gilda, Brady, and the team broke the huddle and ran toward the kitchen.

The young aliens watched the police chase the fugitives through the kitchen doors, then looked back up at the TV, flabbergasted.

Antler eyes lady stared in catatonic shock. Her phone had fallen, and the screen was cracked.

Rushing through the kitchen, Mohawk and Frenchie hit a waitress out of the way. Her tray crashed on the floor. The chefs looked up from their prepping stations of socks and spices.

The fugitives rushed through the double doors to the outside.

Frenchie tossed a long stick to Mohawk, who wedged it through the handles.

The police crashed into the doors.

"You're not getting out of this!" said the cop.

Mohawk pressed his foot at the base of the doors. "Hurry!"

Outside, to the right, was a hovercraft pad to bring socks to the restaurant. To the left, dumpsters were packed with cardboard, trash, and old, grimy, half-eaten socks. Frenchie, Brady, and Bill rolled a dumpster to the doors, adding to the barricade.

"This is treason!" the cop said. "If you turn them in, we can change the declarations on you." Mohawk shook his head. They both knew he had to go by the letter of the law.

More cops came through the kitchen.

"It's blocked. Go around!"

A gate separated the restaurant from the massive field that was the junkyard for old spaceships.

The fugitives crashed through.

An urgent call belted out from inside the restaurant. "They're heading to the repair yard. Close the dome! Close the dome!"

Following the aliens, Brady started to worry. The call meant the Saturn guardians would know their plan. It was already unlikely they'd get out. And they didn't have a spaceship yet. Now it was almost certain they wouldn't.

Bill was shaking his head as they ran. "It's your food. Your frickin' food. Why didn't you tell us? Humans would happily give you socks."

"I thought you knew," said Mohawk. "You didn't know?"

Gilda chimed in, panting. "If it were up to us, we'd have been working with you a long time ago. Insane people think they can only hold their power by manipulation."

Brady couldn't help but think out loud. "It's like this everywhere, isn't it?"

The fugitives rushed through the field.

Standing smack dab in the middle of the sprawling repair yard stood a large "SECTOR 51" sign. The original AREA 51.

"Look everywhere," said Mohawk. "If you see any sign of a working ship, call it out."

They fanned out, racing across the landscape toward the lights.

The fugitives passed rolling hills of metal—mounds of broken machine parts, and old, rusted spaceships. Far ahead, work lights were on, and the area had fewer metal heaps.

"Over there!" Brady said. The others hurried to his call. He pointed ahead at a classic flying saucer, sitting upright in the far distance.

Heavy hydraulics boomed above. The dome started to close.

"Uh oh," said Bill as they raced toward the saucer.

A skinny rock-looking mechanic with long, curly hair bobbed and hummed to music on his headphones. His flashlight was standing up, lighting the underside of the saucer. He screwed in wires on the open electrical box.

Sneaking by him, Brady and company tiptoed up the escalating platform onto the spaceship.

The mechanic sparked two wires together. He picked up the flashlight and shined it on the panel, expecting the power monitor to light up. The indicator bulbs stared back, powerless. He added a silver and blue wire together, connecting it with a metallic conducting tape. Still nothing. He added a gold wire to the red one and twirled them together with metallic tape. The power monitor lit up. "Aha!" He put up his rock fist and celebrated with head moves to the beat of his music, and spun around. "Yeah!"

In the cockpit, Frenchie and Mohawk strapped into the captain and co-captain seats. They looked over the control panel, reorienting themselves to the procedure. Starters, engine power, safety gauge, altitudes, speeds, velocity, thrusters, course maps. They were unfamiliar with most of the panel, but they had the basics down, including automatic flight. With the little time they had, they got right into the protocols. "Space thrusters. Engine power on," said Mohawk.

"Safety gauge set and ready," said Frenchie.

Outside, the mechanic screwed the panel shut. He put his tools in a bag. A job well done. Mumbled yells came from the distance. He turned his head. Several police officers were hovering toward him. He took his headphones off.

"You're letting the humans get away!"

"What?" The mechanic looked back.

A loud force of energy. The saucer blasted off, and a rolling cloud of dust flew out. The mechanic and the police covered their faces.

The saucer swiped by a tall building, smashing the glass windows on its way up.

From the east, a gang of black S.W.A.T. security vessels flew around the building after them. They had round tops and flat bottoms. The leading vessel commanded, "Stop now! That's a direct order!"

Ignoring them, Mohawk continued straight up.

The vessels shot a thunderous barrage of blasts toward the opening of the dome.

The fugitives veered away and circled around a tall building. The S.W.A.T. vessels maneuvered with them.

Shots continued to fire.

A blast skimmed the bottom of the hull, reverberating the saucer. Mohawk swung the saucer to the right.

"Can we shoot back?" Brady asked.

"It's an old ship for scoping missions only," said Mohawk.

A red light flashed on the dashboard. *Engine. Engine. Engine.* The spaceship dipped and began to putter. "That's not good!" said Frenchie.

"No duh!" yelled Mohawk.

The spaceship nosedived.

"Emergency thrusters now!" Mohawk shouted.

Frenchie flipped a line of levers and pulled a yellow knob. "Thrusters engaged!" He shoved a button in with his palm. The spaceship stopped its descent and shot forward like a slingshot, missing a line of blasts before impact. They circled around and back up toward the opening.

The dome was over three quarters closed.

A vessel was hot on their trail. They maneuvered around another tall building. Two other vessels came from the opposite direction, facing them head on. The fugitives zipped up, down, and side-to-side, dodging blasts. The vessels came rushing in. "Thrusting down now!"

At the last second, the saucer dipped, and two vessels collided, exploding in the dome.

"Let's goooooooooo!" yelled Brady.

A "Woohoo!" from Bill.

They headed back up.

Five ship lengths remained in the dome entrance, and closing fast.

"We won't make it. We don't have enough speed," said Mohawk. He kept the throttles all the way forward.

"We can lose the bad engine," yapped Frenchie. "The lost weight could do it. We still have the thrusters."

"Lose it!" ordered Mohawk.

Frenchie ran to the back to a red lever marked "Emergency Engine Unload." Verifying he had the bad engine, he grabbed the lever, and yanked it. The top handle broke off!

The opening was four ship-lengths.

A staccato of shots hit the saucer.

"Going in spin mode!" Mohawk twisted the handles. Gilda, Brady, and Bill held on to their seats. The saucer revolved as it flew toward the slim opening. An unavoidable collision. Blasts missed left and right as they spiraled up.

Frenchie flew into the back wall.

More blasts skidded by the spaceship.

Three ship-lengths.

Not fast enough!

Frenchie got his balance back, pressed his legs against the wall, and grabbed the nub of the lever with both hands. He gripped as tight as he could.

Two ship-lengths.

"Here goes something!" He pushed. The tension of the release point wouldn't give in. He kept at it, pushing—spinning–eerrrrgggh… clink, ffffnnk—crank—it released!

The bottom opened, and the bad engine dropped out, spinning into the line of black vessels. The engine frame smashed into the first vessel, cracking the glass, and ricocheted into two others.

Veering out of the way, the last one got back on the saucer's trail.

Only a sliver of an opening left. Mohawk untwisted the levers—the saucer straightened—and he thrust forward, pushing with all his might. "Full throttle!"

They zipped out as the opening closed, and the last vessel crashed, exploding into a fireball halfway out. Sparks and pieces sprinkled onto the translucent traxtanium dome.

The saucer glided into free space.

"Yeeeehhaaaawww!" Brady and Bill cheered. They unbuckled their seat belts and began jumping and hugging. Bill raised his index finger, like they just won a championship.

Bill let out a loud sigh. "Goodness gracious!" For the moment, Bill wasn't scared at all. Not one iota. The exhilaration had freed him from his usual terror. Even if for a short while.

Disaster averted. Brady and Bill sat back down, smiling.

A minute went by and they couldn't help but notice the aliens were a little too solemn. "What?" Bill got defensive. "That's normal human behavior after a big win."

"We'll be hitting zero gravity soon," said Frenchie. "You should buckle up."

Brady and Bill obliged.

The mood of the aliens was troubling. They had just gotten away, and there wasn't one ounce of celebration from them? Not even in the rush of escaping?

Flashing red lights illuminated the dome city as the saucer streaked to the stars.

Brady peered out the glass canopy, his face blinking red. The seriousness of the situation was dawning on him. The aliens had escaped Saturn, against the guardians, with them as human fugitives. The news would get to Mr. Sock in a hurry.

"What have I done?" said Brady.

Suddenly, the flashing red lights in the dome began alternating between red and yellow.

Brady said, "We're not in the clear, are we?"

"They'll be coming," said Mohawk.

Gilda got deadly serious. "If we don't expose Mr. Sock fast, they'll send a full-scale attack to Earth and pin it on us. The red-yellow combo is the alert that sets protocols for our Planetary Defense Act."

CHAPTER 32

On the executive floor of Saturn's defense building, the marble glass walls were etched with the Saturn planetary solar system. Earth was but a small ball in the diagram.

The council minister raised his three-pronged hand at the table. Stone cold faces looked up, and the whispers quieted.

"We're calling this meeting to determine the course of action regarding the breach of our defenses. The seriousness of the matter shall not be downplayed.

"The evidence is clear. Treasonous saturnites worked in concert with humans to kill our top defense official and escape our home planet. Thus putting the people of Saturn in grave danger."

In the Circle of Doom, officials gave one last look at Norbo, face up on a gurney. They nodded to the doctor who zipped up the body bag.

"By the power vested in me by the committee, I'm putting it to a vote on whether to enact the raid clause in the Planetary Defense Act.

"Red light for those in favor. Yellow light for disfavor."

The entire line of bulbs glowed red, illuminating the vengeful faces of the committee. On the glass wall, the small ball for Planet Human radiated dark red.

Thousands of black triangular spaceships with gold-tops hovered in an undisclosed hangar. There was a flurry of commotion as mechanics examined the ships, inside and out, choosing only the best for the fleet.

As they passed inspection, the raid commander barked his orders. "Go! Go! Go!"

Raid Boys ran to their designated spacecrafts.

The red-yellow lights flickered in Brady's eyes. What did they just stir up for mankind? A bleak future seared in his mind. He could see a world of terror and sorrow. Scorched cities and dead families.

The distress turned into a throbbing headache—starting behind his left eye, and branching out to a full head of agony. He bent over with his hands on his helmet.

He couldn't help but think that had he never investigated the sock mystery, none of this would've happened. But no, he had to persist. He had to "find the truth". Now, not only were his girls in danger, so was the rest of humanity. And he was to blame.

Light became sensitive. Movement made his head worse. He closed his eyes, and tried to sit still.

Dad had said life would always seem unfair. But you keep going. One step at a time. You fight for what's right.

He found it much harder when the entire world was hanging heavy over your head. It was too much pressure. The weight of his mind was beginning to implode.

Then another memory came through. Dad had taught him the mental trick on how to deal with overwhelm. Worrying about all of humanity was too much to bear. You had to bring it down to a level you could cope with. Public speakers did it with crowds. If talking to everyone in the room made you anxious, you took it down to the front row and talked to them. If the front row was too much, you found one person and talked to them. Take it to a level you could handle.

He would need a directed focus. He thought of Mom. Natasha. Tammy. The people he cared about most. They could be his responsibility.

Instantly, his mind cooled, and the headache dissipated to a manageable throb. He relaxed in his seat. That was it. Focus on what he could handle. Figure out how to save his family.

He looked out into the void of space. "I'll do everything I can...."

♪ ♪ ♪

Twenty minutes had passed. The saucer was flying along, but not fast enough. And Brady was getting restless.

"We need to speed up. Is there anything we can do?"

Mohawk said, "Without a second or third engine, we can't use warp mode. We can try a manual trick."

Brady said, "Do whatever you have to."

Mohawk set the destination to Planet Human. "Setting thrusters to automatic with an added turbo-boost-plus to the back thrusters. It's turbo cruise control with an added kick." He pressed a few buttons, then put his hand on a switch. "This disengages the friction protection mechanism needed for warp speed, which we already can't use. Unfortunately, it also disengages the collision avoidance program. It'll make it faster, but it leaves us more vulnerable. It will be slightly bumpier."

"The warning system is still engaged," said Frenchie. "If a rock or other debris is headed for us, an alarm will go off."

Mohawk checked the electronic Saturn planetary systems map and jotted some figures down. He looked over the control panel, verifying that the correct buttons were engaged. "Per my calculations, we can get to one-tenth the speed of light. It's not warp speed, but it's respectable."

"That'll work," said Brady.

Mohawk nodded. "Fasten your seatbelts."

Brady and Bill pulled down on the belt straps. Mohawk made sure everyone was ready, then flipped a switch.

The fugitives jolted back.

The saucer propelled forward with a rush. Once the speed steadied, their bodies relaxed with the effect of the stationary frame of reference, like being on an airplane.

Suddenly, Brady realized they hadn't figured out where the secret compound was. They thought it would be where the train was taking them. "Wait," he said, and turned to Gilda. "The secret sock corporation isn't on Saturn, is it?"

"It's on Earth," Gilda said. "But it's high clearance. It won't be easy to find."

Mohawk said, "We should be back on Earth in twelve to thirteen hours. It's time to get back into Earth form."

The aliens agreed. Brady's and Bill's ears shot up, not sure what they heard.

Above the aliens' heads was a floating light contraption with a curved screen. They pulled it down. On the side of it was a button with a row of squiggly lines. It was the same contraption that Brady had guessed, earlier, was entertainment. The aliens angled them directly over their bodies and pressed the squiggly button.

Beams of light shot down on them. Brady and Bill leaned away.

Mohawk and Frenchie morphed into the hooligans from the laundromat stick up.

Gilda morphed back into the nice older employee from the discount store.

Brady and Bill stared in awe. They were witnessing another miracle. This was how they integrated.

"Holy mother of Saturn," Bill said, and covered his mouth.

"You're that lady from Ginormous Discount," Brady said, realizing where he'd seen her from.

"That's right," she said. "I'm Gilda."

Brady recalled his conversation with Bill after they saw the alien passengers. "They're like humans."

Bill remembered. "Dangomit," he blurted out and covered his mouth again.

Having gotten so comfortable with them as individuals, they subconsciously viewed them simply as people. The translation software helped, of course. Communication between species created a bond of understanding between the intelligent life forms. The connection with the aliens not only felt natural, as well as technical, it also felt spiritual.

Brady thought for a moment. Slightly embarrassed, he asked, "Can we be morphed?"

"We'd have to get a technician to work out the software program," she said. "Would you like that?"

"Probably not," said Brady.

Bill shook his head with a resounding no.

"You'll come around." Gilda smiled.

Brady wondered how many aliens were on Earth. He thought about the other kids in school. The kids that would suck on their T-shirts. Maybe they were kid aliens.

Bill stared at the hooligans, lost in thought.

"We're not zoo animals, you know," said Mohawk.

"I mean no offense," said Bill. "This is simply too amazing for my brain. It's way out there."

"What are your names?" Brady asked.

Mohawk said, "I'm Lievy."

Frenchie said, "I'm Azin."

"Nice to officially meet you. Sorry. It was a little too hectic for greetings in jail. This is my best friend, Bill. And I'm–"

"You're Brady Watts," Gilda interjected. "We know."

"You know who I am?"

"Mr. Sock mentioned you. The way he said it, I knew you were a good person. When I saw you at the discount store, I figured you were investigating socks."

Lievy said, "They ordered us to keep tabs on you. We were about to grab you at the protest when you threw that smoke bomb."

Brady and Bill looked at them. "No way."

Azin scrunched his lips and nodded the way one would say *yep*.

Gilda leaned over. "Do you remember what I said at the store?"

Brady thought about it. "I recall the manager was being difficult, and you helped me get some socks."

"I told the manager, 'If you're nice to them, they might buy something, making them customers. And that will help us survive.'"

"Ha," Bill said. "That right there is a Hall of Fame line."

Brady said, "Your food helps you survive."

CHAPTER 33

It would be a long trek home, and Brady decided they should learn everything they could. The more he knew, the better chance they had. "Can you tell us about your species?"

"Of course," said Gilda. "What would you like to know?"

Brady asked, "How long have you been stealing socks? And how does it translate to food?"

Bill added, "Yeah. And why are socks fine, but not shirts or underwear? Okay—Maybe I get why not underwear, but why not shirts?"

"I'll try to unpack it for you," she said. "To give you the broad picture, we've been stealing the equivalent of socks in other galactic societies for over 4 million years. We've been stealing socks from this sector for about 3,000.

"We moved our colonies to Saturn and several other locations on the universal grid. We came here from Sector 265 after the fallout war 3,000 years ago in the Trogenerack colonies.

"Sector 265 is the origins of where god created our species over four million years ago. When we moved here, after the reconnaissance mission reconditioned our DNA, we contacted your leaders to create a peaceful agreement for assimilation into society. They said it would cause hysteria if the people knew, and they wanted to keep it under wraps. That's what they said. The truth is, they wanted control. And they can only control and manipulate ignorant people. So your planet stayed ignorant.

"As for why socks? Human DNA in sweat form, mixed with cotton, is vital for our cell's reproduction and our adaption to the environment. Our food technically could be shirts and other soft breakable material. However, from experience, socks were easier for humans to lose track of and not care about, making it the best option. On top of that, the fluffier version of cotton absorbs into our cells better.

"Yes, there's an underground market for sweaty shirts, but it's a criminal offense, as it could raise more questions among humans, who keep track of them more readily."

Brady pointed to his helmet. "These were in the saucer. From S4, I believe."

"That wasn't S4," said Gilda. "Who said that?"

"No one. I thought because—Honestly, I don't know."

"S4 is a secret U.S. guardian location. And where you were was a Saturn guardian establishment. A Saturn saucer. You must be mixing S4, the U.S. location, with S4S, a Saturn program. That could be it."

"I don't know what S4S is," Brady said. "Does it include bringing humans to Saturn as prisoners? Are there more humans there?"

"Yes and No. The helmets are from the old S4S program. Which stopped 100 years ago. We keep the helmets in case we have to restart the program. But only for an emergency."

"What was the program?" Brady asked.

"It was called The Human Food Process. It involved abducting men, which normally took place in the woods. Our retrievers would survey the land for a human that was alone. As soon as one was spotted, the spaceship lit up the night sky. This would entice the human out of their truck. When they got close, the spacecraft sent a beam of light on the subject. There's a force in the light beam that pulls the human to the spaceship. Once beamed inside, it zipped off.

"They were put in the human section of the spacecraft where they got tied down by straps—now the cargo hold where you were. The helmet translators are originally set to English, but any language could be programmed in the software, depending on where the subject is picked up. The helmet releases oxygen as well as the exact balance of chemical elements in gas form to keep the human body supplied, so the subjects don't have to take off the helmet to eat."

A lightbulb moment for Bill. "Woah. Are you for real? I haven't been hungry since the helmet went on." He laughed and looked at Brady. "The most crazy part is I was starving when we were on the train. I remember thinking I'd eat a sock if it were food! Holy smoke balls."

Gilda continued. "When they arrived on Saturn, the humans got escorted to the Human Food Processing Plant. It was full of heated rooms called sweatshops—set to 110 degrees. The subjects were only in their undies. Air-conditioning was supplied by the helmet to keep their core cool enough. They were put on a conveyor belt and made to run to induce sweat faster. As the human perspired, large cotton strips wiped off the sweat. Each abductee was used for two hours a day for a month.

"When one hundred bins were filled, the cotton got cut into small sock-sized pieces and sent in orbit to the Inner Ring of Saturn.

"We still use it for our current storage space. They stay ripe and don't lose the human DNA element in space. As needed, a small craft sucks in a load and brings it to the restaurant to be prepared. The socks get heated, flavored, and served. The food supply chains have a contract with the Saturn guardians and pay a percentage of their earnings."

Brady asked, "Are humans in other sectors too? Do the abductees lose their lives as part of the process?"

"To answer the first question: Whatever solar system we integrate into, we need that species' DNA. In this case, human. It helps our cells learn to survive in the sector we're living in. It's how we adapt. Second question: In short, the answer is no. People don't die as part of the process, but humans have unfortunately died in the past. It was mostly from shock rather than other causes.

"Once used up for a month, the abductees got shot with a light blaster to confuse their memory, then were sent back to Earth."

Out of the blue, Brady felt confused and heavy. A cloud of anxiety loomed over him. He grabbed the arms of his chair.

"Are you okay?" Gilda said. "Should I stop?"

He squeezed his eyes tight and blinked. "No, I'm sorry. Please. Continue."

Gilda put a hand on his knee, "You sure?" Brady nodded, and she continued. "The abductees got dropped back in the woods a mile or two from their original encounter. They would go back to their lives, not realizing they'd been gone for a month, and return to where they left off.

"However, the light blaster doesn't affect everyone as strong, and some abductees would tell the media and anyone who would listen that they were abducted. The people would write them off as crazy, and the media would smear their names. When asked for proof, they couldn't show any. We were okay with that at the beginning, but saturnites didn't like the unfair treatment the humans got.

"Because they felt alienated—yes, that's where that saying came from—a lot of abductees would drop the subject after several months so they would be accepted back into society. In other instances, they simply moved to new cities to start over again where people didn't know them.

"Later, some of our leaders got greedy. To cut costs, humans started being used for half a year to a year at a time, and saturnites suffered the consequences. Contamination of unhealthy sweat from sick humans transferred to us.

"It takes about a month before humans are depleted of nutrients, affecting their healthy DNA. Overused, humans became weak as they slopped around in the heat. The sock product became an off color, and hospitals became overwhelmed with sick saturnites. We had to abandon the process plant.

"Many saturnites protested in the streets that it was unsaturnitarian to treat humans so bad. They believed the gods were making us sick in retribution. After all, humans were helping supply us with sustenance. On top of that, with the technology on Earth advancing because of us, our flying saucers got spotted more regularly. Zoom lenses and smartphones came from our computer chip technology. We had to find a new way without being discovered.

"That's where our morphing technology expanded. Now, not only can we survive in the area, it enabled us to add concentrated human DNA and morph into the species. This contraption, the MOR4EVER 3000," she showed them the squiggly logo, "acts similar to a teleportation device. But, instead of transferring to another dimension in space, it 'transfers' and switches out the different cell patterns from alien DNA to human DNA."

Brady and Bill looked lost.

"Think of human DNA and saturnite DNA as being different locations in space. The human DNA is kept in the MOR4EVER 3000 and the beam swaps it with our DNA. It's like copying and pasting on your computer, but instead of data we're switching out the cell patterns in the body. Time stops during the transfer, but only for the individual in the morph beam.

"That became the solution. Qualified saturnites began integrating with humans and morphing to be our sustenance retrievers. So we started our new saturnitarian ways. Just like your humanitarians.

"We began only stealing socks for survival, and a new program was created. Socks 4 Survival. Or S4S for short. That's when we started infiltrating into society more regularly.

"Morphed saturnites became laundromat attendants and laundromat owners. Some became sock store owners and other jobs as their disguise. Saturnites are the ones who made laundromats go mainstream. I was on that first mission. In the early days, humans washed clothes by hand and hung them on string lines to dry. There were only a few laundromats in the beginning. We turned it into an empire, and laundromats popped up all over the world. That was one facet. The most modern achievement of S4S is sock insurance."

Brady and Bill leaned in, gripping their armchairs.

"We set it up like this: Humans sign up at a low cost. When they lose socks in the laundry, they bring their insurance card and get a new pair of socks for free. And we get a fresh supply of non-stale food. The socks you lose on Earth magically appear on a saturnite's plate. Or, if there's no DNA on them, they get repackaged and sold again. It's a good deal. Humans get new socks for free, and we get fed."

"Who is Mr. Sock in all this?" Brady asked.

"The title of 'Mr. Sock' is given to the commander of the SSC—Secret Sock Corporation. They're responsible for keeping our race fed through the programs. Mr. Sock was well respected at first. The SSC started moving on from the Human Food Processing Plant when the morphing missions began. But we couldn't just stop the program cold turkey. S4S would take a little time.

"It was around the end of the saturnitarian protests when Mr. Sock changed. His son worked as the head manager in the sweatshops, and his daughter was the chief technician during the crossover period to S4S.

"A sick human fled from the sweatshop one day, and Mr. Sock's daughter stopped him. When his son came to help bring the abductee back, the abductee swung wildly, cutting both of them across the face. They both got infected. His son survived, but she died a week later.

"That's when Mr. Sock snapped. He schemed the secretive program to make humans sick, ordering Vance to incorporate a poison spray on the assembly line. The long-lasting effects put humans in a state of depression and easy manipulation."

"We found the poison too," said Brady.

"That's why I helped you with the socks. I knew you'd find it," she said. "Early in the phase, a random passerby happened upon the secret compound and was about to spill the beans on the program. He found the compound by chance and was recording the arrival of the barrels of poison. Compound security apprehended him. They shot him with the light blaster and dragged him in front of the executives with a bag over his head. Filled with rage, Mr. Sock ordered the man killed. After that, he ramped up the program.

"His end goal is a slave planet where human live only as a means for Saturn food. They plan to poison everyone. Starry-eyed humans will fill the cities and live on tubes like vegetable zombies.

"Mr. Sock wants Earth to be taken over and inhabited by saturnites with humans motionless in a kitchen. A saturnite would simply put the human in the small sweatshop oven, heat him up, and when sweat fills their socks, he takes them off and eats. And when they're hungry again, they put new socks on the human.

"Saturnites would be enraged if they knew of these anti-human plans. But they are unaware. The media, planet security, and executives run defense for them. The criminal outfit has blackmail on everyone. So they have no choice except to go along with it or be destroyed in the minds of saturnites. The media twisted every story. Pinned it on the wrong people and kept the good people from knowing, and Mr. Sock got drunk on power.

"It's un-saturnitarian. We are a good race, marred by a small percentage of corrupt individuals." She melted in her chair, overwhelmed and mentally exhausted. "They will stop at nothing to get their way."

Brady couldn't help but think of the hell she's been through. And he thought he had it rough? Going up against this level of corruption isn't easy on anyone. "We'll help you make it right," he said.

"No doubt about it," said Bill. "We got you."

Brady leaned over and hugged her.

Bill rubbed her back. "We got each other."

She dabbed her eyes. "I appreciate you more than you know."

"We feel the same about you," said Brady.

Bill nodded energetically and rubbed her shoulders.

"Thank you." Gilda patted Bill's hand, indicating it was enough.

Brady asked, "Do you know where the compound is?"

"We were there once," said Lievy. "I remember we were going to a meeting. But my memory is fuzzy."

Brady said, "In the files at Super Laundry headquarters there was a message from Mr. Sock to Vance about the compound. It said it was in Central America. It noted the whereabouts were to be encrypted? Does that ring a bell?"

"It's a diversion," said Gilda. "There's no part of the production set up in Central America, except laundry machines and sock retrievers, which are around the globe."

Bill got an idea. "Maybe it's in the middle of the U.S. Like Kansas. That's near the 'center of America.' That's a sort of encryption."

Gilda shook her head, no. "I've been there. I didn't know exactly where I was. I only know it wasn't far from the discount store. Forty-five minutes at most."

"When we find it, it'll be a dangerous undertaking," said Azin. "They have a whole operation of lackeys and enforcers who destroy for fun. I know because I was one of them."

"We'll worry about that later," said Brady.

His thoughts went to his sister. She had found Mr. Sock. Which was the only silver lining about her getting caught. If she found him, he could too. "My sister was at my place," he said. "She must've put something together out of my evidence. Some clue. Has to be that."

It was hard for him to imagine her figuring it out on her own. Sibling rivalry was still strong, even subconsciously.

"Give them your home address. They'll punch in the coordinates," said Gilda.

Brady jotted it down and handed it to Azin.

"Why is Mr. Sock concealed?" Bill asked.

"Something is wrong with his morphing," she said. "It glitches, so he hides under disguises. We don't know his Earth identity. So he can manipulate humans and saturnites and no one can connect one to the other. Easier to corrupt people that way. It's another thing we're up against."

"We should get some shut-eye," said Lievy. "We're going to need all the rest we can get."

"He's right. It's going to be a race against the clock when we get back," said Gilda.

Azin checked his calculations. "If we sleep now, that's a good ten plus hours. We're on cruise control. The warning system is activated."

The three human aliens closed their eyes and went right into snoring. Brady and Bill looked at each other.

"What can't they do?" said Bill. He got up close to Gilda, inspecting her eyelids. She really was out.

Having been up for more than 24 hours themselves, Brady and Bill needed their own rest. They closed their eyes.

CHAPTER 34

The quiet hum of autopilot was tranquil. Dark cab, soft snores, and a steady view. The occasional shooting star lit up the peaceful, resting faces.

BEEP! BEEP! BEEP! BEEP!

Lievy jumped for the controls. Azin jerked half-awake and scoured the panel. Eyes bulging out like a fishbowl, searching. Nothing flashed. They peered through the window. Ahead was clear "space skies."

BEEP! BEEP! BEEP!

Bill stretched out and yawned, his vocal cords squealed. "Are we at the arrival destination point yet?" He chuckled softly, rubbing his eyes. "You thought I was going to say, are we there yet?"

BEEP! BEEP! BEEP!

Bill poked Brady, who was fast asleep, slumped over, held up by his seatbelt.

Bill poked him again.

Countdown flashed on Brady's wristwatch. Groggily, he deactivated the alarm. The realization of it lagged, then he was fast awake, eyes wide open. "What's the countdown for?"

He had completely forgotten about it. Confronted with the prospect of aliens and saucers had done the trick.

A disturbed recognition appeared on Gilda's face. "It's the next phase of the slave planet."

Lievy and Azin nodded solemnly.

"What is it?" asked Brady.

Gilda shrugged. "I never got that far in my investigation."

"We'll figure it out," said Brady.

The saucer zoomed along.

An hour later, a flicker of blue flashed in the cab. Out the window, shimmering in space, planet Earth appeared in all its beauty. A large beautiful glowing marble. Mesmerizing.

Brady and Bill gazed at the wondrous blue ball.

"So Earth isn't flat," said Bill.

Brady shook his head. "It would've been enjoyable to experience this once in a lifetime moment without a Wild Bill joke."

"You can't expect a lion not to be a lion," said Bill.

The saucer glided down into the Earth's atmosphere.

Azin pressed the GRAVITY button. "Activating Hover Mode."

Flying overhead, the saucer headed for the mountains. A crowd in the park enthusiastically pointed up, whipping out their cameras and phones. *Flash. Flash. Flash.* Screams of "UFO," "O.M.G.," "The end is nigh," echoed in the air.

The saucer landed in a backyard near Brady's house, settling gently on the grass.

The escalating belt descended, and the fugitives headed down.

Lievy unhooked the panel and entered a code. Once set, he pulled the digital record for the past location coordinates.

Lights systematically scanned inside the saucer and ten feet around the outside, verifying that no bodies were on board and no movement was detected.

A *flash,* and the saucer zipped away.

At Brady's house, the canary yellow curtains were torn, fluttering through the smashed windows. Fragments of glass were everywhere. The front door was off its hinges.

The team entered cautiously.

Whistles of the wind, papers rustling on the floor. The team kept their heads on a swivel. The living room couch was ripped apart. Cotton fibers scattered all over the place. The coffee table lay on its side, its legs broken. The easel was faced down, and the sock mystery board and all the notes were gone.

Brady and Gilda looked under the couch and inside the torn upholstery. Lievy and Azin checked the ransacked kitchen.

At the shattered window, Bill delicately pulled back the curtains. He yelped in a panic, and flailed at the air as a bee buzzed up to the ceiling. "Geezus baneezus," said Bill.

The team looked over, saw the bee, and went back to searching.

Brady pushed the bedroom door open, the hinges whined. He entered. The dresser drawers were in pieces on the floor. The bedding was torn. The mattress was bare, and the side was sliced with its cotton guts out.

In the bathroom, the cracked mirrors doubled the spectacle of the destruction. Lightbulbs were busted. The drawers were ransacked. Brady rummaged through the cabinets, finding nothing for a clue. He caught a glimpse of himself in the mirror. He looked at the surrounding mess. It was up to him to fix it.

He went upstairs to the study. The shelf was toppled over. Books were scattered everywhere. The Gadget Rack was empty. The printer was smashed in. His TV on the back wall was askew—and loud static filled the screen. All the evidence—the drum container, the socks, and the Super Laundry bags—were missing.

Then he noticed the crack in the aquarium. Water dribbling out, forming a puddle. There was a noticeable absence. "Toby!"

The stressed call had Lievy, Azin, Bill, and Gilda rushing upstairs.

"Is everything okay?" Azin asked.

Brady didn't respond. He paced the room, mumbling curses to himself. "We have nothing. I have no idea what my sister saw."

Static scrambled in and out on the TV. The news report came on. Then static appeared again. Brady stared at the black and white balls fighting on the screen—then a clear view. Todd Strout smiling. Then to a whine with long, glitching lines. Something kept his mind on the TV. He rarely, if ever, used it. Why was it on?

"Fix the signal," said Brady.

Lievy and Azin leveled the frame while Bill fiddled with the Wi-Fi box in the back. The static cleared.

On screen, Todd Strout cleared his throat. "Reports from around the country are coming in with random acts of violence. We have made no direct link to the events. An eyewitness sent us this footage. If there are any kids watching, this is disturbing. Be forewarned."

Shaky footage appeared, showing a street view from a third-floor window. A group of thugs were firing a barrage of blasts into parked cars. Windows shattered, tires blew out, hoods and doors punctured. Pedestrians ran for cover. A man got in his car and careened off, ducking his head out of sight.

The view zoomed down the block to a man stepping in front of a car. He had a beet-red face and was bellowing profanities with his chest out and arms inviting danger. The camera zoomed in—seeming to shake in step with the man's rage. Then it angled at the man's legs, revealing his socks in a blur. For a split second, the view cleared up on the socks before it snapped up to the man's face. Suddenly, a commotion of sound came from below the camera. More shaky blurs, then the view cleared up. A thug below took the back of his blaster and busted in a car window.

Brady and Bill noticed the thug's feet. And the logo on his socks. "LFS. See that?" said Brady.

"Oh, I see it," said Bill.

"Give me the remote." Brady rewound it to the previous man, who was yelling, and paused it when the view was clear for a half-second.

The other man was also wearing socks with the LFS logo.

Brady glanced at the destroyed shelf, then at the busted Gadget Rack. Below it, was a toxin tester container that was tipped on its side, and cracked in half.

A bee landed in the container, its furry feet dipping in the solution. Brady's attention fixated on him like a magnet. He moved in closer. His face turned to dread.

The liquid was dark red.

The bee moved around jaggedly, then vibrated, puffing out its body hair. It flew out of the container, barely missing Brady's head, and headed straight for Bill, its stinger pointed forward.

Bill screamed, flailing his arms, and ran around in circles. Gilda, Lievy, and Azin moved out of his way.

From the counter, Brady snatched a jar and snuck closer to Bill. "Stop. Let it come to you." The bee shot up, then around in a loop, and headed back for Bill.

"Are you crazy?" Bill was incredulous.

With its stinger forward and bug eyes glued on him, the bee attacked. Bill gritted his teeth and drew back.

The bee smacked into the base of the jar.

Brady twisted the cap on. "Got it!"

The bee bounced around like a ping pong ball.

"What the heck did I do to the bee?" said Bill.

"Keep facing what scares you, buddy." Brady handed him the jar.

"Easy for you to say when you're not being chased by a killer ninja bee." Bill passed it to Gilda, distancing himself from the fuzzball of fury.

Crouching down, Brady inspected the broken container and the toxin tester liquid. "From purple to dark red. Category six. It's an escalating poison."

The bee buzzed around the jar, thirsting for a hit of red adrenaline.

Gilda stared at the bee with a troubled look in her eyes. "The next phase."

♪ ♪ ♪

Brady picked up a shattered family photo of Momma Jan, Poppa Clark, young Brady, and Natty with their arms around each other. He pulled the picture out of the frame and shook off the shards. It felt like they were smiling at him through the photo. Especially young Natasha. "We should check my mom's house. Maybe we'll find a clue in Natasha's room."

That was the next logical move. And if they destroyed his place, it was likely they would do the same to theirs.

It wasn't as expected, and to Brady's relief. The front of the family house was tidy, with no sign of forced entry. The garden was vibrant and in tip-top shape.

While Brady, Bill, and Gilda went in, Lievy and Azin stayed outside on guard.

The living room and hallways were spotless. In Brady's room, everything was in its rightful place. Natasha's room was messy as usual. Nothing out of the ordinary. Brady opened her dresser drawers and shuffled through.

"What's that?" Gilda said, noticing a piece of paper under the bed.

Bill picked it up. It was the missing person flyer for James Lin.

"Let me see." Brady took it.

While Brady read it, Bill checked under the bed. On top of a mystery novel was a school binder with stickers. He grabbed it.

On the first page, written in bold letters:

THE SOCK MYSTERY.

And under it:

Sock Street, James Lin, Strike at Sock Factory, Mill's Sock Plant, a phone number, an address, and *Adeline Lin*.

"She talked about this." Bill aligned the binder with the missing person notice in Brady's hand. Cross-checking the notes, everything matched.

"What are you talking about?" said Brady. He had recalled no mention of it. He was pretty sure he'd remember. Then he thought of Bill's nagging crush, making it easy for him to re-member everything she said. Just like on the opposite end, the nagging irritation he had with her made it easy to block out everything she said. "When?" he asked.

"The day she came over. Before we went to Super Laundry headquarters. She mentioned the notice."

Brady zeroed in on the home phone number and the ad-dress at the bottom. "This must be where she went." It dawned on him that she figured it out on her own, without his clues. And she put herself in danger doing it. She was just like him. A Mystery Solver to her core. "I think I need to be nicer to my sister."

Bill couldn't believe what he was hearing.

Car horns honked, alarms blared, wheels screeched, and windows crashed. The routine sounds since "the next phase" began. Brady and the team drove to the outskirts safely, avoiding high-traffic streets. They stopped at a small, brown-painted house in a low-income neighborhood. Bars covered the windows.

Worried eyes peered from nearby, run-down homes, and old folks got up from their rocking chairs and retreated back inside.

Brady rang the doorbell. After a minute, the peephole light flickered to dark. A tiny Asian lady with gray hair opened the door.

Brady held up the missing person notice. "Did a girl come by here about this?"

"Sorry, we don't want the troubles," said the lady.

"Are you Adeline?" he asked. She didn't speak. Her fidgeting fingers and shifty eyes told him she'd been threatened. "That girl was my sister," Brady said. "She's missing. I could use your help."

"I cannot," she said, shaking her head.

"More than our families will be in trouble if we don't figure this out. We will help find your husband, and you can help us solve this…" He pointed out to the streets. After twenty long seconds, there was finally a crash in the distance. "That. You can help us solve that."

She looked at him with trust in her heart. "Okay, shhh." She opened the door, and the team entered.

Adeline placed a tray full of teacups on the table. They all declined graciously besides Bill, who took a cup, of course. He would never deny a free snack or drink.

In broken English, Adeline called to her son, "Bring me letter, Li."

A young Asian boy came in with a small letter written in Chinese.

"Is that what you showed my sister?" said Brady.

"No," said Adeline. "Letter came in now. This day. We only tell her where my husband work. That it."

Speaking in perfect English, as second-generation kids do, Li said, "The letter says they have him at a hidden location in Factory City."

"Does it have the address in the letter?" Brady asked.

Adeline shook her head, no. "He don't know where he is. Only our address here to get letter to us."

Li clarified, "He snuck the note in a sock, hoping someone would find it and send it here. It arrived in the mailbox yesterday. My dad says he's in Factory City. He's familiar with the sounds of the area but was blindfolded when he went there and hasn't been outside since."

"It wouldn't make sense to have the secret compound where lots of factories are. The location is hidden. Per confidential files we saw at Super Laundry headquarters, the secret compound is in Central America," Brady said. "Though we know it's not actually Central America. That's only a code word."

"He's in Factory City." Li said it with conviction. "That is what he wrote. I trust that."

Bill stared at the floor, thinking, sipping his tea. "Honduras…. Honduras…. Honduras!"

They all looked at him.

"What?" said Brady.

"Honduras. Costa Rica! Honduras! The streets are named after countries in Central America! It's a street in Factory City. They probably have good coffee!" He looked at Brady, unable to contain his excitement. "I figured something out."

"Hidden in plain sight," said Brady.

For the first time since he lost Tammy, Brady had real hope. They knew where the compound was.

CHAPTER 35

Li got on his knees and begged his mom. "I want to go with them." He looked at Brady. "Please, can I come?"

"We need all the help we can get," said Brady. "But it has to be okay with your mom."

They gave Adeline her space to think it over.

After a short time, Brady snuck over and lightly suggested, "He'll only do non-combative tasks. We'll keep him out of any real action."

Adeline got misty-eyed. She hugged her son tight. "Go bring papa back."

The team packed into the Mysterymobile and drove to the corner store where Oliver, the bum, was begging on the sidewalk. Brady and Bill got out while the others waited in the car. Brady dropped change in the bucket.

Oliver looked up, happy to see a familiar face. "Hi, Brady.... I have something for you." He lifted the bucket. Under it were two crinkled photos. He handed them to him. "The one on top is Vance."

Bill peeked over Brady's shoulder. "OMG. Of course Vance is a pencil mustache weirdo." When Brady placed Mr. Sock's photo on top, Bill said, "I wouldn't want to see what's under that."

"We could use you, Oliver." Brady crouched to his level. "It's dangerous. But it's for a good cause." He put his hand out.

Hesitating, Oliver slowly reached out, then pulled back.

"Yes, we're putting our lives on the line," Brady said. "But what life will we have if we don't try?"

Regret washed over Oliver's face. He grabbed Brady's hand and pulled himself up. Then he exhaled. "I'm tired of being tired."

"Let's change that," said Brady. He turned to Lievy and Azin in the car, hoping it was enough.

Lievy rolled the window down. "We need more."

Azin added, "And I think you know that."

A sigh from Brady. He knew what they meant. "Fine. But before we go, we'll need more evidence. Just talking to them won't do it." He pulled the destroyed phone from his pocket. "The photos from this, and Bill's phone, plus the bee, might work."

♪ ♪ ♪

A soft, calming jingle played in the Printo's store. Brady and the team waited patiently as the clerk spread the photos on the table. The Saturn council dome photo, the photo of alien Gilda in the purple dress, the finance building guards being tickled and kissed, the knocked-out guard sucking his thumb, and more. She handed Bill's phone back. "Is that it, Shakespeare? You some sort of stage play troupe?"

They smiled without answering. She stared back, squinting her eyes. The room got awkward.

"Movie magic, am I right?" said Bill, then he forced a fake, awkward laugh like an impractical joker.

"We'd like these 'printo'ed' too," Brady said, holding up his destroyed phone. "If possible."

If someone used the tag line, *I'd like to get this printo'ed,* she had to smile and say, "Right-e-o." It was company policy.

She decidedly didn't smile and plucked it from Brady's fingers. "I'll see what I can do." She sauntered away, hips seesawing. She patted her curly updo hair—held by a scrunchie––and pushed through the back door.

The gang twiddled their thumbs and waited impatiently. It took several minutes, and still she hadn't resurfaced. Brady told them to be prepared in case they had to make a break for it. Shortly after, two employees poked their heads through the back door. The clerk pushed them aside and sauntered to the counter. She set the photos in front of Brady and spread them out. They were the photos of the responsibility sign from the laundromat, the sock bag with the serial number, rolling bins from the speed train, the train route diagram, and more. She looked the gang up and down.

"They're stills from a short film," said Azin.

"Wild story about socks," said Bill. "Based on true events."

She bunched the photos up and slid them forward with a watchful eye. Brady gathered them, and they were off.

♪　♪　♪

The weekly meeting at Mystery Solver's Inc. was underway. They were watching videos of the mayhem in the city, with Army at the head of the table. He drank a swig of his "Loco" canteen. "When did the chaos start? From there, we go back and find out what was introduced just before. And by who?"

"Potentially an infection of sorts," said Bowl Cut.

Harry said, "Probably something to do with the water. It's the quickest way to infect the masses."

Brady and the team walked into the meeting room with the bee and the multitude of photos. They might try to laugh Brady out of the building again. But he wouldn't let it get to him.

Army paused the video. "What are you doing here?"

"Who are they?" said Glasses, pointing to the unfamiliar faces of Lievy, Azin, Gilda, Oliver the bum, and Li.

"What the hell is this," said Gunner.

"I'll explain," said Brady, preparing for pushback. He noticed someone was absent, piquing his interest. "Where's Slick?"

Gunner tapped a pen to his dome. "He got sick."

"The bug finally got him," said Harry.

"I don't know," said Curls. "He could've been faking it."

"He has been acting off lately," said Gunner.

Army quickly changed the subject. "So, what do you have for us that's so important?"

Brady placed the jar on the table. The bee was buzzing around in a fit. Bill slid all the photos toward the Mystery Solvers, and, almost perfectly, they came to a stop a foot in front of them.

"This isn't that sock mystery jive, is it?" Gunner raised an eyebrow while picking up a photo.

Brady said, "What's going on in the city has everything to do with the sock mystery. Check the evidence, and I'll answer any questions."

As they looked over the photos their expressions changed to awe, worry, wonder, and everything in between. One by one, the Mystery Solvers looked up.

"What in the hell is going on?" Army asked. "This is some high-level editing, or you've contacted aliens."

Brady beckoned Gilda, Lievy, and Azin. "These are our friends from Saturn."

The group studied the strangers, who were clearly human. "Saturn?" Gunner squinted his eyes. "What you mean?"

Gilda said, "With our technology, we change our physical bodies. We morph into our human form when we're here, and into our Saturn form back home. That's where we're from."

"You don't look alien," said Bowl Cut, tilting her head back, observing them.

Bill pointed to the photo of the grand jury testimony. "That's her." He pointed to alien Gilda in purple. "Same dress. And get this: Socks are their frigging food. That's why they steal them. It's a whole thing."

Crossing his arms, Gunner said, "How does this connect with what's going on in the city?"

"We thought you'd never ask," said Bill, eyebrows jumping up and down.

Brady went over the summary of the investigation, including Mr. Sock's plan to make Earth a slave planet. "What's going on in the city is nothing compared to what's coming." He told them about the poison in the socks making people go insane. "It's the same substance this bee came in contact with." Tiny red footprints were all over the jar. He pushed it forward and the bee ricocheted in the glass. "Only a couple of days ago, it was purple. It's an escalating poison, and now a category six toxin. That's what's happening to the affected people. And it'll only get worse."

Blank-faced, worried, and dumbfounded, the group stared at him. Harry covered his mouth. Curls gulped. Gunner sat there, quiet. Army looked confused.

"We need your help," said Brady. "It'll take every one of us or life on this planet is doomed."

The group kept staring with a lost look.

Brady continued, this time more forcefully. And the more he spoke, the more they seemed to lose interest. Why weren't they listening? He might have to throw something at the wall to shake them out of their stupor. "The world needs us!"

The message floated over their heads like it was meant for someone else. It had nothing to do with them. Army rubbed his neck. Glasses scratched his head.

Hope was slipping from Brady's words. Maybe they didn't trust him. Maybe they didn't want to work with him but couldn't say it. He tried from a different angle.

"I know I'm not perfect. No one is. And to hell with my past. There's a world to save. I don't care how crazy the sock mystery sounds or how nuts you think I am. They've poisoned our socks, and plan to turn us into vegetables. What else is there to say to get you on board?"

A few of them were staring off at the screen. There still wasn't one iota of inspiration to act and it pissed him off. He'd only ever spoken his truth to them. Even if he was wrong a time or two, he came from an honest place. They should know that more than anyone.

Suddenly, he felt sick. It was a waste. Their minds had been poisoned against him. Slick wasn't even there, and they were under his spell. "Really, guys?"

He looked around, disheartened. This is what words of negativity do to people. Then, for the first time, he noticed none of them were staring at him with any sort of attitude. He had created that in his own head. There were only blank or worried faces staring back.

A spark from the universe. Through the cloud of frustration came clarity. It wasn't about him. It was about them. The magnitude of the situation was too much for them to handle.

Brady stepped forward with a newfound calm. "Attempts at mass control have gone on throughout our history. This is nothing new. But these guys messed up. They underestimated me and my resolve....

"They took my girls."

Eyes came into focus.

Heads and postures straightened.

The group was out of the fog, with their full attention on him.

"They need you," said Brady. "I need you. And with your help, we can save them. If we do, then possibly, we can save the world."

The Mystery Solvers stood in unison.

"Nobody takes a man's girls," said Army.

Bill pointed to Li. "They also took Li's dad."

"I wouldn't mind messin' up some fools." Gunner put up two hand pistols.

"Mark me down for the cause," said Army.

Glasses said, "I'm in."

"At your service," said Harry.

"I'll help," said Curls.

Bowl Cut joined in. "We got your back."

Brady could feel himself getting emotional, but he pushed it down. It was time to get to business.

Army spoke up, "I've never said this to you. But I've always felt you'd be the best of us one day. And here you are, proving yourself. You have my full commitment to this mission."

"I'd follow you anywhere," said Harry.

"Me too," said Bowl Cut.

Glasses nodded.

"Tell us what to do, boss," said Gunner.

CHAPTER 36

Brady nodded to Bill, who opened the briefcase and pulled out the Factory City street plans. Specifically, the 6-block radius around the secret compound.

After Bill had the eureka moment, he knew where the compound should be based on the Central American street names. He found the only factory with no affiliations—first red flag. He tried to get the blueprints of the building, but there were no access files—second red flag. It involved high clearance, which his blueprint guy didn't have. Pretty obvious what it was. The Secret Sock Corporation.

The best they could get was a layout of the nearby roads and factories. Bill rolled out the street plans on the table. The compound was located deep inside the estate, enclosed with ten-foot-high walls. And a mini jungle surrounding it.

The group, in their Mystery Solver suits, stood at the meeting table with itchy fingers, primed and ready. Brady gathered his thoughts.

"A great man once said, 'The really brave ones are willing to give themselves up so everyone else can be safe.' If you're not up for that, I understand."

There was no chance anyone was leaving.

Brady turned to Gunner. "This mission calls for emergency reinforcements."

Gunner winked. He knew what that meant. He left and came back with the large, black case marked *Arsenal Armaments*. He opened the compartments and handed out blasters. A large blaster went to Army who inspected it, then cocked it. One for himself, and one for Lievy and Azin. Small blasters went to the rest. Besides Bill and Li—who were too young. And Curls. She was old enough, but she didn't want one.

Gunner put his shades on. "Your funeral."

Bill handed the pictures of Vance and Mr. Sock to Brady, who handed them back. "Go ahead."

The unexpected gesture had Bill flustered, but he wasn't going to miss the opportunity. He straightened his posture and squinted his eyes. "Recap: These are the major players causing all the trouble." He showed them the first photo and said in a cool voice, "Before Vance was in the sock business, he was a diamond smuggler. I guess he found a bigger payoff." Next he showed the photo of the monster. "Mr. Sock runs everything behind the scenes. As for why he covers his face—I don't know. Probably the same reason anybody hides. He must look ridiculous!" He nodded to Brady.

"First," Brady said, pointing to the blueprint, "we make our way through the jungle and over the protective walls. When we go in, expect anything.

"Bill, to be on the safe side, you, Curls, and Oliver will take care of the hostages. Find a safe place for them while we handle the rest.

"Lievy and Azin, help round up the scum. You know more than we do who they are. If you see an innocent bystander, get them to Bill in the hostage holding area.

"Gunner and Army, stick together." He pointed to Glasses, Harry, and Bowl Cut. "You're a team. As we take down criminals, make sure they're restrained." He handed them bags of thick zip-tie straps. "We'll find a different place to hold the scum.

"Gilda, you know what to do. Li, you're the lookout. Don't let anyone see you. If you detect anything suspicious, or if you see anyone enter the premises after us, radio me." He handed Li a walkie-talkie and tapped his earpiece.

"If anyone sees Li's dad, get him to the holding area. I'll find my girls."

Army nodded. "Let's give them what they deserve."

"Let's give 'em hell," said Gunner. He cocked his blaster.

♪ ♪ ♪

Sentries stood guard inside the walls surrounding the edifice. Warpaint marked their cheeks. Black uniforms camouflaged their bodies. And bulky blasters held steady in their arms.

From the front gate to the main street, cameras lined the cobblestone path. Outside the cameras' view and a block before the main street entrance, the team darted across the road.

Tufts of tall grass sprang up through bark-scattered dirt in the mini-jungle. Peering from behind a cluster of palms, the team spotted a couple of sentries resting on a tree trunk. One of them heard a crunch and got up. After a brief search, not seeing or hearing anyone, assuming it was the small squirrel, he took a swig from his water canteen and sat back down. Gunner and Army crept behind them like giant ninjas. They pounded down on them with hammer fists. The patrol guards dropped senseless. Further in the jungle, Lievy and Azin knocked out two more sentries.

The team traversed the mini-jungle, subduing sentries and zip-tying them, one by one, all the way to the ten-foot-high walls.

With Army, Bill, and Harry forming the base, and Bowl Cut and Glasses above them, they created a human pyramid ladder and helped Brady and Gunner on the wall. With Gunner's final thrust to the top, the pyramid crumbled.

Brady and Gunner crawled on their stomachs, keeping low, and stopped at the camera angled toward the main entrance. Gunner handed him a mini-Polaroid. Brady set it to silent, then placed it just above the camera and snapped a photo. It printed out. He gently shook the picture until it was clear. He attached it a couple of inches out in front of the camera lens.

Bill gathered pebbles from the edge of the driveway and snuck through tall shrubs to the front gate. He closed his eyes to reset his mind, and crossed his heart. When he was ready, he opened his eyes. He cocked his arm back and threw the pebbles.

Clank-clank-clank-clank-clank.

The guards crept forward, trigger fingers ready. Brady and Gunner silently dropped inside the walls as a sentry peered through the peephole.

Bill was showing his pearly whites. "Is my mom in there? She looks just like me. Except female and older." He smiled again.

From behind, Gunner charged the sentries and clothes-lined them into the gate. They crashed and crumbled to the ground. Out cold. He celebrated with dancing pec muscles.

After ensuring no surprises would come, Brady took a card from one of the guard's necks and swiped it on the gate sensor. It rolled open. The team made their way to the entrance.

Bill, attempting to hype himself up mentally, found his foot buckling on a cobblestone. Glasses and Curls put their hands out to catch him, but he saved himself. "I'm good. Practicing my reflexes." He tried to play it cool, but the heavy breathing indicated otherwise.

Carved into the massive arched doors were symbols and hieroglyphics. Socks, stars, saucers, beams of light, planets, stick figures, and much more. It was the story of saturnite's history on Planet Human.

Before Brady lifted the card to the silver panel, he looked back at the team. "Let's take back our socks."

Apart from the alien humans, the team got in a ready stance. Bill turned to Gilda, Lievy, and Azin, "Don't worry. He's only saying it for inspiration ahead of battle. A last hurrah. You'll get your socks. Nobody wants anybody to starve. You get the drift."

Brady swiped the card. Beep-Beep. A fingerprint scanner lit up on the panel. "Press your hand on the indicated area."

"Bring one of them. Hurry." Brady pointed urgently at the unconscious sentries.

Army and Glasses dragged one of the slump men to the entrance. Gunner lifted him near the panel. Brady flopped the sentry's hand on the reader.

"Thank you. Your weight is excessive. Remove any bags."

They looked down. They were on a scale that blended in subtly with the ground. They stepped back. Gunner kept his arms out, holding the sentry up.

"Weight still too much. Remove any accessories."

Gunner released his grip, and the guard flopped down.

"Thank you. Put your eyes near the scanner for confirmation."

"Wow, for real?" said Brady. "Pick him up." Gunner held the sentry level with the scanner. His eyes were closed. Brady gently tried opening one eyelid. It slipped. He tried again. It slipped again—too delicate to get a handle on it.

"Army, switch with me," said Gunner. Army held the sentry, and Gunner carelessly pinched the top and bottom of his eyelid with his thick fingers and pulled them apart—slurp, the lids came off the eyeball.

Brady saw how he did it and copied him with the other eye.

No pupil materialized.

"Ten... Nine... Eight..."

"You've got to be kidding," said Brady.

Bill dug into his pocket, pulled out an adrenal boost. He handed it to Brady with an embarrassed look.

Brady fixed his gaze on him. We'll go over boundaries later.

"Four... Three..."

Brady poured the adrenal boost down the sentry's throat.

Eyes bulged open, and pupils focused. Army held the sentry's body, and Gunner thrust the man's head next to the panel as it scanned his eyes. The sentry squirmed. Gunner held his head still.

"I didn't take it from her drawer," Bill whispered. "I bought it online in case I could help in an emergency. C'mon, I wouldn't have had it if I wasn't thinking of her." The quick nod was Brady giving him a pass for now.

The scanner finished. "Thank you. Say the code into the voice recognition microphone."

"I wonder if this is the secret compound," Bill said sarcastically.

"Voice doesn't match."

Bill covered his mouth.

The sentry looked around at the sinister faces. Gunner grabbed the man's neck, and squished his face against the microphone. The sentry sealed his lips tight. Gunner squished his head harder into the panel.

"Ouch! That hurts."

"Voice match. Wrong passcode."

Gunner pulled the man's head back and smushed his head against the microphone again.

"Can't do it." The guard squeezed his lips tighter.

"Voice match. Wrong passcode."

One more time, Gunner pulled the man's head back and smushed his head against the microphone. Much harder this time.

Scared out of his mind, the guard said, "Mr. Sock feeds me."

"Thank you. Access granted."

Clink. The arched doors slowly opened.

Gunner pushed the sentry toward the gate and pulled his fist back, hinting at what might come if he didn't leave. The sentry turned and ran away, flailing his arms all the way out to the street.

"Stick together," said Brady. "Li, be patient. We'll get your dad out safe. Now, go."

Li went out the gate and took a left into the jungle.

Brady poked his head in the compound. Four wide pillars guided the entrance, leading to a large open atrium with a glass sunroof. "Everyone, get behind a pillar." They snuck in one after another.

CHAPTER 37

A lackey spotted the trespassers, and yelled, "Intruders!!!" Lackeys, in gray, from the ground level, and enforcers, in navy blue, from the second-floor balcony, unholstered their weapons and fired.

Blast holes riddled the pillars. Sparks flew.

Army leaned out, aiming straight ahead with angular precision, and Gunner fired up to the second floor. The lackey on the ground fell with a thud. The enforcer on the balcony dropped to his knees and fell prostrate, his head bouncing through the porcelain balusters.

Gilda snuck off to the left as blasts howled in the atrium.

To the far right of the pillars, a lackey came charging at them. Brady got on a knee, steadied his weapon, and blasted him off his feet.

Ahead, to the right, Ivan leaned out of the yarn room, aiming his blaster directly at Brady—bang. The blast whizzed by his head, smoking Harry behind him. Harry crumbled to the ground.

Brady looked back. "Harry."

Bowl Cut and Glasses quickly smothered Harry's smoking head.

Brady dragged him behind the pillar out of harm's way. Harry groaned, protecting his head with his hands.

Behind the furthest pillars, Bill and Oliver crouched lower and lower as blasts thundered around them.

"Stick in there, Harry." Brady looked around for where the blast came from. Ahead to the left, he saw the knitting room sign above the expansive wall. Straight ahead in the open atrium were thin pillars at random points. An enforcer hid behind a pillar in the distance. Then he saw Ivan off to the right, smiling in the yarn room's door window.

His spidey senses tingled. Brady recognized the face. The thug with the buzz cut and the shark tattoo. His blood began to boil. "Gunner, Army, take the knitting room. I got the yarn room." Another blast roared by, taking out a chunk of the pillar next to Brady's head. He was so focused he didn't budge.

He beckoned Lievy and Azin over, and pointed far to the right. There was an open room filled with tall bins. Above it read: *Arrival Staging Area*. "That's the spot for the hostages. Take Harry."

Bill was behind the far pillar with his eyes closed.

Brady pulled him to his feet. "You, Oliver, and Curls, follow them. Make a blocking wall with those rolling bins. Go."

Army, Gunner, Glasses, Bowl Cut, and Brady covered for them and fired a barrage out into the atrium.

Lievy and Azin put Harry's arms over their shoulders. When there was a lull from the return fire, they headed out. As they passed the protective pillars, two lackeys charged them from the yarn room. With their free hands, Lievy and Azin smoked them.

Bill, Oliver, and Curls followed closely behind, using them as a shield. A shot from the spiral staircase nicked Azin's arm and he recoiled, almost dropping Harry.

Lievy returned fire, blasting an enforcer off the stairs.

Azin muffled a scream, and they pushed forward. Harry groaned.

When they got to the arrival staging area, a lackey came around a six-foot-tall rolling bin. Lievy took care of him with one shot. Another lackey came out from behind a bin and a shock blast dropped him, too.

The lackey lay there comatose. Oliver's hands were trembling as smoke dissipated from the small barrel. He turned and trained his blaster on another lackey exiting the staging area.

With the unsteady blaster pointing at him, the lackey rocketed his hands up. He clearly didn't trust Oliver's shaky bearing. Neither did Oliver, who stood with his blaster trained on him.

Bill and Curls popped their heads in the Arrival Staging Area, scoping out the scene. It was empty.

The hooligans dragged Harry to a seating area. They laid him down on a table.

Meanwhile, Bill and Curls hastily pulled a row of the bins in a line, blocking the view from the atrium.

Bill called to Lievy, "Can you take over for Oliver?" Then he raised his voice over the bins, "Hey Oliver. Lievy's going to switch places so you can help in here."

Lievy went around the bins, but Oliver had already left his position. They almost hit into each other. Lievy drew his blaster at Oliver and shot. The blast whizzed past his head and hit the lackey coming up behind him.

Realizing what happened, Oliver dropped his head. "Thank you. I'm such a stupid, stupid idiot." He went to the seating area and got right to work.

Azin was favoring his left side with green blood smeared on his shoulder. Bill tossed Oliver a sock. "Clean up Azin's arm."

In the yarn room, hostages fled, stumbling out the door in a half-trance. They wore pale faces with bags under their eyes. It was clear something had been done to them.

Brady leaned against a cabinet. Two enforcers he had stunned, lay woozy on the floor.

Hiding behind a pillar, Ivan let out a sadistic laugh. "Your little girls were terrified when they got here. I think they like it now. Your mother, though. Whoa. She's a brave one, isn't she?"

Brady gritted his teeth. He lifted his blaster, gripping tight on the handle. Where is your damn decency?

Ivan angled his arm out and blasted several rounds. Yarn balls bounced off the shelves. Wood cabinets splintered.

Brady returned fire with reckless abandon, forcing Ivan back behind the pillar.

The noises outside faded to a dull hum.

The sound of Ivan re-cocking his blaster, the moans from the enforcer on the ground, and the hum of the machines had Brady wary. He rolled head over feet, knocked out the woozy enforcer with a quick fist, then unclipped the blaster from his belt and rolled back behind the cabinet. Both blasters sprang up.

"You're going to regret this," said Brady. He leaned out, catching Ivan's eye. A call to action. They ran down parallel aisles with shelves between them, shooting at each other through the wood. Yarn balls flew. Holes blasted into furniture. Light bulbs popped. Dust swirled.

They stopped behind the far shelf at the end of the aisle. Close enough to hear each other's heartbeat. Brady pulled the lever on one of the blasters. There was no charge left. He tossed it.

"When will this end, my friend?" Ivan taunted.

Silent rage simmered. Brady gripped the handle, finger on the trigger. "I'd say now is the perfect time." He listened, waiting for a sign.

The room went silent.

A bump against the shelf. They jumped into the opening, simultaneously blasting at each other, and fell to the ground.

The dust settled.

A searing pain shot through Brady's shoulder. He brought his arm delicately to his chest and closed his eyes.

Listening for movement from Ivan, he was relieved when none came. He got up gingerly, holding his right side, and stepped over Ivan. Seeing him up close, a sudden rage flowed hot through his body. Revenge teetering at the front of his mind. If he incapacitated the scum for good, he wouldn't think about hurting another soul.

As he stared at him, the quiet of the room and the rhythm of his breathing relaxed his mind. He thought better and disciplined his thoughts. He crouched down. "Don't ever speak about my girls."

Ivan lay there, unmoving.

On the far wall, from the floor to the ceiling, stacks of thousands of metal cylinders were welded together like a large honeycomb washing machine, and each cylinder was filled with a spool of yarn. With his good arm, Brady dragged Ivan to the wall. He tossed out several spools from the lower rows and looped a couple of zip ties around a cylinder. He faced Ivan forward with his hands behind his back, and tied him to the honeycomb. He did the same with the enforcers.

Brady peeked out of the yarn room. Down the right side, past the design room, Bowl Cut and Glasses were tying up a lackey. "Hey. Bring him here. This is the holding spot for the lowlifes."

In the knitting room, Gunner and Army snuck behind a row of machines. They hopped on a counter and let blasts fly down the aisle. Shots sparked off panels and knocked down spools of yarn.

Bad guys returned the favor, and plenty more. Shots glanced off screens and metal. The Mystery Solvers ducked for cover. When the onslaught took a break, Gunner and Army fired back.

Workers staggered half-awake toward the exit, moving in start-stop motions. They were fighting in their minds to get out of a trance while simultaneously fleeing the scene. Some of them were talking to themselves.

"What's going on?" said Army.

Shots flew by Gunner's head. "I don't know, dawg, but it's creepy."

More rounds were exchanged, the machines taking the brunt of the action. Punctured metal, damaged wires, and crunched screens.

When the flurry of blasts stopped, the bad guys came out from behind the automated machines. The enforcer held a blaster to James Lin's head. The lackey held another worker in a choke hold, with a blaster to his head.

"Be careful," said the enforcer holding James Lin. "You don't want to shoot a hostage."

James, dazed and apathetic, pushed in his large, square glasses.

Army winked at Gunner. They leaned out from the knitting machine and fired with a one-two punch. Army shot the blaster out of the enforcer's hand—then Gunner blasted him off his feet. James didn't move an inch.

The lackey let go of the other worker and tossed his blaster. "Easy now."

As Army went to retrieve the blasters, the lackey, feeling an itch in his nose, reached to scratch it.

Gunner blasted him back into a knitting machine, and he flopped to the ground.

"Never give Gunner a reason."

Out of view, Gilda was recording. She had gotten photos and videos of the lackeys and enforcers shooting, and the workers in their trance. She snuck to the back, through a door that led to the spray room, and, avoiding detection from the workers and lackeys, recorded the machines dispensing *Nuero Spray*—a blend of nerve toxins and other chemicals—

into the toe section of the socks. Then she took photos showing the toxic classification: purple/dark red.

Lievy and Azin brought in three more freed hostages to the staging area, including Brady's mom, and passed them off to Curls. She sat them with the others and handed them water bottles. "If we can do anything to make you more comfortable, let us know."

Seeing Momma Jan, Bill ran over and gave her a big hug. "Oh, my goodness, Ms. Watts. Are you okay?"

She held tight, relieved to see a friend. "I grew up in a house of Mystery Solvers. I think I'll be all right." She released her hug, and looked around the room. "Where's Brady?"

"He's searching for you and the girls. Do you know where they are?"

"What do you mean, girls? Tammy is here, too?"

Bill felt guilty for giving her the bad news.

Momma Jan wiped her nose with a tissue from her fanny pack. "I should go."

"Please stay," said Bill. "Brady would kill me. You can assist with the hostages." When she agreed, he rubbed her back. "We love you, Momma Jan. You're the best."

Gunner and Army made their way to the staging area with James Lin and the other employee. They passed them off to Bill, who found a spot for them against the wall.

James sat in the last chair. Quiet and sullen.

It took a minute for Bill to recognize the old man as the same guy on the missing person notice. "James? James Lin?"

James stared at the ground. "Me. Yes. Why it matter?"

Bill squared up to him. "Your son Li helped us find you. He got your letter."

The words came out like a slap to his soul. His son's name jolting him back to reality. The trance faded, and he noticed Bill for the first time. He glanced around at the other hostages, then back at Bill. "My son found me? He fought for me?"

James got choked up, holding in his emotions. "That make me proud."

"I would be, too," said Bill.

Watching the emotions, something clicked for Bill. Li had fought for his dad, regardless of the danger. That was true love. Bill looked at his reflection in James's big, square glasses. He saw a child staring back, hiding behind a structure of comfort. "Give me a minute."

He walked to the wall of bins. Out in the open atrium, a group of lackeys were attacking his crew. He looked back to where he was, behind bins filled with fluffy, protective, cotton socks.

His life flashed before his eyes. He could stay in his comfort zone and live life like he always had. Or he could push through the barrier and grow. He had to make a change when he still had the choice to be comfortable. Not in a moment of necessity, like when he pinned Norbo to save Brady, but a decision to change from within.

It was now or never. "I have to go," he said to no one in particular. He called out to Momma Jan, "Can you take my spot with the hostages? I need to be out there with my people."

There was a look of surprise on her face. Then admiration. "Of course, honey. Just be alert."

CHAPTER 38

Bill snuck from the staging area to the atrium. Seeing a fight near the entrance, he darted to the right around the staircase. Specifically away from the commotion by the pillars. He watched in the shadows, trying to summon his courage.

Army was squeezing two lackeys in a headlock. "Take that!" They both passed out.

Six feet over, a lackey held onto Gunner's neck, who was spinning around like a tornado to get him off.

Bowl Cut waited for the right time, playing Double Dutch, as the bodies revolved. She jumped on the lackey and got ahold of his shirt. As they spun, she unclipped the blaster from her belt and stunned him. He went stiff and let go. They tumbled off, rolling to a stop.

Army turned around, got on a knee, and smoked a lackey, who was exiting the knitting room. He winked at Bowl Cut.

She smiled. "Me like that."

Bill couldn't shake the nerves. He snuck his way back to the staging area.

In the security room, three guards leaned back in their chairs, watching the large wall of screens. But it wasn't security footage they were watching. It was the movie *Acting Hero,* filling the entire wall of monitors. An action-packed adventure with loud explosions—sounds that muffled the commotion in the real-life compound. When the movie ended, the screens flipped back to the monitors, and the guards jolted from their seats.

"We're in a lot of trouble," said the main guard.

Highly embarrassed and confused were the words to describe their collective faces as they came out into the atrium. The sounds of the movie had blended too perfectly.

The melee of Mystery Solvers vs lackeys was in full swing.

Gunner came around a pillar and pile-drove the first guard into the ground. "Hello there." He grabbed the second guard's wrist, which was holding a blaster, and swung him into the third guard, knocking them both out in the process. "Strike!" He jumped up and felt his hair to make sure his flat-top was still smooth.

Outside the design room, a lackey yanked Glasses' blaster from his belt. Pulling the lever, he recharged it, and aimed it at the mystery solver's chest. Then he fired the trigger.

As the shot went off, a large bin rolled over the lackey, knocking him to the ground and the blaster loose.

The shot barely missed Glasses, who patted his body in terrified relief. "Thank goodneth."

The bin rolled over the lackey again. Wild Bill was at the helm!

Just then, an enforcer stepped behind Bill. "Congratulations. You're a hero…. And heroes die."

Bill eyed the blaster on the floor. The enforcer saw it, and shot it to bits. As he did, Bill snatched a mound of socks from the bin and flung them back at the enforcer. Scattering out in slow-motion, the socks covered his entire line of sight.

The enforcer unloaded blasts at the socks. When they settled on the ground, no one was under them.

Bill kicked at the enforcer's wrist from the side, but couldn't get his leg high enough. "Then I'll show you this!" He hit the blaster down with a balled fist.

Glasses was at the enforcer's legs immediately, and they wrestled him to the ground. While Bill squished the man's head with his protruding belly, Glasses coerced the man's arms behind his back. They sock-cuffed him with double knots.

From the second floor balcony, Brady watched, smiling, as his honorary brother was turning into a man before his eyes. A day he thought would never come.

His attention was pulled from Bill when a lackey snuck by a pillar, heading to the hostage staging area. He leaned over the railing and blasted him off his feet.

Brady turned back to his best friend. "Hey! *Wild* Bill!"

Bill looked around to see where the noise came from.

"I'm proud of you," said Brady.

Bill saw him on the second floor and waved excitedly. Then he pointed to Brady. Brady pointed back. They smiled. Spiderdudes.

"Your mom is helping with the hostages. Also, we got Li's dad."

Brady nodded, relieved. "Good. Two more to find."

Going along the balcony, Brady stopped at the first door, *Workers Quarters*.

Slowly, he twisted the handle. It unlatched. He sprang through the door. An enforcer at a desk pulled out a blaster. Brady's trigger finger reacted first, shooting him two times. He pivoted, searching for others. No more bad guys sprang into action.

He extended his hearing to the far ends of the room. No sound besides snoring and the humming of an A/C unit. The place was filled with cots like a military camp. Ten men slept in silence. Shockingly not awakened by the blasts.

To his right, a colorful light mechanism was set up in front of a seating station. Out of the blue, Brady felt heavy and on edge. That strangeness again. Pictures scrambling in his head.

He sat down to stabilize himself. His mind was being pulled in a million directions. Why does this keep happening?

He finally forced the thought through his skull. Something was re-activating it. He read the sign by the front door.

"Before you go, don't forget to take your picture."

The thought circled back that all the hostage workers were in a daze of consciousness. He glanced behind the light mechanism. Colored bulbs circled the lens, with metal contacts on a computer board. On the wall across the room was a chart showing the workers' day/night shift schedules. And before each slotted work shift was a scheduled "light photo."

And there it was again. A tidal wave of emotions: Coldness. Hopelessness. Rage. Restraint. Sadness. Vengeance. All balled into one. The emotions twisting him into torment.

Mental images of the last time with Tammy rattled like a series of mini-exploding snappers on pavement. The screams. The taunting, the turtle sock swaying. The electromagnetic cuffs. The cold ground. The faint colors of light.

He looked back at the contraption and the colored bulbs around the lens. That's what happened to him.

♪　♪　♪

The enforcer sprawled out over the chair. Sleeping hostages quiet in their cots. The schedule of the "light photo." Brady pieced it together. Each rotation of workers got flashed at the start of each working day, keeping them in a trance.

Brady shot a blast in the air. "Wake up!" He shot again. "Wake up!" Workers rose groggily from their slumber. "Wake up your friends and come with me!"

Workers robotically shook their cot neighbors, who stretched and yawned and rubbed their eyes to clear the "morning fog."

"It's already time?" said one worker.

After all ten workers were on their feet, Brady gathered them at the front door.

A pudgy man cleared out his eye-boogers. "But we haven't had our photo taken yet."

"There will be no more photos. Follow me." He took them outside to the spiral staircase, and sent them down to Azin.

Brady went along the balcony past the workers' quarters to the next door. *Executive Quarters*.

He burst through with a searching aim. The door closed behind him—shutting off the outside noise. There were several small rooms behind closed doors to the left. The rest of the space was empty, including an office to the right. Quietly grabbing the handle of the first room, he turned it. Then flung it open and steadied his blaster. A soul-less space with an empty pod for a bed. And a small lamp on a nightstand.

At the next door, he turned the handle and pushed it open. Seeing someone facing him, he jumped back, almost firing. He steadied his blaster. "My goodness."

In the middle of the room, a mannequin was dressed in a Mystery Solver suit with pins in its head. It looked a lot like Brady. "That's just wrong." As he was about to leave, he decided he had better take precautions. He pulled the pins out of the mannequin.

The last door was locked. He stepped back and blasted a quick couple rounds at the handle and kicked the door in. The room was empty.

Leaving the executive quarters, the atrium noise returned. He snuck down to the far end of the balcony and around to the other side of the building. She's got to be here somewhere.

Halfway along the balcony, a small wooden table sat between the boardroom and the executive office. A variety of designer socks were laid out on the table with a carved label that read *Needs Approval*. At the same spot on the balcony, connected to the railing, was a cable descending to the design room on the first floor across the way.

Suddenly, the boardroom door opened and Brady flattened himself against the wall. An enforcer snuck out, with a shaky blaster leading the way. When the enforcer glanced to the left, Brady's barrel was staring at him. He turned to shoot, but Brady had already pulled the trigger.

Hit, the enforcer lost his balance, wobbled back to the railing, and twisted, falling over the edge. And on schedule, a thud.

Brady entered the boardroom. Rolling chairs surrounded the meeting table. A large map of the city covered the entire lefthand wall, littered with small magnets of buildings and little washing machines. He didn't get a sense anyone else was there.

He found a cabinet and combed through the top drawer. It was filled with paperwork, timestamps, and work schedules, including the daily "light photo." Nothing pointed to the girls. He opened the next drawer.

In the staging area, Harry drank the small bottle of water Momma Jan had given him. He forced himself up. "I should get back out there," he said. "I'm feeling a little better."

It appeared he was pushing it. "You should rest," she said.

"They think I'm down. I can hide. If needed, I can come out as a surprise."

"Only if you're positive you can."

He grimaced and nodded.

In the yarn room, bad guys groaned on the "honeycomb" wall. Azin and Lievy forced three more lackeys inside. Ignoring the yaps from the bound criminals, they zip-tied the newcomers.

"Traitors," said Ivan. "You'll never be free working with them."

"We were loyal," said Azin. "You forced our hand."

"Then plead your case with the council. I have ranking. We can change the word on you." He got an idea. "I can also add bonuses."

Azin ignored him, and headed for the door.

"I'll be right there," said Lievy. He punched Ivan in the gut.

Azin smiled as he walked out.

Lievy turned to Ivan. "You make me sick." Then he leaned in and whispered, "Full restoration? Expunged record?"

"My word is my word," said Ivan, unaffected by the fake punch.

Out in the middle of the atrium, near a thin pillar, Wild Bill and Glasses held a lackey still while Gunner zip-tied him. He added a sock around his wrists for added strength.

Slipping behind Glasses and Bill, Ivan yanked the blasters from their belts. He tossed one to Lievy and pulled Bill back.

Lievy, with no remorse, trained his blaster on Azin.

"Really?" Azin let go of the lackey.

"I'll spare you from doing it yourself," Ivan said to Lievy. He adjusted his blaster to full stun. "This is 'hello' from Mr. Sock." He shot Azin in the chest.

Vibrating, Azin staggered back and dropped, unconscious.

Lievy wrestled the blaster from Azin's belt. He had the lackey pull his arms apart and—*Bang*, the zip-ties and socks blew off.

They turned on Gunner, who was switching his aim from Ivan to Lievy, and back to Ivan.

"Sorry," said Lievy.

"Yeah, you're sorry," said Gunner.

Ivan put the blaster to Bill's head. "Give up the blasters or he gets it."

"No way, Jose," said Gunner.

With the nozzle at his temple, Bill said timidly, "Maybe, yes way, Jose?"

Ivan yelled, "Come out!"

Lackeys and enforcers exited the yarn room. Lievy tossed them extra blasters, and they rounded up Army and Bowl Cut. Soon after that, they had control of the atrium.

Gunner handed over his weapon and put his hands up.

Bang—Gunner vibrated and crashed to the ground. An enforcer smacked him in the face with the butt of his blaster.

The lackeys and enforcers knocked the rest of the Mystery Solvers to the ground.

Biker girl, in her leather pants, dragged Natasha out of the design room by her hair, and pulled her to the center of the commotion. "Look what I found." She slapped Natasha.

Natasha gathered herself, then darted forward and returned a blow.

"That's more like it." Biker girl licked her teeth and struck Natasha again.

They exchanged slaps and flung their arms at each other wildly.

The enforcers and lackeys gradually stopped hitting the Mystery Solvers, and, one by one, turned to watch the fighting girls.

A slap here. A smack there. "Oooooooooooo..."

Smack. Punch. Slap. Smack. "Aaaaaaaaaaaah..."

Weak and battered, Natasha fell to the floor, nursing her cheek. She scooted away from the crowd. She pulled the last adrenal boost from her pocket. Her hand was trembling.

No. She couldn't do it. "He's with me in spirit," she whispered to herself, then flung the pill across the atrium.

Bill pushed away from Ivan and shielded Natasha. "No more!" He leaned in quietly. "You are amazing, by the way. Are you okay?"

"I think so."

"You ruined all the fun, Fatboy." Ivan rubbed his buzzed head. "Line them up on the wall."

The lackeys and enforcers corralled the Mystery Solvers on the far wall at the end of the atrium.

On the second floor, Brady came out of the boardroom with nothing to show for. He passed the table of socks and snuck to the executive office. As he was about to go in, he heard a whimper over the balcony.

"No.... Please...."

It was a voice he had heard his whole life.

Natasha!

He peered over the edge. The Mystery Solvers were lined up at point-blank range to the firing squad.

"Impress them," said Ivan, smirking. "Blow them away."

The blasters lifted in succession along the line of Mystery Solvers.

Brady watched, half horrified, half at a loss for words, as Bill stepped in front of Natasha.

CHAPTER 39

Brady snatched a sock from the *Needs Approval* table. He flipped it around the descending wire, jumped off the railing, and glided down, holding the looped ends of the sock in one hand. His blaster in the other.

Precise. One shot.

Ivan flew off his feet.

The lackeys and enforcers turned around and fired up at Brady. A flurry of sound. Blasts whizzed by left and right. One nicked him, and a burning pain seared through his ribcage. He let go of the sock, hit the ground, and rolled. The land knocked out his earpiece. He grabbed his side in pain.

Before the lackeys knew what hit them, the Mystery Solvers tackled them from behind.

In the commotion, Biker girl passed Bill and went straight for Natasha. Bill reached for her, accidentally grabbing a clump of hair. Biker girl stopped in her tracks, and he let go apologetically.

Natasha came forward and smacked her square in the nose.

Biker girl fell on her butt and covered her face.

Natasha forced her arms behind her back while ignoring the malevolent threats spewing from her mouth.

Wild Bill sock-cuffed her wrists extra tight.

Without warning, Brady hobbled to Natasha and embraced her. He didn't want to let go. "You deserve better from me." He stepped back, looking her over. "How are you?"

"I'm all right," she said, nursing her knuckles. "I threw away my adrenal boost...."

"That's big, Natty. And you're sure you're okay?"

Now he was being way overprotective. "I'm okay."

He got the message but hugged her again, anyway.

His focus turned to Tammy. Still one more person to worry about. "Bill," he said. "Get Natty to the staging area. Make sure she's safe. Or, more realistically, Natty, make sure he's safe."

She smiled.

A soft hand took Bill's, and he blushed instantaneously. A euphoric jolt. Surely, his childhood self was doing all the dances and cheers.

"Bill, go be excited in the staging area," said Brady.

Bill tried to play it off. "It's all cool. Yeah, totally." Natasha let go of his hand, and they snuck off.

Brady ran up the staircase.

♩ ♩ ♩♩

"**P**olice are coming," Li whispered into his radio as a cop car pulled up to the front gate. Officers Tager and Martin got out.

Tager swiped his card, and the gate opened. Seeing the unconscious sentry, he put a finger to his mouth.

Li called into the radio, "Police are entering the compound."

The sound of a fig beetle and soft wind was the only reply.

Officers Martin and Tager unholstered their blasters and stepped over the unconscious man. They went to the left of the main entrance. Tager pulled out a key and unlocked a side door.

Li whispered louder into the radio, "Hello?" He snuck out from the shrubs and jumped inside the gate before it closed.

In the atrium, the Mystery Solvers had control of the scene. They had the enforcers and lackeys cuffed with what was left of the zip ties, and sock-cuffed the rest.

"Police! Put your hands up," ordered Officer Martin.

"We're the good guys," said Bowl Cut.

"You're not police. You shouldn't be playing hero," said Tager.

Gunner said, "Stop with that nonsense, dawg!"

"Then tell me exactly what's happening here."

Army was fed up. "They've only been keeping hostages, among other crimes, including mass theft and poisoning your citizens."

"We're glad you're okay," said Officer Martin. "We'll take over from here. Please hand in your blasters so we don't have to add it to the report."

Gunner shook his head. "Not a chance."

"We'll have to report you. We don't want to do that," said Officer Tager. He pointed the blaster at Gunner. "Hand them over."

Gunner almost laughed. That wasn't happening. Something was fishy about them. "I ain't giving up my blaster this time."

"It's an order!" barked Officer Martin.

Glasses, Bowl Cut, and Army looked at each other, sensing what the others were thinking. They turned and pointed their blasters at the police.

Officers Tager and Martin dropped their blasters on the ground. "You're making a big mistake," said Tager.

"Trust me. We're not," said Army.

Outside, Li found the side door cracked open. He entered, cautiously. "Hello?" To the right, he could see the large pillars by the entrance, and further at the way end, he could see the blockade of bins in the arrival staging area. Hearing mumbled noises coming from the atrium, he snuck over, passing the knitting room and the security room. To the left, far down in the open atrium, the cops had their hands up. Gunner and Army were patting them down in a reverse uno. Li called out as he walked toward them, "Sorry. No one answered on the radio."

His dad came around the wall of bins from the hostage staging area.

Li stopped. "Poppa?!"

"Son!"

An injured lackey stumbled into the atrium from the knitting room. He saw James and Li running toward each other. Teetering, barely able to stay up, he pointed his blaster, and found Li's back in the middle of his scope.

Bang—the blast ECHOED... Echoed... echoed.

The space fell silent.

The lackey grabbed at his chest, and dropped.

Gunner blew away the smoke from his blaster. "Not on my watch."

In the executive office, above the wainscot paneling was a long glass display of socks. Next to each pair were photos of men and women.

At the back of the room, on the mahogany desk was a translucent computer and an organizing pad with pens, notes, and an approval stamp. The monitor was visible from both sides. Behind the desk was a bookshelf, and an aquarium locked at the top. Trapped inside was an adorable little turtle.

"Toby!" Brady hurried over. He pulled at the lock. "Hang on." In the drawers, he found the normal desk amenities, but no key. A stapler wouldn't work. He took a metal pen and wedged it against the lock loop. The pen broke in half.

Toby put his front foot on the glass. Brady kneeled down and touched the glass. "It's nice to see you, too, buddy." He looked around for something else he could use.

The sock display grabbed his attention.

He made his way over to it. As he looked at the collection, he noticed the photos next to each sock weren't random people. They were famous faces in history. Included in the collection were the first socks on record, the first designer socks, Queen Elizabeth's socks, and other notable people from past and recent cultures. Aristbotle. Plado. Sherlock Abodes. Research maven—Miss Pinky. Confucius. Nancy Wrote. And the Hardy Men. Most of them investigators, truth seekers.

Recognizing another pair in the frame, he became unsettled. In the center was a pair of blue cashmere socks with a design of dancing turtles. Next to them was a picture of him and Tammy.

What is wrong with these people?

With his attention fixated on the picture, he failed to hear Toby frantically tapping on the aquarium glass, or the hidden door open on the opposite wall.

A massive body crept behind Brady. When he felt the ground move, he whirled around.

Mooch cracked his knuckles.

Standing behind the brute, Vance scowled. "All-you-can-eat buffet."

Mooch picked Brady up and smashed him into the frame. The glass shattered, and shards fell with socks and photos. He tossed Brady to the back corner.

Wheezing, Brady held his side.

The brute stomped over, lifted him, and shoved him into the wall. His massive fist swung back.

Brady barely leaned out of the way as the fist shot forward and smashed a hole by his head. With a hard thrust, Brady kicked Mooch's stomach.

The effect was moot. "Childs play." Mooch punched Brady in the gut, dropping him to his knees, and he keeled over. Mooch threw him into another wall. *Crash.*

Brady used all his power not to sink into the floor. He was in a bad dream. The kind where the enemy wielded a boulder, while he brandished a pebble. He staggered to his feet. Mooch marched over. Brady threw a limp punch, glancing off his arm.

Vance tossed Mooch one of Brady's turtle socks from the shattered frame. With glazed eyes, Mooch wrapped the sock around Brady's neck and pulled back, slow and steady. Brady grabbed at the sock, struggling to get his fingers under it.

♪ ♪ ♪

Down the hall from the executive office, in a hidden room, Mr. Sock schemed on a velvet maroon couch. His green eyes were deadly flames, flickering through his cloaked face. He let out a guttural snarl, and switched the knob of his light blaster to shock flash–full range.

Tammy sat on the floor of the cage, emaciated and chained. Mr. Sock opened the cage door and pulled Tammy to her feet. With her frail body, she couldn't resist. He disconnected the brace, and pulled her out of the cage.

He pressed a button on the wall. A hidden door materialized, then slid open. He dragged her onto the second floor balcony.

"You won't get away with this," Tammy cried out.

From above, Mr. Sock glanced down to the first floor. The intruders had finished sock-cuffing the lackeys, and he caught a glimpse of Ivan's unconscious body.

The green in his eyes darkened with a smoldering rage. He yanked Tammy, pulling her around to the other side of the balcony.

Gunner and Army followed the sound of Tammy's cries. They aimed their blasters up as her voice got closer.

Mr. Sock angled his light blaster over the edge and pulled the trigger. A wide net blast of light hit the whole area, flashing the Mystery Solvers and the tied-up lackeys.

They closed their eyes from the blinding light.

Mr. Sock switched the light blaster to full power. In a calculated rage, he blasted the Mystery Solvers one by one. Gunner. Army. Bowl Cut. Glasses. He followed it by blasting the lackeys and enforcers who didn't do their jobs. An extra flair of hatred for them.

Then he hovered at the spot, gazing down at Ivan, who lay motionless.

There was no retaliation from the Mystery Solvers. Gunner mumbled loudly to himself. Army karate blocked phantom demons. Glasses took off his spectacles, cleaned them, put them back on, took them off, cleaned them, put them back on. Bowl Cut stared straight ahead as far as she could see, like she was trying to understand the meaning of life. Enforcers and lackeys ranted and raved. The yells and screams echoed off the walls.

Footsteps below scurried to the staging area. Mr. Sock pulled Tammy along the balcony, following the sound. They passed the executive quarters and workers' quarters to the spiral staircase.

Wild Bill had heard a faint cry coming from the atrium. He told everyone in the staging area to be quiet and went to check it out. Out of direct view, he saw the shock flash sweep the whole area. When he crept over to get a better look, his mates were staggering from the blinding light. He became aghast as Mr. Sock flashed the Mystery Solvers from the balcony.

Instantly, they were bewildered and lost. He rushed back to the staging area.

On the other side of the balcony, near the boardroom, Gilda was recording.

Down the spiral staircase to the first floor, Mr. Sock dragged Tammy with him. He pushed her into the arms of a lackey. "Hold her."

Momma Jan stepped out from the staging area to see what Bill was running from.

As Mr. Sock approached, her jaw dropped, and she fainted, falling sideways. Her arms flopped, and she collapsed like an inflatable tube man without coming back up.

Mr. Sock paced around the bins to the staging area full of shocked faces. He pulled Oliver out of the crowd and switched the light blaster to shock flash–full range.

The hostages stared in horror. Bill and Natasha forced a fake smile.

Flash.

CHAPTER 40

Mooch gripped tighter around the sock and dragged Brady to the desk for Little Toby to have a better view. Brady was barely holding on. Face beet-red.

"Want to know what happened to the last person who got in our way?" Vance slugged him in the stomach…. "He begs for socks now."

Black spots flickered in Brady's eyes. The little air he could breathe whistled through his nose. Mooch leaned back and choked him with more leverage.

Faint gasps, eyes fading, Brady was losing consciousness.

"As for your precious turtle." Vance busted the top of the aquarium. Glass fragments dropped around Toby, and stuck upright in the sand, shards sprinkled in the pond. Vance reached in.

Like a mini snapping turtle, Little Toby jumped up and bit him.

"Ow!" Vance shook his hand. "You little #$%." He reached back in.

Brady lifted his feet with his last ounce of energy, pushed off the desk, and jumped backwards with force, scraping by Mooch's face and flipping over him.

Stunned by the unexpected blow, Mooch momentarily released his grip on the sock. Brady snatched it.

Vance drew his blaster.

Brady rolled forward and slapped the sock around the barrel. He pulled back, yanking the blaster out of Vance's hand and into his.

Unloading three shots, he took care of Mooch. The brute dropped. The floor rumbled under his weight.

Weak and tired, Brady plopped on his butt. He pulled the re-charge lever, aimed the blaster at Vance. "Where...is...she?" He could barely get the words out.

Vance smiled. "Why would I tell you?"

"Where... is... she?"

"Mr. Sock has a death grip around her. He's dealt with your mystery boys by now. He'll take everything and smash you like the insect you are." Vance headed arrogantly for the door.

"I don't think so." Brady adjusted the knob to full power. He pulled the trigger.

Vance flew back into the wall with a crash. Black soot discolored his face.

Brady pushed himself to his feet and limped to the aquarium. He delicately removed the shards and pulled Little Toby out. "I got you."

He grabbed several historical fluffy socks from the collection on the wall and arranged them in a mound by the corner. He placed Toby on top. "Wait here."

♪   ♪   ♪

Mr. Sock called out his name with a nasty bite, the sound echoing in the atrium.

Mustering the nerve, Brady snuck a peek over the balcony. The monster had a strong grip around Tammy's neck. Her face was smudged, her hair was disheveled, and her shoulders frail.

Brady's heart sagged. I'm sorry I took so long.

He grabbed a sock from the approval table, wrapped it around the cable, and stepped off the balcony.

Gliding down the wire, he let go and landed with a thud. Pain shot like lava through his legs. He limped and hobbled behind a pillar, grimacing, keeping his blaster trained on the monster.

Tammy fought Mr. Sock's grip. "Don't worry about me. Don't listen to him." She had a glazed look in her eyes.

"I'll get us out of this," said Brady.

Looking behind Mr. Sock, he could sense something was off. The lackeys and enforcers surrounded his team, who had zero fight in them. But it was more than that. Gunner was staring at the ceiling. Bowl Cut talked to herself like a street weirdo. Curls pulled her hair straight, then let go, and it sprang back into tiny curls. Army saluted while speaking poetic Spanish. Glasses excessively blinked. Bill mimed, and Natasha counted fingers.

He couldn't understand. Only a moment ago, they were in complete control. The lackeys and enforcers were subdued. And, in a flash, it was over. His entire team squashed to a nub. With no spirit.

He felt himself losing strength. It was already an impossible mission as a full team. What could one person do? He was alone. And weak.

Mr. Sock had a wicked glint in his eye. "Not only are you responsible for them, you'll also have a lot more to answer for in short order." He let the thought stir. "Our raid fleet is on their way. Earth, as you know it, is dead!" His voice boomed.

In formation, the triangular fleet of 1000 black spaceships with gold tops flew out of the Saturn dome toward the outer rings.

Brady wished he could act, make one last valiant effort. But deep down, it wouldn't matter. He was exhausted and he didn't have a single soul to back him up. Why did he think solving mysteries would make a difference? There was too much evil in the world. And, apparently, the universe.

He had failed humanity. He had failed the Mystery Solvers, who finally put their trust in him. He failed his father. His mother. Natasha. Tammy. He couldn't save one of the people he loved. And now Mr. Sock would have free rein to enslave humanity.

He looked at Tammy apologetically. "I'm sorry."

Her worried eyes stared back.

The look from her gave him pause. Wait. Was she present? Right then, time seemed to stop. He looked closer. Yes. There was mutual recognition. She wasn't entirely gone. He still had a faint chance....

If I can save one person, he told himself.

He glared at Mr. Sock. "Do what you want to me. Leave her out of it."

Mr. Sock snickered. "Just like that? Her for you?"

"Her for me." Brady adjusted his stance.

"It'll go how I want it to. I control the cards." Mr. Sock waved the light blaster. "Do you know how this thing works?" He called for Oliver.

Lackeys brought him forward with barely a struggle.

"I told you we couldn't win," said Oliver, with his head down.

Brady kept his eyes glued to the monster's trigger finger.

Mr. Sock said, "I left him un-flashed so you could see for yourself what happened to your friends." He pulled the trigger.

Colors swirled in the chamber and burst into Oliver's eyes. His face lit up, pupils dilated. Tilting his head to the atrium top, Oliver mumbled incoherent nothings. After the light vanished, he went limp.

The lackeys dragged him away. Another crushing reminder of what happens to those who take on these monsters. Mr. Sock placed the light blaster on Tammy's head with a smile in his eyes.

A tear rolled down her cheek.

Brady tried to speak, say something to comfort her. But nothing came.

"I'm going to enjoy killing her. And I'm going to enjoy killing you," said Mr. Sock. "Just like your pathetic father."

♪ ♪ ♪

The shock of the words hit Brady with a numbing blow. He lost all feeling in his body. The depraved soul of the monster smoldered in vignette and the rest of the world faded away.

As the outer edges of his mind billowed in a dark cloud, memories rushed through. The family picnics. The laughter. Dad teaching him to ride a bike. The Mystery Solver suit. The proud smile.

Brady clenched his jaw. His grip on the blaster tightened. His hands trembled.

"Your father tried to destroy my mission," said Mr. Sock, eyes glaring. "He thought he would turn us in."

Aching to shoot, Brady's mind went to the time Gilda spoke of a man filming the barrels of poison at the secret compound. He was brought to Mr. Sock with a bag over his head. Then to the time the bum mentioned being approached by a Mystery Solver approximately his height.

His dad. His hero.

He had been investigating something right before he went missing.

The Sock Mystery.

Brady looked around at the chaos in the atrium. At his friends in a trance. His hands shook harder, fingers digging into each other. His jaw was clenched tight and grinding.

The pain. The loss. Sadness. Rage. His whole life had been destroyed by a single evil.

He looked into the monster's eyes. They glowed with a sense of achievement. *Keep going*, they were saying. *You're almost over the edge.*

"I'll give you the first shot," said Mr. Sock.

How badly he wanted to. He had good aim and the monster's head was clear above Tammy's. All he had to do was squeeze.

Thoughts of Bill's words materialized in his mind... Giving in to the anger was what they wanted. Part of him wanted that, too. Give him what he deserved.

Suddenly, Brady felt himself mentally detach from the moment. He looked at Bill, who was twirling around in a trance.

A moment of clarity.

Don't agree to it.

The tight grip around his blaster loosened, relieving the pain in his hands. He relaxed his jaw. And with it, the marionette strings snapped free from his mind.

If the monster was going to hurt him, so be it. He wasn't going to continue hurting himself.

Out of the corner of his eye, a frantic motion pulled his attention. It was Bill. Present. Not in a trance.

Bill signaled to close his eyes and avoid the light. Then he took a deep breath, ran his fingers down his own face and went back to miming.

Brady stared at Bill in disbelief.... Then he smiled ever so slightly. Emboldened, he turned to Mr. Sock. "A very good friend of mine gave me a special power." Brady wiggled his body, then rolled his fingers down his face. "Transfer complete."

Mr. Sock's demeanor changed. "You're outnumbered. The planet is going to be gassed. You're as good as dead!"

"I have a power you wouldn't believe," Brady said.

Mr. Sock gripped Tammy tighter. "And what is that?"

Brady nodded to the light blaster. "That thing doesn't work on me." He came out from behind the pillar and tossed his blaster on the ground. There was a long, confused standstill between them.

Irritation festered in Mr. Sock, and he raised the light blaster. "Suit yourself."

"You're just a smelly fart face, aren't ya?" Brady said, doing his best Wild Bill impersonation.

Mr. Sock pulled the trigger. Light spun in the chamber. Brady closed his eyes as it shot out. The light swirled around his head. He tensed. His body trembled…. The light faded away.

"Whoa…." Brady patted his head, making sure it was still intact. "Told ya." The monster fired again. Brady's eyes closed just in time.

His body shuddered. He held on until the light faded away.

Relieved, Brady checked his surroundings. He felt a little wobbly this time. "That's all you got, smelly head?"

Switching the light blaster off and back on, Mr. Sock adjusted the knob to full power. Bang-Bang-Bang.

Eyes shut tight, Brady gritted his teeth. His body convulsed. He could feel the light prying at his eyelids. He grabbed his face, shaking, holding on with all his strength.

The light faded away.

Then his body went stiff, and his eyes bulged open.

"Why I is here? Who am you?" Brady twirled in a daze.

Bill looked on in horror. Mr. Sock's eyes glinted.

Rigid, then Brady relaxed. It was taking a toll on him, but he kept his goofy composure. "I'm kidding. I have the power. For realzies."

Mr. Sock yelled at the lackeys, "What are you waiting for?!"

The first lackey charged. Brady stepped to the side and put his leg out, tripping him. Two lackeys flanked him. They swung their fists, and he ducked—smack. They grabbed their knuckles and screamed. Brady jumped and split-kicked them to the ground.

"Take him!" yelled Mr. Sock. A gang of six lackeys tackled Brady.

In a haze of commotion, kicks and punches flew about. As the blur expanded, Brady's voice yelled out, "We can become friends, Mr. Sock. Maybe frolic on the beach somewhere. Sip on wine!"

"You're dead!" Mr. Sock flashed shots into the brawl. Lackeys went stiff and fell over. Mr. Sock traded his light blaster with an enforcer's enormous gun blaster and pressed it against Tammy's head.

When the dust settled, Brady had his blaster back in hand and a lackey as protection. "Surrender, and I'll forgive your crimes."

"Not in a million years," said Mr. Sock.

Brady said, "Why not get involved in charity, dude? An honest way of life."

"Shut up!"

"Random side note, Mr. Sock. You can use my foot powder for your smelly head any time you want. Completely free." He winked at Wild Bill.

Mr. Sock's green eyes narrowed. "What are you talking about?" Then he grumbled, now mad at himself for asking.

"Well," Brady said, "that makes your head sweaty, I imagine. So, any time you need, my foot powder is all yours."

"Stop it!"

Bill wasn't acting out anymore. He watched and smiled, enjoying the humor transformation.

Mr. Sock pushed the large blaster harder against Tammy's head. Her eyes cried for help.

Brady winced inside, but kept his outside cool. "Eh... one person? What will that do? You got to go bigger than one person. Right?"

"How about an enslaved planet?" said Mr. Sock, the words rolling off his tongue with pleasure.

A mental sidestep, Brady let the acid of his words go by. He knew deep down who he was dealing with. Addressing Mr. Sock without judgement, Brady became sincere. "You're in a lot of pain. We can all feel it. But none of this is going to bring your daughter back."

Mr. Sock's head moved back, affected by the words. "Your whole world deserves to feel pain."

"One tragedy isn't worth the enslavement of an entire species," said Brady.

Mr. Sock raged, "One tragedy?! A slave planet is your most desirable outcome. There's an item in our raid policy that little know about. Let's just say your guardians are too proud not to fight back.

"And I have to thank you. None of this would've happened without your persistence. You are a great Mystery Solver. If you never investigated socks, if you never found the secret airport, if you never made it to Saturn. And if you never escaped. A raid would've never been commanded. You're one of a kind, as I expected you'd be."

Brady held the protective lackey tighter under the neck. "You're just saying that because I figured you out. You're jealous, admit it. You can't stand that a young man beat you." He looked closer at Mr. Sock's eyes. "C'mon. You can't be this rotten, can you? Why do you hide your face? Let's see it. Let's see that ugly face of yours. Is that you, Slick?"

Mr. Sock grumbled. "He was just a pawn," Two lackeys brought a beaten and disheveled Slick from the design room. They each held an arm stretched out.

Slick pleaded.

Mr. Sock pulled the trigger. Slick blew out of the lackeys' grasp back into the design room, the door ricocheting shut.

"You don't need to stall," said Brady. "Show me. I dare you. Unveil that tantalizing fautch of yours. 'Fautch' is 'Face' by the way."

"Quiet!" said Mr. Sock.

"You're clearly procrastinating. Are you scared? I get it, dude. I would be, too, if I was as ugly as you." Brady tilted his head, thinking. "Hey, that rhymed.... I would be, too, if I was as ugly as you. I would be, too, if I was as ugly as you."

"I said stop it!"

"It's okay. Most people fear revealing their true selves," said Brady. "You're a scaredy pants. Chicken b-b-b-bock-bock."

"Shut up!" Mr. Sock ripped the black sheet off his head.

Brady stared, dumbfounded.

Wild Bill said low and slow, "One hundred snaps of sniggities."

It was Harry.

CHAPTER 41

Taking out the voice modulator from his neck, Harry said, "None of it matters anymore. This planet is finished."

Brady couldn't move. Could barely think. It was the person outside his family that he looked up to the most. The only one at Mystery Solvers who defended him when he was too new to fend for himself. "When? How?"

"I infiltrated Mystery Solvers after I killed your father..."

In the meeting room at Mystery Solvers Inc., Harry appeared in the first team photo after Clark Watts was gone.

"...It was the only group that could get in my way. When I realized you were going to get the promotion, I planted the fake bribe report and pinned Slick against you.

"When you brought the poisoned socks to the meeting, I switched them out before passing them around."

Brady said, "But you were shot when we got here."

"Fake powder."

Gilda called from the balcony, "Thanks for incriminating yourself, Mr. Sock." She showed Harry the video recorder. "An Emergency Live View Code was needed to share this, so thanks for sending me home, too. You're being broadcast on Saturn as we speak."

Enraged, Harry fired several rounds at her. Gilda ducked and retreated from the edge as balusters blew to bits. He turned to Brady with a sinister stare. "What made you investigate socks?"

Slowly, Brady got a grip on the back of the lackey's gray shirt.... "Ask my father." He yanked the lackey to one side, jumped parallel to the ground, eye on the target, and pulled the trigger.

Bang—Harry's head exploded! Slimy green goo splattered all over the floor. Tammy stumbled away.

Brady, on the ground, and Bill, with his mouth wide open, stared at the green goo and the headless body convulsing.

Bone-reformed. Clumps of mass filled out. Harry's head grew back with green-tinted skin, splotchy marks, and indents in his skull. His body grew, tearing the black cloak.

Brady got up with his blaster ready.

"Sniggity a million snaps!" yelled Bill.

The lackeys and Mystery Solvers backed away, partially awakened from their trance.

Mr. Sock switched the blaster to full power. He fired at Brady, who ducked, dropping flat to the ground. The shot zoomed by his head, chunks of a pillar crumbled behind him. Mr. Sock fired again, and Brady jumped and rolled, the floor cracking underneath.

Noticing where they were, the mob of lackeys and Mystery Solvers backed away, half in a trance, half in reality. A few lackeys with their hands tied tripped.

Bill slipped backwards, past the crowd, and raced to the spiral stairs.

Leaping behind the next pillar, Brady avoided another blast. Mr. Sock unloaded on the column, crumbling it to pieces. Brady ran, leaped, and rolled behind another column.

And, moments later, it blasted to bits. Brady ran to the open, vulnerable.

Above Mr. Sock, Bill had made his way up on the second-floor railing. He took a nervous breath. "Up here, monster!" Bill jumped down as Mr. Sock glanced up, and he bounced off the large alien body and hit the floor.

Mr. Sock whacked him, sending him sliding into the wall all the way on the other side of the atrium.

Bill groaned, holding his stomach. When the pain subsided, he wriggled his body around. It wasn't too bad. "I think I'm officially brave-brave." There was a visible relief in his face. Then worry. He realized if his weight kept saving him, he'd continue using it as an excuse.

The distraction was enough to get Brady out of harm's way. He slipped behind Mr. Sock and placed the blaster high up to his head. He pulled the trigger.

More green goo splattered everywhere! The large body fell to the ground. Brady watched, anticipating, hoping that was the end.

Mr. Sock's body began convulsing more forcefully. His head grew bigger. His body grew thicker and stronger, with darker scales. He rose up, towering ten feet above them. The blaster got stuck in his finger.

"What am I doing?" said Brady.

Bill called out, "I don't know, but stop?"

Mr. Sock crushed the blaster in his hand—the last charge from the blaster shot out, inadvertently taking down an enforcer.

The hostages, Mystery Solvers, and lackeys scattered.

Swooping by, Wild Bill pulled Tammy and Natasha with him, rushing through the atrium into the knitting room.

Mr. Sock's eyes fixed on the trio, then he tore after them. The floor reverberating under his weight. He broke through the wall, and hit over knitting machine towers.

Brady followed behind Mr. Sock. "C'mon, think," he said out loud as he jumped through the open wall. He dodged broken machines, ran down the main aisle, and jumped a few more obstacles to the back, where the monster had Bill and the girls cornered.

Beyond the last knitting machine, Wild Bill and the girls flattened themselves against the wall away from the monster's sharp claws.

Mr. Sock ripped the last machine out of the ground. He threw it aside, and shrieked. His bad breath and saliva speckled all over the trio.

Hesitant to shoot, Brady leveled the blaster at Mr. Sock's head.

It would only postpone the inevitable.

Natasha saw Brady's indecision and had a flash bulb moment. The solution was from the book they had grown up reading. Their favorite book. She yelled out, "If Aliens Attack! Brady! If Aliens Attack!"

Brady's eyes went big. He got it. Just as the monster's claws reached out, he stuck the blaster to Mr. Sock's butt and fired.

Bang—Pink goo burst through his pelvis, and splatted all over Bill and the girls. The goo slowly dripped down their shocked faces.

Mr. Sock spotted the hole in his pelvic region. His face went blank. He wobbled and crashed to the floor. The ground shook.

Brady, Bill, and the girls waited for another convulsion....

It didn't come.

"Phew." Brady relaxed.

Disregarding the goo, Tammy and Natasha hugged Brady. Bill joined them. They looked back at Mr. Sock on the floor.

"How did you know what to do?" said Bill.

"Natasha reminded me," said Brady. "*If Aliens Attack*. Not all alien brains are in the head area. Sometimes it's in the pelvis or stomach. I made a lucky guess."

Bill thought about it. "Was it lucky, though? I mean, he was a *butt*-head."

Crickets. Silent stares. Then smiles. They went in for another group hug.

Spools of yarn from the knitting machines and socks were used to clean up and wipe off the goo.

Brady felt a sudden nagging. An alarm in the corner of his mind with no snooze button. They weren't out of the woods quite yet.

The raid.

CHAPTER 42

Outside the rings of Saturn, beyond the field of the planet's electron zone, a wormhole appeared. The raid fleet of 1000 spaceships shot through.

In the executive office, Vance and Mooch slept unconscious against the wall with their hands and feet tied.

At the desk, Gilda typed the hashtag *#Saturnity* into the live stream as she spoke to the audience.

Brady was on the other side of the monitor, but he couldn't understand what she was saying. It was in Saturn tongue. Among the foreign rant was a familiar "Mr. Sock," "human," and "the Earth."

Unable to help, Brady felt useless. "Can I do something?" he whispered, breaking her concentration.

Gilda leaned out from the monitor. "Our only route is to get a groundswell of support to push the council to stop the raid. I'm making progress. The message is spreading. However, there's no guarantee of anything. The raid has already been commanded." She faced the monitor and continued the live stream in Saturn tongue.

Natasha, Bill, and Tammy entered the room quietly. Seeing Mooch and Vance by the right wall, and the glass shards scattered by the left wall, they huddled in the middle of the room behind Brady.

Little Toby came out from the shadow and scurried to Tammy's feet. She felt a bump and looked down.

"My little baby." She picked him up and hugged him and kissed him. "Oh my goodness. I missed you." She rubbed her cheek against his cute little face. He smiled, happy as a turtle. Then he rested his head little on her arm.

On Saturn, videos of the live footage were playing on billboards, news stations, social media, and the internet comm boards. Flurries of messages were filling the airwaves. "Stop the Raid," "Humans are our life source," "Treat them the way we want to be treated, within reason," and many other messages were shared and echoed from the hearts of saturnites.

Also spreading were messages of "Treason," "Saturn life over human life," and "Enemies of the state!"

Back on Earth, in the executive room, Brady paced back and forth, watching the double-sided monitor. If he could speak on the live chat, he could help from a human perspective. But he didn't have a helmet. He needed the translation. He leaned over to Gilda, palms on the table. "Can we add in a translator to the live feed?"

An incoming video call appeared on the top corner of the monitor. *Unknown Source*.

She accepted it. On screen, the council minister appeared. Gilda's eyes lit up.

Speaking Saturn in a blunt tone, the minister was visually irritated. Gilda said something, and the minister nodded, waiting.

In a blur of fingers, she pulled up a file and downloaded the human translator app. She connected it to the chat window. "Hello, Minister. Do you understand me?" Gilda asked.

"What is going on here?" said the minister.

It worked. Brady got excited but quickly realized the minister's attitude wasn't that of a supporter.

"The raid needs to stop," Gilda said. "Innocent lives are at stake."

"It's not that simple. Standard procedure is standard procedure. You know this." He scratched under his eye.

"With all due respect, sir, it's based on false reports and undue process. You can't forge ahead. I have exposed the truth about Mr. Sock. The people have spoken."

"You, as well as I, know, once a raid is in progress, there's no stopping it. Our survival is most important above all other species. You should've thought hard about escaping Saturn with human fugitives."

"We were falsely accused," said Gilda.

"We are done here," said the minister. He reached his arm out, and his screen disappeared. A gut punch. Gilda dropped her head, defeated.

Realizing it wasn't a good idea to show a lack of hope, she switched the screen to the video clip of Mr. Sock's confession, and added #Stoptheraid.

A moan stirred on the right side of the room. Mooch moved his nose and struggled with his arms, slowly coming alive.

Bill and the girls scooted back. "Brady...," Bill pointed to the brute coming out of his deep sleep.

Brady clicked his blaster to stun. The waking giant's eyes opened as he approached, and he stunned him back to sleep.

Vance was still out. He stunned him, too.

Down in the atrium, Oliver, Glasses, and Curls were collecting blasters. They tossed them in a large, white rolling bin while Gunner, Army, and Bowl Cut brought lackeys and enforcers to the yarn room.

Back in the executive office, Brady paced in a three-foot radius, scratching his head. He went around the desk to her side. "Let me speak to them."

"If it's not the council, it won't make a difference," she said. "The minister was our best chance. Citizens can't stop it."

"Give me a shot."

His persistence worked. She switched the computer to the live feed. Brady adjusted the video recorder on himself with Gilda in the background.

He considered what to say. What would be too much for them, and what could they take. If he over shared on Mr. Sock's plan, they might not believe it and latch back onto the propaganda against them. If he under-shared, it might lose the urgency, and he could fail that way, too. Give them enough.

"Hello. My name is Brady Watts. I was one of the human fugitives on Saturn who broke out of jail and escaped with Gilda. We did it out of necessity, because it was our only chance to expose Mr. Sock before it was too late.

"Along with Norbo and corrupt members of your guardians, they plan on making humanity a slave society, where we live as vegetables. Not the healthy kind. And where we have no life of our own. No freedoms. No will to live by our choice."

Army, Glasses, Curls, and Bowl Cut piled in behind Bill and the girls.

Brady continued, "I'm sorry, but life doesn't work that way. If their vision becomes a reality, we will become sick and contaminated. You can't kill off what sustains your life, or you'll die. You also can't poison what gives you life. If you do, common sense says you will be poisoned.

"Consider why the 'Steal for Survival' (S4S) program was launched. It was your solution to humans being unjustly used by your greedy guardians and corporations, causing planet-wide sickness.

"This raid and what has been set in motion won't lead to an unlimited food supply or survival in the way Mr. Sock has tricked your leaders into believing. It will lead to certain sickness and eventual death."

On Saturn, the green faces were in awe as crowds in the public square watched the large screen.

"On Earth," Brady said, "we had a similar problem. Fake philanthropists and greedy corporations found ways to increase the food supply for profit. But they poisoned our soil, our plants, and animals, treating them to horrible sanitation and disease-infested quarters. It didn't give us better survival. It gave us higher rates of disease, sickness, and death. Which led to bigger hospitals, more drugs, and more sickness.

"On the surface, it's only about greedy corporations. But you have to look deeper. Corruption comes from all sides. When taxes are raised, that puts good farmers in a bad spot. And because they have to survive, they look for shortcuts. Guess what that leads to? Spraying insecticides to make up for the natural losses from critters. Or they won't have a farm left.

"You'd think to ban toxic pesticides and find natural solutions for the problem. Which there are many. And make organic farms tax-free. But if you looked even deeper, you'd find that insane leaders think they need a world in turmoil to keep their so-called power. And so the people pay.

"Everything in life has repercussions. You'll be setting yourself up for a similar fate if the raid continues. It might not be immediate. But come it certainly will."

The "Treason" hashtags faded away and "Stop the raid" hashtags took over, gaining ground. Groups of green, loving aliens formed around large public squares, cheering.

Chants from every sector broke out. "Stop the raid! Stop the raid!" Banners flew in the streets.

Back in the executive office at the compound, another video call appeared in the corner of the screen. *Unknown*

Source. Brady and Gilda looked at each other. This could be it. She accepted the call.

The council minister greeted them. "You guys drive a hard bargain. I have seen the groundswell of support for your cause. Very impressive."

"Thank you for responding," said Gilda. "This means so much."

The minister raised his three-pronged hand. "Unfortunately, what is done is done. Stop wasting your breath. Goodbye."

The screen went black.

Brady and Gilda stood there frozen, not sure what just happened.

The energy in the room flatlined.

Outside earth's atmosphere, a wormhole materialized. The black triangular fleet zoomed through.

"What else can we do?" said Brady.

"We've done it." Gilda held her head with her hands. "Even if we had communication with the raid itself, we'd have to convince half of them to disengage to break the command. And they're prohibited from outside connections when a raid is under way. There's nothing else to do."

"We are not going out like this. Let's keep the groundswell going. Put me back on live."

A futile gesture. But she obliged. It was better than giving up entirely. She connected the live video. "It's impossible to get one ship, let alone half of a raid, to break off. It's never been done."

"I don't care what it takes." Brady adjusted the frame. "We'll break through."

"Hi, saturnites. As you have seen, the council isn't on board. But when have you counted on so-called guardian leaders to make things better for you? You haven't. There's only one course of action left. We change it ourselves. If you know anyone, or if you know anyone who knows anyone...."

On Saturn, Nita's bags were packed, ready to go hunting for a new place to hide. She wiped off smeared mascara as she watched the live stream. It was coming through, translated into Saturn tongue. She had betrayed her good friend and was now realizing she had betrayed her own kind as well. "I really messed up."

Suddenly, it was as if Brady was speaking to her. She could do something. She jumped off the yellow seat, rushed to her phone, put in her earbuds, and dialed rapidly. "If she feels it in her heart, she better forgive me."

The phone rang... then disconnected.

She dialed again. It rang, and rang... then disconnected.

She dialed again. "Pick up, Tanex, you macho specimen. I know you see it."

The connection went through. "This isn't a good time. We're setting formations," said Tanex.

"You have to stop the raid," she begged.

"Are you crazy?" The phone disconnected.

Nita took a deep breath. She put the phone down.

She thought about it, arguing with herself. Then she picked up the phone and dialed again.

The connection went through. "What?"

"I met the humans," Nita said. "They are good people. You can't go through with this. It's not the saturnitarian thing to do."

"Gilda conspired with humans against us. You want them to destroy our race? I have to go."

"Wait! Have you not seen the live feed? It's all lies. Mr. Sock is a manipulative piece of corrupt you-know-what."

"What are you talking about?"

"The video of Mr. Sock confessing! He organized everything and is blaming it on the humans. Norbo was in on it, too. You have to believe me. If you go through with the raid, it'll be a grave mistake. I'll prove it." She pressed a code on her phone and put it next to the TV. It scanned and transferred the video. "Watch this."

CHAPTER 43

Synced up as a unit, the raid fleet zoomed into Earth's atmosphere.

Panic blanketed throngs of eyewitnesses on Earth. Men, women, and children pointed to the sky, and recorded as the massive fleet of UFOs approached.

Lights beeped through the gold tops, and gas projectiles jutted out from the bottoms.

A single spaceship in the middle of the formation turned its lights off. It swerved out of line and whooshed around to a point ten feet in front of the general's spacecraft.

In response, three escort raid ships from the fleet shot forward, surrounding the general in a circle.

The lights on the general's ship blinked blue—a wave signal, setting up intercom to the entire fleet. The general, wearing a dark tinted face mask, pressed the *comm* button. "Get in formation! You are messing up the coordinates."

The single ship didn't move.

"Declare yourself!"

"This is the representative of the people of Saturn."

"You are breaking command. What's your number?" The general zoomed his view screen to the gold cockpit window. It was blacked out. He zoomed to the left side. Acid spray had eroded the numbers.

"Declare yourself now!"

"This is Tanex, acting as the representative of Saturn. Planet Earth is our life source in this sector. Mr. Sock and his chain of command have been exposed as criminals against saturnity and humanity. The will of Saturn is that you end it. I'm the face of this cause. And if I must, I will die trying."

"Get out of the way, or you will be taken down with force. Per raid code: 1915311!"

Three other raid ships turned their lights off. The gas projectiles reversed into the ships, and they flew out of the formation. Another two raid ships followed.

"Back in formation, now!" ordered the general. A red light blinked on his craft. Then a red light on Tanex's.

The motor controls on Tanex's ship clamped down and, against his will, he zoomed back twenty feet and halted.

Three six-barrel blasters jutted out from the escort spaceships.

BAM-BAM-BAM-BAM-BAM-BAM-BAM-BAM-BAM-BAM!!!!!!!!!

Tanex's ship exploded in the sky.

Crowds on Earth scattered in the streets. Spectators watched in horror. Witnesses in headlights.

"The rest of you are ordered back into formation!"

Two of the disengaged spaceships fell back in line while another five disengaged.

A news reporter angled his camera away from the falling debris of the spacecraft and zoomed the camera back on the formation.

Live coverage was spreading throughout the country and the world.

The airwaves were captured and transferred to Saturn, where the live coverage circulated in a flurry.

Nita watched, shaking. Streams of tears pouring down her face. "Tanex, my baby!"

More communications made their way to the Raid Boys, and more ships fell out of line.

"There will be hell to pay!" The general pressed a series of buttons. Red lights blinked, and another disengaged spaceship's motor controls clamped down. The craft was guided twenty feet in front of the general's spaceship.

Blasts discharged from the escort ships.

A wall of sound—in loud, rapid succession.

BAM-BAM-BAM-BAM-BAM-BAM-BAM-BAM!!!!!!!!

The raid ship exploded into a fireball.

"We can keep this up all day!"

Hysteria continued spreading below on Earth.

Two more fleet ships fell back in line. Another twelve ships disengaged.

Another raid ship's motor controls froze and zoomed in front of the general. It was BLASTED to smithereens.

Three more raid ships glided back in line. But then when fifteen more ships disengaged, two of those three changed their minds, flipped around and went back out.

Another twenty raid ships turned their lights off, disconnecting from the formation.

Cheers escalated on Saturn. Communication with the Raid Boys was spreading like wildfire. Friends and familial connections. The momentum was building.

In a contagion of inspiration, one hundred more spaceships disengaged. Then fifty more.

Another flurry of 250 spaceships retracted their gas projectiles and flew out of the formation.

Then the final fifty ships disengaged.

503 total.

Stalemate.

The red light on the general's ship turned yellow. He had no more authoritative power.

The general groaned. "You better be right." He turned his ship around, facing the formation. "Disengage from protocols."

The rest of the fleet turned off their lights, reversed the gas projectiles, and spun about face in the opposite direction with the general.

The five hundred-plus disengaged ships fell back in their positions.

On Saturn, jubilation erupted in Sector 1 square!

In the executive room on earth, Brady and Gilda were all smiles, watching the live footage of the fleet turning around.

"I can't believe you pulled it off," said Gilda.

Brady hugged her. "I knew we could do it."

Flying out of the clouds, a silver, U.S. guardian saucer with "S4" marked on the hull headed straight toward the fleet.

The pilot pushed the throttle forward. Red-faced. A twitch in his eye. And wearing sponsored LFS socks. "Bring it on, beasts!" He fired into the formation.

A raid ship exploded, and pieces rained down from the sky.

CHAPTER 44

The fleet moved apart in one movement and spun around. A swarm swooped in and surrounded the silver S4 hybrid, unloading blasts in a revolving onslaught.

The S4 exploded!

Red and black lights flashed on the general's ship. The code spread instantaneously to the entire fleet. "The raid clause is enacted. Protocols for a new sector are engaged. Attack with deadly force."

The hive mind took over the fleet. Missiles and blasters jutted out from the saucers, and the raid descended toward Earth.

In the executive room, blinking eyes and petrified faces stared at the scene.

Missiles shot from the front line of the fleet, hitting two tall buildings. The top-half floors imploded, crumbling into rubble, and dropped below.

Lines of buildings and stores exploded, spreading a frenzy of terror in the streets. Throngs of dots scattered.

A company of 400 silver S4 hybrids glided over the northern hills toward the invasion of the skies. They spread out, launching a blaze of attack against the raid.

The front of the Saturn fleet angled its attack straight ahead, and the rest launched missiles below.

Several projectiles shot down from the raid. A group of S4 hybrids zoomed over, focused their blasters on the projectiles, and blew them out of the sky.

Two more missiles launched. A lone S4 hybrid streaked left and right, spun about, and shot them into a raging fire.

A black swarm encircled the lone silver S4. Before crunching under the onslaught and dropping off into wreckage, the S4 took one of the raid ships with it.

In a swift movement, stacking like a spread-out Jenga game, the entire Saturn fleet halted and shot up from low to high, forming a towering wall in the sky.

The S4 band of hybrids followed suit.

Thirty feet apart, they hovered in place and fired at each other relentlessly. Saturn raid ships and S4 hybrids took turns crunching and exploding.

The hull of an S4 hybrid plummeted to Earth. It crashed on the street, flipped over, tumbling and skidding to a stop. Up close, on the left side of the hull was the "S4" marking, followed by an "S" that was etched out.... An original "S4S" ship of Saturn.

♪ ♪ ♪

In the executive office, the room fluctuated between worry and hopelessness. Faces were pale, fingernails were bitten, palms rubbed together, and legs bounced restlessly.

Gilda shook her head in disbelief. "The S4 hybrids won't hold up for long."

After considering options, the craziest idea pinged through Brady's head. Perhaps it was the only one that could work. "Are there any spaceships here?"

"There may be a hybrid stashed somewhere," said Gilda.

"Let's find out," said Brady. "Bill, go convince Lievy to re-join our side. I'm flying up. Army, find out if someone knows where a hybrid is. They're absolved if they help."

Bill and Army rushed out. Bowl Cut tagged along.

"You're really going up there?" said Tammy.

"If I don't, there might be no us. Or anyone else."

She nodded.

In the yarn room, Gunner watched over the restrained criminals who yapped and complained. A few tried to bribe him. He just smiled and petted his blaster like it was a family pet. Now and then, he practiced centering them in the blaster scope if he wanted to shut them up.

Army, Bowl Cut, and Bill entered. First, Army asked the tied-up criminals if they knew of any available spacecrafts. No one answered. Then he appealed to their senses. "If this planet becomes a wasteland, do you think they will care for you? You will only be an afterthought. That's it."

Bowl Cut added, "We're all dead if we don't stop it."

One pair of tied hands rose above the crowd, "I'll show you where the hybrid bunker is."

Army nodded, and Gunner uncuffed the enforcer. The other lackeys and lowlifes glared from their restraints. In response, Gunner centered one of them in his blaster scope. They shut up immediately.

Wild Bill explained to Lievy the plan to fly Brady up, but he rejected the offer.

Lievy said, "I should've turned you in on Saturn."

Bill couldn't believe it. "But this is the right thing to do."

Lievy shook his head. He was re-committed to Mr. Sock.

That failing, Bill found Azin in recovery, resting on a layer of socks. Momma Jan and Bill got him up against his rejection. Bill explained the scenario.

"I'm useless. I barely have an arm." Azin tested his shoulder movement, wincing as stabs of pain shot through. "I can't do it. I'm sorry."

"You'll be perfect." Bill wouldn't take no for an answer. He gently put Azin's good arm around his shoulder, told him he didn't have a choice, and brought him to the executive office. Momma Jan went with them.

Brady finished explaining the plan to Gilda as they came in.

"Lievy turned us down," Bill said. "But we got someone better."

"Good to see you're okay," said Brady.

"Not really." Azin let go of Bill and Momma Jan, adjusting the weight on his feet.

Army brought the enforcer forward. "He knows where the hybrids are stashed."

"They're out in the field," said the enforcer. "Back of the compound."

"Let's go," said Brady.

"Be confident out there," said Momma Jan.

"Yes, mom." Brady kissed her on the cheek and put a hand on his heart. Then he kissed Tammy on the head. "Love you."

Brady and company rushed out the back of the atrium. Into the jungle they went, following a thin, beaten path of dead leaves, and came to an open field surrounded by palms. Army and Bowl Cut carried Azin.

The enforcer ordered everyone to the edge and kicked up bark at a few spots, revealing a hidden tarp. "Get that side." He and Bill pulled the camouflage tarp off the bunker.

Embedded in a slab of cement was an access panel. The enforcer entered a code.

The bunker top disconnected from the side walls, and rose to a ninety-degree angle. Below were two hybrid spacecrafts. Dark green with rounded bodies, and each held four seats. The cockpit canopy was a glass bubble.

Brady and Gilda descended the ramp.

Bowl Cut and Army helped Azin down, each movement taking more energy than he had. "Maybe you should try Lievy again," Azin said, keeping his bad arm to his chest.

"You'll do great," Brady said as he climbed the ladder to the cockpit. "You can rest when we're done. All we need is one quick-twitch arm."

The top of the hybrid slid back. Brady hopped in, and Gilda scaled the ladder. Brady took the co-captain seat. Gilda took a back seat. Army and Bowl Cut helped Azin up the ladder, then exited the bunker.

Brady said, "Let's go."

Azin buckled up. He took a deep breath and exhaled. "Okay."

He flipped the power switch on. Red lights flashed on the panel: *"NO CHIIP. NO CHIP. NO CHIP."*

They went quiet.

"You're not chipped," said Gilda.

Azin opened a cupboard and grabbed a pointed tool. Shoving it in the sensor indicator, he yanked it around until it cracked. The red light warning turned off. "I guess that makes me a master," he quipped.

A beep, then the console power lit up. Green lights trickled across the dashboard. Fully operational. Azin set protocols.

"Do you think this will work?" Gilda asked.

"It has to." Brady looked at Azin. "You ready?"

Azin didn't answer with words. He flipped the switch and a green light flashed on top of the craft.

The rest of the team moved to the edge of the palm trees.

Energy exploded from the base. The hybrid shot up out of the bunker. They passed the jungle, and raced to the skies.

A cacophony of blasts and flashes howled around them. Black raid ships and S4 hybrids exploded, plummeting below. Azin flew the green hybrid right through the front lines of the battlesky toward the heavens.

Shots from both sides aimed at the green hybrid. Azin veered the ship left and right, barely dodging impact. A single blast skidded off the hull, and they banged around, holding onto their seats.

Azin grimaced as they flew past the upper range of battle.

The carnage escalated, and spaceships continued to fall.

The general thrust down on the intercom button, "Escort Craft 840. Take care of the intruder." A black escort raid ship veered out of line, going after the green hybrid.

The entire S4 fleet was down to one hundred and thirty hybrids, and dropping fast.

Out of the back view, Azin spotted the escort raid ship coming after them with shots of fury. "Hold on!" He yanked on the controls, swerving the ship down and left, then in a wide loop.

"Go into their fleet!" said Brady. Azin looked at him like he was crazy. "Do it," Brady said.

Azin swung the hybrid around, and headed for the fleet. They flew between the raid spaceships, weaving in and out. Artillery from the spaceships aimed at them but didn't fire.

As the green hybrid made figure eights around the formation, Gilda waved through the glass, yelling, "Stop the raid!" Brady joined her, waving frantically.

A handful of Raid Boys squinted through the gold glass tops, trying to make out who they were. One thought he saw Gilda. "Isn't that...? No, couldn't be."

Left, right, up, and down, the green hybrid evaded the *840* raid ship hot on their trail. "Can we set up intercom?" Brady asked.

"Only the general's ship can," said Azin. They continued weaving through the fleet as more S4 ships fell.

They were down to 100 hybrids.

Blasts ringing in his ear. The dropping hybrids. The rumbling motions of the ship. The pulling force on the maneuvers.

As they zipped around, Brady could feel their hope dwindling. They were going nowhere fast.

At his feet, "hull boots" was engraved on a cupboard. Brady opened it. Inside were a couple pairs of traxtanium boots. Gray space boots wide enough for shoes to fit in. He picked up a set.

On top was a small stick/un-stick sensor. He touched it. The boots flew out of his hands and stuck to the side wall. Light bulb moment. "I have another crazy idea."

♪ ♪ ♪

While Azin evaded escort ship *840*, Brady fit his shoes in the magnetic boots. A sensor beeped, and the lining closed in snug around his feet. "When I'm ready, we're going back to the front lines." Brady tested the boots on the floor. The strength of the hold was stable. Then he checked the movement. He was satisfied. "Open the top."

Azin jerked the hybrid left, avoiding another blast. "I don't know if this is a good idea."

"I brought this situation upon the world," Brady said. "It's my fight. If I die, I'm going down swinging. And we're all dead if we don't stop it, so you're joining me." He took a deep breath. "Open the hatch. And when I say 'now,' fly to the front."

The craft zoomed down through the bottom of the raid fleet, the escort ship followed close behind. The hatch disconnected, and the top slid back.

"Coming on your left!" yelled Gilda.

Azin swerved away from another line of blasts.

Brady forced his way up through the turbulent wind, holding onto the edge. He put his left foot out, and it stuck to the hull. Then his right foot—Fffthnk. Pushing off his hands, he stood up.

It didn't take him long to get used to the balance. Easier than zero gravity. The boots had the dual magnets, firmly connected while letting him move. He made his way to the middle of the hull.

"Now!" said Brady.

The ship veered around and flew up to the front lines.

Waving his arms wildly back and forth, Brady got the S4 fleet's attention.

Gilda watched with bated breath as Azin dodged blasts with zigzags and veers. They swooped around in a figure eight and back up as shots raged on.

An S4 pilot spotted Brady flailing on the hull. "Who is this nut?" Others noticed, too, and the S4 hybrids ceased firing at them.

Hope ignited in Gilda. In a surge of inspiration, she unbuckled her seat belt and made her way to the co-pilot seat. She opened the cupboard and grabbed the extra pair of hull boots.

"Are you sure?" said Azin.

"If it gives us a better chance." Gilda put the boots on. When she was ready, she reached up to the edge of the opening. Step by step, she climbed the inside of the hybrid and got one foot out the top. Then the other. She pushed herself up on the hull and made her way to Brady.

Boom—A blast rocked the hybrid. Brady and Gilda hit hard against the hull as it teetered out of control. The hybrid sputtered. The engine failed to reignite. And the ship fell out of the sky.

The escort ship *840* zoomed by and glided back into position next to the general.

Azin pushed the motor ignition button. It did nothing.

He pulled it out and pushed it again. Sparks flew. The engine came to life.

Grabbing the controls, Azin favored his bad shoulder and veered from the battle in the direction of the compound. "I'm sorry. I can't do this. We'll find a better solution."

Brady forced himself back up. He called to Azin. "No. Go back!" He pulled Gilda to her feet. "Are you okay?"

She looked hurt but nodded.

Azin looked at Brady.

Brady said, "We have to keep fighting. There's no other way."

The look on Azin's face was one of sheer disbelief. "This crazy dude." He grabbed the controls, turning the hybrid around and toward the front lines.

A raid ship and two silver S4s exploded.

Azin deftly avoided the falling debris.

"Face your side," Brady said to Gilda. They waved frantically at both sides of the battle as they flew up.

Several aliens peered through the gold glass tops. "Isn't that Nita Townsend's friend?" "That's Gilda's human form." "Yep, that's Gilda."

Blasts ceased from the Raid Boys at their level.

The general barked a command, and the raid fleet spread apart, leaving his ship and the escort ships in clear view of the green intruder.

The red light on top of the general's ship blinked. But no red light blinked on the hybrid. He couldn't control it. Switching on the blue light, the general ordered the escort ships to attack.

Gatling-blasters from the escort raid ships jutted out. BAM-BAM-BAM-BAM-BAM-BAM-BAM-BAM-BAM-BAM!!!

Azin veered left, then right, dodging the line of blasts.

When the firing ceased, Azin floated the hybrid back in front of the general.

The escort ships aimed their Gatling-blasters, this time directly at Brady and Gilda on the hull, firing another barrage.

Azin yanked back on the controls, angling the hybrid up to protect them.

The blast struck the edge, rocking the ship, and knocking Azin unconscious on the whiplash.

The hybrid flipped over, then over again, and dropped.

A nearby S4 exploded, the shock wave knocked Gilda and Brady into the hull, and the ship hurled toward Earth.

CHAPTER 45

Plummeting. Twisting. Loose objects floated out of the cockpit. Azin rocked around in his seat, passed out and strapped in.

Mumbled calls from Brady made it to Azin's ears, and his eyes opened. He looked down. The size of earth-bound objects were expanding by the second.

Recognition forced its way in his skull, and he jerked awake, grabbing the controls. He yanked back, and the ship slowed its descent just before Earth appeared life-size. He flipped the ship upright. It puttered and leveled out.

Azin exhaled, taking a rest on the controls. He looked out the cockpit for his friends. Thankfully, the hull boots had done their job.

Sprawled out, Brady blindly reached for Gilda. Relief came when he made contact. They sat up, dizzy, tired, and beaten.

An S4 ship crashed down on a tree thirty yards from them. The three of them looked up at the raging sky, then at each other, barely able to hold themselves up. Their bodies couldn't take anymore.

The sky ignited, rumbling with fire and black smoke. Dark clouds rolled in, suffocating the horizon. The last of its beauty was dying away. Raid ships and S4s blasted out of existence.

The violent, scattered sound of explosions hit Brady at his core, and he winced with each reminder. Another S4 ship disappeared in a fireball. There were only 40 hybrids left.

Everywhere his life had gone wrong, and everywhere it went right, still led him here. Each new moment in its own time. For a new decision to be made. He looked at Azin. "I've been close, but I've never fully given up. And I'm not about to start."

Azin nodded. Gilda smiled.

"Back up?" said Brady.

Azin's eyes focused.

Brady said, "Get me right up to that bastard so he can see my face."

Azin veered the ship around, and shot up to the battle.

They whooshed through the front lines, dodging falling ships and blasts, and got level with the general.

Seeing the pesky green hybrid, the general barked more orders.

Another barrage of blasts discharged from the escort ships.

BAM-BAM-BAM-BAM-BAM-BAM-BAM-BAM-BAM!!!

Azin veered the hybrid down and away this time, then back up.

Frantic motion from the general's cab.

Azin noticed a blue light on the console. He pressed it, accepting the connection. The intercom crackled and cleared up. Spitting Saturn tongue, it came out as muffled words to Brady on the hull. But not to Azin. He pulled out the microphone and flipped the translator on. He disconnected the mic from the radio port and plugged it into a cordless attachment. "The general is on the line." He tossed the microphone to Brady.

"Get out of our $#% way," commanded the general. "It will not end well for you." Before Brady could respond, the general ordered the escorts to take them down.

BAM-BAM-BAM-BAM-BAM-BAM!!!!!!
Azin veered up and away as blasts ROARED by.

The hybrid shook.

"Get closer!" said Brady.

The green, dauntless hybrid turned around and zoomed closer to the general's ship. Out of nowhere, with no warning, Brady clicked the unstick sensor on his boots, ran down the hull and jumped off...

Awestruck, Azin watched as Brady flew from the hybrid to the general's ship, blasts exploding all around him. Brady clicked the stick sensor on his boots at the last second.

Phffnnk. Brady landed.

The general leaned back.

The raid escort ships zoomed out of line and angled their blasters toward Brady on the ship. They focused, honing in on him.

"Go ahead," said Brady, turning around, inviting an attack.

"Don't shoot!" barked the general.

Brady got down in front of the gold-tinted canopy. Face to face with the general. He pressed the radio button. "We are not enemies. We need each other."

Blank, unkind eyes stared back.

"If you want both of our races to die," Brady said, "you'll continue this raid. And if you do, you'll kill me, anyway. So, go ahead." He beckoned Azin, and the green hybrid zoomed over, nose to nose. Brady stepped back on.

The general pressed the intercom.

No words. Just static.

Brady spoke into the mic, "Don't order one of your little protective escorts to do it for you." He pointed directly at him. "Do it yourself, General.... Or you go down as a coward." Brady threw the mic in the cockpit. He put his arms out, then placed his hand on his heart.

Copying him, Gilda put a hand on her stomach where her heart was.

In the executive room, Momma Jan, Tammy, Natty, and Bill stared at the scene as the hybrid floated in front of the raid fleet. Brady standing tall with his hand on his heart.

The room watched in silence.

A smile from Momma Jan. "He's always with you." She put her hand on her heart. Natasha and Tammy did the same.

The firing ceased. And the air stood still.

The remaining S4 spaceships retracted their blasters and backed off.

The camera in the general's ship zoomed up close to Gilda and Brady on the hull. They kept their gaze up at him. Not with a death stare. Not with hatred, nor fear. But with faith.

The battlesky was at a standstill.

The general let out a disgruntled moan. He pressed the intercom. "I hereby call an end to this raid."

The red and black lights on top of the entire fleet switched off. "By the powers conferred on me, the raid clause is null. We are going home."

The Saturn fleet retracted their missiles.

Brady nodded to the general.

Gilda thanked him, then blew kisses to the fleet.

Turning back, Brady acknowledged the S4 company, who lit up in morse code lights, then spun around, and flew over the hills.

The Saturn fleet rotated towards space as one unit. White lights blinked through the ships, then they zoomed out of the atmosphere.

Brady and Gilda dropped to their knees, exhausted. They hugged each other tight, holding on for a long time. Their heads rested on each other's shoulders.

Throughout the world, people who were watching the live coverage erupted in celebration! In bars, in living rooms, in school classrooms. A single man in his bed, eating beef chips, jumped up and down on his blanket. Similarly, a single woman in her pajamas cheered with a pint of mint ice cream.

On Saturn, celebrations flowed in the streets. Saturnites waved the Saturn flag and the Earth flag.

Nita watched the screen, wiping her tears away. "You are my hero, Tanex. I will sing for you every day... you will always be in my heart." She dried her eyes with a cloth. "I hope you forgive me, Gilda."

On Earth, an expansive lawn of spectators waved to the empty spot where the UFO fleet had occupied earlier. A burly man in a tank top fainted. His family tended to him.

With Brady and Gilda still on the hull, Azin flew the hybrid back to the bunker.

The Mystery Solvers and freed hostages were gathered in the field, waiting. They celebrated as the green hybrid touched down. Brady and Gilda double high-fived and shook their hands together the way old folks do.

Momma Jan, Tammy, Little Toby, Wild Bill, and Natasha whooped and hollered!

Gilda said to Brady. "I've never seen anything like it. What you did for this sector was incredible."

"What all of us did."

♪ ♪ ♪

Administration agents covered Mr. Sock's giant alien body on a stretcher. They rolled him past the cleaners, who were mopping up the goo in the knitting room, and took him the side exit.

Agents in hazmat suits sealed off the Spray Room with red *toxic warning* tape.

The Mystery Solvers had the lowlifes wrangled outside. Brady grabbed Vance by the shirt and shoved him in front of Oliver. "Now is the time to do or say what you will."

Oliver hesitantly stepped to the ominous Vance, whose face was still covered with soot, and his mustache bent out of shape. Oliver gained a little courage and got up real close to him. "In your face!"

Vance flinched.

Oliver walked away. A weight lifted and his posture straightened. Then a smile plastered his face.

James Lin squeezed his son's nose and patted his head. "You is my hero." Li smiled and hugged his dad.

Brady winked at Li and showed him a *hang loose* sign.

When the police got there, they walled off the compound with yellow barricade tape.

Gunner and Army passed the criminals off to them. "Take these fools away."

The officers shoved Vance, Ivan, Mooch, Lievy, Biker girl, Officers Tager and Martin, and all the lackeys and enforcers into police cars.

The captain slapped the leading car, and they drove off.

The team looked back one last time at the sinister building. They had successfully put an end to the dark side of the sock enterprise.

The police captain shook Brady's hand, then Bill's. "What you all did was brave. We will have you sign an NDA for obvious reasons."

"Non-disclosure agreement? The whole world saw it," said Bill.

"The world knew about the Roswell incident too. There are ways to change minds," said the captain. Then he shrugged. "It's embarrassing how easy it is."

"I'll be proposing a change," Gilda said. "Humans and saturnites should work together to keep this sector safe. It's our home."

"Whatever you say, we're with you," said Brady. They did an awkward, badly timed fist-pound. "Gilda. It's saturnites like you that give me hope for the universe."

"And humans like you. Let's make sure the good ones win," Gilda winked, and went on her way.

Brady smiled at Bill. "We did it."

"I'm not gonna lie," Bill said. "It feels pretty good to show a little courage."

"And I'll try to use humor more often."

"Please do," Bill said. "You know, you're not the worst of all time at it. Could be better, but it wasn't bad."

"You're not too bad yourself at being brave."

They did the French-fry handshake.

"We're like double-zero-six, mission always-possible," said Bill.

"Spy Turtles," Brady added.

"Getting to the bottom of a real mystery against all the opposition in the world—and sector—and we pull out on top? We're real blipidy-blopidy-blipin' heroes."

"Whoa. Don't swear," said Brady.

"I didn't. I 'bleeped' it out. We're real 'blipin' heroes." Bill smiled and added a bad robot dance.

Momma Jan gave Brady a metronome hug. "My baby."

Brady joined in the swaying.

Bill said, "It's good to see you're doing okay, Momma Jan."

"Why do you say it like that?" she asked, perplexed.

"Before Mr. Sock flashed everyone in the staging area, you fainted."

At first confused, then she remembered. "He was the same monster I had nightmares about. I knew right away that he must have had something to do with Poppa Clark. I wasn't ready for it."

"I'd say Mr. Sock was lucky you fainted," Bill said. "You would've destroyed him by yourself." They smiled.

Natasha came over with Tammy and Little Toby.

Momma Jan squeezed Brady's and Bill's cheeks. "This deserves a family dinner. That includes you, Bill."

"That would be awesome," said Natasha.

"I'm not mad at that," said Brady.

"I love it...and I'm not above it," Bill said. "We are world savers. And world savers deserve feasts. Was about to say, I'm famished." He patted his belly. "Definitely starting my diet after, though."

Natasha smiled. "You're growing on me."

A happily shocked expression teleported on Bill's face.

Brady nudged him and tilted his head toward his sister.

Bill swallowed the lump in his throat. "I mean, I am pretty awesome. You saw what I did in there, right? So, yeah, I get it."

"I don't know about that," she said. "But I'm thinking maybe we could hang out more?"

A nervous breath came out of Bill. "If we're going to be something."

Natasha interjected. "Let's not go that far just yet. Why don't we start with a date?"

"I should get something off my chest." Bill knew he would have to say it at some point. Honesty was admittedly his best policy. "Do you remember the two laundromat criminals who stole your socks?" He couldn't believe he was saying it.

"Yeah, I told you about it," she said.

"That was us." He showed his pearly whites, embarrassed. Then an attempt at forgiveness. "We wanted to get your help without Brady having to ask. I'm so sorry."

"No, you didn't." She hit his arm. "You have some explaining to do."

"I wanted to be around you more. Because," he paused, "I've always liked you."

"You're adorable."

He smiled back expectantly. He was waiting for her to say it was okay to make a move. On a spark of inspiration, he decided he was going to take it into his own hands. He went in and gave her a hug.

She stood there being hugged, shaking her head. When he let go, she grabbed his face and—Smooch!

Bill's eyes went big. Butterflies fluttered in his stomach, spreading to the rest of his body. Best. Day. Ever.

Tammy looked at Brady and said, "Why do they get all the exciting romance?"

"That's young love. We're old hat." Brady smiled, then said, "Okay, fine," and started peck-kissing her all over her face.

Her cheeks turned rose-red, and she giggled.

"I have something for you." Brady went in his pocket and pulled out her pair of cashmere socks with dancing turtles.

"You owe me more than that," said Tammy.

Brady said, "Vacation in the City of Lights?" Her eyes lit up. He pulled her in close, and they locked lips. Little Toby smiled up at them and snuggled his cheek against theirs.

In the background, fireworks went off, lighting up the night sky.

The family walked away in the sunset of fireworks.

In silhouette, Bill pointed up to the sparkling explosions. "So random. Right?"

The front of *Investigation* magazine spun into view on the TV screen—*Kablam*. A picture of a fading sock with the caption:

THE SOCK MYSTERY

CHAPTER 46

EPILOGUE

Investigation magazine issue titled "The Sock Mystery" was in the top left corner of the breaking news report. Todd Strout whipped his hair back and winked at the camera. It was going to be a juicy story.

He angled his head ever so slightly and furrowed his brow. "Big Sock—the crime syndicate—has been stealing socks since forever. And recently, it was found they've been poisoning them for over a year. A clean-up is underway to restore the natural order of things and to put trust back in the sock business." A video played. Trucks with *Poison Sock Waste* stickers were converged at an intersection. Citizens tossed in their contaminated socks. "Go to your nearest discount store or go online to thesockmystery.com to get replenished."

♪ ♪ ♪

Back in the Saturn council dome at the grand jury, Gilda showed the evidence of Mr. Sock and his un-alienitarian activities on Earth. The crowd gasped at each new video, including the sock poisoning, the light blaster brainwashing, the workers' quarters, and more.

The Saturn guardians filed the official documents, chronicling the atrocities against humanity perpetrated by Mr. Sock and his cronies.

Across the skywalk in the Circle of Doom, Vance, Ivan, Mooch, Biker girl, Ethan, Cliff, Officer Tager and Martin, and the rest of Big Sock were electromagnetically strapped to the walls. They grumbled in their Saturn form as they awaited the results of the grand jury.

♪   ♪   ♪

Momma Jan, Brady, Tammy, Wild Bill, and Natasha ate from the table of meats and fruits and vegetables and breads and desserts, laughing and having a grand old time.

From his propped-up position on the table, Little Toby ate seaweed from a mini bowl.

Bill wrapped a chicken drum in a waffle and dipped it in syrup. He sucked it off the bone in one slurp. "Tomorrow my diet starts. I promise."

"Yeah, right," said Brady, followed by laughter. "Seriously though. I love you no matter what, but when you're ready, we need to get you healthier."

Bill winked, dunked another drum in the syrup, and slurped it.

♪   ♪   ♪

On Saturn, in the election ceremony, the leader of the council meeting put a special hat on alien Gilda. The new title of Mrs. Sock. The crowd cheered.

Christening the ceremony was none other than her best friend, Nita Townsend, the diva singer, who emotionally sang her heart out with her tentacles dancing on top of her head.

"We get a fresh new start because of fallen heroes... we love out loud because we care... to make a change in the lives of many... only happens because we daaaaaarrrreee!" She wiped a tear away. "I love you forever, Tanex!" Nita kissed her hand and threw it up to the sky.

♪　　♪　　♪

On Earth, at the White House, Gilda was in alien form, shaking hands with the President. In attendance at the sector summit were members of the United Worlds.

Mixed in with the summit panel were several saturnites, proudly showing off their alien form.

A treaty had been made to inform the population that not only were aliens real, but that they'd been on Earth and in this sector for at least 3,000 years.

Gilda spoke, "We are going to move forward, working together and being in each other's lives. No administration—not anyone, has a monopoly on the 'truth' about 'aliens.' It's time everyone was in the know on the secrets of the universe."

Outside on the lawn, camera crews from around the world were recording.

From Earth to Saturn, in expansive fields, the event was being watched on large screens. Crowds of alien-loving humans on Earth, and human-loving aliens on Saturn showed off their signs while watching the sector summit.

♪　　♪　　♪

At Mystery Solvers Inc., Brady ran the show with Bill as his assistant. Slick had resigned, and the group gladly chose him to be the next president. It was a seamless transition. He was the natural leader for Mystery Solvers Inc.

At the meeting, the group listened respectfully as Brady finished the day's news. Being that it was the end of the meeting, it was time for announcements.

Brady talked with composure—on the outside. Under the surface, a giddy excitement bubbled. "I'm thrilled to introduce the newest member of Mystery Solvers Inc.... My kick ass sister, Natasha Watts!"

Bill and the rest of the Mystery Solvers cheered loudly, clapping and hollering. Natasha smiled coyly, and Bill's eyes took in her cuteness.

♪ ♪ ♪

It was July 5th, Interdependence Day, and the UFO Festival was underway. Humans were dressed in alien costumes, and aliens were dressed in human costumes. It was the festival of the year.

Human children learned and played Saturn board games. Aliens in different shapes and sizes signed autographs and took pictures at the booths.

Of course, Mystery Solvers had their own booth, signing autographs for their part in the sector's victory. People mostly wanted Brady's and Wild Bill's autographs and photos, but they were just as happy to get anyone of the Mystery Solvers, including Natasha. They would be valuable in the future.

Later that night, near the end of the festivities, the alien rock band "The Saturnites" performed music in front of an excited crowd. They started with a new song titled "Welcome Human Friends" and ended with "Sector Defense." That was a crowd favorite.

♪ ♪ ♪

Soon after the festival, entrepreneurial aliens began setting up morphing booths at fairs. "Watch an alien turn into a human with the MOR4EVER 3000!" People came in droves.

The new administration added zero taxes for saturnites, which provided a great boost to the economy.

As the integration between aliens and humans took place, a mutual admiration between the species began—for their symbiotic survival.

Aliens began sharing more technology. Some wild humans even decided they wanted to become aliens, and one declared he would be the first to move to Saturn full-time. Upon reverse DNA engineering, once the technology was perfected, the human could take saturnite DNA, along with the light contraption sessions with the MOR4EVER 3000. Eventually, it would make saturnites out of Earthlings. But that was still quite a few years away.

Naturally, aliens ran all the laundromats and held all the jobs regarding cleaning clothes. Part of the treaty was that from each load of laundry, a sock could be taken using the software program already installed in the Super Laundry washers.

Humans liked the saturnites so much that they would offer a sock to an alien manager as a thank you. A regular occurrence enjoyed by the managers. Their double-mouths would shoot out with razor-sharp teeth, chomp it up, and slurp it down. And that, of course, was on top of the treaty initiative of "One Sock Per Load," or OSPL for short.

Aliens began having drinks with humans at local bars. When the humans got sloppy drunk, they would offer up their socks. But drunk human socks didn't taste very good, so aliens would say, "I appreciate it, but I've already eaten," putting their hand on their chest as a show of gratitude. They did it so often that they got as good as earth celebrities were at avoiding getting drunk with fans.

An alien laundry attendant at the NBA arena pushed a hamper through the locker room, picking up the dirty socks and uniforms to be cleaned. He stopped at Curry's locker. His eyes danced with joy. He peered around, making sure no one saw him, and smoothly picked up the highly sought-after sports sock. He slid it into his pocket and threw the rest of the clothes in the hamper.

♪ ♪ ♪

When things were finally back to normal, Brady took Tammy on the highly anticipated trip to Paris. They went to all the tourist attractions. The Eiffel Tower, the Louvre Museum, the oh-so romantic Paris Seine River boat ride. They ate at the most expensive high-class restaurants. Tammy was in heaven.

When the trip came to a close, they gathered their belongings and began filling up their suitcases. All their clothes were neatly folded and packed away... besides one lonely sock.

Brady shrugged. Tammy smiled, then leaned over, planting a kiss on his cheek.

Through the hotel window, the Eiffel Tower lit up the night sky. The sparkling lights exposing the dark—the way truth brings to light the mysteries of the universe.

ACKNOWLEDGMENTS

So many people helped make this story what it is. From an early movie script to a full-length novel.

But before I thank them, I want to thank you. Because a book isn't a story if people don't read it.

If a tree falls in the forest, but no one is there to hear it, does it make a sound? I say no. So, thank you for letting my book make a sound.

A very special thanks to Kevin Keele for the amazing cover art. I can't explain how happy I was seeing my characters come to life. I mean—I have explained it. But it doesn't do it justice. It feels like the characters really are alive.

To my family and friends who helped along the way. Thanks to my dad, mom, and broski. Greg, Joni, and Ryan, for your encouragement, love, and helpful feedback. JJ and Davan, for going through multiple versions of the story. I sincerely appreciate it. Rodrigo, Lizzie, Cody, Tom, Michael J., Brent, Christian, Stephen, Gio, and Marco, thank you for giving me notes and suggestions and, as well, for reading my story. Many of you were there in the very early versions. And look where it got to—a published book! And thanks to Darren. On the fateful day when you said the line. Had those words not been uttered, who knows if there's *The Sock Mystery*. So thanks for being an inspiration.

Thanks to all the editors, and proofreaders, and beta readers who found mistakes that I couldn't see no matter how closely I looked. Also, I appreciate everyone who gave me encouragement along the way. There were too many of you to thank individually. People don't understand how hard writing is and how tough creativity can be. Those little signs of support mean a lot to us. So, thank you if you've ever acknowledged an artist.

Also, thanks to the many authors, storytellers, teachers, and podcasters from whom I gained great insight into story, drama, and suspense. It helped the writing get better with each revision.

I hope you liked the story, the characters, and the truth behind where all our socks go. Hopefully one day, this will be on the big screen as an animated feature. How cool would that be?

Lastly, if you would like to, you can tell family and friends to read the book. You can also review it. Every little thing helps authors.

Thanks again for reading my story!

"OUTTAKES"

Outside *Family Laundry*, officer Tager and Martin interviewed a victim.

"And he did something really rude to it," said the girl.

Breaking character, Officer Tager, Officer Martin, and the girl started laughing uncontrollably.

"Did something really rude to it," said Officer Tager.

Officer Martin said, "He farted on it."

♪ ♪ ♪

Outside the corner store, Brady said to the bum, "Let's go somewhere more comfortable."

Oliver wearily put out a dirty hand. Brady put his nose up and drew his hands back. "Ew. No, thanks." He grabbed a sock from the bum's bucket and wrapped it around his hand while plugging his nose.

Onlookers gave him a dirty look, then started laughing.

"What?" Brady said with a deadpan expression. "I don't know what he has."

Oliver laughed, then rubbed his fake dirty hands all over Brady.

♪ ♪ ♪

On the dinner date, Brady reached his hand out. Tammy put her hand on his, and he pulled her up. He led her into a slow dance as the jazz melodies played.

He took her hand, turned her out, and spun her back and into a dip. Tammy's eyes sparkled.

Grabbing hands, they spun in a circle, gazing into each other's eyes—they slipped, and Brady fell on top of her.

"Oops. Sorry," said Brady.

Tammy looked up at him and said, "Shall we dance?"

The actors playing "patrons" and "staffers" gave Tammy and Brady strange looks–per the script, then started laughing.

A few of them had that look in their eyes like they were so excited to possibly make it on the blooper reel. They laughed extra hard, staring directly at the camera.

♪ ♪ ♪

Outside Super Laundry headquarters, the large receptionist rolled after Brady and Bill on the Segway.

The roll of motors got closer. Brady and Bill looked back.

"Uh oh," said Bill.

"Go!" urged Brady.

The big man caught up pretty fast, getting hot on their trail. "I wanted to apologize. I was only joking! Seriously, have a good day." The large man slowed down, and when he went to turn around, the Segway spun out of control, going in circles.

"Aaaaagghhhhh." He fell off.

The next take, the same thing happened.

Brady and Bill rolled on the ground, laughing. The guard got up panting, which made Brady and Bill laugh harder.

♪ ♪ ♪

On the speed train, Bill took the unconscious guard's thumb and put it in the guard's own mouth.

Bill smiled and took a selfie with him. *Flash.* "Great Insta-pic."

The guard started sucking his thumb. "I'm a baby."

On the next take, Bill put the guard's thumb in his mouth, and the guard yelped and pulled it out. "Ew!" said the guard. Bill laughed.

♪ ♪ ♪

With the light blaster, Mr. Sock charged around the wall of bins to a room of shocked faces. The hostages stared in horror.

Brady and Natasha forced a smile…. Bill made a weird face. *Flash.*

"Cut! Let's go again," said the director. "Without the face, Bill."

On the next take, when Mr. Sock went around the bins, Bill started laughing before Mr. Sock got on his mark.

"Sorry. I'll get it right."

On the next take, Natasha started laughing as Mr. Sock came around the corner. Bill was already making a face.

"Don't do that!" she said.

Bill laughed.

Mr. Sock shook his head and started guffawing.

♪ ♪ ♪

Gilda and Brady danced on the hull of the green hybrid, with the raid fleet and S4 company around them in the battlesky. Gilda was in her Saturn form.

They did the Moonwalk.
Then they did the Pulp Fiction dance with peace fingers.
Then the waltz.

♪ ♪ ♪

Brady was eating at craft services. Bill snuck behind him, hummed the investigation melody, and softly mumbled, "Make the notes, ask the questions, see if anything starts connecting."

When Brady noticed, he rolled his eyes. "Not now, Bill. Get out of here."

Bill laughed.

The cast, crew, directors, producers, camera crew, Mystery Solvers, and all the Saturn aliens shouted, "Make the notes, ask the questions... see if anything starts connecting. Make the notes, ask the questions... see if anything starts connecting!" Brady shook his head, and joined in. "Make the notes, ask the questions... see if anything starts connecting!!!

♪ ♪ ♪

ABOUT THE AUTHOR

SHAWN LABAQUI is an author, screenwriter,
and creator. He was born and raised in
Hollywood, CA. One of the only few.
It's wild. He's been writing stories
and comedy since he was
a small little lad.

This is his first
novel.

CONNECT ONLINE

thesockmystery.com
@ShawnLabaqui
@thesockmystery

www.ingramcontent.com/pod-product-compliance
Lightning Source LLC
Chambersburg PA
CBHW011148190726
48288CB00010B/3220